The Fourth Chair

A Marcus Clemens Novel

(Book Three)

James E. Anderson

i

Also by James E. Anderson

In The Marcus Clemens Series

The Trials of Marcus Clemens
(Book One)

Retribution
(Book Two)

ISBN 978-1-7379692-7-3 (paperback)

This work is dedicated to my wonderful children,

Traci, Angie, Sean, Adam and Jamee.

All of you, each special in your own unique and

individual ways, are the apples of my eye.

You mean the world to me.

Table of Contents

Prologue

It was but a scant few minutes past 11:30 on the quiet and cloudless Friday morning, but the July 7th sun had nearly reached its peak high in the pale blue sky. The intensity of the unencumbered solar rays was unforgiving as they pounded mercilessly on the exposed, unprotected, and mournful gathering below. For some of those in the sparse and loosely huddled group, Independence Day, on Tuesday past and just three miserably long days ago, had begun as a time of jubilation and excited celebration. It was, after all, the one hundred and ninety-first birthday of this great nation. On that July Fourth afternoon, however, at least for those gathered in a semicircle here today, the much-anticipated revelry had been brought to a sudden, screeching, and sobering halt. The days and accompanying nights immediately following had been both solemn and grievous for all involved, for those touched directly, and for others who were affected more peripherally.

"We have received a precious revelation today: God has acted on our behalf and provided for us solution to our need. As stated in Psalm 23:4, '*Yea, though I walk*

1

through the valley of the shadow of death, I shall fear no evil'."

"Our revelation and proclamation this day is that life has triumphed over death! Mercy and grace have triumphed over sin! And justification has triumphed over condemnation!"

Reverend Enos Jackson spoke eloquently at the graveside service, offering solace to the assembled mourners. Reverend Jackson served as the current pastor of the Old Hills Baptist Church, the house of worship attended by Marcus Clemens and his stepmother Margaret for most of the past eight years, beginning shortly after the tragic death of Margaret's husband and Marcus' father, Elijah, in 1959. The formal funeral service today had been performed in the spacious sanctuary of the large First Baptist Church, located on White Street, and had been officiated by Reverend Arthur Drummond. First Baptist had become Marcus' secondary church as he would alternately attend there with his girlfriend, Cassie Worthington, along with her parents, and younger brother, Charlie.

Reverend Jackson continued, "There comes a time, as the Bible describes, when we are 'absent from the body' and 'present with the Lord'. As Paul said in Philippians 3:20-21, *'For our citizenship in heaven, from which we also eagerly wait for the Savior, the Lord Jesus Christ, who will transform our lowly body that it may be conformed to His glorious body'*. And as Charles Spurgeon rightfully said, 'We shall rise again, we shall be freed from all corruption; no evil tendencies shall remain in us'. As so it shall be with our dear young friend Ellis Compton, a poor soul

2

whose misdirection had been redirected. From all indication, I believe he saw the light, and I believe that he accepted the truth of our Lord and Savior. Believe, my friends, there will be no separation in Heaven. Heaven, for us, will be a place of perpetual reunion."

Yet once again, tears formed in his eyes as Marcus gently squeezed Cassie's hand. His grief was imminently shared by Cassie. She had disliked Ellis; to be precise she verily hated, from their very first meeting, the Ellis she had originally known. He had, after all, intended to kill her, or at the very least maim her. He had aided in her kidnapping. But after paying his court-ordered penance, he had forced his way back into her and Marcus' lives. She gradually had grown to accept him, understand his background and the distinctly evil influences of his youth. She had come to appreciate the wonder of his rehabilitation, had witnessed first-hand the effort he had put forth to earn the trust of her, Marcus, and both of their families. Ellis had endeared himself to both of them and had made the ultimate sacrifice while attempting to protect Marcus. She most definitely felt the grief and shock of losing him and could not help herself from wondering what a delightful relationship could have continued to grow between him and Marcus. Ellis had quickly become the elder sibling influence that Marcus, as an only child, had previously not had the opportunity to experience; she now knew how terribly Marcus was suffering with the loss of his brotherly figure.

"We thank you, Oh Lord, for Ellis' life here on earth, and we recognize that the body lying before us is not his, but merely the house in which he resided. We know that Ellis is rejoicing now, in your presence Lord. As such, we will now commit his body to the earth, from whence we were created, and we will rejoice in the steadfast knowledge that he is now with you. We pray Oh Lord, that in the coming days, weeks and months, that Your Spirit will strengthen, sustain and comfort Ellis' friends and family. In Jesus' Name, Amen"

Reverend Jackson closed his bible and waited patiently as the bronzed casket was carefully lowered into its permanent resting place. Duty accomplished, the Reverend respectfully offered handshakes, condolences, and words of comfort to Ellis' adoptive mother, Alicia, and Marcus' Cousin Judy, who all now were aware had been revealed as Ellis' biological father. Marcus, Cassie and Margaret followed the Reverend as they made their way to Alicia and Judy to pay their final respects and offer words of solace and shared empathy. Cassie's parents led the remainder of the queue, consisting of a handful of Ellis' high school chums and a few other assorted acquaintances. Due to his involvement in the murderous spree of his adoptive father, Oliver Compton, local townsfolk were both hesitant and unprepared to present a sympathetic display toward his unexpected demise. Although Marcus and Cassie had made a concerted effort to be seen publicly with Ellis in an attempt to repair his image, the endeavor had been largely unsuccessful.

With the conclusion of the service, Marcus and Cassie walked with her parents, Jack and Debbie, who along with her young brother Charlie, were headed toward their car over on the gravel road some fifty yards to the south. From the cemetery, they planned to make the forty-five-minute drive to Alexandria for a late lunch at Alicia's new home. Although everyone in attendance for the funeral had been invited, the five of them, Cousin Judy, two of Ellis' classmates, and three of Alicia's new neighbors would be the only attendees. Margaret and Harvey Franklin both had to be back at their jobs as soon as possible, and the remaining mourners declined the invitation for various reasons. Marcus wished he already possessed his driver's license and could drive himself, but he was still a few weeks shy of turning sixteen.

Alicia had made good on the vow she had made to Ellis to again move back to Alexandria following the death of her ex-husband Oliver Compton, settling into her new home just more than one week prior to Ellis' passing. A few of her new neighbor ladies had brought food and desserts to her new home yesterday and this morning and had promised to help her out after the service and for the next few days. Judy had felt it was imperative that as many relatives as possible should be at Alicia's house after the service to show their support and, as a show of goodwill, the Worthington family had happily agreed to be there.

Following the meal, Cassie suggested to Marcus that they take leave and go outside for some fresh air. They stepped out onto the front porch and, after smoothing the back of her dainty taffeta black dress, Cassie carefully sat on the top of the three stairs leading down to the sidewalk. Marcus sat, joining her, as Cassie prepared to get out the words she had been holding back for well over an hour.

Attempting to use a hushed tone, in an effort not to be overhead, she asked, "Marcus, did you notice the two strange men at the cemetery?"

"No, I think I pretty well knew everyone there. I mean, honestly there weren't a lot of folks. Aside from a few of his classmates, there really weren't that many people there. Mr. Franklin, of course he came, and a couple of others," Marcus thought for a moment trying to recall any unfamiliar faces. "No, I don't recall any strangers. Who did you notice? If you describe them, maybe I can tell you who they were."

"I know it's not a big deal, but while the preacher was talking, I was kind of looking around and I saw two men that I didn't remember seeing at the wake or the funeral service at the church." Cassie explained. "I didn't think either of them looked familiar. And they both kept their distance."

"What do you mean, kept their distance?" Marcus looked at Cassie quizzically.

"I don't know, I mean they definitely weren't together. One was standing over by the parked cars, toward the very end of line and leaning against a car. He seemed strange, was kind of heavyset looking, and he had something in his hand. It kind of reminded me of a spy glass, you know like a pirate would use to look for land. Actually, now that I think of it, him and the last car in the line, the black one he was leaning on, they were both gone before the service was even finished."

"That's sort of weird," Marcus said. "I wonder why he'd have left early, I mean, if it was somebody who knew Ellis; you wouldn't think they'd hightail it would you?"

"No, I wouldn't think. And the other guy, he was standing way up by the tree line, looked kind of like a soldier that was standing at ease maybe, holding his hat down in front of him. He seemed to just kind of disappear, too. I didn't see him walk toward the cars or anything."

"That does sound strange, Cassie. Up at that tree line, I don't think there's nothing back there but forest. As far as I know, the only way out of the cemetery would be the road where all the cars were parked." Marcus was at a loss about either of the strangers. Shrugging his shoulders slightly, he said, "Maybe they were employees of the cemetery or something."

"You know what, Marcus," Cassie concluded, "I'm probably making something out of nothing. It was probably just a couple of guys that live out there in Monticello that have a thing about sitting in on funerals, right?"

"Probably so, Cassie."

Marcus elected to change the subject and suggested they make a detour on the way back to Cassie's house and ask her parents to drop them off at *Franklin's Five and Dime*. Cassie had no objections, actually feeling that his plan sounded superb. She did her utmost to put the funeral and cemetery conversation out of her mind. She sat, quietly enjoying the wooded scenery across the road from Alicia's house.

Cassie's parents were agreeable to their request, and a quarter past four that afternoon, the two were sitting side by side at the *Five and Dime* soda counter, occupying the same seats where they'd had their initial encounter with Ellis, four years earlier. Billy, Marcus' friend

Denny Wallace's brother, and still part-time soda jerk, took their drink and sandwich orders. In a few short minutes, their lunch had been delivered. But before digging in, they faced one another, and as planned, shared a toast with their chocolate milk shakes.

"To Ellis," Marcus offered.

"To Ellis," Cassie responded, with a sad but sincere smile.

April 6, 1969

"Marc, let's take a break!" bellowed Jude Allensworth as he plopped onto the worn green tufted sofa that he'd grown quite accustomed to during his sporadic visits over the course of the past six years. The faded, but reliable piece may have been in the neighborhood of fifteen years old, but the durable cotton upholstery still offered firm support and unbridled comfort. Far more than the exceedingly expensive and morbidly stiff living room set that adorned his own home in St. Louis. Each time he visited he was tempted to ask Margaret where she and Elijah had purchased the set and who the manufacturer had been, but he feared it would make him look small and tasteless. After all, he was a successful businessman, enjoying all the trappings that accompanied his status. Judy always strove to project an appearance of being upscale and well off, even around those with whom he shared a close relationship.

"Give me a minute Judy, I'll grab you and Louie a couple of beers and some Cokes for Denny and me," Marcus responded from Margaret's bedroom, where he and Denny had just carefully situated the new mattress and box spring set onto the beautiful, and also brand-new, four-poster bedframe that Margaret had recently purchased and had been delivered on Saturday to their new abode. She had gone mildly into debt to secure the new bedroom sets for both herself and Marcus. In anticipation of Marcus' eventual "fleeing from the roost", Margaret had upgraded his well-worn bedroom set from the twin that he had known all his life to a more appropriate and comfortable queen-size. Quite frankly, he had outgrown the old one several years ago.

Margaret and Marcus had reached a new plateau in their lives. Now, in April of 1969, and nearing the end of his junior year in high school, Marcus was pulling down a decent three and half dollars an hour at Walt's Tire and Auto, albeit still only working part-time during the school year. But fortunately he had been able to squirrel away some cash during the past two summers due, in no small part, to Walt allowing him to work full-time hours and occasionally even being rewarded with some overtime. Over the course of his employment, he had also become a fairly skilled, though still relatively novice, mechanic under the tutelage of Walt's master craftsmen, Louie Dupree and Chester Bernstein. Margaret had received a promotion to floor manager at the *Gold Mine*, in charge of the scheduling and performance of the restaurant's hostesses and servers, although she still occasionally helped out waiting tables when the staff was shorthanded. Both had seen substantial increases in their weekly paychecks and as a result had decided to move out of their apartment and into a house, a quaint two-bedroom rental with a covered carport. It was located on North Seventh Street, only about a block and a half from Marcus' friend, Denny Wallace, who resided with his family over on Jamison Street.

When Marcus had asked Louie if he could lend a hand with the move, he was mildly surprised when, even though they were moving on Easter Sunday, Louie had immediately and enthusiastically agreed. Sundays were the only full off days on Louie's busy schedule. He regularly worked five and a half days, each and every week. Aside from vacations and holidays, Frenchy, as Marcus affectionately had come to call him, appeared to never miss a day of work; the man seemed to be a living miracle as he had never gotten sick, not so much as a case of the sniffles, in the entire time Marcus had known him. He was a real professional who truly loved his craft. Nearly thirty years of age and unmarried, he lived alone in a rented room in a boarding house located on the south end of town. And when Louie was not working or busy reading the latest French-Canadian ice hockey journal, he could generally be found out behind Walt's shop tinkering with the latest addition to the ever-rotating small collection of off-road motorcycles that he bought, repaired, and sold as a hobby. Louie had grown quite fond of Marcus and made every effort to share his vast mechanical knowledge with the teen.

Denny Wallace had remained Marcus' best friend through everything, and still worked part-time manning the movie projector at The Meridian, which was still the only theater along U.S. Highway 61 between Hannibal and the Missouri-Iowa border. Denny had so grown to love the aura of the movies; he was hopelessly attracted to the allure of Hollywood. He was determined, upon graduation from Lewis and Clark High School next spring, to venture west and join the growing parade of young aspiring actors and actresses who were likewise seeking fame and fortune. Although acting was Denny's deepest desire and passion, Marcus had doubts that Denny's strict father, Doug Wallace, would be supportive of his plan. In Marcus' opinion, it seemed far more likely that Denny would either find himself drafted into the army, or follow in Doug's footsteps, and enlist in the navy.

Shortly after its grand opening, the area's new, but now one-year-old 8-lane bowling center boasted in its employ an intelligent and eager, but quite inexperienced, red-haired, freckled and, of course, pigtail wearing concessionaire in the form of Marcus' true best friend, Cassie Worthington. She had made the decision, with the end of her sophomore year coinciding with the opening of *Riverwalk Lanes*, that she was ready to begin earning her own spending money rather than having to rely on her measly two dollar per week allowance. Cassie had also begun to feel guilty about her dependency upon Marcus, as he paid for just about everything, from eating at *A & W* or the *River's Edge Diner*, to going to the movies, playing pinball, or making the occasional shopping trip to Quincy. She felt better about herself and enjoyed a slight feeling of independence and self-reliance knowing she could share some of the financial responsibility in her relationship with Marcus.

During an earlier visit with Margaret and Marcus, Cousin Judy had learned of the planned move onto North Seventh Street and had insisted upon driving up from St. Louis to lend assistance. Although Judy was only in his mid-forties, it had become apparent that he had been a desk jockey his entire adult life, and no longer possessed the stamina to keep up with the teen-aged Marcus and Denny, nor the ten years younger Louie Dupree. As the day wore on, Judy found he needed rest periods far more frequently than those required by the youngsters. In Marcus' opinion, there was little doubt that Judy's habit of three or more packs of unfiltered cigarettes per day were the root cause of his fading energy. Marcus was quite aware of the dangers associated with smoking, as the subject had been a debate topic in both social studies and health classes in school. Congress had even ordered back in 1965 that cigarette packs must contain labels with health warnings, and now, in 1969, rumors persisted that a likely ban on cigarette advertising on television was being seriously considered. Largely thanks to his enlightenment on the subject, Marcus had thus far, other than some brief experimentation with a corncob pipe, managed to steer clear of the addicting grasp of tobacco.

Marcus brought a chilled, condensation-covered bottle of Budweiser to Judy, who was splayed on the couch, eyes closed, legs spread wide apart, with shoes kicked off and appearing, for all intents and purposes, as if he likely would never vacate the space he was now inhabiting.

"Is he alright?" Denny whispered to Marcus with sincerity.

"I'm sure he is Denny," Marcus whispered in response. His face bore a smile, but Marcus' expression lacked any real sense of conviction.

Denny continued out the front door, where he met up with Louie, and handed him a cold brew. The two sat in the shaded, and somewhat relative, comfort of the screened-in porch and enjoyed their respective cold drinks.

"So Frenchy, where did you find that motorcycle? Is it a Triumph?" Denny asked innocently enough. A simple pair of questions, to be sure, about the sleek red motorcycle parked in the Clemens' front yard. Little did Denny realize the floodgate he had opened, nor the intense education he was about to receive concerning the history and mechanical breakdown of a one-year-old Kawasaki C2SS enduro bike. There was only one thing Louie Dupree loved as dearly as working on motorcycles, and much to Denny's chagrin, it was talking about them.

"Judy," Marcus said, trying not to startle his obviously dozing cousin.

At the sound of his name, Judy stirred, snapped to, and quickly sat up, gratefully accepting the beer that Marcus held in his outstretched hand.

"Sorry Marc, I wasn't asleep, I swear. Just resting my eyes for a minute," said Judy as he adjusted his posture from nearly prone to upright. He took three hefty gulps of the refreshing beverage and turned to his cigarette pack on the end table to his left. After packing the smoke by tapping both ends on the table, he lit up, inhaled deeply and, through a raspy cough, exhaled a string of smoke clouds that were larger, in Marcus' opinion, than several well-ripened cantaloupes.

"You know Marc, whenever I have moved, I generally have hired some dirt bags to do the manual labor for me." Judy said in a somewhat condescending manner. "Apologize to Mags for me when she gets home later. Instead of volunteering to help, I should have just contracted with some outfit to do this move for her. I gotta admit, I don't much have it in me anymore for this kind of work."

"Don't worry about it Judy." Marcus felt a little bad for him. "I'll tell her what you said, but me and Denny and Louie, we don't mind doing this, and we....especially me, really do appreciate your help. It means a lot to me and Mama just that you came and offered. You really didn't have to make this long drive, you know. We would have managed just fine."

"I guess I know that Marc," Judy shrugged before continuing, "but I guess I kind of saw it as a way of getting a little closer to you and Mags."

"That's nice of you to say Judy." Marcus said. "I wish Mama could have been here too, she had planned to be here helping too, but with what happened at the restaurant, she didn't have much choice."

Margaret had specifically asked for the day off from the *Gold Mine*, but two of the waitresses were sisters, and they had experienced a death in the family. Both were out on bereavement leave and had gone to

Indiana. Margaret was reluctant to put all the burden of the move on Marcus, his friends, and Judy, but she was left with little alternative. Marcus took the news of the emergency in stride; he had matured a great deal in the past couple of years and had developed a great knack for handling and dealing with personal responsibility. He had never doubted that he could oversee the move effortlessly. He was no longer the young boy who might lock the front door and just wander away, totally unaware that he had left the housekey lying on the kitchen table. No, he was seventeen now and quite mature. In a few short months' time, he would turn eighteen and be required to register with Selective Service. He couldn't help but realize that in another year he might well find himself in Southeast Asia with a rifle in hands defending his country. If he was going to be mature enough to handle that type of pressure and responsibility, he figured that he surely ought to be able to oversee moving into a new house.

As Judy tilted his head back, finishing off his bottle of beer, Marcus looked at the wrinkles beginning to really take root around Judy's eyes. Then as Judy dropped his head back down, he noticed the pronounced sag in the jowls and the not very subtle development of a double chin. Judy was really beginning to show his age, and Marcus couldn't help but wonder how his own father would have looked today. Sure Elijah would have been three or four years younger than Judy, but he would have had to have begun showing signs of aging as well, wouldn't he? He would have been what, forty-one already? The first memories Marcus had of

Judy; he was probably only in his late thirties. And Marcus remembered that Judy already was showing premature gray hair. Since Judy and Marcus' father came from the same paternal bloodline, would Marcus' dad have displayed similar physical traits at this age? Marcus realized that, unfortunately, the question was unanswerable. It was only himself and Cousin Judy that were the only surviving members of Clemens' bloodline. Of course, there should also have been Ellis.

Thinking back, Marcus realized that he could recall several similarities between Judy and Ellis. Their height and general shape were not identical, but they certainly had silhouettes that were indistinguishable. Seen in dark surroundings, with their faces unrecognizable, and despite their age difference, no eyewitness could have been able to tell one from the other. In Marcus' memory their facial profiles were nearly mirror images, and with the obvious exceptions of hair color and the maturity of their facial hair, there was no doubt that they were father and son. The similarities didn't end with just the physical make-up. It occurred to Marcus that it had to be mental and personality-wise as well. Despite growing up and not knowing Judy at all, being raised by Ollie and Alicia Compton, the two even had the propensity to dress alike. Unless he had been dressed for a business meeting, in every memory that Marcus had of Judy, he was dressed in blue jeans or slacks and was wearing a white tee-shirt. Just as he had been today. Today, Judy had worn brown corduroy slacks, and predictably, was sporting a white tee-shirt, with a pack of Chesterfield cigarettes rolled up in the left sleeve. In almost every encounter Marcus could recall, Ellis had been attired in either blue or black jeans and always sported a white tee shirt.

Shaking himself of his mental wandering, Marcus asked Judy if he'd like one more Budweiser.

"No, Marc, but thank you for offering," Judy said as he stretched his arms out forward, as if trying to relax a tight lower back. "I think it might be time for me to hit the road and head back to St. Louie. I think all the heavy work is about done here, ain't it?"

"Oh, yeah, for sure, Judy," Marcus replied, still partially entrenched with his earlier thoughts.

"You know, sometimes, Marc, I wish Ellis was still here. Wouldn't it have been nice to have his young strapping self here helping out today?" Marcus was taken back by Judy's seemingly off-hand comment. Ellis was a topic that rarely was mentioned by Judy. Since Ellis' death, it had always seemed to Marcus that Judy had adopted an out of sight, out of mind philosophy. And unfortunately, Marcus had found himself in a similar situation when in the presence of Judy. The last time Marcus had initiated a conversation with Judy, which concerned Ellis, had been the most difficult interaction with Judy he had ever suffered. It had occurred just a short few weeks before Christmas of 1967. Marcus, as he had been instructed a month earlier, had passed along the message that Opa had sent from beyond.

"Judy, I don't really know a decent way of telling you what I have to tell you. It's so hard, but I have to do it," Marcus stammered. How could Opa have possibly

asked an immature sixteen-year-old kid to give a message like this to a grieving father?

"What is it Marcus, I mean, hell, it sounds like something bad. So what is it? Is something wrong with Mags, or your girl? What?" In his own way, Judy had a habit of sounding pushy and condescending whenever he spoke. And especially after Ellis' death. He had been troubled deeply by the loss, and while Marcus had terribly dreaded delivering the message, he knew it had to be done. It couldn't be put off any longer. He was deathly afraid of the possible consequences and was truly worried about the reaction he would receive from Judy. With a deep breath he had continued.

"Judy, I was given an anonymous message, and told that it was to be relayed to you," Marcus began.

"Anonymous? Who gave you this message?" Judy asked as his mind raced through possibilities of the contents and source of this 'message'.

"I'm sorry, Judy, but I can't tell you where it came from." Marcus knew he would have to lie a little bit to preserve the truth that could not be revealed. "It was typewritten and left on the windshield of my Metro during school about a week ago." Marcus had to tell a wild story and try to make it sound somewhat plausible. He had to keep the knowledge to himself that Opa had delivered the message through Cassie more than a month ago. It had to come out like he'd just received it, and this was the first opportunity that he'd had to deliver the message face-to-face.

"Is it somebody going through you to try to bribe me or something? Oh, Jeez, just get to it Marc." Judy's impatience was threatening to turn into anger.

"Okay, Judy." Marcus was blunt. "It said to give you these eleven words. 'This is all your fault, Jude. You are responsible for Ellis'.'"

Judy threw a ceramic ashtray onto the floor, shattering it. "Nobody calls me Jude, nobody. Who sent that note Marc? I have to know; I'll kill the son-of-a.....who sent it Marc?" The seven other startled customers at the 'River's Edge Diner' gazed in astonished amazement at the seemingly unprovoked display.

Before Marcus could respond, he saw Buster, the cook, out of the corner of his eye and he was fast approaching.

"What's the problem over here fellas? Marcus, you of all people and you, Judy? What the hell?"

Surprisingly, Judy composed himself quickly and apologized to Buster. "I'm sorry man, I was telling Marc here about a guy at work that pissed me off, and I guess I just got a little too animated, I'm really sorry. Hey, you got a broom and dustpan? I'll clean this up for you."

"Nah, don't worry about it, just don't pull this kind of stunt again, okay?"

"I won't, Buster. You got my word. Hey, add two bucks to my bill to pay for the ashtray, would you?" Judy offered in an attempt to smooth things over.

"You bet I will, thanks Judy," said Buster as he looked up from gathering the shards that had splattered across the floor.

The two sat in silence until the bill was paid. When they got back out to Judy's Corvette, and before he even put the key in the ignition, Judy, eyes focused straight ahead and not looking at Marcus, said, "Not another word about the message. I don't want to know who gave it to you or why. But I don't ever want to hear another word about it from you." There wasn't a doubt in Marcus' mind that while the matter might have been concluded between the two of them, Judy wouldn't rest until he knew who had sent the message.

True to his word, Judy had never brought up the message again. Marcus had no idea of how Judy had processed the words, or to what lengths he may have gone to try to locate the person who had originated the message. Judy rarely mentioned Ellis, and Cassie had often told Marcus that she thought it strange that Judy never seemed to want to discuss Ellis. Cassie had developed an interest in medicine and its many related fields. She was an inquisitive sort by nature, and not only was interested in the physiological, but also liked to look into the psychological aspects of medicine. Cassie was in the beginning stages of making plans to attend college in the fall of 1970, but she had yet to make a definitive determination about whether she would prefer to study medicine or if perhaps psychiatry or psychology would be her ultimate calling.

"Yep, you're right Judy. I really wish Ellis was here. You know, he had become kind of like a brother to me. I had begun to confide in him a lot." It was true that Marcus did find himself still thinking a lot about

Ellis and all that had transpired. But at this moment, for fear that he may have upset Judy, he wished he had not said as much about Ellis as he had.

"Oh, I know you did Marc," Judy responded. "Him and I had developed a really close bond, and he had sort of gotten that way with me, too. You know, the confiding, the soul baring type of stuff. He used to tell me a lot, yeah, he did." Judy paused as he put his shoes back on. Standing, he offered his hand to Marcus. "I know I wasn't much help, but I enjoyed seeing you and your friends. Give Mags a hug for me when she gets home, will you?"

"Yeah, I will Judy. Drive careful, won't you?"

By 6:00 p.m., Denny and Louie had also left and Marcus found himself sitting alone staring in an exhausted trance at the television, which wasn't even turned on. At a few minutes past six, there was a light knock and the front door swung open. Standing somewhat silhouetted in the doorway, with the setting sun casting a burnt orange aura around her, was a sight for sore eyes. Clad in black pants and a white shirt that was generously decorated with various minor stains, a mishmash of reds, yellows, and with a smattering of smeared green pickle relish, Cassie Worthington and her lovely red pigtails stood waiting patiently to hear Marcus' invitation to enter.

"I'm sure glad to see you Cassie!" Marcus exclaimed with a good deal of enthusiasm, especially considering how tired he actually felt. "Come on in and sit down. Do you want a Coke?"

"No thanks, Marcus. I just had one on the way from the bowling alley," Cassie said as she took a seat next to him on the couch. "How did the move go?"

"Oh, it went really well, Twigs." Cassie might have let her red hair grow back out, after experimenting with a pixie cut a couple of years ago, but the nickname that Marcus had so cleverly bestowed upon her had lived on. He still called her Cassie in most instances, but the choice of which moniker he used depended a great deal upon the prevailing mood.

"Everything is in its place and I even swept all the floors. I think Mama will be pretty impressed," Marcus said with a combination of both pride and confidence.

"The house sure looks nice, Marcus. I think she'll be happy with what you guys did." Cassie had to admit, the house did look pretty presentable. She felt a bit proud of Marcus for the finished product.

"How was your Cousin Judy today? Did he provide a lot of help?" Cassie asked.

"Oh, he was fine," Marcus said. "You know Cassie, I'm just a little bit worried about him."

"Why so?"

"Well, he just seems like he's aged a lot the last couple of years, you know, since Ellis, you know." Marcus said somewhat glumly. "He seems like he's aged a lot, he's getting wrinkly, putting on weight. And all those cigarettes he smokes, you know that can't be good for him. He couldn't keep up today. He spent more time on the couch than doing anything. I just hope he made it back to St. Louis okay. Even the way he drives, that's still a two-hour trip you know."

23

"Oh, I'm sure he's fine," Cassie reassured. "He's not that old, you know it's not like he's seventy or something, right?"

"Yeah, you're right," Marcus agreed. "How was your day? How were your tips today?"

"Pretty good, I think," Cassie answered. "I made six dollars and eighty-five cents. Not bad for a little more than five hours of work, right?"

"Yeah, I'd say so," Marcus was proud that Cassie did well at her job. She was very congenial and fun-loving, never failing to provide service with a smile. "I'm sorry I couldn't call you this morning before you went to work, but the phone was shut off at the apartment yesterday and this one won't get turned on until tomorrow. And to be honest, I didn't even think to stop by a payphone this morning."

"Oh, that's okay Marcus, I understand." Cassie hesitated for a moment before adding, "I do kind of wish you could have called though. It would have been nice if I could have heard your voice. I had an awful dream last night."

"You had a nightmare? I'm sorry, Sweetie." Sweetie had been a relatively new nickname in the rotation and had its own specific usages. It was reserved for sad, sorry, or emotional situations where caring, empathy or sympathy were the order of the day. Marcus was going to be eighteen soon, and with his maturity, he was learning rapidly - or so he had convinced himself - how to respond to Cassie's needs.

"Well, maybe it wasn't really a nightmare, just a brief, really uncomfortable dream."

"So tell me about it, get it out in the open, so you can put it behind you, okay?" Marcus suggested.

"Well Marcus, I found myself just suddenly sitting at a nice round table, with an absolutely beautiful tablecloth; that's the very first thing I noticed was the beautiful tablecloth. Then the cup of tea in a lovely English style cup with a matching, very old-style tea pitcher in the center of the table. The room was kind of dark, the only light coming from a few candles that were scattered around and a little distance away from the table." Cassie had been speaking with her head down, concentrating on her memory of the dream's details, but now she looked up to try to gauge the look she would see on Marcus' face. He appeared to be listening intently, but she sensed he wasn't terribly impressed with her discussion of the tableware. So, she continued, "It was when I noticed the candlelight that I looked around a bit and also noticed who was sitting across from me. Marcus, it was Ellis. He looked exactly like he did when he died. I mean, he wasn't in his jeans and tee shirt like we always saw him. He was in a suit, just like the one he was wearing in his casket."

"Well now Cassie, that only makes sense that you would see Ellis that way in your dream. That was the last vision you had of him; it was in his casket. Of course that's why you'd remember him that way in your dream. That's why a lot of people don't go to funerals, they don't want to see a person in a casket because that's not how they want to remember them. People want happy memories of the dead." Marcus tried to explain away the negative thoughts Cassie was having in regard to her dream.

Cassie sat quietly, carefully absorbing Marcus' words. But, after a moment's consideration and upon further reflection on the images her mind had conjured, she elaborated on her original narrative.

"But that wasn't all, Marcus. Sitting to my left was a lovely lady with beautiful long red hair. Her face seemed, oh...I don't know the word," Cassie muttered in frustration, "but it was kind of blurred. And now I remember Marcus. Ellis called her mother, very politely. I could swear I heard him ask her, 'more tea, mother?' and he seemed to have a smile, a really sad, kind of forlorn smile. Marcus, we have to look that story up again about Paula Sue Schaeffer. I have to see her picture. I have to know if that was her in my dream."

"That is a pretty weird dream, Cassie," Marcus said, quite unsure of the proper response, "but it really doesn't mean anything, I mean, not really. I've had dreams about Ellis, and I'm sure you've dreamt of him before last night, too. And maybe you were just seeing that newspaper clipping picture of his mother, like in your subconscious or something. It's nothing. You and I both know that. It was just a silly dream. You need to just put it out of your mind, okay?"

"Maybe it was just a silly dream, but I don't think I can just put it out of my mind and forget it." She seemed to shudder as she shook her head and closed her eyes. Suddenly, another aspect of the dream burst into Cassie's mind. "Oh my God, there's another thing I just remembered Marcus! And I'm telling you, this really does scare me. Sitting at the table, off to my right, there was a little girl with red hair and pigtails. And her face was really, really blurry, even more than the woman's. And Marcus, nobody was moving in the dream. They all just sat there, not moving, just staring straight ahead. Or maybe not, maybe they were looking at me. I'm not sure. Marcus, I think they were all sitting there dead. It was like Ellis was dead, his mother was dead, and even the little girl was dead. All of those people were dead Marcus, everybody but me. And now I'm afraid. It makes me scared Marcus. Marcus, I couldn't see that little girl's face. She had my hair. Marcus, what if that little girl in the dream was me?"

The Stranger

Harvey Franklin, "Dutch" as he was known to friends and employees, or "Old Man Franklin" as his abundant young pre-adolescent and teenage clientele generally referred to him, gingerly lifted a full case of Kleenex tissues onto the roller conveyor and carefully sliced along three edges and flipped back the top before stamping the boxes with the current price. Opening and pricing merchandise was but a small part of the daily routine with which Dutch had to contend, six days a week and fifty-two weeks a year. When it came to owning and operating *Franklin's Five and Dime*, the tasks were endless and the work never seemed to get done. He had been the sole proprietor, performing the hiring and firing, overseeing the buying and selling, and basically, he had shouldered the sole responsibility for keeping his customers happy for the better part of thirty-five years now. He had taken control of *Franklin's Mercantile*, as the general store had been known during his father's ownership, as an eighteen-year-old way back in 1934, following his father's sudden death, the result of a massive heart attack. Benjamin, as his father had been graciously named, had moved in 1931 to northeastern Missouri from Chicago, Illinois, bringing along a wife and teenaged son. He had fallen upon hard times following the stock market crash of 1929 and the ensuing Great Depression, but had been emboldened by a highly enthusiastic, yet somewhat pragmatic, vision of opening a general store in what had years ago been a booming little river town known as Tully. Word had spread that a new lock and dam was about to be built on the Mississippi River, and Benjamin was convinced that the project was going to lead to a massive revitalization of the former site of Tully. Construction workers and engineers would soon populate the area, and he envisioned unprecedented growth. Benjamin anticipated the creation of a budding metropolis, somewhat similar to Quincy, about twenty miles to the south, on Illinois' eastern bank of the river. And while there initially was an influx of workers concurrent with the commencement of construction, by the time of the dam's completion in 1935, the area had seen a mass exodus of those anticipated residents. As a result, the eighteen-year-old Harvey Franklin found himself owning a small general store with a scarcity of customers. But the young "Dutch", as he had mysteriously come to be known, had stuck to his guns, carried on his father's dream, and had somehow persevered. Despite a sparse local population, he had managed to carve out a solid reputation with a meager, but fairly thriving business.

"Hello, Mr. Franklin," the overweight gentleman, dressed in neatly pressed black slacks and sporting a very unique bright orange blazer and matching tie, got up and extended a meaty right hand as he strode toward the approaching store owner. The stranger had been seated on a metal folding chair and waited patiently, just outside the slightly elevated small office that was located a dozen or so feet inside and to the right of the store's front door. The small office served Harvey Franklin well, for its slightly raised platform allowed him a vantage point from which he could oversee both cash registers, the candy shelves – which occasionally were the object of aspiring young shoplifters' desires – and the small soda fountain and its nearby magazine rack.

Dutch Franklin had been notified by the store's long-time and trustworthy morning cashier/bookkeeper, Mrs. Lewelyn MacGregor, who had hurried down to the basement storeroom to inform him of a gentleman who had insistently requested to speak with the store manager and was now waiting at Dutch's office. After reluctantly trudging up the dozen steps, Dutch approached the man and accepted the invitation to shake hands with a gentleman that he could only assume that, even though it was Saturday, had to be a sales representative intent upon introducing a new product into *Franklin's Five and Dime*. Somewhat surprisingly however, the stranger introduced himself, not as a sales rep, but as a private detective hailing from Connecticut.

"My name is James Burgess, Mr. Franklin," the stranger announced as he shook hands. "Thank you for taking the time to speak with me. I've traveled a long

31

way to see you. You see, I'm investigating a case that we're working on back in Hartford, Connecticut."

"That's an awfully long ways from here Mr. Burgess," Dutch replied. "What in the world could you be working on that could possibly involve me? I've never been any further east than Chicago in my entire life. Certainly never been to Connecticut."

"Oh no, relax Mr. Franklin. I'm not here for anything that directly concerns you. I am just interested in compiling some background information that might help us to solve a little malfeasance that occurred back east several years ago."

"What kind of malfeance? Is that the word? What's that even mean Mr. Burgess? I guess I'm not really familiar with the word."

"Oh sorry. It's malfeasance. In this particular case, it's an illegal act that causes someone monetary harm. You'll have to excuse me, but I can't go into much detail, but we're investigating a case that has to do with property that might have been stolen from a citizen of Connecticut. I guess it wouldn't hurt to let you in on the fact that the victim is a rather well-known former resident of this general area."

That information being shared by Mr. Burgess rather puzzled Dutch. He had lived in this area for more than thirty-eight years and was familiar with a large percentage of the local population. He certainly didn't know of anyone who would have been considered either "well-known" or that had been a former resident and was now living in Connecticut.

"Well, that doesn't really mean anything to me, sir. I've known a lot of the folks in these parts, but it sure don't mean nothing to me." Dutch had absolutely no clue as to who or what Mr. Burgess might have been referring.

"Let me get into some specifics then, Mr. Franklin. Do you mind if I call you Harvey, sir?" the man asked.

"Most everybody calls me Dutch; you can do the same, Mr. Burgess," he replied.

"Good, good. And please, feel free to call me Jimbo, Dutch. I prefer informality whenever possible. I guess what I need to ask you is pretty forthright, Dutch. As you yourself said, you're pretty familiar with the folks in this part of Lewis County, right?" The private investigator didn't hesitate to stare Harvey Franklin directly in the eye.

Dutch sized up his interrogator, wondering what he was about to be asked.

"Dutch, I'm sure you hear a lot of scuttlebutt, rumors, and innuendo, you know, being in the position you're in, here in a small-town little store like this. I imagine you get to know your customers pretty well and are privy to some juicy tidbits about people and their business, you know goings on and such." Jimbo paused, seemingly for effect, before continuing, "Before I go digging and delving too far into people's lives, it would be a lot easier for everyone involved if I could get a firm grip on the right track, I mean, right from the get-go, you see what I'm getting at?"

33

Dutch realized this man was going to expect him to divulge someone's deep and dark secrets, and the thought of such a request made him extremely uneasy. He knew his customers well, and yes he did know a lot of secrets. He'd heard lots of rumors. Things like romantic affairs and petty crime. Hell, he even had knowledge of some really deep secrets that he had preferred to keep to himself, things he probably would have been wise to have shared with the Lewis County Sheriff's Department. He had always been a believer in discretion being the better part of valor. And now this man, this stranger, was preparing to ask him to give up information on someone, perhaps someone he knew quite well, perhaps even someone who was a good friend. And Dutch suddenly realized, he didn't know this man from Adam. This fellow had just appeared out of thin air. He hadn't sent advance notice of his visit or prefaced his appearance in any way. He had just shown up, unannounced.

"Yes, Jimbo, I think I do see what you're getting at. But it occurs to me that I don't have even the slightest clue of who you really are," Dutch was wary of saying anything more.

"Hey, listen Dutch, I know where you're coming from. And I don't blame you at all for wanting to protect your friends and acquaintances. I should have sensed that about you before I even started talking." Jimbo reached into the breast pocket of his loud, and to be quite honest, obnoxious orange jacket and proceeded to pull out a thick, heavy duty black leather identification holder. Flipping it open, he offered for Dutch's inspection an official looking Connecticut private detective identification card and badge. While everything appeared to be in order, Dutch couldn't shake the thought that the badge didn't appear too terribly more authentic than the children's sheriff and deputy badges that he sold just two aisles over in the toy section, right next to the cap guns and holsters.

"I hope that makes you feel better, Dutch," Jimbo said with a reassuring smile. "Let me just get to it, Dutch. I really don't want to waste a lot of your time, and I've got a few other people to talk to and plus, I've got budget and time restraints myself."

"Alright, Jimbo," Dutch relented, resigning himself to help this seemingly busy fellow. "Go ahead, ask away."

"Dutch, have you heard any kind of scuttlebutt about anybody round here that might have either cashed in on a big inheritance or maybe was in line for one?"

"No sir can't say that I have. I mean Hubert Tompkins got his dad's farm after he passed last summer. And the Fuller kid down in LaGrange, his granddad down in Hannibal, when he died, Tommy got the old man's '56 Belair. But that's all I heard about the last year or so, I'd say."

"That's it, huh? Go on back a few years, maybe even '65 or '66. Nothing else at all comes to you?" James Burgess sure seemed to be searching for something in particular, definitely not just idly fishing for random information.

"Well, there was that killer. That guy Oliver Compton from Monticello. Right before he got himself killed in prison, he sold his house and land to that body shop guy. Schofield was his name. But then Schofield got himself killed, too. I don't actually know what happened to his place." Dutch was trying to recall what he could from that black mark on county history. "I don't really think he had any family. Seems like maybe it all went to probate or something. I know that they had a hard time selling that property. Everybody around here felt like it was cursed. Heck, the last three people that lived there, they all three got themselves murdered. I think it finally got unloaded this past winter, some folks from out of town bought it. But I think they just took it on as an investment. So far as I know, nobody's ever moved in there."

"That's it? Nothing else comes to mind at all?" Jimbo asked.

"Nothing else comes to mind, no."

James Burgess took his time, obviously contemplating his next move. Just how much did he feel comfortable revealing?

"Okay, Dutch. I don't want to hold you up any longer, but let me just throw out a name at you, okay?"

"Yeah, shoot. Whose name?" Dutch asked, a little frustrated with the length of the conversation, and about ready to wrap up this interview.

"Do you know anybody named Marcus Clemens?" The question took Dutch back just a bit. Of course he knew Marcus Clemens. Unless you lived under a rock, everyone in the county knew Marcus.

"Yeah, I know him. He's a pretty popular kid around here," he said.

"Really? Well, what do you know about him?" Jimbo asked, suddenly seeming to be very interested.

"Ah, he's just a local kid. Him and his little girl-friend used to come in here a lot, you know, for magazines and milkshakes mostly, but not so much lately though, since he's nearly grown now."

"That's it? Nothing special about him?" the man dug deeper.

"Well, probably nothing to it, but rumor has it that he's a descendent of that writer Mark Twain, you know the fellow who wrote *Tom Sawyer and Huck Finn*? He came from Hannibal back in, what was it, the mid 1800's?" Dutch related. "Probably nothing to it though. I mean, I've been here since 1931. I knew the kid's dad from when he used to come in here back when he was just a kid. I never heard anything like that when he was alive. That crap just started a few years ago. It all coincided with all the killings that went on there for a few years."

"Killings? What killings are you talking about?" James Burgess had now become highly interested.

"Well, it started with the girl over at the river," Dutch began. "Marcus was the one that found the poor girl's body. Then Oliver Compton, or Ollie like we all knew him, remember, I mentioned him earlier? Anyway he got convicted of killing that girl, but then he got killed in prison. And then a little bit later on there were something like five murders out at the Schofield property, the one I told you about before, the place that people think is cursed. Anyway, Oliver Compton's son Ellis, who used to work here by the way, as a soda jerk, well he was one of the five that were killed that day."

"Gosh, Dutch. That's a pretty involved story. So where does Marcus Clemens fit in exactly?"

"Well, turns out he and Ellis were related, and the word is that Ollie Compton figured that out. And supposedly, and now this is only rumor mind you, but he also or so they say, figured out that Marcus was, somehow or another, in line for an inheritance from Mark Twain. And Ollie thought if he could get Marcus out of the picture that he could get his boy Ellis in there to collect the inheritance. Or so the story goes. But, who knows? I mean, it's all just rumors. Until I see Marcus Clemens driving around in a new sports car, I think the inheritance crap, well it's just a bunch of hogwash."

"Well hey, thanks for your time and the information Dutch," Jimbo said as he suddenly seemed to have heard enough. He offered his hand once again. "I appreciate you talking to me. You might have helped me a bit, we'll see. But thanks again. You have a good day now, okay?" James Burgess seemed almost in a hurry as he headed back out into the sunlight. Dutch Franklin watched from the large storefront window as the private eye got into what looked to Dutch like a somewhat rusty black 1956 Pontiac Sky Chief Safari. Dutch was relatively sure of the make and model because he had owned an identical vehicle, except for his being red with a white top. As Burgess drove off, it occurred to Dutch that a private detective traveling all the way from Connecticut and apparently working on a very high-profile case involving an inheritance, would surely have sported a newer and more reliable mode of transportation than the fifteen-year-old clunker that he had just pulled away in.

The more he thought about it, the more uneasy Dutch felt. He wondered if he wasn't beginning to piece some nagging, but ill-fitting puzzle pieces together. By early evening, he had nearly convinced himself that perhaps he had seen both the private investigator and his familiar vehicle somewhere once before.

At the traffic light and safely out of sight of any prying eyes, Jimbo Burgess made a right-hand turn and headed south on U.S. Highway 61, searching for the first available payphone. Spying the first unused phone booth just off the shoulder of the road, he pulled into the *A & W* parking lot. Entering the booth, Jimbo quickly glanced around to make certain there were no bystanders who might inadvertently overhear his conversation. After dialing "0" and being connected, he recited to the operator a long-distance number and requested the charges be reversed. In a matter of seconds, Jimbo heard the man answer and accept the charges.

"Hello, Sarge? It's Jimbo," he said, his excitement hard to contain.

"That was quick. Did you learn anything?" The voice on the other end seemed to have no desire to indulge in small talk.

"Yep, the first person I talked to pretty much verified everything. He sure seemed to know a lot about everybody around here."

"So it's just a matter of following through with the plan, then. You know the mark, where he lives and everything?" Sarge asked.

"I'll find out soon enough. It's a small town, won't take much effort," Jimbo answered.

"Good. It's been a long wait. I'm glad we're finally beginning to see the light at the end of the tunnel."

"Yeah, I wish we could have solved this little mystery two years ago, when I first started staking out these characters," lamented James Burgess.

"Hey, just like taking on any new job, you've got to do probation, right? I'm sure the reward is going to justify the time and effort Jimbo. Good work so far. Now let's see it through. Get it done and get back here as soon as possible," said the voice on the other end.

"Will do, Sarge."

"Keep in touch," were the last words that Sarge uttered before the line clicked and went dead.

Jimbo replaced the receiver, pulled on the booth's accordion door and stepped back out onto the hot asphalt parking lot.

"Well, enough for one day," he said to himself as he wedged his large frame back behind the steering wheel of his Chevy. James Burgess suddenly felt parched, and luckily for him, he had discovered a favorite local watering hole on his first night in the area. With the success of today now in the rearview mirror, the allure of a frosty cold mug of beer was too much for

40

him to resist. He felt confident that he would be able to gather the remaining information that he needed in the morning, and that it would just be a matter of another day or two until his mission would be accomplished. In the meantime, Jimbo considered himself off the clock and continued driving south on Highway 61 toward La-Grange. From there he would head west on County Road C and rediscover the infamous *Bar None Saloon.*

A Bad Day Indeed

"So, think back, Marcus," Cassie said as she half turned to her left, placing her left hand on Marcus' right thigh. It was Monday, the day after the move, and the two had just exited the Lewis and Clark High School parking lot. Behind the wheel of his Nash Metro, Marcus was intending to take Cassie to the *A & W*, planning to treat her to a root beer float. He wasn't scheduled to work today at Walt's Tire and Auto Repair, and as such, it was one of the rare afternoons that the young couple were celebrating some uninterrupted time together. Unfortunately, it appeared that Cassie was intent upon continuing the uncomfortable conversation that had begun during lunch break but had been halted, to Marcus' great relief, when his best friend Denny had sat down at their table, shouldering up to Cassie and effectively forcing an end to their private discussion. The topic of the aborted conversation was a matter that did trouble Marcus deeply, and actually was a source of extreme angst in his young life.

"I know you would never have been foolish enough to have told Denny, but is there anyone else, besides me and Margaret that you discussed any of this with, anyone at all?" Cassie continued her questioning because, in her eyes, Marcus was suffering from a great deal of internal and emotional distress. The question posed by Cassie really wasn't even a new one. Many times they had repeated much of the same nonsense regarding both Marcus' potential inheritance and the gold bars that he and Ellis had discovered. Of course, Cassie knew all about the contents of the footlocker, the document binder, all of the legal paperwork, the stock certificate, newspaper clippings, the letter from his father, and the note mysteriously left by his grandfather. She had seen everything first-hand. And with all the tragic events, including the death of Ellis, on July 4, 1967, Marcus had been very open and had withheld nothing from Cassie. He had freely, and without hesitation, discussed what he and Ellis had found in the remote cave on the Illinois side of the Mississippi. Last summer, the two had even borrowed Doug Wallace's canoe and made the painstaking excursion downstream and back on the river so that Cassie could see the bounty with her very own eyes. No, the topic wasn't new by any means, but it certainly seemed to hold far more of Cassie's intense interest and attention than Marcus was comfortable with. Although he would prefer the subject be dropped for good, he knew she meant well and only was concerned with his well-being. Marcus was sure that Cassie felt it was in his best interest for him to talk through everything and hoped that eventually it would aid in clearing his conscience and eventually alleviate his emotional strife. However, even with all the understanding Marcus could muster, he felt it did little to diminish the amount of guilt that he still felt, nor the heavy burden of responsibility that Marcus shouldered over the death of Ellis and all the others who had perished that day.

"Cassie, we've been over this a hundred times now, haven't we? I told you and Ellis, and that's all. You two were the only people in the world that knew every detail. Mama knows what's in the footlocker, but to this day, I still have never mentioned the gold bars to her." Marcus had long ago grown weary of having to go through all of this, rehashing everything over and over again. In many ways, he wished he had never even known about the items they had found in the footlocker. And besides, Marcus was completely confident that his girlfriend had done a thorough job of researching and investigating the Detmeyer Drydock and Machine Company of St. Louis, and from what Cassie had learned, the stock he was about to inherit in the Detmeyer company apparently was going to be worth absolutely nothing. Her research revealed that the company had gone bankrupt and dissolved some forty years ago, falling victim to the combination of both the stock market crash of 1929 and the decline in need for steamship production in the early twentieth century. All in all, it turned out that the very existence of Marcus' supposed inheritance had come at the expense of at least nine or ten people's lives. Had it not been for Opa stepping into his life, either he or Cassie, and possibly both of them could have been included in that toll.

45

"I know what you've told me over and over is the truth, Marcus." Cassie said sincerely for the umpteenth time. "But for the life of me, I just cannot fathom how so many people somehow seemed to know about what's in that footlocker. It just doesn't make sense. All those people that died because they wanted what you're about to get."

"And now we both know; it was all for nothing." Marcus shook his head, expressing a bewildered and disbelieving look as he parked his car in a space adjacent to the intercom and small menu board at the *A & W*. "That's why, after all this time, I just can't get over the fact that Ellis died over what is probably nothing but nonsense."

Marcus ordered a pair of root beer floats, and the two sat in the car quietly. Neither felt compelled to utter a word. Silently, they calmly held hands and waited patiently for the carhop to skate out with their order.

Cassie finally broke the pensive mood with another question.

"Marcus, those two motorcycle guys that you said Opa took care of out there at that house. Do you think since they showed up out there at the sandbar, do you think they knew anything about those gold bars? I always kind of wondered if they might have followed you to that cave and knew they were there."

"If they did, they never said anything about it. And if they did know, it sure looks like they never told anybody else or the gold wouldn't still have been there when we checked on it last summer. I'm pretty sure all they were doing was following orders and that all they were interested in was just getting us to that Schofield guy so he could get his stupid hat back." One of the biggest things that was still unknown to Marcus was how Max Schofield had apparently known about Marcus' inheritance. He hated to think of the possibility, but he at least had to admit to himself that Ellis might somehow have divulged the information. He couldn't imagine any other possible source. Sadly, Marcus realized that he really was fortunate that whoever had been the one to give up the information, or who had ended up possessing the knowledge, had all gone to their graves. Now, it was only him, Cassie, and Margaret who knew about any of it, and there were no doubts that the secrets were safe within their circle.

"That would be true, wouldn't it?" Cassie replied. She took a few moments to collect her thoughts before continuing with an idea that had been circulating through her brain and had sort of been percolating for a while now.

"Marcus, have you considered or given any thought to maybe going to see like, I don't know, like a psychologist or therapist or something, maybe?" She had been worried about even breaching such a subject, unsure of the type of reaction she could expect to receive from him. Cassie was concerned for his mental health and really was troubled that there may be possible long-term effects of the stress that she knew he was feeling subconsciously, if not overtly displaying on a regular basis.

"You think I'm crazy, Cassie?" Marcus asked. He was obviously offended by her suggestive question.

"No, of course not, Marcus," she replied, defensively.

"Yes you do, Cassie. Only crazy people go to therapists or psychiatrists."

"That's not true, Marcus. People go to therapists to help themselves solve problems that they have trouble working through in their minds. And I didn't suggest a psychiatrist, I said psychologist. They're not the same. Maybe crazy people probably do go to psychiatrists, but psychology is a totally different discipline." Cassie regretted bringing up the subject. She had hoped that Marcus would be more open to the idea and thought it might be helpful if he could talk to a professional and perhaps learn to shed some of the guilt that seemed to weigh so heavily on him.

"Psychiatrist, psychologist. They're all the same, Cassie. I'm not nuts and it bothers me for you to imply that I am."

"First of all, no, they're not the same. You're not crazy Marcus. You just carry a lot of guilt and remorse. Believe it or not, I do too." Cassie had to figure out a way to get through to him. "You know I do a lot of reading, Marcus. And mental health interests me a lot. Look, you feel guilty about Ellis dying. Guess what, I do too. I used to hate him, but after all that happened, I actually grew to like him. And yes, it made me very sad to see him die. But you, Marcus, your situation is different. You hated Ellis when you first knew him, too. But after you learned that you were related to him, that he was Cousin Judy's son, your whole outlook did an about face. That made all the difference in the world, and you found yourself loving him like the brother you never had. And then he died, and he died because he loved you, too. Ellis gave his life trying to protect you. Opa even said it, Marcus. Ellis developed a life-long commitment to you, just like the one I have. And you know that. And that's why it's so hard for you to let go, Marcus. That's why you can't stop talking about him, about how much you miss him."

Marcus sat, eyes closed, a thousand thoughts running through his confused and angered mind. *How dare Cassie sit here, in my car no less, and try to psycho-analyze me. Just because she likes to read doesn't make her an expert.*

"Marcus, I'm really concerned about the toll this all might be taking on you, and you can't even realize how much it's bothering you. Please think about what I've said and give it some real consideration. I really think it could help you and make you feel better." Cassie decided she had said enough and thought the time was right to let the subject rest. Marcus didn't say a word for several minutes. Finally he rubbed his face with both hands and reached down, pulling on the switch to flick his headlights several times to notify the carhop that he was ready for her to come and pick up his window tray.

Cassie endured the silence on the short drive back to her house, finding it unbearable. When Marcus stopped at the curb, didn't turn off the ignition, and made no move to get out and open her door, she realized the depth to which she had upset him.

"You're not coming in?" Cassie asked.

"Doesn't look like it does it?" Marcus retorted without even looking at her, and in a tone to which Cassie was quite unaccustomed.

"Fine," she said as she reached for the door handle. Before she could get out of the car, Marcus spoke.

"This is because of all that stupid reading you do. Driving back here I remembered that book that you asked for and I got you for Christmas. I know this whole discussion is because of that stupid book."

"*One Flew Over The Cuckoo's Next*? You think the reason I care so much about your well-being is because of a book? That, Marcus, is an insane and absolutely dumb thing to say. I just can't believe you sometimes." Now Cassie found herself reaching a state of anger with Marcus that had never been approached before in their relationship. She pulled on the handle, pushed open the door, and stepped out. But before slamming the door shut in anger, she leaned back into the car for a final parting word.

"Don't you even call me to say you're sorry, Marcus. I won't answer the phone. I might not even be home. I might go to the bowling alley and play some pinball games. Maybe there might be some nice boy there who will show civility and treat me with some respect." With that, Cassie slammed the door and stormed off toward her front door.

Through the open passenger side window, Marcus leaned over and called after her, "You just did it again, Cassie. You just called me insane again, didn't you? Well I'm not crazy Twigs. And you know what, I hope you do find yourself a Prince Charming at the bowling alley, I really do."

Marcus slipped the Metro into first gear and did his very best to peel out as he pulled away from the curb. But unfortunately enough for Marcus, the Metro lacked sufficient power for a burn-out and all he actually managed to do was embarrass himself when he abruptly killed the engine.

* * * *

The day started off on the wrong foot for James Burgess. He'd had to wait until Monday to get into the nitty-gritty of his real workload. He knew that the primary subject, Marcus Clemens, would be gone attending school. And he knew from his prior surveillance, performed two weeks earlier, that by later in the morning, the woman who lived in the apartment would have headed out for her job in LaGrange. All he had needed was a bit of corroborating information, which had unknowingly been provided by the apparently not-so-bright Harvey Franklin. Jimbo was sure he would have several hours to complete his work and make himself scarce. However, to his great dismay, in mid-morning he found that the address he had secured for the Clemens family was no longer valid and led him to a dead end. He had arrived, carrying lock picking tools in a handy small leather bag, at the prescribed address only to find a vacant, no longer occupied apartment. When he inquired of the lady and gentleman, whom he had found busily cleaning and performing touchup painting, if they might know of the whereabouts of the apartment's former residents, neither had any inkling of who they had been or where they may have moved. At first Jimbo was flummoxed, he had expected this to be a quick in and out situation, but as luck would have it, he now found himself needing to perform some bona fide detective work. Luckily, he had actually at one time, in a prior life and many years past, been a police officer in St. Louis and thusly had a pretty good idea of how to proceed and remedy the situation.

Jimbo walked into the local U.S. Post Office branch and approached the counter with identification holder in hand. Aware that presenting himself as a private detective likely would not be a sufficient form of I.D. to acquire the information he so desperately needed, he quickly flipped open and shut his identification holder. As if to share a secret, Jimbo leaned forward on his left elbow and in a whispered voice told the elderly, and quite surprised, clerk that he was a United States Marshall involved in a top-secret surveillance case. The unwitting, but duly impressed clerk was very acceptive of his request, no doubt quite eager to assist a fellow government employee in his quest to serve justice. It took only moments for her to acquire the new address, and less than one hour after arriving at the first and recently vacated residence, James Burgess found himself standing at the front door of the newly rented Clemens house on North Seventh Street. Occasionally looking over his shoulder and doing his very best to hurry, Jimbo skillfully picked the lock and entered the Clemens' home. It was only a two-bedroom house and he was correct in assuming that these folks would not be the type to own a safe. The bounty he was in search of would most likely be located in one of the bedrooms. He started in the room which seemed most obviously to be inhabited by Marcus. He checked every nook and cranny, beneath the bed, behind furniture, and searched the closet with a fine-toothed comb. With the boy only being a few months shy of eighteen years old, Jimbo would have bet his own house that the boy would have stored his most valuable possessions in his own bedroom.

Giving up on the temptation to further explore and totally destroy the youngster's closet, Jimbo moved on to the bedroom containing a four-post bed with silky white sheets and covered by an obviously feminine comforter. Not much digging was required to uncover the old green military looking footlocker. He knew this had to be the mother lode and time was running short. But Jimbo had to be sure, he certainly could not make a mistake and risk incurring the wrath of Sergeant Roberts. He pulled the footlocker out of the closet and set it upon the cedar chest that was located at the foot of what could only have been the boy's mother's bed. Carefully, James Burgess once again utilized the lock picking equipment on the old combination lock. Lifting the lid, he was gratified to see a very old document binder. He was positive the binder had to contain what he was looking for. Once again, Jimbo nimbly picked the small binder's lock and peeked inside. To his glee, he immediately recognized the stock certificates, easily identified by the raised and embossed print. He reclosed the binder and did a quick, perfunctory search of the remaining contents and, with the exception of a handgun and accompanying ammo, saw nothing that seemed of any real value. As much as he would have liked to have taken the gun and ammo for himself, Jimbo wanted to leave the contents as much as possible just the way he had originally found them. His hope was that the missing binder would not even be noticed until sometime far into the future. Of course, he had been smart enough to wear latex surgical gloves so to ensure there was no fingerprint evidence left behind. His objective was that he would leave with there being no sign whatsoever that the old green footlocker had ever been tampered with. If he were fortunate, the absence of the binder would come as a massive surprise, and not be recognized until months from now.

After replacing the now relocked footlocker in the closet, Jimbo picked up the document binder, put it beneath his left armpit, and made his way toward the front door. Carefully he looked around, searching everywhere he had been, making sure that, as far as he could be certain, everything remained just as it had been when he had entered the house. He carefully relocked the front door and retraced the steps taken after his arrival. As he was about to get into his car, he noticed what appeared to be a youngster approaching from a quarter block away. Jimbo sat in the car, hoping his presence would go unnoticed. Half slumped down in his seat, he continued to curiously keep his eyes on the rearview mirror, watching as the young male casually approached. Just as the figure neared the right front quarter panel of his car, what Jimbo now realized was a crew-cut wearing teenager or perhaps young adult, turned his head nonchalantly to the left, looking right into Jimbo's car. Their eyes met for but a brief instant before the young man made a right turn on the sidewalk and began walking toward the Clemens' front porch. Jimbo nervously, and without hesitation, turned the key, put his Chevy into gear and inadvertently kicked up some loose gravel as he tried to ease away, unnoticed.

* * * *

Marcus was having a bad day. After dropping Cassie at her house, he had noticed his Metropolitan's steering seemed to be pulling to the right. Sensing he was low on tire pressure and in danger of having a flat, he had headed straight to Walt's and pulled into an empty bay. Checking the right front tire he found the problem. There had been a sheet metal screw embedded an inch or so into the tread. Thankful now that he worked at Walt's, and with the problem being something he had tended to on other vehicles numerous times over the past two years, he instinctively knew what to do. Marcus grabbed the handle of a small hydraulic jack, pulled it over, proceeded to raise the Metro and remove the tire. After extracting the screw and inserting a tire plug, Marcus uncoiled an air hose and prepared to reinflate the tire. As he was about to attach the hose nozzle to the tire stem, he heard a familiar voice as it approached from behind.

"Say Marcoos, have a flat tire, *Monsieur?*" Louie Dupree said in his heavily accented and lilting voice.

"Hi Frenchy. Sheet metal screw," Marcus said, shrugging his shoulders.

"Ah, too bad *mon ami.* And on your day off too, you are here working. Where is zee *beaute rousse*?" He asked with a smile. Marcus knew that *beaute rousse* meant red haired beauty in French, it was the nickname Louie had bestowed upon Cassie. Louie was very fond of the young lady, and Marcus was in no mood to confess to him that they had just had an argument.

"Oh, I just dropped her off at her house," Marcus said, hoping that Louis would let that topic die and pick another subject to talk about.

"Is too bad. I always enjoy speaking with the girl. She has learned the French language oh so well." Louie always tried to speak some French with Cassie. She was finishing up her second year of French in school, and Louie always complimented her language skills, saying that she had learned well. He once told her that if she were to one day travel to Quebec with him that he could pass her off as his sister. She always thought he was no doubt just being complimentary, but Louie did claim privately to Marcus that her French actually was good enough that even native French speakers would be surprised to learn that it was actually her second language.

"She had a lot of homework today, so we stopped by *A & W* for a bit and then I just took her straight home. Oh, and thanks again Louie for helping with the move yesterday. Mama and I are very thankful. *Merci beaucoup.*"

"*Je t'en prie*, it was my pleasure, Marcoos," Louie said with a grin. But the grin quickly faded and Louie's expression turned grimly serious. "Listen, there is something that I regret to have to tell you. I just got the news this morning, and I just went in and spoke with Walt."

"What news Frenchy? Not bad news I hope. I would sure rather hear some good news today, my friend."

"I put my two-week notice, Marcoos. I must be going back to Quebec." Marcus felt like he'd been punched in the stomach. Ellis had represented the only thing he had ever had that even resembled a brother. And after his loss, Louie Dupree had been right there to step in and occupy the void, partially taking over and helping to replace that newly discovered and precious spot in Marcus' life. Marcus had learned so much from Louie the past two years, and he had been such a good friend. Louie had been there, offering so much support, and always providing an ear that Marcus could bend when he was feeling down and out. Louie had represented a number of things to him over the past couple of years, he had been a friend, a mentor, and a confidante. And now he was but two weeks away from also exiting Marcus' life.

First the argument with Cassie, now he was losing Frenchy. What other bad news could surface today? What a lousy day Monday had turned out to be.

More Than Meets The Eye

The circumstances surrounding Oliver Compton's death in the exercise yard of the Missouri State Penitentiary, just prior to Memorial Day of 1967, had never been the subject of a final and sufficient explanation. Questions remained unanswered and nary a single suspect amongst the handful of prisoners present in the yard that day had ever been identified. Their numbers had totaled eight on that fateful day, all under the charge of three veteran corrections officers. When the fracas had started, the three had done their best to maintain order, but the wild melee had quickly become uncontrollable and the resulting violence too much for the three of them to corral. An additional dozen officers were summoned to the yard before the brawl had deescalated and order restored. Four inmates had been transported to the infirmary requiring medical attention. None of their injuries were deemed serious, with only two of them receiving a handful of stitches for what were essentially nothing more than minor lacerations. There had been some assorted bruising and a couple of lingering headaches, but seven of the inmates had survived, and for the most part, none were the worse for wear. But then, there was the other inmate. Oliver Compton had suffered two stab wounds. Both had resulted from the use of a homemade shank. One wound had penetrated his lower abdomen and was considered neither severe nor life-threatening. But the fatal wound, a slash to the throat, had been perfectly placed and definitely well-intentioned. The gash had extended from the larynx area and across to the left side of the neck, effectively severing his jugular vein. Oliver Compton had essentially bled out right there in the exercise yard. Even though the shank had been recovered, fingerprint dusting had produced no discernible evidence. Either the weapon had somehow been thoroughly and miraculously cleansed of any prints right there on the spot, or the perpetrator had possessed enough foresight to have worn gloves or had managed to wrap and handle the weapon securely in cloth. Regardless of just how the fatal deed had been done, the fact was abundantly clear to everyone that the murder had not occurred as the consequence of a normal inmate fight. According to the conclusions of the ensuing investigation and the words of its accompanying report, it was obviously clear that the entire scenario had been preplanned, and that the violence had been artificially initiated purely as a cover up for the prearranged murder of Oliver Compton. No motive had ever been established and not a single one of the other seven inmates was willing to shed light on the subject. All remained silent, disavowing any knowledge of a preplanned plot. None admitted to seeing anything at all happen to the victim. All claimed ignorance of the murder. Nothing could ever be established to provide a clue or give any indication as to why Ollie had been targeted.

Even though she and Ollie had been divorced for the last half decade of his life, Alicia Compton had been devastated by his murder. Admittedly, Alicia had been most certainly appalled by the severity of the crimes he had committed and had in no way sympathized when he was sentenced to the electric chair. Making matters even worse for her, Alicia had been thoroughly horrified to learn that, following their separation, Ollie had managed to brainwash their adopted son Ellis, cajoling and inducing him into acting as an accomplice. She deeply despised Ollie for his despicable actions and had begun mentally preparing herself for the day when her former husband would pay his penance. But Alicia had never considered, even in her wildest dreams, an outcome such as this. She was not prepared in the least bit for the sudden and violent way in which Ollie's life had ended.

Immediately after receiving the news of Ollie's death, she had lashed out in rage at Ellis' true father, Jude Allensworth, flat-out accusing him of bearing responsibility for Ollie's death. Truth be known, Alicia knew far more about Judy than he could possibly have even been aware. She had been acquainted with Judy since his wild youth and galivanting days, well aware of the violent tendencies he had exhibited as a young man. She knew first-hand that he had never undergone any type of mental therapy or treatment for his erratic behavior. Alicia was also certain, even though he had seemed to learn to cope and control himself publicly, that he was still far from a changed man. She was positive that he had merely developed mechanisms to help him to handle himself outwardly in a somewhat organized and civil manner. Alicia had no doubt of the demons that still lived, burrowed deep within his demented mind. After all, Judy had told her about his visit with Ollie in prison just a week or so before his death. He had told her of his concern over the threats that Ollie had made in connection to Paula Sue's death, and Alicia had convinced herself that Judy had come to the realization that he could not possibly risk having Ollie's accusations ever being uttered publicly. She had always harbored a strong suspicion that Judy indeed had killed Paula in an out-of-control rage. And his angered reaction to Ollie's threat only served to fortify her suspicions. With her knowing the relationships that Judy maintained within the penitentiary, and the influence he exerted over key personnel at the facility, she was certain that he had masterminded and coordinated Ollie's murder.

Alicia had gained a massive amount of information from her tenure working in the employ of Max Schofield. She had been privy to the finances and inner reaches of Max Schofield's arm of the illicit drug trade in northeastern Missouri, Iowa, and on into northwestern Illinois. As a result, she had learned a great deal about the hierarchy of the business. Alicia had long suspected a lot of things about Judy but had never possessed sufficient supporting facts to affirm her assumptions. Amongst others, Max had proven to be the primary source that had aroused most of her suspicions. The entire matter had stewed inside her over the course of the past two years. In some ways, she really wished she was able to discount some of what Max had told her. Alicia carried an unbearable amount of hatred and resentment toward him. Max had been the person who had followed up on Ollie's evil misdeeds by knowingly and maliciously taking advantage of the young, vulnerable, and impressionable Ellis. Max paid him what was relatively but a pittance, while Ellis risked his entire future by making drug deliveries all over northeastern Missouri. Even though, on the face of things at the time, she had convinced herself that all Ellis was doing was securing a financial base and foothold that would catapult him into a successful future, Alicia knew that what he was doing involved an element of risk and danger. She continually tried to convince herself that Ollie had done the same work for years, with never a hitch, nary a problem either legally or socially. Even when Ellis had expressed doubt about the work he was doing, she had found herself defending the job, telling him that Ollie had done it for years, with never a problem. Deep down, Alicia knew she was to blame for Ellis' employment. But she could not bring herself to admit that fact. Instead, and despite Judy's protestations and claims of ignorance about Ellis' true profession, she blamed Judy for allowing him to be hired by Max. She always felt certain, despite Judy's claims of thinking that Ellis was only innocently delivering auto parts, that he knew the truth. She always felt that Judy had the ability to intervene at any point and force Max to terminate Ellis' employment. In Alicia's mind, Judy was responsible, not only for Ollie's death, but also for Ellis'. If Judy had just stepped in, as a true father should have, Ellis would not have been working for Max. And, in turn, Ellis would never have been at that pond on the Fourth of July. And if he had not been there, Ellis could not have taken the stray bullet that Max had intended for the Lewis County Deputy. Alicia felt she had many reasons for holding a grudge against Judy and was confident that she would one day get her retribution.

* * * *

Looking up from writing in his order book, Dutch Franklin took off his glasses and rubbed both eyes briskly with the heels of his palms. Then, using the ring fingers of both hands, he proceeded to drag the matted sleep and crusty flakes that had formed on the inside corners of both eyes down, and safely onto his cheek. Pulling a white handkerchief from the back pocket of his slacks, he wiped his eyes again, making sure to clear the debris from his cheeks. Replacing the handkerchief in his pocket, Dutch put his glasses back on and, from his perch in the elevated office, he surveyed the roughly thirty percent of the store within his line of sight. Dutch noticed, and immediately recognized, a pair of Lewis County Deputies sitting at the soda fountain counter taking lunch break. Stepping down from his office he sauntered past the cash registers and magazine rack, on over to the counter where he took a stool just to the left of Deputy Mitchell Daniels.

"Afternoon Mitch," Dutch said patting Mitch's left shoulder as he sat. Leaning forward slightly, he nodded in the direction of Deputy Wilcox, "Good to see you as well, Helen." Dutch spoke to Mitch and Helen on a first name basis, having known them for years, as both had been customers since their respective youths. And, as always, they still frequented *Franklin's Five and Dime* often, regularly stopping by for a quick sandwich and Coke. Although they patrolled the entire county, the primary focus of both deputies was the U.S. Highway 61 corridor, and even though they did travel in separate cruisers, they were considered partners. They often handled cases and many situations in tandem and were largely inseparable.

"How's business, Dutch?" Mitchell asked before taking another bite of his grilled cheese.

"Good, good," Dutch replied, smiling broadly. Abruptly adopting a more serious demeanor, he said, "Mitch, there's something that's sort of been on my mind since Saturday, and I hope you don't mind me bringing it to your attention."

"No, no not at all, Dutch, shoot."

"Well Mitch, and you too, Helen, have either of you heard anything about a private detective making the rounds the last few days?" Dutch had felt a wee bit uneasy ever since the unannounced arrival of Detective Burgess at the store late on Saturday afternoon.

"I haven't heard anything, no. What about you Helen, you heard anything?" Mitchell asked as he turned to his right on the swivel stool.

"No, can't say that I have Mitchell." She answered. "Actually, I couldn't tell you the last time a private eye ever even visited these parts."

"Where did you hear about this private eye, Dutch?" Mitchell's interest was piqued just a bit. "I mean, these types of guys are generally hired to look into a cheating husband or to help out with missing person cases and such. I can't say that I've heard any rumors out there about marital infidelity or anything, not that it doesn't happen more than we'd probably suspect. And I haven't heard any reports of any missing persons around here."

"No, no. It's not anything like that." Dutch went on to explain the cause for his concern, "This fellow just showed up Saturday afternoon out of the clear blue. I'm downstairs, you know processing some product and Lewelyn comes down the steps and says there's this fellow that wants to see me, that he's waiting, you know right over there at my office. Hold on a sec.... Hey, Billy! Hey, get me a Coke will ya?"

Mitchell and Helen waited patiently for Dutch to continue, but he took his time, nervously swallowing two gulps of his freshly delivered drink.

"So, what did he want, Dutch?" Helen finally asked.

"Well, he told me he was working for a client from Connecticut that'd had some property stolen. I guess he was trying to track it down. He seemed pretty evasive,

66

you know?" Dutch was trying to remember exactly how the conversation had begun.

"Connecticut?" Mitchell said, somewhat surprised at where this private eye had said that he had come from.

"Yeah, that's what he said. But that seemed fishy to me, cause when I looked out the front window right there when he left, I seen that the car he was driving, that it had Missouri plates on it, yes it did." Dutch nodded and said confidently.

"Well, that is a little odd, but tell us more about the conversation," Mitch wanted more information on the man and his purpose for talking with Dutch.

"Well, I don't know Mitch. I mean, one thing just seemed to lead to another, and next thing I know, I'd told him stuff I probably should have kept under my hat, you know?"

"Like what?" Mitchell asked.

"Well, like he asked me if I knew anybody around here that might have gotten an inheritance in the last few years. I told him I didn't know nobody." Dutch reconsidered his words, "Well no, that's not really true, because I did mention Hubert Tompkins inheriting his dad's farm, and I guess I might have mentioned Tommy Fuller getting his grandpa's Belair after he'd passed."

"Yeah, but none of that had anything to do with anything in Connecticut, I wouldn't imagine," Mitch said, not sensing a connection. "Dutch, what was this man's name? Did he show you any identification?"

"Yeah, Mitch, actually he did show me his badge and identification. He had it in a nice expensive folder, too."

Mitchell pulled a notepad from his shirt pocket and prepared to write. "Name, Dutch, what name did he give you? I'll call the station and see if this guy has checked in with us. It would be a professional courtesy, if he was here on official business, to have checked in with us, you know, let us know he would be canvassing the area so as not to raise any suspicions. Like he apparently has with you. So, what was his name again, Dutch?"

"He said it was Burgess, James Burgess. But he said he preferred to be called Jimbo." Dutch felt there was more he needed to relate to the deputies. "He also told me that his client back in Connecticut was, what he called anyways, a well-known former resident of the area. I didn't have a clue who he might have been talking about, do you?"

"Nope, I don't know any prominent citizens of Lewis County that have moved to Connecticut." Mitchell was also stumped over who the reference could have pertained.

"Listen Mitch, one thing kind of led to another and I think I spilled the beans about some other things that he really seemed to take an interest in."

"Such as?" Helen interjected with her question.

"Well, I mentioned the shootout and all the killing out there at the Schofield place in Monticello a couple of years ago. And that seemed to get his attention."

68

Mitchell looked to Helen and back and then asked of no one in particular, "Why in the world would he be interested in that insanity?"

"Well maybe because I let the cat out of the bag a little?" Dutch was beginning to realize that he had quite possibly made a tremendous mistake. "He asked me if I knew anything about Marcus Clemens, and of course I did; Marcus used to come in here all the time, though not so much anymore. And then he found out that Marcus was related to Ellis Compton and that Ellis used to work here. And all the rumors that Marcus was supposed to get an inheritance from Mark Twain and all that stuff."

"Dutch, you told a stranger all of this about Marcus?" Mitch asked.

"Yeah, I guess I did. I told him about Ellis' dad's plan to steal the inheritance from Marcus and that it probably was what ended up causing all that killing over there in Monticello."

"How could you give up all that information like that, Dutch?" Mitchell, quite frankly, was severely disappointed in Dutch's lack of discretion.

"Well, Mitchell, the guy had identification and everything, but like I said, when he left and I didn't see a Connecticut license plate, well, it made me wonder." Dutch wished he had been a bit smarter Saturday, had not been so free to share information that he would normally have held close. This was such a small and basically tightknit community and it bothered him to the core that he might have betrayed any of the locals. But James Burgess had put forth such an official appearance. Even though, in the moment, when he couldn't really see the harm in talking to the man, Dutch now feared he might have misplaced his trust and been played for a fool.

* * * *

As the clock was slowly approaching closing time, Dutch Franklin was mildly surprised to see Deputy Wilcox stepping through the front door. As she entered, Helen spied Dutch looking down at her from his office and immediately noted his furrowed brow and puzzled expression. He put down his pen, removed his glasses, took the two small steps down to the sales floor and waited as the deputy approached.

"Helen, a bit surprised....uh, and pleasantly so I might add, to see you again so soon, uh, on such short notice." Dutch stammered through the greeting.

"Well, Dutch, after talking to you over lunch today, Mitchell and I decided to put some folks to work back at the station and we did a little research of our own, as well." Dutch suspected what the research involved and he was definitely interested in hearing the results of their labors. "First off, we tasked the staff with consulting the Connecticut state government to ascertain what governing body was in charge of the regulation of private detectives. Simple enough, and with a telephone number in hand, Mitchell placed a call to the office of the Commissioner of Emergency Services and Public Protection. That is the agency that licenses and oversees the registration of all of the state's private detective services. Each licensed service is required to register every one of its employees with the state."

"My God, Helen, please tell me James Burgess was registered." Dutch nearly found himself pleading.

"No, he was not, I'm afraid," was her unfortunate response.

"Oh gosh, that's not good then, is it, Helen?"

"No, Dutch, on the surface it's not." Helen went on to explain, "But in the long run that information, while a bit disappointing, did set us off on the right track. With four of us dialing nonstop, we placed phone calls to most of the hotels and motels within a fifty-mile radius of here. With the description you provided of both Mr. Burgess and his vehicle, it was just a matter of time until we hit upon a particular Motel 6 just south of Hannibal that had a James Burgess registered in a room from Friday through Monday morning. Now, while he did check out of the facility this morning, the desk clerk who had assigned his room had fortunately required him to list his license plate number on his registration form."

"That's wonderful news, Helen. With his license plate number, now you won't have any problem finding out where he lives and going and arresting him then, right?" Dutch was immeasurably relieved to hear that the man's true identity had been so quickly uncovered.

"Well, actually, Dutch, I'm afraid that's not the case." It was obvious that Dutch was severely disappointed with Helen's response to his hopeful question.

"You see, Dutch, there are no grounds to even consider arresting Burgess. So far he hasn't committed a crime. All he did was talk to you and ask you some questions. Really, there's nothing illegal about what he did when he talked to you." She knew that Dutch was not happy with her explanation, but the facts are but the facts.

"What about the I.D. badge and his papers? Isn't that impersonating a police officer, Helen?"

"No, I'm afraid not. He never claimed to be a police officer did he, Dutch? A private eye yes, but that's a completely different ballgame." Helen hated to see Dutch looking so forlorn, but she decided to make an effort to lift his spirits. "But that's not to say we didn't learn some interesting facts about James Burgess. Through his plate number, we obtained his address in Jefferson City and discovered some tidbits about his background."

"Such as?" Dutch's ears seemed to perk up.

"Well, Dutch, it seems our friend Mr. Burgess had at one time been employed as a police officer in Clayton, Missouri, which is a suburb of St. Louis. He had walked a beat for about eight years, before he got himself caught up in a little money laundering scheme. Maybe there had also been some incidental drug trafficking involved as well, but the state prosecutors opted to let that slide for the more likely conviction of money laundering for some small-time marijuana distributors." Deputy Wilcox felt a bit of pride when she realized the amount of information she and Mitchell had put together in only a brief three-hour span.

"To get to the gist of it, Burgess served six years in the state pen at Jeff City. He was paroled almost

72

exactly two years ago, in March of '67. He did another two years of supervised probation there in Jefferson City, and he finally got his total Get Out of Jail Free card last month. Up until then, it was incumbent upon him to keep his nose clean. But I guess now he feels like maybe he can spread his wings a bit." Helen had revealed all there now was to know about the "private eye".

"I'm glad to know all of that, Helen. Thank you for letting me know," Dutch said gratefully.

"It's no problem, Dutch. Mitchell and I felt like you were entitled to know the truth." Deputy Wilcox now felt she had done her duty in an official capacity. But, she had more to say, unofficially.

"Off the record and just between us, Dutch, if that fellow comes around again, let Mitchell or me know about it right away, would you? We both, and especially Mitchell, are concerned about Marcus Clemens." Although her words were unofficial, Helen was now speaking from the heart. "With that fellow nosing around, asking about inheritances and the like, and then specifically mentioning Marcus, well that seems pretty suspicious. We had enough crap that went down in '67. With that boy about to finally turn eighteen and ready to claim his inheritance, well we sure don't want a repeat performance."

Old Friends / New Friends

Marcus couldn't help but laugh to himself yesterday afternoon when he had momentarily sat red-faced, with his car just nudged away from the curb, sitting catty-corner, and barely nosed onto Fernwood Drive in front of Cassie's house. He had been trying to emphasize a point, wanting to drive home his displeasure with Cassie, by peeling out from in front of her house. Marcus had genuinely been offended by the insinuations Cassie had made concerning his emotional health, and it truly did bother him that she sincerely thought he might be experiencing mental problems. Restarting the car and leaving her house in a calmer manner, he couldn't help but wonder if Cassie hadn't stood there on her sidewalk, giggling at him and shaking her head at his childish behavior and the embarrassing consequence of his immature display.

Instantly upon starting down Fernwood Drive, Marcus had noticed that something was amiss. He'd felt the steering wheel pulling to the right and had immediately headed straight for Walt's. It was while there that

Louie had floored him with the bombshell revelation about the imminent departure for Quebec. It had certainly been a disheartening Monday and Marcus had known of only one way to get things back on an acceptable track. As soon as the tire had been remounted, he had gone straight to the western edge of the parking lot, exited his car and dropped a dime into the payphone.

"How about a piece of pie at the diner?" Marcus had asked sheepishly, before Cassie could even finish saying, "Hello." Try though he had, Marcus was fully aware that he could never stay angry with Cassie. And he knew that to be especially true when she was being earnest with him, holding only his best interest and well-being in mind.

"Well," Cassie had paused for dramatic effect, "maybe, but only if the offer is accompanied by a sincere I'm sorry." Cassie had really wanted to be firm sounding in her demand, but she found herself just as guilty as Marcus in her understanding of their relationship. After all, as angry as she had briefly been, it was only seconds after storming away from the car and toward her house that she had stood laughing on her sidewalk as Marcus had embarrassingly stalled his car in the street. They had been through too much over the past six years and both were in-tune with the fact that they would be together, forever and eternally joined at the hip.

Before Marcus even had an opportunity to respond, Cassie had asked him, "Where are you calling from? I'll get my shoes on."

As she had waited for Marcus, she'd had thoughts nearly identical to those that had simultaneously floated through his mind. Marcus was sure that no matter what life had to throw at him, that Cassie would be there, with him and for him. There was no denying their mutual resolve. There could never possibly be any doubt, not after the explanation given to them by Opa. He had laid it all out in his conversations with Cassie. He had explicitly described to her the concept of their mutual and lifelong commitment. He had demonstrated to Cassie through his uncanny ability to communicate with her that there were supernatural forces in effect. If it were not all true, they would not have been singled out for this extraordinary journey that they had the fortune to experience daily.

Parking at the curb, Marcus had run around the car and waited patiently at the passenger side door as Cassie approached the Metro. Marcus greeted her with, "I'm sorry, Sweetie," giving her a warm kiss and heartfelt hug before helping her into the car. Following pie, Coca-Colas, and pleasant conversation, Marcus had driven Cassie back home, promising to come to the bowling alley after leaving work on Tuesday to visit with her and drive her home when her shift concluded at ten o'clock.

* * * *

Late Monday afternoon, Jimbo had returned to the *Bar None Saloon*. He had ended up sleeping (passing out) in his car in the parking lot. Tuesday morning as he turned south onto U.S. Highway 61, Jimbo Burgess had an empty, gnawing feeling deep in the pit of his gut. Of course he had overindulged, drinking far too much last night. It was a problem he had struggled with and that was beginning to get out of hand all over again. Going back to his days with the police force, Jimbo had always told himself that he was in firm control of his drinking. It hadn't been until later, when things had really begun to snowball, that he had accepted the fact that he was spiraling out of control. By the time of the realization, his efforts to rectify had been too little, too late. His excess drinking had led to gambling. At first, just petty little things like football parley cards, and then occasionally, the horses over at Cahokia Downs; before he knew it he had advanced to the bigger scale bookies in East St. Louis, and that's when the debts had really started to concern him, to pile up, and rapidly become unmanageable on a modest policeman's salary. He had to find a way out of debt and, to his misfortune, Jimbo had soon dug himself in even deeper with the wrong types of characters. Before he could even fathom to what depths he had fallen, he had been caught up in a black-cop sting operation. Soon, Jimbo was staring out from the inside. In short order his position had switched, and he was suddenly on the side of the jail cell bars where he had once been sworn to put criminals. He had done six difficult years at the Missouri State Penitentiary, and during that time had become hardened to the realities of life. James Burgess came to the comprehension that there was a blurred line between good and evil, just as there is a fine and blurred line between genius and insanity.

Jimbo had come to believe that he could see no future in trying to adhere to the straight and narrow. It seemed to him that despite his best efforts, no matter how hard a man tried, no matter the effort he put forth, there was no way possible for the average Joe to ever get ahead by being honest and hardworking. Unless a man was born with a several spoon in his mouth, unless he had a brilliant head start handed to him, he was destined to work his fingers to the bone in order to just scrape by. It took going up the river for six years, meeting a few people like the fellow cons he had learned from in the big house, and it took a real and experienced mentor like Sarge Roberts for him to really see the light. But now, James Burgess finally did see the light, the truth. You have to be a little shady, to be just a little bit dishonest, and to be smart enough to take advantage of an opportunity when one is presented. It was with all this in mind that Jimbo was feeling the tightening knot in his stomach.

He had been succeeding in his new life. After his release from prison, after more than six years free from alcohol, he had learned that moderation was key to maintaining a controlled lifestyle. But, for reasons unknown, this weekend he had somehow begun to provide a crack in the door. He was allowing an old demon to have the opportunity to regain a foothold in his life, and he knew he would have to nip it in the bud. Jimbo was going to have to force himself to close that door and close it for good. He thought back to last night. Last night, and for the third time since he had arrived in Hannibal on Friday afternoon, he had visited the *Bar None Saloon*. For sure, it had been calm last night, it was a Monday after all. Nothing at all like the scene on

Friday and Saturday nights. Now, those two nights had been wild. The place had been loaded with rednecks and motor bikers, and certainly had not been lacking for action. Heavy-duty fisticuffs had broken out on at least three separate occasions over the two nights. There had been plenty of pool being played with a ghastly number of gallons of beer and whiskey being consumed. Actually, it had all been a bit too much, far too loud and violent, for Jimbo's sensibilities. But last night was very different, indeed a welcome respite, and a lot quieter to be sure. But because of the lack of action and mayhem, last night posed a uniquely different situation and that is what made it so obviously clear to Jimbo that change would have to be effected immediately. He didn't have the motivation of noise and activity that Friday and Saturday nights to compel him to drink in celebration of happiness and good times. It had been quiet and he had still allowed himself to drink well beyond reason. In the somber mood of Tuesday morning, Jimbo realized he could not be as loose and vulnerable as he had proven to be last night at the *Bar None Saloon*.

The place had been almost empty after seven o'clock. When he had originally arrived, about three hours earlier, the bar had been empty. Between five and seven it had picked up with the after-work crowd and the bar and several tables had been occupied. But as the moments passed, the crowd steadily began to dwindle. By the time *The Avengers* had begun airing on the small black and white Zenith television located behind and just above the bartender's head, the establishment was bereft of customers save for five or six at the bar proper and three couples spaced across three of the more than a dozen available tables. Most of the patronage had finished their after-work cocktails and headed home for dinner and to join their families. Finding himself alone and with nothing to do but watch *The Avengers* in near silence, Jimbo had ordered up a full fifth of whiskey and prepared for the next hour to share in the company of Patrick Macnee, the beautiful Diana Rigg and of course, his old friend *Jack Daniels*.

By the time *The Dick Cavett Show* was deep into its first guest, Jimbo had nearly finished his fifth of whiskey and had had gotten to know quite well an old and very proper seeming English gentleman by the name of Neville Naughton. By that time, they were two of only four patrons still inhabiting the *Bar None*. The yawns of the bartender were plentiful, and with Jimbo's watch indicating that it was fast approaching eleven o'clock, he assumed the barkeep wouldn't have been disappointed had they all decided that they'd had enough for the night.

But the old Englishman seemed he had nowhere else to be and was certainly in no hurry.

"Here, here, barkeep. Splash me with another ale if you would, my kind sir," Neville said with a broad smile. He had been enjoying a marvelous conversation with Jimbo, although he found the name ridiculous and insisted upon calling him James. Neville had been very forthright with Jimbo, offering a most complete autobiographical sketch of himself. Their manner with one another had been easygoing and neither had seemed to encounter any difficulties in discussing even the more

81

intimate details of their personal lives. Jimbo had been pleasantly surprised to learn that the two of them shared a background in law enforcement. Neville, it seems, had served in World War I as a British Army Intelligence Officer. But he had begun, enlisting directly upon graduation from secondary school, as a London Metropolitan Police Officer. However with the beginning of the war, and with the forming of the Intelligence Corps in August of 1914, he was among the first to volunteer. He had served two years behind enemy lines and had planned for a promising future in the field of intelligence. However, the end of the war had brought the disbandment of the Corps, and in 1919 Neville was once again employed as a lowly Constable in the Metropolitan Police Force. It was while patrolling in that duty that he began to take notice of the underbelly of London, and within a couple of years Neville was, what was then termed, "on the take" in the local vernacular. He was doing quite well for himself, but because of his true passion, he volunteered again for his country in World War II as a British army intelligence analyst. At the war's conclusion, he had managed to retire for good in 1946. During retirement, Neville had been fortunate to travel extensively, and with his militarily obtained mastery of the French and German languages, was always in a position to pick up extra spending money working as a translator for various and often-times shady operatives world-wide.

Jimbo was fascinated by the tales of Neville Naughton and longed to be able to have such yarns to spin in his old age. He was so intrigued that he had gone so far as to ask Neville if he saw any possibility that Jimbo could eventually secure a position in such an international drama. Neville explained to him that the life was not one for every man, and that a great deal of special talents were required. He warned Jimbo that not the least of those talents was having the ability to perform deeds outside the parameters of what would normally be deemed socially acceptable or even, for that matter, legal.

"In other words, my dear James, dishonesty and corruption are but common prerequisites for a successful transition to this type of vocation," Neville warned.

"Listen, Neville, I was born for a lifestyle like that. I'd be a natural, I just know it." Jimbo pleaded his case vehemently.

When Neville asked if he could provide examples of some of the underhanded deeds he had been involved in, Jimbo didn't hesitate to describe his qualifications in explicit detail. He talked about the gambling and drug professions in which he had dabbled in the past, the money laundering scheme that had cost him six years in the penitentiary, his experience within the walls of the penitentiary in handling the procurement and distribution of numerous and sundry illicit items ranging from tobacco to heroin, and even the project with which he was now involved. Jimbo probably would have done just about anything to have gotten into the good graces of Neville Naughton. And Neville did appease Jimbo by having him write on a cocktail napkin his address and a telephone number where he could be reached in the evenings.

But all that was last night. He had allowed himself to get drunk and had no doubt gotten carried away with pipe dreams. This morning, he was hungover, he had a fire in the pit of his stomach, and the heat he was feeling was definitely not burning desire. The acid burning the pit of his stomach was caused by guilt and worry. Jimbo could not honestly remember the vast majority of the lengthy conversation he'd had with Neville, but he was quite worried that he may have said more than should or would have been wise for him to divulge. Jimbo strongly hoped that his new friend Neville had been every bit as drunk as he had been last night, and that he was also having trouble remembering this morning. Jimbo desperately wanted to convince himself that Neville was an old man, probably at least eighty years old. There should be no way the man could have that good of a memory. No way.

* * * *

Finished up with the last of the sweeping, and while Chester Bernstein was locking up the shop, Marcus headed out to his car. Able to leave about fifteen minutes earlier than he had anticipated, Marcus had decided to hurry home for a quick shower and a change of clothes before heading over to the *Riverwalk Lanes*. Whenever possible, he tried to avoid going to Cassie's workplace in his shop clothes for fear he might embarrass her. When he got home, Margaret would be at work at the *Gold Mine*, and with Marcus now independent, with money of his own to spend and able to fend for himself, she no longer had to make sure to leave meals in the fridge for him. He quickly showered, carefully making sure to degrease his hands and arms thoroughly. Marcus dressed and by eight sharp was on his way to see Cassie.

Marcus sidled up to the snack bar and was immediately greeted with a smile and complimentary fountain Coke, a benefit of having a girlfriend behind the counter.

"How was work, Marcus?" Cassie asked, as she leaned forward with both hands splayed on the counter.

"It was good, Twigs. Changed out a radiator and a water pump, not bad for a three-and-a-half-hour shift. How about you? Been busy tonight?" Marcus replied and asked.

"So-so." She answered, toggling her hand side-to-side. "Marcus, did you see the flyers up at the counter?"

"No, what are they for?" He inquired, wondering if someone was putting on a yard sale or car wash.

"An old-style tent revival," she said. "Here, I've got a few of them over here." Cassie scurried a few feet to her left and snatched one from the small pile she had stashed near the small sink.

"*Kaisenreicher Family Prayer and Salvation Ministry* is what it's called." Cassie read from the page before handing over one of the flyers.

"I've never been to a revival, have you?" Marcus asked as he looked over the paper curiously.

"Nope. But it sounds interesting doesn't it, Marcus?" Cassie seemed to be slightly intrigued.

"Maybe, I don't know." Marcus wasn't as interested as Cassie seemed to be. "I mean, it might be kind of fun to hear the word from maybe someone different than Reverend Jackson and Reverend Drummond. What do you think?"

"I think it might be interesting." Cassie wouldn't come right out and say so, but Marcus could tell her heart was already set on going. "It's on a Monday night, and we're both off work on Mondays, so maybe it's meant for us to go. What do think, Marcus? At least we'll be able to say we've been to a good old fashioned tent revival, right?"

"I don't know, when is it, Cassie?" Marcus looked back down at the flyer in search of the date.

"It's on Monday, May 12." She had already committed the date to memory. "What do you think, Marcus?"

"Yeah, I guess so Cassie, I mean why not?" Marcus had resigned himself. If Cassie had decided she wanted to do something, it would take an act or event more exceptional than Clarence Darrow's finest argument to talk her out of it.

"Oh good, Neville even said he thought it would be good for us to go." Cassie said with a smile.

"Neville, who is Neville?" Marcus asked.

"Oh, you haven't met him. I think he's in the restroom right now, but he said he'd be right back. He said he was going to put some of these flyers out in his car and use the restroom."

"He's not one of these pinball playing guys you threatened me with yesterday, is he?" Marcus felt a jealous tingle on the back of his neck. He hadn't forgotten Cassie's remark during their little dust-up yesterday afternoon about coming here and playing some pinball and having somebody show her some respect.

Cassie laughed heartily, actually feeling a bit flattered that Marcus was displaying a measure of jealousy.

"No Marcus. As a matter of fact here he comes now."

A quite old and well-dressed man retook his seat two stools away from Marcus. With an impressive English accent, the gentleman politely asked Cassie for an order of chips. She turned, grabbed a paper plate, and began taking the lid off the potato chip container. She was about to reach in for a handful of chips when the gentleman spoke up again.

"Oh, no, no miss. I'm dreadfully sorry. And I apologize for my mistake. I sometimes forget myself and where I am. I fully intended to ask you for a basket of your french fries, I'm so sorry. Do accept my apology, that was obviously my error. Where I am from we call sliced fried potatoes *chips*." The Englishman stumbled all over himself in regret for not remembering the American terminology.

"That's okay, Mr. Naughton. It will just take a few minutes for the french fries." Cassie emptied a small carton of frozen fries into the basket and gently dropped it down into the scalding oil.

Aside from interviews with British musicians like the Beatles or Rolling Stones on television, Marcus had never heard an English accent, and especially not in person. And he was pretty sure that Cassie hadn't either. He thought the man's voice actually sounded really fascinating.

"Please my dear, once again, please call me Neville."

"Okay, Neville," Cassie said smiling. "This is my boyfriend, Marcus Clemens," Cassie said in a manner of introduction as she motioned with her right hand toward Marcus.

Neville stood and took a step toward Marcus extending his right hand.

Mindful of the impeccable manners instilled by his stepmother, Marcus stood as well, and as he reached to shake hands said, "It's a pleasure to meet you sir."

"Pleasure is all mine, Marcus. And please do call me Neville." The man seemed to hold the grasp longer than Marcus expected, but he assumed that was probably just the European style of handshake. "I've only spoken briefly with Cassandra here, but in the few words we have exchanged, she has spoken very highly of you. I feel that I already know and am quite fond of you."

"Thank you, sir." Marcus said, feeling a little abashed. It felt good to hear that Cassie had spoken well of him to this stranger.

"Neville, son, call me Neville." The man said with a broad smile.

"Neville," Marcus said with a nod.

Cassie pulled the fryer basket, setting it on its holder, and went to wait on two new customers who had just taken seats at the far end of the counter.

"Listen Marcus, I know it's not any of my business, but the young lady seemed to have a sincere desire to attend the traveling revival that is advertised on that flyer there before you. It's nice that you've agreed to take her to it. I would think that it will be a good experience for the both of you." Neville stood and reached to again shake hands with Marcus. As they shook, the old Englishman reached out with his left hand and patted Marcus' right shoulder.

"I must leave now Marcus. I left five dollars there for the french fries and the young lady's tip. Help yourself to the fries, won't you?" Neville took just a step before stopping and turning back to Marcus. "Once again, none of my business, but won't you try to look up an older gentleman by the name of Othello Paige. He lives now in a village called Fairfield, in Iowa. I don't know with any certainty, but perhaps, just perhaps, he may be in possession of something of interest to you. Or it may be that he has knowledge about the origin of something very valuable that you may be intimately aware of. Whether any of that is true or not, I'm sure he would benefit greatly from meeting you and receiving any assistance you may possibly extend toward him."

Neville Naughton affectionately patted Marcus' shoulder once again, smiled and walked toward the building's front doors.

Marcus sat back down, wondering what that had been all about. Who in heck was Othello Paige? It only took a second for the question to form in his head. Could the old man, Neville, be referring to someone who was somehow related to Jeremiah Paige? And if so, how or why would this old Englishman know anything about him?

In a few moments, Cassie returned with Neville's order of french fries.

"Where did he go?" She asked as she set the basket on the counter. "Is he in the bathroom again?"

"No, he left," Marcus said, as he stared straight ahead, an obvious look of confusion on his face.

"Well, what about his fries?" Cassie asked, wondering why he would order food and then just abruptly get up and leave.

"He didn't want the food. He just wanted you to leave for a bit so he could talk to me, Cassie."

"What?" Now Cassie really felt dumbfounded. "Why would he want to talk to you without me around? Marcus, what's going on here?"

"I don't know. Did you tell him that you really wanted to go to that revival?"

"No. He saw the flyers and asked for a few and took them to his car. We didn't discuss it at all, why?" Cassie asked.

"Because, he said you really wanted to go and that it would be a good experience for us. Plus he said it was nice that I had agreed to take you. You didn't talk about any of this with him?" Marcus was at a total loss with what had just transpired.

"No. None of that. He just sat down and introduced himself, he said his name was Neville Naughton. Then he asked my name and when I said Cassie he asked if that was an abbreviation for Cassandra. Then, when I said yes, he asked if I had a boyfriend named

Marcus. That's when I said yes and I told him what a great guy you were." It was beginning to dawn on Cassie how strange the conversation had actually been. At the time, words had just seemed to flow, nothing had seemed out of the ordinary. But now, at Marcus' prodding it was starting to feel weird. "Then he asked me about taking a few of the flyers. He said he was going to put them in his car and then use the restroom. And then, well that's when you came in, while he was outside."

"That seems strange that I didn't see him in the parking lot when I came in," Marcus commented as he shook his head slowly.

"Maybe he was already in the bathroom when you came in." Cassie gave a logical reason for Marcus not seeing Neville in the parking lot.

"Cassie, did you say anything to him about the gold bars?" Marcus asked.

"Well of course not. I wouldn't mention that to anyone, especially a stranger." Cassie was surprised that Marcus would even ask. "Why would you even ask?"

"Because he told me to find a man named Othello Paige who lives in Iowa." Marcus had no idea how Neville could know about this man, especially if it turned out that Othello really was related to Jeremiah. "He said it was possible that man could know something about the origin of the gold, at least that's what I'm pretty sure he was getting at. He never actually said it, but he referred to something of value that I was aware of. The gold bars are the only thing I could think of. And he also hinted that this fellow might have something in his possession that would be of interest to me."

"Marcus, how could Neville know about the gold?" Cassie asked.

"I don't know, Cassie. How does he know anything" You said when he first met you he asked if I was your boyfriend. How does he know who I am? Who is that guy, anyway?" Marcus jumped up from his stool. "I've got to see if he's still in the parking lot." Marcus ran to the front double-doors and out into the small parking lot. He looked every direction, but there was no sign of the old man, Neville Naughton.

Simon Macawi

Tuesday, the fifteenth of April 1969. Another day amongst many that would likely stick with Marcus for the rest of his life. As he would every weekday afternoon, with the exception of his off day on Monday, Marcus drove Cassie home from school, walked her to her front door, and then headed to Walt's Auto and Tire Repair for his scheduled shift. As always, he went straight to the corner of the shop where everyone's work shirts were neatly hung next to the oversized private employee restroom. Hurriedly removing one of the shirts with his name, *Marcus*, emblazoned in bright embroidered red above the left breast pocket, from the clothes rack, Marcus went inside and changed into his work attire. Wanting to start his shift on the right foot, he gazed into the mirror, checking his hair and rubbing his index finger across his top front teeth. Satisfied with his appearance, Marcus was ready to hit the time clock and check in with Chester to receive his instructions for the day. As always, he hoped there would actually be a bit of mechanical repair work that Chester would assign to him.

He didn't particularly mind performing tire duty but plugging and replacing tires had become rather dull and routine a long time ago. Marcus had developed the same opinion when it came to taking parts inventory or stocking supplies. He would much prefer the prospect of getting his hands dirty as he actually performed the work of making repairs in the shop.

Clocked in and ready to go, Marcus didn't immediately see Chester at his work bay, so he went to Louie seeking guidance. Much to his disappointment, Louie gave him the unpleasant news that it had been a slow beginning to the week, and the bulk of the work that had been left over from Saturday, he and Chester had handled yesterday. He had already taken care of the inventory and had stocked all the supplies earlier. In fact, Chester had been sitting idle-handed most of the afternoon and had just gone home less than an hour ago. Walt was planning to call it a day shortly, and unless someone came in with an emergency problem or flat tire, they had nothing on their plate for the next three hours. It dawned on Marcus that if it were that slow, there stood a chance that Walt might just send him home early. He certainly hoped that wouldn't be the case, he had become quite fond of his weekly paycheck and when the opportunity arose to supplement it, he always made himself available for any additional hours. Marcus was shaken from his thoughts by the sound of Louie's voice.

"So, Marcoos," he advised, "make sure to have a broom in your hand when he come out of zee office. When he leave, we play rummy for a while, *oui*?" Louie laughed aloud, but he wasn't joking about playing cards.

"Sure thing, Frenchy." Marcus laughed in return, but then asked, "So, if it's so slow, what is Walt still doing here? Usually when it's this quiet he's out of here by noon." Walt was no longer a young man, the effects of age and the years of doing hard manual labor were beginning to show, as Marcus was well aware. Though still quite capable, Walt seldom came out into the shop and performed any real work anymore. He had plenty of faith in Chester and Louie and, whenever it was convenient, he would call it a day as soon after lunch as possible.

"Interview, *mon ami*. Walt is talking with *le jeune homme* right now just as you and I speak. He will be taking over my position when I return to Quebec next week." Louie explained to Marcus. "I tried to tell you Marcoos, you could have quit your schooling as did I and applied for the position. I know Walt would have hired you, you are *tres bon mecanicien*." Marcus had heard Louie's story many times over. He had quit school when he was only sixteen years old and gone to work at his uncle's gas station which had doubled as an outdoor repair shop. Louie had literally been trained by a shade tree mechanic, but apparently his Uncle Pierre had been a good instructor because Louie had obviously turned out to be a master.

"Well, number one Frenchy, I'm *not* a very good mechanic, yet." Marcus told him once again, explaining why he could not consider giving up on his education. "I'm still learning. And two, I'm not going to drop out of school. I plan to go to college after I graduate next year. And I don't say this meaning to offend you, but as much as I love working on cars, I really want to do more with my life." Marcus was sincere in not wanting to offend Louie. The Canadian was, after all, probably the best friend he had outside of Denny Wallace.

"Oh, that cuts me deeply, Marcoos." Louie put both hands over to his chest, feinting a heart attack, and dropping to one knee. Fortunately for Marcus, he had seen the pantomime many times before and knew Louie was only playing with him. "*Mon ami,*" Louie made his best crying face, "that hurts me so much more that you will let me here to die!" They both broke out in simultaneous laughter and Louie stood and pulled Marcus into a warm embrace.

"You are a good man, Marcoos. I will miss you when I have gone."

"I'll miss you too, Louie Dupree. I owe you so much." They still had a few more days, until Saturday to share one another's company, but Marcus was already feeling the sadness creeping into his heart.

Just as Marcus had begun to sweep around the tire changing station, the office door swung open and a well-tanned teenager stepped out followed closely by Walt McMurphy. Walt placed his hand on the youngster's shoulder and led him toward where Marcus and Louie were attempting to give the appearance of being busybodies.

"Louie, Marcus...I want you to meet our newest mechanic. This here is Simon Macawi. Simon is from over Quincy way." Simon, Louie, and Marcus all exchanged handshakes and pleasantries as Walt looked on. He then continued the introduction, "Simon tells me he's been toiling on cars for a couple of years now and it seems that he's graduated from a trade school over there in Quincy. Called his boss and the man gives him a glowing recommendation. So, assuming he gets a room over at that place you're at Louie, he'll be starting on Monday. I'll give Lois a call over there, see if she's got anything. If there's not a room open right now, I'm sure we can work something out until your room gets vacated, Louie."

"Walt, I will be leaving on Sunday morning, so my room will be open." Louie said, hoping to be helpful.

"Well, if that's the only room, I'd think Lois would want at least a day or so to clean up after your filthy butt, Louie!" Walt joked, demonstrating an unusual amount of enthusiasm. "We'll get it worked out, I'm sure."

"We'll figure something out, Walt. If need be, I can always sleep in my car for a night or two." Simon said confidently.

"Well now, that ain't gonna be necessary, Simon. Push comes to shove, you can bunk at the McMurphy's for a few days, long as it don't become habit." Walt laughed and then turned to Louie. "I'm heading out Louie. See you in the morning." Walt shook hands with his newest mechanic and said, "See you Monday morning, Simon. But I'll call you and let you know about whatever living arrangements I get worked out, either at the boarding house or at my place for a couple of nights." Walt turned and headed in the direction of the bay door.

"Okay, Walt. Thank you again for the job and for your help with the room, sir." Simon certainly sounded grateful. Walt raised his right hand and waved without looking back. He continued across the parking lot, and upon reaching his truck he shouted, "Don't you boys forget to lock up tight!"

As soon as Walt McMurphy's Dodge pick-up had disappeared from sight and he was satisfied that it was tracking to the west, Louie cleared the leftovers from the small table that hosted their lunch and morning breaks. Marcus and Simon took their seats as Louie went to his toolbox to search for his deck of cards.

"You're going to enjoy working here Simon. Chester and Louie are both good guys to be around, they've taught me a lot since I've been here." Marcus instantly recognized the need to correct himself. "Well no, I guess that's really not right, Louie will be gone when you start Monday. But you'll like Chester...and Walt, too. He's a really good boss to have."

"Oh yeah, I'm sure everything will be cool, Marcus. I can't wait until Monday, I'm looking forward to getting started, you know getting my feet wet," Simon said with a broad and friendly smile, flashing a mouthful of pristine pearly whites.

Louie returned, slapping the cards onto the table. "*Un coca?*" he asked as he reached into his pocket for some loose change.

"Yeah, I'll take one, Frenchy. Thank you. Simon?" Marcus looked to his left toward the new man.

"Uh, are you asking what I think you are? A Coke?" Simon said with a slightly quizzical look on his still smiling face.

"*Oui*....uh, yes, a Coca-Cola for you?" Louie clarified himself, realizing that with Marcus and Chester he could intersperse a small amount of French, that they had grown accustomed to hearing it and could usually decipher what he meant. Simon, on the other hand, was probably completely caught off guard by the question.

"Yeah, Louie, thank you. I appreciate it." Simon responded gratefully.

"So you're already working as a mechanic now, Simon?" Marcus was curious just how much experience Simon possessed because, in his opinion, the new man's youthful appearance would suggest that he should right now still be in high school.

"Yeah, Marcus. I work at my dad's shop over in Quincy. Been there just over a couple of years now." Simon offered up his information, well aware that Marcus was doubtful of his age and experience, just as Walt had been. He then threw a similar question to Marcus. "How about you, Marcus, you've been doing this for a while?"

"Almost two years exactly," Marcus answered.

"Did you go to trade school for it?"

"Oh, no. I just kind of learn on the job. I only work part-time, I'm still in high school, but I'll be a senior this fall." Marcus felt almost shy to admit he was still in school. "It kind of surprises me that you've already worked for a couple of years, I mean, to be honest,

I only figured you to be about my age. I mean, no offense or nothing, you just look young for your age, I guess."

Louie returned with the sodas and took a seat.

"How about you, Louie? How long have you been pulling wrenches?" Simon quizzed, still with a smile on his face. Marcus was beginning to wonder if it was a perpetual grin that Simon wore, it hadn't faded since he'd left Walt's office and entered the shop thirty or so minutes ago.

"Oh let's see, this is 1969, so I guess about twelve, thirteen years now. I quit zee schooling when I was sixteen. *Mon père* had grown ill and *mon frère et moi,* we both had to leave school and go to work to care for zee family." Louie knew that Marcus was already well-versed regarding his background, but he thought there was no harm in relating some of his personal details to Simon. "So I went to work for *mon oncle Pierre* and *mon frère Lucian* found employment pushing gurneys at zee hospital. In a few years, I had become a good mechanic and Lucian had made his way to nursing school and now he still earns his living at zee same hospital."

"That's really interesting, Louie. Marcus and your boss both have told me that you're an excellent auto repairman. I wish I could have spent some time working beside you, I'm sure you could have taught me some things." Simon was grateful that Louie had shared his story and wanted to be complimentary in appreciation of his openness.

"So then, Simon, what is your story? I must confess you look to me to be not much older than *mon ami* Marcoos here." Louie asked the question that Marcus was about to present just before Louie had returned with the Coca-Colas.

"Well, I'm going to turn nineteen in June and believe it or not, I guess my life is not too much different from yours, Louie. I quit high school at sixteen also, although not out of need, as in your case." Simon was not glowingly proud of his circumstances, but he decided to go ahead and tell his story. "When I determined that I couldn't deal with school anymore, I didn't want to flounder about, and my stepfather is definitely not the type of person who would have put up with any nonsense. So, as soon as I was able at the next available term, I enrolled in a local trade school there in Quincy to learn auto mechanics. A year later, there I was working for my stepdad, and that's where I've been ever since. At least until this coming Monday."

"I'm curious, Simon," Marcus could not resist knowing, "why did you quit school. You said you couldn't deal with it anymore."

"Well there were some seniors, and a couple of juniors too, that ... well, honestly, they were prejudiced against me and my kind." Marcus and Louie looked at one another, a little confused and taken back by what Simon was saying.

"I'm a little bit mixed up I think, Simon. Why were they prejudiced toward you? I don't understand." Marcus could not conceive of a reason that anyone would have a bone to pick with Simon. "What did you do to bother them?"

"Haven't you two noticed that my complexion is just little bit tanner than yours? I'm Native American, a descendent of the Pottawatomie Tribe. And there are still a lot of people who don't like our type. In the eyes of many, we are still relegated to a lower tier by people who still hold onto these outdated beliefs." Simon had finally lost the smile that he had displayed all afternoon. "Maybe you don't see it over here in Missouri, or maybe you don't have folks like me around here, but there are still parts of society that are prejudiced against us. Just like they are against black folk and some foreigners, heck in some places they really don't like the Polish and Chinese. I mean let's face it, it just depends on where you are in this country. Someplace or the other, if you're not Anglo-American, you're just not the same. Now, I sure hope that I haven't offended you two fellows, I mean I don't mean to imply that y'all are like that."

"No, for sure you haven't offended me," Marcus said. He had seen enough on television over the past few years to understand and sympathize with the plight of blacks in the country, but he had never envisioned that American Indians were still faced with the same type of discrimination in these modern times.

"Me either, *mon ami*, no offense here," said Louie in agreement.

"So anyways, that was why I quit school, that's my story," and with those words, the smile returned to Simon's face.

But Marcus' curiosity had not been satiated, "Okay Simon, so you were working for your stepfather for a couple of years, but now you're quitting and coming here. Why are you changing jobs, I'm just wondering."

"Mostly just because Frank, my stepdad, and I don't get along very well. I don't particularly like the way he treats my mom and then he also withholds part of my paycheck every week. He says I owe it to my mom for her troubles in raising me. But I know she doesn't see any of it, I'm sure he just puts it straight into his pocket. So anyhow, we just kind of came to a mutual agreement that I would find another job in another town and then we would both be rid of one another." Simon felt a bit humiliated for airing his dirty laundry and kind of wished he would have tried to be just a bit vaguer about his reasons for leaving Quincy and coming across the river to work at Walt McMurphy's shop. But honesty and openness had always been among the strongest of his natural traits, and for the most part, they had served him well in his young life.

A car pulled up outside of Louie's bay and Marcus quickly recognized the driver as a stock clerk he knew from Dempsey's Grocery. The man approached the three of them at the table and stated that he hoped they weren't too busy because he was hoping to get his oil changed during his dinner break. Marcus started to rise from his chair, but Louie put out a hand to stop him.

"I've got this one, Marcoos," he said. "You keep getting to know your new friend. You will be together for a long time and you should get familiar with each other more better." Louie turned to the young man and instructed him to go ahead and pull his Chevy into the bay. As they walked toward the roll-up door, Marcus could faintly hear Louie inquire of the fellow if he had any preference regarding oil weight and filter brand.

"Have you lived here all your life, Marcus?" Simon queried as he attempted to restart the conversation.

"Yep. My parents were both from here and I was born right here too."

"That's good, it must be pretty nice in this area if they have stayed here all their lives," Simon said, still smiling.

"Well yes, but no. I mean it is nice around here, but both of my parents have passed away. But yeah, I guess technically they did spend all of their lives here." The subject was still sobering to him, but Marcus had long ago come to terms with the reality of their absence. Memories of his mother had faded, but thanks to the family photos that Margaret had carefully preserved for him in an album, he still was able to reimagine and relive times with her and his father. Being seven years old when his father's accident occurred, his recollections of Elijah were far more vivid than those of his mother, Betty Jo.

"Oh man, I'm sorry to hear that, Marcus," Simon sincerely offered. "I couldn't imagine how difficult that must have been for you. To be orphaned at such a young age had to be traumatic for you."

"Actually, Simon, I was really lucky to have my stepmother there." At this point, beginning to feel quite comfortable in Simon's company, Marcus felt compelled to tell his family history. "See, my dad had gotten remarried after my mom died, and Mama, her name is Margaret, but I have always called her Mama, she has always taken the best care of me. You would never guess that she was a stepmother, she has always treated me just as if I was her real son."

"Wow, that's a really good story to hear, Marcus. I'm glad you were able to have your stepmother there to help you through losing your dad."

"Oh, for sure. Mama has been a real rock for me, absolutely," Marcus had never doubted Margaret's devotion to him and thanked God for her in his prayers every night.

"What about your grandparents? I guess they must live around here too, I mean since your parents were both born and raised here, right?" Simon logically assumed that would be the case.

"Well, no. They are all gone now as well." Even though they had all passed on, Marcus was comforted by the fact that his paternal grandfather was still being vigilant, keeping a watchful eye over him. Or at least he assumed that Opa was still in the neighborhood. Cassie and he were fairly certain that they had spotted him on a few occasions, most notably when they visited Forest Park Cemetery. But Opa had not spoken to Cassie nor made any contact since the October day in 1967 when he had come to them as they'd sat on Cassie's front yard wooden swing. That was the day he'd given Cassie the message that Marcus had been obligated to pass along to Cousin Judy. A day that he'd dreaded with every fiber of his body and soul.

"Gosh Marcus, that's terrible. You don't have any family aside from your stepmother? That's got to be tough for you." Simon's heart went out to Marcus. From his perspective, and in his life experience having relatives all about, he couldn't conceive of the pain and solitude of not having family involved in his daily life.

"Nah, it's not so bad. I do have one relative, my dad's cousin that lives in St. Louis. You got to promise you won't laugh if I tell you his name, though." Marcus smiled and almost laughed himself, even as he was asking Simon not to.

"Okay, Marcus, I promise," Simon said as he made an 'x' across his chest with his index finger. "Do you want me to pinky swear?"

"No, not necessary," Marcus said as he chuckled just a bit. "His actual name is Jude, but he's always been called...."

"Judy!" Simon blurted, and despite crossing his heart, he started laughing. "I could see that one coming from a mile away." After they both laughed for a few more seconds, Simon told Marcus, "There ain't nothing wrong with that name. You should hear some of the names in my family!"

"Okay, enough about me. Let's hear your story, I've never known any Native Americans, especially from the Powertonie tribe." Marcus was ready to learn about this young man who he was beginning to realize would probably turn into a good friend.

"Well, first off it's Pottawatomie not Powertonie. My people have been in this part of the country for at least three hundred years, but there are few left nowadays." Simon felt like he may as well give Marcus a little history of his tribe. "We mostly started out up in Michigan and Wisconsin, but through the years we filtered down south, into Illinois and Indiana. I guess around 1830, the Second Treaty of Prairie du Chien is what got the process started of relocating our tribe. Most of the folks in Indiana got moved to Kansas and a lot of my ancestors were sent to Nebraska."

"Wow that's terrible. They had to give up all their land and just start all over in a strange place?" Marcus had heard tales of how Indians all over the country had been forced westward and onto reservations.

"Well, everybody didn't get relocated. Some of them fled into Canada, some were able to assimilate into the local populations all over Michigan and Wisconsin. A lot of us, including my family, were able to settle in Quincy back around 1838 or so. Apparently, the people there were very accommodating. The story is they also took in folks from the Church of Latter-Day Saints that had gotten run out of Missouri too, as well as providing shelter for a lot of our tribe." Marcus was finding the history of Simon's tribe to be very interesting.

"That's pretty cool that those people took everybody in like that. I had never heard any of that about the Latter-Day Saints people getting run off like that. I'll have to do some reading about it." Marcus was anxious to hear more.

"I'm a descendant of Simon Pokagon. He was a tribal chief in Michigan and part of a delegation that went to Washington, D.C. like a hundred years ago. He wrote some books and was kind of famous. Actually, I was named after him. I think he was like my mom's great-great-grandfather or something." Simon thought about it and then added, "If I remember right, I believe his grandfather was Leopold Pokagon. He was a chief in the St. Joseph River Valley in the early 1800's, so I guess you could say I come from a long line of royalty, right?"

"Yeah, sure sounds like it." Marcus had to admit that he was quite impressed by Simon's heritage. "I hope you don't mind, but I think you've earned a nickname here already. I think you're gonna be known as Chief around here."

"*Chief?*" Simon yelped in a high-pitched squeal.

"Oh man, I'm sorry, Simon. If that offends you, I'll never use it again, I promise."

Simon nearly busted his gut laughing. "I'm just joking, Marcus. I'd be proud to have a good friend anoint me as his chief."

The two new friends shared a handshake and returned to their Cokes.

Sarge

James Burgess was just finishing his dinner when the knock came at his door, catching him off-guard and taking him completely by surprise. He lived in the second to last room, at the furthest end from the office of the 'L' shaped, single story, and family-owned motel that was situated in not one of Missouri's most sought after nor most desired locations. James "Jimbo" Burgess had discovered the run-down enterprise a few miles north of Jefferson City along U.S. Highway 63 almost midway from the capitol city and a small town of several hundred people called Ashland. He had immediately decided that it seemed like a pretty decent place for a freshly released ex-convict to hunker down unobtrusively while he rode out his two-year probation at the conclusion of his six years in the state penitentiary. Originally renting the room weekly for a reasonable thirty-five-dollar rate, it gave Jimbo the affordability he desperately needed along with the flexibility, had it become necessary, to pack up and disappear on a moment's notice. The *Sundance Motel* was fairly popular amongst newly released cons who lacked family or resources to make solid starts elsewhere and were just in need of someplace inexpensive to temporarily hang their hats until they got some footing. Even though his probation had been successfully completed, and the weekly rate had seen a significant increase, Jimbo had made the determination that the room was comfortable enough for his needs. Additionally, the work he was presently doing was not exactly what would be deemed respectable, and as such, he thought it prudent to try and project a public image of simplicity and relative poverty. Since his release, he had been diligently working locally on a part-time basis as a gas station attendant, maintaining a low profile and keeping quietly to himself.

Jimbo emitted a deep, grease-infused belch as he set the remnants of his fried chicken dinner next to the three empty Miller High Life beer cans already occupying space on the small side table next to the easy chair. With some effort, he stood and made the four-foot journey to respond to the knocking. He cracked the door just enough to peek out and identify his visitor. Recognizing the guest, he pushed the door shut, unfastened the chain, and then reopened it, welcoming the man in.

Stepping inside carrying a brown paper grocery bag, the guest spied only one chair and took it for himself, relegating Jimbo to either sitting on the edge of the bed or standing. Oscar 'Sarge' Roberts set the bag on the floor between his feet, reached inside and pulled out a document binder, which he promptly tossed onto the mattress next to Jimbo.

"What?" Asked Jimbo, rather dumbfounded by the way Sarge had just entered the room and silently produced the bounty that he had recently procured for his boss.

"Worthless." Sarge muttered disgustedly.

"What do you mean worthless? By the looks of that leather and the certificate inside, that's probably about a hundred years old. Those stocks should be worth a fortune by now. What are you getting at boss?" Jimbo was dumbstruck. When he had peeked inside the binder and saw the contraband it contained, he had assumed the value had inflated tremendously over the years.

"That kid's gonna be pretty disappointed when he opens this and finds out his inheritance ain't worth the paper it's printed on, Jimbo." Sarge had planned to be in possession of something with a significant amount of value. He had trusted the information he had gotten from Ollie Compton. He had gone to a lot of trouble having Jimbo pull reconnaissance on the Clemens kid. He'd been gathering and verifying information ever since he'd taken care of Ollie. Jimbo had traveled up north to put eyes on the kid at Ollie's son's funeral. And after Jimbo had cleared his probation, Sarge had set him up with official looking identification and had him verify some of the intel he had gathered. Thanks to the stupid old man at the dime store who had been kind enough to corroborate the identity of Marcus Clemens and the whole inheritance story, Sarge was confident that when Jimbo secured the goods that there would be a nice little payoff coming. He had even promised Jimbo a five

111

percent cut of the take on top of the fee he'd already shelled out to him. But, when he had produced the stock certificates to his fence, he was met with doubt. His contact initiated some research and, with a few phone calls, learned that the Detmeyer Drydock and Machine Company of St. Louis had gone belly-up some forty years ago.

"Turns out the company went out of business back during the Great Depression. Those three hundred shares ain't worth nothing anymore. Looks like old Mark Twain might have had good intentions but didn't do the kid any favors after all. Or me, for that matter." Sarge wasn't happy to relay the news, he'd been looking for a nice return on a minimal investment.

"Nothing at all? I thought stocks were guaranteed forever." Of course, Jimbo was no financial whiz, but he sure thought there would have to be some value still. In the back of his mind, he had an inkling of doubt and an uneasy feeling that Sarge might be telling him a tall tale to avoid shelling out the five percent that he had been promised.

"Not according to my source. Sorry Jimbo." Sarge's apology was cavalier, it wasn't as though he was really concerned for his minion. "But I do want to make sure that our little indiscretion in obtaining the binder continues to go unnoticed."

"What do you mean boss?"

"Well, you were up there running all around town, asking questions, making yourself known to a few people. So when the kid does go to open up that box..."

"It was a footlocker, Sarge," Jimbo interrupted.

"Okay footlocker, whatever," Sarge continued with his thought. "Anyway, when he opens it and the binder ain't there, it's gonna raise a red flag. Then, if the cops get involved, it will just be a matter of time before somebody figures out that a stranger had been snooping around and with you being an ex-con, well, you used to be a cop, what do you think?"

"So are trying to tell me that I'm going to have to break back into the house and *put it back*?"

"Yeah, that's exactly what I'm telling you." Sarge spoke firmly. He was dead serious.

"Don't you think that's risky, Sarge?" Jimbo asked.

"Sure it's risky, but I've got faith in you. Look, when it's back in the footlocker, everything is back to how it was. There's nothing to raise any suspicion about you or the questions you were asking when you were there. Everything is totally rewound. But," Sarge implored, "make sure you examine that footlocker carefully, make positive there is nothing else of value in it." Sarge made it sound simple enough and it certainly was logical thinking. All Jimbo had to do was slip back into the house and simply replace the document binder. Ten minutes inside and he would be home free, no worries. And Sarge was right, if no one knew he had returned and there was no evidence of the original break-in, then there really was no reason that his earlier visits would have raised any suspicions at all. There was no way for anything to go wrong.

"Call me when everything's taken care of," Sarge said as he left the motel room.

Driving back to his house, Sergeant Oscar Roberts had a long list of items that ran through his mind. He had a mental checklist that constantly required attention. He had to pick up cigarettes from his bootlegger in Columbia, he needed to run by the hospital to pick up some new syringes, and he still needed to make a run to St. Louis to see the Bossman. That was definitely the most important item on the agenda. It was Sunday, and he had to gather the week's supply of cocaine and heroin. He also was delivering the take that he had managed to collect since Monday. But most importantly, today was payday. Sarge had calculated that Bossman should have a cash roll ready containing six one-hundred-dollar bills and four twenties as compensation for his week of hard work. They say a side job won't make you rich, but the alternate employment that Sarge Roberts had procured back in 1965 had produced an income that made his salary as a corrections officer pale by comparison.

Newly promoted to the rank of Sergeant in 1965, Oscar Roberts had been discreetly approached by a man identifying himself only as *Bossman*. It had taken only a few clandestine meetings and a sampling of product to convince the thirty-four-year prison guard supervisor that there was money to be made. He had agreed to be the middleman between Bossman and inmates at the Missouri State Penitentiary in Jefferson City, Missouri, supplying both prisoners, and eventually a few select guards, with their weekly fix of drugs in addition to a few other items of contraband that could not be easily had behind the walls and bars of *The Big House.* He had soon realized that an assistant would be required and Sarge had done well in recruiting James "Jimbo" Burgess to fill the position. As a former police officer, Jimbo had experience and training that would turn out to serve him well in collecting and making good on debts that were owed inside. He seemed to have a way of dealing with his fellow convicts and he was exceedingly successful in providing the necessary muscle that allowed Sarge's operation to thrive. He served well in handling the tasks he was assigned, and when he had received his parole in early 1967, Sarge felt it would be in his best interests to continue to employ Jimbo on the outside as well.

Sarge had been very successful with his operation and Bossman was responsible for making him a great deal of extra cash. He had grown to have the utmost trust in just about anything Bossman told him and had willingly agreed to whatever the man had asked of him. When he was offered a thousand dollars to have one of his inmates killed, Sarge's hesitation was only momentary. He had agreed, and when he was told the name of the victim, he was only too willing. It had so happened that the ill-fated inmate was one with whom Sarge had become quite intimate. Over a period of months, the two had engaged in numerous conversations in the exercise yard. They had discussed many topics, but the conversations that had become most interesting to Sarge were the ones centered on the reason the man had been caught and sentenced for crimes unrelated to the situation that had been the cause of his arrest. The inmate was a death row prisoner, sentenced to the electric chair for the murders of two young women. However, he insisted he would never have been cited for the murders had it not been for mistakes made in a get rich scheme that had gone off the rails.

Oliver Compton had been too bold, too foolish to have stuck to a sane plan to contrive to have a certain young man incarcerated or eliminated. Either outcome would have sufficed. So long as the boy were taken out of the picture, Oliver was quite positive that his only adopted son, him being the only remaining blood relative of the youngster, would be the rightful heir to a fortune left by the world's most famous writer, Mark Twain. Sarge had found the tale remarkable and had begun brainstorming, trying to figure out some brilliant way that he might somehow finagle his way into getting his hands on that huge inheritance. Finally, Sarge concluded that after Jimbo Burgess' probation had been satisfied, he could simply have Jimbo utilize his skills and basically just steal what he was after.

When Bossman made the request to have Oliver Compton taken care of, Sarge didn't have to take much into consideration before agreeing. It only required one night's thoughtful planning and the promise of a few weeks' worth of either cocaine or heroin for him to secure the aid of three death row inmates. In return, they had agreed to instigate an exercise yard riot that was designed as a punishment for some unknown offense committed by Compton. If executed to plan, the brawl in the yard would provide cover while the dastardly deed was completed. Sarge knew that he could not trust any of the inmates to perform the execution. There was too much likelihood or possibility that he would fall victim to some type of blackmail plot if one of them actually did the deed. No, his plan was just to have them instigate a small riot, rough Compton up a bit and then, when he and other officers attempted to quell the melee, he would pretend to subdue Compton. In the process, Sarge intended to take care of business himself. He would then start screaming that Compton had been stabbed. Of course an investigation would surely follow, but if he had performed his job correctly (and he had), no one would have seen what actually had happened and there would be not a shred of evidence pointing toward anyone. Just as he had envisioned, there was never a culprit identified. All the inmates had been on death row and as such, whoever the guilty party had been, he was still destined to meet his maker. There was no need for the state to finance a trial when the punishment had already been prescribed for whoever the killer had actually been. Everything involving Oliver Compton had gone perfectly by design. Everything except for the pot at the end of the rainbow. The pot had turned out to be empty.

Arriving home, Sarge had quickly run in to let his wife know he was heading to St. Louis to finish his Sunday duties. Darla Roberts had no earthly idea what exactly it was that her husband did in St. Louis every weekend, and she honestly didn't care. As long as she was kept in the finest clothing that either Sears and Roebuck or their rival, Montgomery Ward, had to offer and her kitchen appliances were the most up to date and modern the market had to offer, she had no interest in the side job from which Oscar had been deriving his extra income.

As he cruised eastward on Interstate 70, Sarge found himself thinking more about James Burgess. Jimbo had been very helpful, both inside the prison and now on the outside. However he wasn't so sure anymore. He'd gotten a concerned call from the Bossman earlier in the week questioning him about reports he had received from some acquaintances in Hannibal who had quizzed him about a certain heavyset individual who had apparently had some loose lips while drinking at a place called the *Bar None Saloon.* Bossman told him that this person was reportedly running his mouth about working in the "pharmaceutical" field. He told Sarge that the man's description was reminiscent of Jimbo's and wanted to make sure that Sarge hadn't sent him up that way to run some errand. Bossman had been assured that Jimbo had not had a reason to be anywhere near that portion of the state, that he had no business to handle that far north. The entire conversation had made Sarge nervous. That was Bossman's territory, all the way up into Iowa he thought. Sarge also knew that if Bossman suspected someone horning in on territory that was his would be met with severe repercussions. It was en route to St. Louis that Oscar Roberts reached the conclusion that Jimbo Burgess was developing into a liability and that after returning from this assignment that his employment under Sarge's command would have to be terminated.

Reaching the warehouse in west St. Louis County that was the designated rendezvous point for his supply collection, Sarge exited his flashy lime green Javelin, the relatively new sports model that American Motors had begun producing the year prior. Sarge had special ordered his, just picking it up from the dealership yesterday. Pulling a handkerchief from his back pocket, he quickly wiped the driver's side of the windshield to remove any bugs he might have picked up on the drive. The large warehouse door suddenly slid left to right, opening wide. He re-entered the car and pulled inside the dimly lit structure. As he opened the car's door, Sarge was immediately met by a loud and angry voice.

"What the hell is wrong with you?"

Turning to his right, Sarge saw Bossman alongside two of his associates.

"What do you mean?" Sarge asked in a confused and startled tone.

"What the hell are you doing driving something like this?" Demanded a visibly agitated Bossman. "Where's the Impala you've been using for the last two years?"

"I traded it in for this yesterday. Why Bossman?" he asked.

"Why? Why, you ask? What are stupid or something? You can't be coming here in some crap like this. For Christ's sake, are you trying to draw attention to yourself?" Bossman was incredulous. "You can't be driving something like this hauling hard drugs. Jesus, what a damned idiot."

"I don't get it Bossman. You just bought a new red Corvette a couple of weeks ago. I figured folks like us ought to have classy rides, I mean why not, right?" For a pretty smart fellow, Sarge was totally missing Bossman's point.

"Folks like us you say? Okay, let's get something straight, you ain't like me, and never will be. And listen, Einstein. Get this through your thick skull. I drive a Vette because I'm the Bossman. And guess what genius? I don't carry freaking drugs in my trunk." The point was starting to sink in now. Bossman was worried that with a wrong move Sarge would get himself pulled over and risk having his week's supply of goodies being discovered.

"You're right Bossman. I apologize. Listen, I'll use the wife's car from now on." Sarge was trying to be as apologetic as he knew how. "I promise I won't show up in this again, okay? I'm sorry, boss, I really am."

"Be sure of it. My luck, cops will spot you leaving the warehouse, you'll get pulled over leaving the complex, and we'll all be busted. I'd have to call in a ton of favors and hope for the best. I swear, you get pulled over and risk my operation, you're a dead man, you got it?" Bossman was still seething and somewhat red-faced. Sarge had never seen this degree of temper from him. "Get him loaded boys, get his ass out of here."

The boss started to walk away, but was delayed when Sarge again spoke up, "Uh," he paused and cleared his throat, "excuse me, uh, Bossman. Today's payday ain't it, uh, sir?"

Without looking back, Bossman stopped and sarcastically asked, "It's Sunday ain't it?"

"Yes sir, the twenty-seventh if I ain't mistaken," Sarge replied.

Bossman stood for a minute and in an obviously disgusted manner, shook his head. Reaching up, he unrolled the left sleeve of his bleached white tee shirt and pulled a Camel cigarette from its pack. After alternately tapping one end and then the other against the pack, he placed the smoke between his lips. He slowly and deliberately rolled the pack back into his sleeve. Pulling a lighter from his jeans pocket, he silently lit the cigarette and took an unhealthy but prolonged drag. He slid the lighter back into the watch pocket of his jeans and then reached into his left side pocket, extracting a roll of green, hard cash wrapped in a rubber band. Casually, he tossed it over his left shoulder, landing it about two feet to Sarge's left.

Without turning or bothering to look back in Sarge's direction, his words rang out loud and clear. "I don't want to see that damned car again, got it?"

Another Lazy Sunday

Marcus stepped onto the front porch of the two-story, one-hundred-year-old Wallace residence and rapped five times quickly, paused, and followed up with two slower more deliberate taps. It had been his habit since the second grade to use the signature knock, and he still remembered when his father had originally described it to him. It was a simple cadence that Elijah told him he had heard used by an old-timey shill at Union Station – the rail depot in downtown St. Louis - who was trying to lure customers to a nearby barbershop. *"Shave and a haircut, six bits"* was the first and only verse Marcus could still pull from his recollection of his father's tale. Over the course of ten years, the familiar rapping had become his personal calling card. When the cadence sounded, everyone within the Wallace household was aware of the caller's identity, and if he were home, it was Denny's sole responsibility to respond.

After the second time through the ritual, the front door was opened and Denny stepped outside. "How's it going Marcus?" Denny asked, with a touch of raspiness still in his voice.

"Good, how about you? Are you better? You sure you're up to getting out and about today? You still don't sound so swell." Marcus was a bit concerned about his friend's well-being. Denny had come down with a pretty severe case of the flu and hadn't been to school since getting sick right after Easter. He had been there helping with Marcus' and Margaret's move on Easter Sunday, but had felt under the weather and stayed home from school the day following. From there, he progressively worsened, eventually having to see Dr. Fleming on Thursday of that week. There's an old saying, *'If you take medicine for a cold, you can shake it in seven days. But if you don't, it could last up to a week!'* Unfortunately for Denny, his condition far exceeded the common cold that he and his parents originally thought he had contracted.

"Oh yeah, lots better. No more fever or chills, just a bit of a lingering cough, but I feel a whole lots better. Going back to the *Meridian* tonight, I can't afford to miss any more work, you know what I mean?" Denny didn't earn a lot operating the projector at the theater, but he was very proficient at putting his earnings away. He was deadly serious in his quest to eventually set out for Hollywood and was fastidious when it came to saving and planning. When the time came, Marcus knew that Denny would have a foolproof blueprint devised that would almost virtually guarantee his success, or at least provide him with the utmost opportunity to achieve his goals.

"Are you sure you're ready, Denny? Coming back to school tomorrow, too?" Marcus asked as they walked toward his car.

"Yeah, I think I'm good to go. Don't worry, I'm not contagious or nothing." Denny wanted to assure Marcus that he needn't fear catching the miserable affliction he had suffered through. "And besides, you know *If It's Tuesday, It Must Be Belgium* just opened this week. God, I'd marry Suzanne Pleshette right now if she showed up in front of me and asked. She's so beautiful, don't you think, Marcus."

"She's okay, I guess," Marcus replied. "But Denny, you know darned well that I'm partial to redheads!" They both enjoyed a good belly laugh as they climbed into Marcus' Metro.

Fifteen minutes later they stood at the snack bar of the *Riverwalk Lanes*, waiting for Cassie to finish serving a customer. When she noticed Denny standing alongside Marcus, she was relieved to see he was out of quarantine and back among the living. Wiping her hands on her apron, she proceeded to prepare two fountain Cokes and deliver them to her friend and boyfriend.

"How are you doing stranger?" Cassie asked, setting the glasses on the countertop. "Long time no see. Feeling better it appears."

"Oh for sure, much better. Thanks for asking Cassie. I figured I'd treat your boy here to a couple of games, haven't been able to beat him bowling since before Easter." Denny had to laugh at his own comment. He may have always been a better baseball player and able to run faster, but when it came to bowling and other physical matters such as strength and endurance, he had always been Avis to Marcus' Hertz. Almost always finishing as second-best. "Speaking of which, we'd better get started so we can get a couple of games in before Marcus has to drop me at the *Meridian* at four o'clock."

"Oh good, you're going back to work tonight?" Cassie asked.

"Yep. I have to get back to my normal routine, rejoin the human race, right?" Denny was actually quite relieved after being cooped up for the better part of two weeks. Giving Marcus a playful punch to the shoulder, Denny said, "C'mon Marcus, let me go kick your butt, son."

Marcus smiled at Cassie and begged his leave, "Let me go take care of my light work. Be back in an hour or so." He winked and headed to the counter twenty feet away to join Denny in renting bowling shoes.

Midway through game one, Denny remembered something that had slipped his mind while he was sick and he had never thought of mentioning it to Marcus whenever they'd spoken on the phone over the past couple of weeks.

"Hey, Marcus, did I ever tell you about the day after you moved, when I came by your house that afternoon?" Denny asked.

"No, didn't know you had come by. You never said anything, why?" Marcus was a little curious as to what Denny was getting at.

"Well, I knew you weren't working, you know with it being Monday and all, and even though I wasn't feeling so hot, I thought I'd walk over to see you, you know, and get some fresh air. Just as I turn the corner down the street from your new place, I see this fat guy walking down the sidewalk from your house and get into his car." Marcus wasn't sure what the point was, it was probably just a door-to-door salesman or something like that.

"So what about him?" Marcus quizzed.

"Well he was carrying a package or satchel or something under his arm, and when he got in his car he sat there for a long time."

"What do you mean a long time? And I don't see what is so suspicious. You're making out like the guy was a secret agent, a James Bond or something. It was just probably like an encyclopedia salesman or something. You know, I'm sure they get leads when new people move in and stuff, and I'd imagine that's all he was. I mean, nothing got stole or anything that I know of. Mama would have told me if her jewelry was gone or something like that."

"I don't know Marcus; I'm guessing you're probably right. But it just seemed odd. It was like the closer that I got, I had this feeling like he'd seen me and knew I was approaching. His head got lower, like he sort of slumped down in his seat. Just seemed odd. When I got up to his car, I took a peek over at him. He looked nervous; you know? Kind of like a pitcher with the bases loaded and one out, knowing he's got to either get a strikeout or a double-play type of nervous." Denny squinted as he thought back. "And he was dressed funny. He had like a suit coat or jacket on and it was orange. Who wears an orange jacket? Sales people usually dress kind of conservative, don't they?"

"I would think," Marcus offered. "But who knows? Man, times are changing fast. I mean, look at all the tie-dyed shirts and stuff. This is the psychedelic age Denny, the world is different, bright colors are in these days. You've seen all that stuff on television. Heck, just look at *Rowan & Martin* and all that psychedelic stuff on there. Bright colors don't make you stand out anymore."

"Yeah, you're right." Denny conceded. "But it still was odd. He seemed like he left in a hurry after I looked at him, too."

"I wouldn't give it anymore thought, Denny. It's nothing." Marcus picked up his ball and prepared to take his position to throw the second ball of the ninth frame.

"Hey buddy," Denny intoned, hoping to rattle Marcus. "If you don't mark here, and I throw four strikes in a row, I'll win."

"Fat chance of that," Marcus laughed, almost uncontrollably. "Man, you've never made more than two in a row in your life." With that remark, Marcus landed his hook shot squarely between the one and three pins and cleared the deck, putting the game safely out of reach. To use Denny's metaphor, he was the pitcher who struck out the side with the sacks jammed.

Marcus returned to the *Riverwalk Lanes* after quickly running Denny over to the *Meridian*. Once again he sidled up to the snack bar counter and waited for Cassie to bring his complimentary Coca-Cola. Before she had even noticed that he had returned, Marcus felt a gentle hand on his shoulder. Turning to his right he found himself somewhat bewildered to see Dutch Franklin from *Franklin's Five and Dime*.

"Hello young Marcus, although young doesn't so much apply as it did when you and your pal Denny Wallace used to come by when you were little kids, does it?" Dutch had a remarkable knack for remembering all of his customers. He took pride in that quality and it did seem that the man never forgot a face.

"Hi, Mr. Franklin. I haven't seen you in a while," Marcus said as he recovered from his surprise, both in seeing the man and realizing that Dutch remembered him and Denny so readily. "I have to apologize that I don't come in as often as I used to, you know, with school, and all. Oh and I have a job now too, you know?"

"That's quite alright, Marcus, quite alright. I understand how busy you are. I was a teenager once myself, years ago back in Chicago. Priorities change as people age." Dutch had seen it many times before. Youngsters came in for toys and candy and then, when they traveled through puberty, it was for magazines and milkshakes. Suddenly the children were teenagers and the milkshakes were more often purchased over at the *A & W* or the in the more grown-up atmosphere of the *River's Edge Diner*. But then, just as suddenly it seemed, those same kids were having kids of their own. And eventually, voila, here they were back at the *Five and Dime*, spending their hard-earned dollars on diapers and household goods. And of course, toys and candy. A never-ending cycle of life that Dutch had been witnessing for decades.

"So Marcus, this being my day off from the store, I was about to throw a few games with the missus when I noticed you sitting over here." Marcus wondered what reason could have prompted Mr. Franklin to approach him but didn't have to wait long for the answer to his unspoken question. "And I felt that I needed to come over and ask you something. I know you and Deputy Daniels have a history together and I couldn't help but wonder if Mitchell might have spoken to you."

"No, Mr. Franklin, I haven't spoken to Mitch for a couple of months I would guess. What makes you think he would have wanted to talk to me?" Marcus asked, with his curiosity now piqued.

"Well, maybe it's not my place to be telling you anything, Marcus." Dutch was hesitant to be the messenger of what had transpired at the store three weeks earlier.

It was obvious to Marcus that Dutch, when he found that Mitch Daniels had apparently decided not to talk to him, was now in a quandary. "No, please do Mr. Franklin. You can't tease me with something and then withhold it from me."

"Well, I know I shouldn't, but I guess my mistake was even coming over here. I hope Mitchell and Helen forgive me for overstepping my bounds, but someone came into the store the Saturday before Easter asking questions and your name eventually came up." Immediately, Marcus was overcome with a feeling of dread.

Dutch Franklin proceeded to provide Marcus with the details surrounding the visit and questioning by James "Jimbo" Burgess. When Dutch got to the part where Burgess had specifically asked about him, Marcus had a terribly uneasy feeling come over him and his stomach sank drastically. He had been through quite enough over the past six years or so with this supposed inheritance. He and Cassie had already done ample research on the Detmeyer Drydock and Machine Company and, with barely minimal effort had learned that the outfit had long ago gone out of business. They already were aware that the stocks had no value whatsoever, although they could not admit that to anyone. Marcus and Cassie were the only people on earth with the knowledge that Ellis had long ago opened the document binder, revealing its contents. The binder was not to be legally breached until Marcus turned eighteen years of age and then it could only be done in the presence of a licensed attorney. Whoever this Burgess character was, Marcus wished he could tell him he was wasting his time if he were looking for some form of treasure. But, even more than that, he felt a twinge of fear for both his and Cassie's safety.

Dutch added to the information he had already revealed by letting Marcus know what Helen had subsequently told him. He related that Burgess had not been a private investigator as he had claimed, but in fact was an ex-con who, before prison had actually been a police officer.

"If I were you Marcus, I wouldn't be too concerned. Helen told me that they have already tracked this guy down, they know where he lives, what he drives, all about him. If he shows up again in these parts, I'm pretty sure he'll wish that he'd never ventured into Lewis County." Dutch was a little worried that he might have caused undue concern, and sincerely hoped that he had eased Marcus' mind by telling him about the man's identity being positively known and that the local authorities were well aware of him.

"Well, Mr. Franklin, it is all good to know and I'm glad you were open with me and I appreciate it. I'm sure that if this fellow comes back, Mitch will keep an eye on him." Marcus was relieved that Dutch had notified the deputies at the Lewis County Sheriff's Department, and that they had found out the truth about James Burgess.

"Well, I guarantee you this Marcus. If he comes back dressed like he did that day, he certainly won't blend in with folks around here and will be easy to spot," Dutch said. "He'll stand out like a sore thumb."

"What do you mean, Mr. Franklin? Dressed how?" Marcus wondered aloud.

"His choice of clothing was ridiculous, Marcus. Kind of stuff I'd never be able to sell around here even if I was to stock it, which I wouldn't." Dutch explained, but not to Marcus' satisfaction.

"Why do you say ridiculous, Mr. Franklin?"

"His jacket, Marcus, he was wearing an orange blazer or suitcoat."

As soon as possible after Dutch Franklin had left to rejoin his wife, Cassie scooted over to where Marcus sat with a visibly shaken look on his face. "What was that all about, Marcus?" Cassie asked. "I was occasionally able to catch bits and pieces but missed most of your conversation. Did I hear that somebody is looking for you? What did you do? Why would someone be looking for you?"

"I don't know Cassie. I'll give you the whole story when you get off at five, but I guess someone is wanting to get their hands on the stupid inheritance again." Marcus didn't want to alarm Cassie, but knew he had to be honest with her. "Listen, I'm going to go use the payphone to call Mitch Daniels. I need to get some answers from him."

"Well, I'm done here in another twenty minutes, I guess I can wait," she said, not happy but understanding the circumstances. "Just one question. Should I be worried for our safety again? Is somebody out to kill us?"

"No, Sweetie. According to Mr. Franklin, everything is under control," Marcus said trying to allay Cassie's fears. "I'm going to go call Mitch now and I'll know more about things in a few minutes, okay?"

With it being Sunday, Mitchell Daniels was off duty and sitting in his backyard. He was enjoying the relaxing sight of his two daughters wearing out the swing set as he slowly sipped from a can of Budweiser. When the phone rang, his wife answered briefly and, setting the receiver down on the kitchen counter, hurried outside to let him know that Marcus Clemens was on the line.

"Okay Peggy," Mitch said before draining the can. "Watch the girls for a minute?" Mitch entered the kitchen through the back screen door and curiously picked up the call.

"Hello, Marcus," Mitch said. "What can I do for you?"

Marcus immediately went into the details of the conversation that he'd just had with Dutch Franklin. He made sure to express to Mitchell that while he had the most absolute faith in the abilities of the deputy and his department, he was quite nervous to learn that someone had been snooping around once again concerning his upcoming inheritance. For his part, Mitch did his very best to calm Marcus, explaining that they were fully aware of James Burgess. He filled Marcus in on everything they currently knew about the convicted former police officer and assured him that they were also in contact with the Boone County authorities. In so far as the Boone County Sheriff's Department could ascertain, the man had been a good citizen since his release from prison. He had served a satisfactory two-year probation period and up until now had appeared to be keeping his nose clean. However, after being informed of the suspicious behavior Burgess had displayed at the *Five and Dime*, including the impersonation of a private investigator, the Boone County officer that he'd spoken with had assured Mitch that a close eye would be kept on him and guaranteed that Burgess would be extended an extremely short and taut leash.

"Well, things seem a little better after talking to you Mitch," Marcus said, feeling a certain degree of relief. "But I'm still a shade concerned that he was at my house when no one was at home."

"What?" Mitch responded incredulously to the last words that Marcus uttered. "He was at your house? When? How do you know he was at your house, Marcus?"

"I guess I left that part out when I told you about what Mr. Franklin had talked about." Marcus was disappointed with himself for omitting such an important part of the story. "I just learned today that the day after we moved into the house on North Seventh Street, on the Monday after Easter, my friend Denny had come by my house. He said that he saw that same guy leaving my house and getting in his car. Denny said he looked nervous and just kind of seemed suspicious."

"Wait a minute Marcus." Mitchell was thinking of the time frame. Burgess had spoken to Dutch on Saturday and now Marcus was saying he was at his house on the following Monday. Marcus said he had just moved on Sunday. On Easter Sunday. How could Burgess have known where Marcus had moved to? Maybe he had been doing surveillance during the move? And how would Marcus, or Denny Wallace for that matter, know that this was the same man that had been at the *Five and Dime* interrogating Dutch just two days prior?

"Marcus, I guess maybe I'm confused." Mitchell had to get some facts straight. "Was your friend Denny at Dutch Franklin's store on Saturday and see this Burgess fellow there?"

135

"No, at least I don't think so. You'd have to ask Denny. But if he did, he never told me, Mitch." Marcus didn't understand why the question was even asked, or what Mitch was getting at.

"Okay, Marcus. You're telling me that Denny told you he saw a guy at your house on Monday, coming from your front door and then going to his car, and that it was the same guy who was at the *Five and Dime* on Saturday asking about you?" Mitch was struggling to see how Denny or Marcus had made the connection.

"No Mitch, that's not it. I know it was the same guy because of his description. And the jacket. Mr. Franklin said he was overweight and wore an orange blazer. And that's how Denny described him, too. He said he was fat, looked nervous and was wearing an orange jacket," Marcus explained. "That's how I put two and two together and figured it had to be the same person."

"Marcus, I never asked you before. Your inheritance. Where does it come from, where is it? Is a lawyer holding it? Is there paperwork, a will, just what do you know about it?"

Marcus wasn't about to tell Mitch that Ellis had opened the binder two years ago. He couldn't admit that he knew what the inheritance was nor that he already knew it was nothing more than worthless paper. But he could at least tell Mitch where it was.

"It's in my house Mitch." Marcus admitted. "It's in an old army footlocker that belonged to my dad and it's in Mama's closet."

"Have you seen it inside the footlocker, Marcus? You're sure it's there?" Mitch asked.

"Yes, Mitch, I've seen it, it's in a locked document binder in the footlocker."

"Are you at home right now, Marcus?" Mitchell had another question that needed to be answered pronto.

"No, right now I'm at the bowling alley getting ready to pick Cassie up from work. Why?" Marcus asked in response to Mitchell's question.

"Marcus, as soon as you can, go home and look in that footlocker and call me right away. As soon as possible, alright?" Mitch hoped Marcus would be able to leave and go home immediately.

"Okay, Mitch. Cassie gets off in less than five minutes. I'll go straight home and check. I'll call you back right away," Marcus promised.

On the drive back to his house, and to the best of his ability, Marcus attempted to fill Cassie in on everything he had learned this afternoon. Arriving at his house, they raced inside and straight to Margaret's bedroom where they anxiously pulled out the footlocker.

Twenty minutes after concluding the conversation with Marcus, the Daniels' phone rang once again.

"Marcus?" Mitchell asked expectantly.

Prior to Mitchell's asking, Marcus blurted, "It's gone."

An immediate All-Points Bulletin was issued in Lewis and nearby surrounding jurisdictions, complete with a description of James Burgess and his vehicle, a black 1956 two-door Pontiac Sky Chief Safari. Deputy Mitchell Daniels called the Boone County deputy with whom he had previously consulted, requesting the department to immediately pursue the apprehension of Burgess tentatively under the suspicion of trespassing, breaking and entering, and robbery.

The Return To The Scene

"Hello," Sarge's wife slurred groggily, intensely aggravated that her nap had been disturbed. The afternoon siesta had become a highly anticipated activity after lunch each Sunday afternoon. It had become a routine, a therapeutic method for Darla Roberts to counteract the boredom that would always set in while Sarge was out galivanting all over Missouri gathering supplies and securing the inventory necessary to sustain his distribution network for the coming week.

"Hi Darla, it's Jimbo," the voice intoned from the other end of the line. "I guess Sarge ain't there is he?"

"He's never here on Sundays, Jimbo, and you know it," Darla replied tartly. She knew without a shred of doubt that Jimbo was perfectly aware of her husband Oscar's weekend schedule and whereabouts. "Why would you even ask? Unless you're just a complete numbskull, you know exactly where he is."

"I was pretty sure he wasn't there, but it's okay, because really it was you that I wanted to talk to anyway." Jimbo came right to the point of his call. "I have to make a trip to northern Missouri tomorrow, it's business for Sarge. But I was just there a few weeks ago, and I've got reservations that I might be recognized if I take my car."

"So I guess you're wanting to borrow my Falcon?" Darla correctly surmised.

"If it's convenient for you," said Jimbo. "Of course, I'll leave my car with you, you know, in case you need to run any errands or anything."

"Yeah, I guess so," she replied. Darla wasn't really aware of the extent or details of her husband's enterprise, but she was wise enough to know that if James Burgess was worried about being recognized in his own vehicle, then it would probably be wise of her to allow him the use of her Falcon to help him to maintain his anonymity.

"Good, thank you, Darla. It will be a quick in and out operation, most of the time will be involved in the commute. If I can come by around eight in the morning, I should be back just a bit past noon. Eight isn't too early is it?" He asked cautiously.

"No, Oscar leaves around 7:15 so that'll be alright." Darla felt a bit anxious, even though she liked Jimbo and felt that she could trust him, she was still nervous. Jimbo provided her regularly with no-cost uppers and bluebirds that he skimmed from the personal stash he was allotted from Sarge's weekly supply. Jimbo wasn't a user himself, but he made a few extra dollars from flipping the product he was given. Due to the hush-hush arrangement – her husband would blow a gasket if he knew - Darla was in no position to turn down this simple request from him. She could ill afford to alienate him for fear he would inform Oscar of her habit. On the one hand she felt confident she could trust Jimbo just because of the faith Oscar had in him. They had been working together for a long time, both in the pen, and now, for more than two years on the outside. There should be no obvious reason for her to be concerned. But on the other hand, there still were the two considerations leading to her trepidation. First was the supplier issue. Secondly was the fact that the last employee Oscar had used on the outside, back in 1966, had borrowed and ultimately stolen her car. That fiasco had resulted in a sticky situation because they couldn't just simply report the theft to the police. There existed the very certain possibility, if and when the culprit was caught, that the man would rat out her husband and bring him crashing down. She never learned how Oscar had managed to locate and retrieve her Ford, but he somehow had recovered it in just a few weeks' time. Following that debacle, Oscar had made it abundantly clear that she was never again to loan her vehicle to anyone. With that in mind, she warned Jimbo, making it crystal clear to him that he had better be careful and on his best behavior. "And Oscar can never know you borrowed it," she warned. "Never."

"Guaranteed," was Jimbo's one word affirmation.

* * * *

James Burgess arrived once again at the front door of the Clemens' residence on North Seventh Street just past ten o'clock on Monday morning. The plan was for a quick in and out. After picking the door lock, and already familiar with the layout of the home, Jimbo made his way directly into the master bedroom. Opening the closet door, he instantaneously noticed the first red flag of the day. The lock had been removed from the footlocker. With the lock gone, the fact became painfully obvious that someone had opened, and no doubt rummaged through the contents of, the footlocker. That realization logically led to the further assumption that the absence of the document binder had also been noticed. He removed the green footlocker from the closet and opened it. It was then that he became aware of the second red flag. The Ruger single-action .22 caliber pistol was missing, along with the box of ammo. New questions had now entered the equation. Had someone opened the box specifically to remove the gun and bullets? Had the missing documents been noticed at all? Had the absence of the binder been discovered and the gun removed with the intent being to search for and perhaps punish the thief? The final scenario seemed highly unlikely and certainly not a cause for concern.

But Jimbo had made himself somewhat known locally, albeit not necessarily by intent. He had only engaged in lengthy conversations with the old lady over at the Post Office who, considering her age, he doubted would even have the mental capacity to remember him, and the storekeeper at the *Five and Dime*. Dutch Franklin was the only person he could recall who might offer a plausibly accurate description. A decision would definitely have to be made concerning his fate. The need to eliminate a potential witness would have to be discussed with Sarge. While seeming to Jimbo that it was distinctly necessary that the storekeeper be removed from the equation, he knew that he had to give Sarge an opportunity to either concur with or reject his opinion. Regardless of Sarge's thoughts, the fact of the matter was that the whole mission had been an exercise in absolute futility. The documents he had stolen had proven not to be worth a plug nickel. And now here he was trying to return them. They had hoped that by doing so would avert any possible suspicion. But now he knew it was just another wasted effort because in all likelihood the disappearance of the documents had already been discovered. It occurred to Jimbo that the best thing for him would be to get out of Dodge before Marshal Dillon and his cohorts discovered him.

Replacing the documents inside the footlocker and returning it to the closet, Jimbo retraced his steps to the front door. Making sure that this time there were no pedestrians occupying the street or sidewalks, he relocked the front door and returned to the borrowed Ford Falcon. Taking care to stay below all posted speed limits, he drove cautiously all the way back to Jefferson City.

Arriving back in the state's capitol city, Jimbo stopped and refilled the gas tank before proceeding to the Roberts homestead. Apparently, Darla Roberts had been watching anxiously through her front bay window as she awaited his return, because before he could park the Falcon in the driveway and shut off the ignition, she had bolted through the mudroom door and was making haste in approaching the car.

"Tell me something, Jimbo," she demanded as he opened the car door. "What have you done to stir up the deputies around her?"

"Why nothing, Darla," he pleaded as he handed her the key ring. "Why in God's tarnation would you even ask such a question?" Jimbo was caught dumbfounded by the confrontation. It wasn't yet one in the afternoon and he hadn't even been gone the five hours that he had estimated the round trip would take.

"I needed spaghetti sauce for tonight's dinner, so I took your car to the grocery, just as you had offered." Darla began explaining the trauma of her morning. "When I left I noticed a Boone County deputy parked out in the street. He followed me all the way to the I.G.A. store, but when I turned in, he kept on going. I thought it was a wee bit strange, but I shrugged it off as just a coincidence."

"Well, I'm sure it was just coincidence, Darla." Jimbo theorized. "I've had that type of stuff happen to me a few times, too."

"Yeah and that's what I thought as well," she seemed to agree, "until I came out of the store. Now there was a different deputy sitting two rows behind where I was parked. I left there and went to Miller's Pharmacy to pick up a prescription and some feminine items and was followed all the way again."

"Okay, now that does sound a little strange, I admit, but still." Jimbo was slightly confused and became a tad alarmed by Darla's tale.

"Yeah, tell me about it. And when I left there, a deputy in an unmarked car was behind me all the way back home. What do you make of my excursion, Mr. Ex-cop?"

"Well, what you're calling an unmarked car, what makes you think that was a cop, anyway?" Jimbo asked her.

"Because he wasn't trying to hide anything, he was wearing a uniform. Now what I'd like to know is why were they following me?" Darla wanted Jimbo to come clean and provide some answers. "Unless it was your car. That's what came right to my mind. I think they were looking for you, Jimbo. What I would like to know is why? And does it have anything to do with my husband? I sure hope not. You'd better not have done anything that puts me, my husband, or our livelihood in danger."

"No, nothing Darla, I swear. Whatever their motivation was, I don't know, I'll figure it out though and take care of it." Jimbo wanted to be reassuring but, in reality, he had his doubts. He was also fearful that Darla would tell Sarge of the events of her day, including him borrowing her car, an absolute cardinal sin. "I can tell you this much, there weren't any cops out in the street when I pulled back in here. They were probably just looking for an old black Pontiac for some reason or another and my car fit the description. Then after following you around they realized you weren't who they were looking for."

"God, I hope you're right Jimbo, I really do." Darla's voice did not exactly exude confidence in Jimbo's words.

"Everything is fine, I'm sure," he reasoned. "Just don't mention any of this to Sarge, okay? All that would do is open a can of worms, you know what I mean, right?"

"I'm not stupid, Jimbo." Darla said with an attitude. "If he knew you took my car, he'd have my ass on a platter." She flipped Jimbo's keys to him and stalked back toward the mudroom.

On the drive back to the motel, Jimbo Burgess mentally rehashed his entire day. It had been a lot of driving and he was dead tired. He thought about the green footlocker and the possible ramifications of finding it had been opened. Then he had to consider the missing Ruger and what consequences that could entail. It was highly unlikely that he would have to deal with anything as a result of that, but then there was always the chance. By the time he had gotten out of the city limits, he had firmly reached the conclusion that he wouldn't even bring any of this to Sarge's attention. He would report the mission successfully accomplished. Documents restored to their original location, and with everything copacetic. There was no need for him to even make mention of the storekeeper. He knew the man's name and it would be a piece of cake to learn his address, or perhaps he would just follow him home from the store one afternoon and take care of matters.

Heading north on U.S. Highway 63, one final thought had to be satisfied. The matter of the deputies following Darla today. What could have been the motivation for Boone County deputies to tail her? Was it truly her they were looking at? Or was it his car they were tracking? Was he the subject of an investigation? Luckily, he had experience behind the badge and could easily fit his size thirteen feet into their shoes. He knew he hadn't done anything in Boone County to garner their interest. It almost certainly had to go back to the old man, Franklin. Jimbo theorized that the old man must have talked about the interrogation he'd been subjected to the day before Easter. He had to have talked to the cops. And with the open footlocker, the kid must have reported the missing stock portfolio. It all started to fit together now. The kid filed a robbery report, the old man squealed, and somebody along the line must have gotten his license plate number. To top things off and actually the worst of all was that, while trying to play private eye, he had been stupid enough to use his real name. Why the hell didn't he get fake identification? It wouldn't even have cost him twenty bucks. Stupid. A fake I.D., a stolen license plate, and no problema. Just plain stupid on his own part.

On the trip back to the motel Jimbo had picked up a pizza and a cold six-pack of Pabst Blue Ribbon beer. As he pulled off the highway and into the motel parking lot, he scoured the area, performing a little reconnaissance before settling the car in front of room thirteen. Once again he looked around, checking his rearview and side mirrors. Satisfied there were no unexpected surprises lurking, Jimbo picked up the pizza and beer and went into his room. Leaning forward to set his dinner on the small table located just inside the door, he was startled by two uniformed deputies stepping from the small bathroom, weapons drawn and trained directly on him. Instinctively raising both hands, Jimbo was compelled to utter, "How the hell did Tweedledee and Tweedledum both fit in there? It's barely big enough for me to take a dump."

"James Burgess, consider yourself under arrest for breaking and entering, trespassing, and robbery. If you would place your hands behind your back please while Deputy Morton applies your restraining cuffs." The nametag of the deputy speaking read W. Thornberry.

As the handcuffs were being applied, Jimbo decided to ask questions of his own. "Gentlemen, may I ask who or what I am being charged of robbing? And where exactly did this trespass occur? And for that matter, what building or residence did I allegedly break into and enter?"

"Not at liberty to say, Mr. Burgess," Deputy Thornberry responded. "Someone will discuss those matters with you at the county facility in Columbia."

As the two led Jimbo out of the room, a deputy cruiser appeared from behind the end of the motel. That explained why Jimbo had not spotted it when he'd pulled in. From his perspective, entering the lot from the south, the car had been comfortably hidden from sight. With Jimbo securely situated in the back seat of the cruiser, Deputies Thornberry and Morton stepped into an unmarked Ford Fairlane. The two vehicles containing James Burgess and three officers began the twenty-five-minute journey north on Highway 63 toward the Boone County Jail where Jimbo would be officially fingerprinted and processed.

* * * *

Oscar Roberts was working on his third Budweiser of the evening as he watched the tail end of an episode of *The Big Valley* on ABC. The western drama was a weekly standard as it featured one of his all-time favorite actresses in the person of Barbara Stanwyck who, alongside relative newcomers Linda Evans and Lee Majors, brought the late nineteenth century lives of the fictional Barkley family to life every Monday. Having only a single television, the color Zenith set located in the living room, he and Darla had reluctantly reached agreements regarding network fare for each night of the week. Earlier, he had been forced to endure thirty minutes of the nighttime soap opera *Peyton Place*, but the last two hours of the evening were reserved for his western dramas, first *The Outcasts* and now *The Big Valley*. Their strict household rules dictated that Sarge never be disturbed when his most cherished shows, such as *The Big Valley*, were being broadcast. As such, it was Darla's responsibility to answer the ringing telephone that was now posing a distinct threat of distracting him from the climactic final fifteen minutes of the show.

Darla hurried over to the small telephone table, hoping to minimize the number of rings, and answered in a hushed tone. The male voice on the other end requested to speak to Sarge.

"He's a little busy right now, but he'll be available shortly. May I have him call you back in a few minutes?" Darla asked in a polite and professional tone.

"Actually, Mrs. Roberts, this call is fairly urgent," was the response.

"Is it business? Is this the penitentiary calling?" If the call was official, it would be perfectly acceptable to interrupt her husband. If not, then she would refrain from disturbing him and instead insist that the man accept a return call.

"No ma'am, I'm not from the pen, I work over here at the Boone County Sheriff's Department and it's very important I speak to your husband." Darla realized the man was speaking with clarity and serious intent. The mere mention that he was with the Sheriff's Department shocked her system and sent fear coursing through her body.

"Just a minute, I'll get him." Her hand trembling, Darla laid the receiver carefully atop the phone book on the table and called out to her husband. "Oscar, honey, it's someone at the Sheriff's Department. He's saying it's important and can't wait."

"Damn," Sarge muttered as he rose from his chair and crossed the room. "Pay attention to the rest of the show, will you? Let me know what I miss."

Darla resumed her station on the couch and, try though she did to monitor with the activity on the television, she struggled mightily as her mind was occupied with three things simultaneously. On her husband's orders she was forced to pay some reasonably adequate attention to the television show, and at the same time tried to eavesdrop and ascertain the topic of the conversation her husband was having. All of this while at the same time worrying about her encounters earlier in the day. She had been followed by Boone County Sheriff's deputies as she drove Jimbo's car while running errands. There was no doubt in her mind that for some unknown reason the deputies had been looking for Jimbo. Her deepest fear right now was that, at this very moment, Oscar was being informed of her driving Jimbo's Pontiac. Darla worried because she had specifically been forbidden to allow anyone to drive her car. If indeed her husband found out that they had swapped vehicles for the day, she was apprehensive, to say the least, as to the possible repercussions.

The man on the other end greeted Sarge with a serious and rather somber sounding, "Good evening Sarge, it's Dale." Dale Snyder, as a booking officer at the county jail, was a member of the small network that Sarge had managed to establish over the years to help keep himself and his few associates at a safe and secure arm's reach of potential issues involving his side business. It wasn't often that something arose requiring his attention or putting his interests in jeopardy, but this certainly was one of them.

"They arrested James Burgess this evening," Dale was hesitant to lay such sour news on Sarge. Dale himself had processed Burgess, and while Jimbo did not know him, he was aware of Jimbo's connection to Sarge. "The warrant was issued in Lewis County, but the charges seem relatively minor and I wouldn't be surprised if Judge Deavers released him tomorrow morning on some insignificant monetary bond. With him being an ex-con, I'm sure it won't be on his own recognizance."

The two continued the conversation for another fifteen minutes, discussing the severity of the charges. "I'll be honest with you, Sarge," Dale spoke openly, offering his unsolicited opinion. "From what I've seen in the reports that I could access, there's not really much of a case. Apparently, whatever was stolen in the robbery has not been recovered. He had nothing in his possession. There were no witnesses, except for a teenager that claims he saw Burgess sitting in his car at the scene of the crime. But of course, that doesn't prove anything at all."

"That doesn't mean jack," Sarge agreed. "I happen to be sitting in my car at the gas station waiting for my wife to use the ladies room, and some jerk robs the cashier inside, well that sure as hell doesn't make me guilty does it?"

"Nope, sure doesn't," said Dale, before delivering more unwelcome information. "Speaking of wives though, I think it's only right for you to know Sarge that our folks had been looking for Burgess all day. And it turned out that his car was spotted later on this morning."

These words definitely grabbed Sarge's attention. Jimbo was supposed to have been gone today returning the stolen merchandise to the footlocker from whence it had come. Why in the name of God was his car spotted around Jeff City late in the morning when he should have been out on the road? Sarge's internal rage was palpable. If that idiot didn't return that binder today and it ends up being found; Sarge knew all it would take is a slip of the tongue by Jimbo and he could end up being linked to the heist. The chance was there that the nimwit might have jeopardized his entire operation.

Sarge was forced to present some obvious questions. "Where, where did they see his car, was he there? And if he was, why didn't they pick him up then? And then you said speaking of wives. What did you mean by that?"

"Sarge," Dale knew this bit of news was not going to be taken well. "His car was seen in your driveway." Sarge's immediate thought was a suspicious one, that his wife was carrying on with Jimbo, but common sense quickly prevailed. Darla was an attractive woman. There was no way in the world that she would ever have any interest in an overweight and sloppy ex-con like Burgess. However, his remaining question of why the car was here, at the house, was about to be clarified.

"When the car had been located, a deputy was assigned to a stake-out, hoping that Burgess would get in the car and leave. At that point he would have been detained and arrested. But Sarge, when the car did leave your house, it was your wife driving it."

"What?" It was hard to subdue the volume of his response. Sarge was now furious and struggling to keep his voice down and emotions in check.

"Yes sir. It was her driving." Dale reiterated. "Deputies tailed her, and apparently she just went to the grocery and drug stores and then back home. Later in the day, a white Ford Falcon that is registered to you, and had not been at the house all day, was seen parked in the driveway and Burgess' vehicle was gone."

As the ten o'clock news was moving into the weather segment, Sarge finally replaced the receiver in its cradle. He went into the kitchen, removing two more frosty bottles of beer from the refrigerator and returned to his easy chair. Darla wanted to continue to focus her attention on the weatherman but could feel the imaginary heat of Oscar's gaze penetrating the right side of her skull. Anticipating the severity of the lambasting she was afraid might be coming her way, she momentarily closed her eyes before turning toward her husband.

"Do want me to tell you how *Big Valley* finished up?" She asked calmly.

"No, not really." Sarge had practically chugged the first bottle of Budweiser in an effort to ease his nerves. He took a relaxed swallow of bottle number two and asked in an even and relaxed tone, "Would you care to tell me anything about your day today, my darling?"

Iowa

After an enjoyable tuna casserole dinner at the Worthington residence, Marcus suggested that he and Cassie take a ride over to the lock and dam for old time's sake. The change to Daylight Saving Time had just occurred over the weekend and as a result the sun would be setting an hour later, giving them a bit more time before the mosquitoes began their quest for unsuspecting victims. It had been several months since they had last visited the dam to watch a little boat traffic and enjoy the twilight. Additionally, the weatherman had reported a forecast calling for a beautifully clear and cloudless starlit night. The sun wouldn't set in the west and at their backs until right around eight o'clock. Marcus envisioned they should be able to enjoy roughly a half hour of complete darkness to carry out some stargazing. Astronomy was one of Cassie's more favorable scientific studies and she could be counted upon to effortlessly identify a number of constellations. Marcus, on the other hand, was less than enamored by the subject, and it was only through Cassie's constant reminders that he had finally been able to locate and name, without her assistance, the Big Dipper and Orion constellations. If he were patient enough, sometimes he could even locate Aquarius without Cassie's hints.

As they sat quietly watching a second barge navigate its way through the lock system, a thought passed through Cassie's mind, a matter that neither of them had discussed since the night that the strange Englishman had visited with them at the snack bar of the bowling alley. It had been weighing on her mind a bit and she was curious if it was something that Marcus had given thought to as well.

"Marcus, do you remember the Englishman a few weeks ago?" She asked.

"Yeah, I remember him, Neville was his name. Neville something," the last name of the gentleman was lost to him at the moment. "He seemed like a nice enough chap now, did he not?" Marcus tried, without much success, to mimic the man's unique accent. The effort did warrant a giggle from his girlfriend before she continued with her thoughts.

"You've never mentioned it, but have you given any consideration to what you said he told you before he left?" She asked as she turned her gaze from the river and back into Marcus' green eyes.

Neither of them had really been compelled to discuss the man's presence at the snack bar that late afternoon. Subconsciously, perhaps they both had recognized his appearance as strange and unusual. Marcus, especially, had wondered if there wasn't something really out of whack about the entire conversation, and as a consequence he had been at least fairly successful in clearing the entire incident from of his mind.

"No, not really," he replied. "I mean, I guess it crosses my mind every once in a while, but honestly, what he said kind of creeped me out a little."

"Me too." Cassie concurred. When Marcus had told her of Neville's suggestion that he look up someone in Iowa followed by the intimation that the man possibly had some information that Marcus might find useful, Cassie had honestly been freaked. They'd had no idea who Neville was and had never seen him again since then. But just the familiarity with the name that he had mentioned was enough to send chills down her spine. Othello Paige. They probably would never have given any other name a second thought, but in this case there existed the eerie chance and likely connection to Marcus' friend Jeremiah Paige. Before Jeremiah's death, he had not only been a friend to Marcus in the here and now but had also been Opa's childhood friend. The unspoken implication was there. Although she was almost certain of the answer, the lingering question in Cassie's mind had been, *is Othello Paige related to Jeremiah?*

"But, Marcus, it has gotten me to thinking. With all that has happened over the past few years with Opa in our lives, we know now that there is more to the human existence than just living out our lives and then rotting in the ground when we die." Cassie paused and looked up into the sky. "There is way more up there than we could ever even imagine."

After a brief pause, she asked, "Marcus, what if Neville was another messenger, kind of like Opa, but maybe different? I mean after all; he spoke to both of us. But didn't it seem to you that he might have been like, I don't know, like otherworldly or something?"

"You could be right, Cassie." Marcus had to agree. As far as his own thoughts and feelings were concerned, he had kind of wanted to pretend that Neville had never even been there. They had certainly already dealt with enough of the strange and unusual without inviting more into their lives. "Heck maybe Neville is a ghost and maybe his sole mission was to get me to go see Othello Paige in Iowa. We just don't know, do we?"

"What do you mean, 'get you to go see Othello Paige in Iowa'?" Cassie used air quotation marks and a mocking voice to emphasize her point. "If anybody is going to Iowa, it will be *we* and not just you, Mister."

"Wait a minute, Cass. I never said I was going to Iowa. Don't go putting words into my mouth, Sweetie." Cassie had a way of pushing hard to get whatever she was after.

"No, I guess you didn't, did you? But *I* think we are going. This Sunday as a matter of fact. We can miss one week of church, right?" Cassie was a bullheaded lass if ever there had been one.

"Now hold on Cassie, don't go putting the cart before the horse." Marcus sensed the necessity to gently apply the airbrakes to this runaway train. "First of all, there's really no need for us to drive all the way to Iowa. They've come up with this new invention that I'm sure you're familiar with. It's a little contraption this old fellow named Alexander Graham Bell developed, do you follow me, Twigs?"

"Ha-ha, very funny wise guy, but once again ol' Cassie is a step ahead, smarty pants. I've already checked and there is an Othello Paige that lives in Fairfield, but guess what? He doesn't have a telephone, or at least there's not a number listed to that name." While Marcus was most definitely impressed by Cassie's level of intelligence, he sometimes found himself at wit's end, frustrated by her uncanny ability to consistently outsmart him or be otherwise prepared to offer a counter to just about anything he could think or try to do.

"So, I guess that means I'm driving the Metro to Fairfield, Iowa Sunday morning then, eh?" Once more, Marcus had found himself forced into an unenviable position of subservience. "How are you going to explain this little excursion to your parents?"

"Easy, I've already planned that out as well. It will be a fact-finding trip to learn and gather information about the birthplace of Harry Harlow who, as it just so happens, was born there in Fairfield on Halloween of 1905. And while we're in town I'll get a few quotes about him from some of the residents of Fairfield." Cassie was *always* a step ahead.

"Oh my God, Cassie. Who on earth is Harry Harlow?"

"He's a well thought of psychologist who specializes in maternal-separation and dependency needs. And it ends up being convenient because I do have to come up with an independent study biographic report for my futuristic science class. My guess is that a psychologist would be as good a topic as any. Whatever notes I can pick up while we're there will actually be a bonus." As if

159

she wouldn't have, and as always, Cassie had all of her bases covered.

"Twigs, is there ever anything that you aren't prepared for? Anything at all?"

"Of course Marcus. You! My heart was never prepared for how marvelous and wonderful you are." She threw her arms around Marcus' neck and locked lips with him just as a shooting star streaked across the now darkening sky, painting a beautiful picture on the canvas above them, but going completely unnoticed by the two.

Somehow Cassie always spoke the right words at the right time

.

* * * *

Sunday couldn't arrive quickly enough for Cassie. She had requested and been able to receive the day off at the bowling alley. That had been the only hurdle that had to be cleared for the excursion to take place. The slight exaggeration in regard to the upcoming science report had served her well. Jack and Debbie Worthington always offered unbridled support when it came to matters of education. They had always held lofty expectations for their children and would gladly jump through hoops to ensure their academic success. A short day trip into rural Iowa to perform research for a school report was definitely not too much to ask. The only caveat had been Debbie's insistence that the two of them start the day with a healthy home cooked breakfast, a proposition that she knew Marcus could not refuse. He absolutely loved having meals with Cassie's family. Not as an insult to Margaret, but wherever Debbie had studied home economics, the instructor must surely have been a gourmet chef. A restaurant dish did not exist that Cassie's mother could not replicate. Marcus was surprised when he learned that Debbie did not even need to refer to recipes, she worked strictly off the cuff, much like a musician blessed with the talent to play by ear without the necessity of sheet music.

As Marcus devoured his newest favorite breakfast, french toast and warm buttery biscuits slathered in white country gravy, Cassie idly picked at her food. She had been far too excited to eat and was bursting with nervous energy. She had suffered with anticipation all week. She had been anxiously looking forward to today ever since they'd sat on the bench at the riverfront and she'd convinced a reluctant Marcus to commit to making the trip. Cassie was more than enthusiastic about meeting Othello Paige. She had really just briefly known Jeremiah, but in a short time had grown quite attached to him. The knowledge that he and Opa had been childhood friends had only served to enhance their connection. The trauma of his sudden loss had been devastatingly hard for her. Neville's suggestion that Marcus look Othello up had only heightened her curiosity about him and his relationship to the gold that Marcus and Ellis had found in the cave. She knew that Jeremiah and Opa had been the first to see the treasure, and she hoped that, based on what Marcus had told her, perhaps Othello had been the person who had described its location to Jeremiah all those years ago. Marcus was intent on learning of the gold's origin and wanted to find if there was a rightful owner that he might be able to locate or track down.

By eight-thirty a.m., and with a bloated and satisfied belly that would surely keep him fulfilled for the bulk of the day, Marcus literally squeezed behind the wheel of the Metro. He and Cassie left the Forest Park Subdivision, driving north and then east on Missouri Highway 457 toward U.S. 61. At the intersection they would turn left and proceed toward Iowa.

Nearly sixty miles and just more than an hour into the journey, and at Cassie's request for a pit stop, they pulled into a service station in Mount Pleasant, Iowa. Marcus was glad that Cassie had requested the break. At nearly six feet in height, it was beginning to become evident to Marcus that he was soon going to need a newer vehicle with a little more ample leg room. The Metro was fine for local transportation, and the relatively short jaunts over to Quincy. But for drives in excess of an hour or so, the constriction of the small coupe was difficult to handle. It was nearing ten o'clock in the morning and with neither of them in a hurry to continue the remaining forty-five minutes or so, they decided to grab a couple of bottles of Coke from the vending machine and take a breather. They settled at a picnic table that had been strategically placed beneath a large elm tree about twenty or so feet from the restrooms.

"How much further, Marcus?" Cassie asked.

"I think maybe thirty or thirty-five miles still," Marcus replied. "Why, are you getting tired of riding?"

"No, not at all, just wondering," she said, taking her first sip of the soda.

"Are you sure you have the right address, Twigs?" Marcus really didn't doubt that Cassie had procured the correct address but felt the need to ask just the same. "How did you find it anyway?"

"Fairfield Post Office. All it took was just a phone call." Cassie answered the question, then offered a suggestion, "You should try taking charge sometime, Marcus. Do you think you'd have been able to find out where he lives?"

"Sure I could have. I'd have done the same thing, you know, called the good ol' Post Office of course." Marcus spoke with an air of confidence.

"Marcus, I almost doubt that you would have even figured out how to get the phone number to the Fairfield Post Office." Cassie laughed at her own little dig.

"Sure I would've." Marcus shot back, acting offended.

"How?" Cassie asked, egging a little more.

Marcus had to laugh himself. "Heck, I don't know." After they had both caught their breath from the laughter, Marcus suggested they go inside and pay the four cent deposit for the two bottles and take the Cokes with them.

At a quarter of eleven they eased into Fairfield, Iowa, population 8,054. They turned left off of U.S. Highway 34 and onto Iowa Highway 1 for less than a mile before heading west on 227th Street. Five minutes later they were sitting at the curb looking at a single-

163

story abode with shake siding, the home of Othello Paige.

"I sure hope he's home." Marcus said.

"Me too. He could be at church you know." Cassie replied, not taking her eyes off the house.

"Might be. But we've got all day, we can always come back you know. If need be, we can grab some lunch or go scope out the town until somebody is home. We'll just play it by ear." Marcus knew one thing for sure, he wasn't leaving Fairfield until he had spoken to the man.

The two exited the Nash Metropolitan and, while holding one another's nervous hands, they apprehensively strode up the sidewalk approaching the front door. There was no doorbell visible, but the maroon colored door did feature a medium sized brass knocker. Opening the screen door and with the seriousness of the visit weighing on his mind, Marcus reached for the knocker, opting to utilize a solemn and simple rap-rap-rap.

Nearly a full half-minute passed before the maroon door slowly opened. Marcus and Cassie were greeted by a beautiful young lady dressed in an immaculate outfit, a white three-piece ensemble consisting of matching white skirt, long-sleeved blouse, and jacket. She wore a neatly coiffed four inch afro hair style and her age appeared to be somewhere in her early to mid-twenties. It seemed fairly obvious to Cassie that she had most likely just returned from attending church.

"Yes, may I help you," she warily asked the unfamiliar young couple.

"Good morning, uh, yes ma'am," Marcus stammered. "We don't mean to bother you, but we were hoping we might be able to speak to a man named Othello Paige."

"And just what business might you have with Mr. Paige, if you don't mind my asking?" The woman was by no means rude, on the contrary, she seemed perhaps to be protective and cautious.

"Well, um," this type of conversation with a stranger obviously took Marcus out of his comfort zone and forced him into an unsteady and somewhat clumsy state. Sensing Marcus' nervous discomfort, Cassie decided it was time for her to assume control of the dialogue.

"Yes ma'am, my name is Cassie Worthington and this is my boyfriend, Marcus Clemens. We, um, especially Marcus, we were friends with Jeremiah Paige, um, before his passing. We thought that perhaps Jeremiah and Othello Paige were related. Um, Jeremiah had told Marcus some things, and we think he was talking about the Othello Paige here in Fairfield." Cassie took a deep breath hoping that she had said enough that she may have earned them an audience with the man.

"Who sent you? Somebody sent you or you wouldn't have known to look for Othello. I doubt you'd even have known his name."

"Nobody sent us, ma'am," Cassie said, skirting the truth.

"Don't lie to me, miss. If you're gonna stand here and lie to me, I'll just shut the door and y'all can be on your merry way." The woman seemed dead serious with her threat.

"Neville," Marcus said hesitantly. "A man named Neville told me to look up Othello Paige, that he might have answers to some questions that I have."

"Should have said that to begin with. My name is Wanda," she said as she pulled the wooden door further open. "Ya'll come on in. Actually, I been expecting you."

Marcus and Cassie gave one another looks of surprise and uncertainty, wondering why the lady said she'd been expecting them. They entered and Wanda pointed to a red velveteen couch, motioning for them to sit. "Iced tea for you'se? I'm gonna get myself a glass."

"Yes ma'am, thank you," Cassie answered for both of them.

"No more ma'am, Cassie. My name is Wanda and I prefer that to ma'am. I'll be right back." Wanda crossed the combination living and dining room and passed through a doorway that seemed to lead into the kitchen. Marcus and Cassie politely sat in silence, listening to the tic-toc of the antique maple grandfather clock that stood stoically in one corner.

Wanda came back a few minutes later carrying a tray containing a pitcher of tea, three glasses, two spoons, and a sugar bowl. She set the tray on the coffee table in front of them, poured the tea and invited them to help themselves to the sugar.

"I take mine unsweetened," she said as she took a seat on the matching love seat. Cassie prepared both hers and Marcus' teas and thanked Wanda for her hospitality.

"My pleasure, sweetheart. You know I thought it was grandpa's Alzheimer's speaking for sure, but he told me you two would be coming to see him. I thought he was just crazy; the Lord knows all though don't he? Here you are." Wanda shook her head slowly, as if in disbelief.

"He told you we were coming?" Cassie asked. "I wonder why he would have said that?"

"Same person told you to come here it appears to me." Wanda said with a broad smile. "Maybe God does work in mysterious ways...maybe."

"Neville?" Marcus asked.

"That's what grandpa said. He told me not two weeks ago I guess. Yep, he said Neville told him a young white couple would be coming to see him." Wanda couldn't contain her wide grin. "He sure knew more than me, didn't he?"

"Neville Naughton, the old Englishman?" Cassie could not understand how such an unlikely thing could have happened.

"Don't know about no last name, but grandpa did describe him as an old Englishman, that much is right." Wanda confirmed that they seemed to be talking about the same person.

Marcus looked at Cassie and said, "That confirms it Cassie." He looked back to Wanda and asked, "Wanda, were Jeremiah and Othello cousins?"

"Of course, they were. Are you just realizing?"

"Wanda, where is he? Can I talk to him?" Marcus asked. "I mean if it's okay, I know you said he had Alzheimer's."

"No Marcus, you can't. Even if you could, you wouldn't be able to understand him. He was born with a harelip and his speech was almost impossible to understand. Only a handful of us knew what he was saying." Wanda explained.

"Jeremiah did, didn't he?" Marcus said more than he asked.

"When they were young, yes, I suppose." she said. "They grew up together and was always close."

Cassie had a sad revelation come over her. "Wanda, I noticed you've said *was* several times," Cassie said, emphasizing the word *was*.

"Observant Cassie. I did say was. Grandpa died this Tuesday past. I buried him in the church graveyard day before yesterday, on Friday morning." Wanda said looking down at the carpet.

Marcus felt terribly depressed. Why didn't he act on Neville's words sooner, he could have been here a week or two earlier.

"Don't look so forlorn, Marcus. Grandpa said he knew you were coming and what you wanted to ask so he told me some things about him and Jeremiah before he left. I don't know if I have your answers, but I can try." Wanda's words were encouraging, but it didn't alleviate the pain he was feeling over Othello. Even though he had never met him, he almost felt as if he had lost Jeremiah all over again.

"Go ahead, Marcus. Let's try one," Wanda suggested. "Is it about the gold?"

Cassie was taking in this conversation in an utter state of awe. Neville was not what he had appeared to be at all. He definitely had to be an angel or something. He had come to her and Marcus, and now they'd learned that he had visited Othello Paige as well. Unless Wanda was pulling off some exorbitantly elaborate ruse, everything had to be true and it all seemed beyond the normal realm of human understanding. Most people would say this was impossible, but Opa had spoken to her many times, over and over. At this point, she had no choice other than to believe in Neville.

"Oh my God," said an exasperated Marcus. "How do you know about the gold before I even asked about it?"

"Grandpa told me about it, Marcus. He told me that's what you wanted to know about." This was just amazing. Marcus was mildly surprised that Wanda seemed somewhat nonchalant about it all.

"Did your grandpa put the gold in that cave?" Marcus asked bluntly.

"Let me save you some time, Marcus. Grandpa told me he only knew about the gold because Jeremiah had told him that him and his friend John..." Wanda was interrupted by Marcus.

"John Clemens, he was *my* grandpa. It was him and Jeremiah that found it when they were teenagers." Marcus began spilling what he knew of the story. "Jeremiah told me that part. Jeremiah said it was his uncle that originally found the cave. Oh okay, I think I get it now. Jeremiah's cousin was Othello, and Othello's father was Jeremiah's uncle, right?"

"Exactly right, Marcus." Wanda nodded in the affirmative.

"So then, I guess here's my only real question Wanda. Do you think that it's possible that your great-grandfather put the gold there?" This was the question Marcus and Cassie had come here hoping to have answered once and for all.

"Unfortunately, no. Grandpa told me that his father never even had seen the gold. He had been told where it might possibly be, in a cave somewhere. But he never found it. He had an idea and tried looking for it, but in the end, I suppose he just gave up. Wish he would've been the one hid it though, because then it would be mine now, wouldn't it?" Wanda laughed dryly at the prospect that she would now have been filthy rich. "But I guess though, since Jeremiah and your grandfather found it and because Jeremiah never had any children, guess what, Marcus?"

"No Wanda. I know you were gonna say it's mine, but it's not. Somebody put it there and whoever did has got to have descendants. I'll find them somehow, even if it takes me the rest of my life, I'll find out whose gold that is." Marcus certainly seemed steadfast in his stance on the treasure.

"If you're telling me the truth, you are a good and honest man, Marcus," Wanda was sincere as she stood from the love seat and reached to shake Marcus' hand. He stood also, but before he could take her hand in his, Wanda pulled him into a bearhug and whispered in his ear. "I wish you luck, Marcus. I truly do. I wish grandpa could have met you and Cassie."

As they drove east on U.S. Highway 34, Marcus broke the mutual silence by glancing toward Cassie and saying, "Well, I guess your friend Neville sent us on a wild goose chase, didn't he?"

"I don't see how you could say that, Marcus," Cassie responded sternly. "If we could have acted a week sooner, you would have met Othello, but as it is you got to meet Wanda and she seems precious. I hope as time goes by we can stay in touch with her."

"Yeah, as usual, you're right Cassie. I really liked her."

"And you did get your question answered, Marcus," Cassie was sympathetic to the whole purpose of the trip. "Maybe it wasn't the answer that you had hoped to hear, but it did satisfy what you needed to know. And now at least one possibility has been eliminated."

"That's true, Cass. But now, where do I turn with the next question?" Marcus asked rhetorically.

A Time To Every Purpose

Boone County wasted no time in the case against James Burgess. The morning after his arrest, at eleven a.m. sharp, he was escorted from his cell to the back of a waiting deputy cruiser, and soon thereafter the two-hour journey to Lewis County had commenced. Jimbo had hoped that Lady Luck would smile upon him, that he would have his bail set early on Tuesday morning and would be immediately released by a Boone County judge. But, since the arrest warrant had been issued under a different jurisdiction, the local judge had no imminent authority in the case. And so here Jimbo sat, glumly watching from the backseat as the spring scenery rapidly passed him by. As a former police officer, he had a rough, though somewhat basic, understanding of the judicial system and its procedures. He was almost positive that he could now expect an appearance on Wednesday morning before an unknown Lewis County Associate Court Judge and was hopeful of having his bail set at that time.

However, the Lewis County court docket was crammed full and backlogged, and when Wednesday morning arrived, his case was not scheduled to be heard. Jimbo was forced to wait in lock-up nearly a full week until Tuesday, May 6 before he was finally taken, in handcuffs and shackles, to face the judge for his preliminary hearing. His normally calm demeanor was being thoroughly tested by the unusual delay, and as he waited in the courtroom, he was feeling uncommonly nervous. He knew that Sarge would surely have made arrangements for someone to post his bail and then drive him back to Jefferson City. But still he found himself in an uneasy situation. There was no guarantee that the judge would even set bail. He was an ex-convict who had only recently completed a mandated two-year supervised probation. The fact that he had completed it satisfactorily was a plus in his favor and he had been very careful the entirety of those two years, fastidiously keeping his nose squeaky clean.

The only occasion in which he had assumed some minimal risk was when he had taken to the trip to Monticello, right after his release, to attend the funeral of Ellis Compton. But his behavior while there had been perfect, almost to a fault. When Sarge had explained to him all the details that he had managed to extract from Oliver Compton concerning the Mark Twain fortune, Jimbo had felt duty-bound to at least familiarize himself with the key actors involved in the scene in which he would eventually play an important role. With the promise of his ultimate reward in mind, he had ventured to Monticello, where he deftly separated himself from the thin and scraggily assemblage of mourners, acting as an uninterested observer during the funeral. He had made sure to maintain a safe distance, remaining a few hundred feet away, over near the short line of parked cars. From his unnoticed vantage point, he was able easily and discretely photograph most of the small gathering and then make his leave well in advance of the service's conclusion.

As he impatiently waited for his case to be called, Jimbo thought back to a few of the errors he had committed, most notably the use of his actual name. That had definitely been his most glaring mistake and undoubtably had been the precipitating factor that had led to his arrest. He was confident that even if the case ended with him actually facing the charges in a trial, he would certainly prevail. No witnesses could actually place him inside the kid's house and there had been no forced entry. The lack of evidence therefore dictated there was absolutely nothing to the trespass charge. There had been positively no crime committed in approaching someone's door, knocking, and with there being no response, returning to one's car. And as far robbery, he had safely gotten the binder replaced back into the footlocker. There was nothing missing; hence no robbery had occurred. Jimbo had no doubt he would walk. Hopefully, the kid had looked again yesterday, seen the binder and had notified the local cops. The best case scenario, and the one that he felt the lack of evidence pointed most directly toward, would be for the judge to call his name and announce that all charges had been dismissed.

Two hours after taking his seat in the courtroom, James Burgess was finally called before Judge Alex Wathan. Apparently the kid had not yet noticed the returned documents, as all three charges were read and his bail set at five hundred dollars. Twenty minutes later he was back in his cell, awaiting his delicious county jail lunch. Jimbo knew it would no doubt be dried out bologna between two slices of stale bread and accompanied by a lukewarm carton of milk. He also knew from his past experience that county jail lunches typically consisted of a nutritionally bare minimum. He was thankful that one of Sarge's men would be posting his bail and he would back on the outside after being held almost a week in captivity. His was more than anxious to stop somewhere on the way back home for a reasonable dinner. Apparently, the jail personnel handling paperwork were in no immediate hurry. Time dragged on mercilessly, and when he finally was allowed to step out into the fresh air it was nearly ten p.m. Jimbo saw two men, neither of whom he recognized, waiting next to his own Pontiac that was parked at the curb.

"Thanks fellas, I'm kind of surprised you drove my car all this way. I wouldn't have expected that you'd be giving me a ride back in my own vehicle," Jimbo said with a confused expression on his face.

The taller of the two handed him his key ring and said, "Naw, we got us another assignment to take of care that's more important than driving you home. Sarge said to bring your car and you could look out for getting yourself home."

"That's alright, I don't mind. But it's been a long day. I do think I might have a beer and a sandwich on the way. Thanks again guys. I appreciate the helping hand." Jimbo nodded as he opened the driver's side door.

"No problem, bud," the shorter and stockier man said.

Jimbo fired up the Sky Chief and made haste in anticipation of grabbing a cold one. He thought about just making a quick stop to grab a six-pack and bag of chips for the road but nixed that idea. The last thing he needed was to get pulled over late at night with an open container in his car. Remembering a nearby place where he could both enjoy a cold beer and a freshly made sandwich, he instead opted for a home away from home, a place where he'd been comfortable on his weekend visit just a few weeks ago. Jimbo drove twenty minutes out of his way to whet his whistle at the *Bar None Saloon. Hey,* he thought to himself, *maybe Neville will be there again.* He had enjoyed his last long conversation with the old man.

Jimbo parked his Pontiac at the end of the Arcadian porch near the old worn payphone located just off the west end of the building. Opening the car door, he stepped out with his left foot and began to push against the steering wheel to lift his heavy frame from the seat when he heard a voice say, "Shouldn't have been so stupid, cop." Before he could even look upward toward the source of the words, a tire iron smashed into his right cheekbone. Several severe blows followed, and as he landed face-first, the realization didn't register that the gravel of the *Bar None* parking lot was the last sight James Burgess' eyes would ever see.

* * * *

The first Tuesday of May was Chester Bernstein's day off at Walt's Tire and Auto Repair. Before the end of his second week at the shop, Simon had already earned Walt's trust. The first two off days for Chester after Simon's hiring, Walt had stayed to lock up. But following the second off day, he had given Simon Louie's old set of keys, complete with the worn retractable belt harness, telling him he could begin taking turns with Chester securing the joint at closing time.

Just past seven o'clock, as he was finishing up his sweeping, Marcus called over to Simon, "Hey, what are you doing for dinner tonight?"

"Oh, I don't know, probably a couple of wieners and some chips. Can't afford to go to the diner every night on these paltry wages, know what I mean?"

"Well, hey then," Marcus leaned on his broom as he spoke. "You want to go with me to the bowling alley? We can have those hot dogs at the snack bar. Cassie is working tonight so I'll get a ten percent discount plus free Cokes. I'll treat." Marcus had grown to really like Simon. They seemed to have a lot interests in common. They hadn't had much of an opportunity yet to hang out, although they were planning to. Between Marcus' schedule, working and going to school, and then keeping up with Cassie's work schedule, not to mention the limited time they were able to spend in each other's company, there just hadn't been much time to hang with Simon. Marcus was hardly even able to spare any opportunities to see his pal Denny much these days either. If they spent any time together, it was also usually at the snack bar so Marcus could also see Cassie while she was working.

"Yeah, that sounds cool, Marcus, but we're going Dutch. I don't want you paying for mine." Simon sounded adamant, so Marcus quickly agreed. Simon asked if Marcus could allot him time to go back to the boarding house so he could clean up and change clothes.

"I'll try to meet you there about eight-fifteen," Simon told him.

"Perfect," Marcus said. "That's gives me time to do the same."

Simon had already seated himself and greeted Cassie when Marcus arrived a few minutes before the agreed upon eight-fifteen.

"Hey, Simon, you're early," Marcus said as he sat down and swiveled the stool a half circle so he could wink and wave at Cassie.

"Yeah, thought I'd get here a little early to make a pass or two at the redhead behind the counter," joked Simon.

"Sorry, my friend, she's taken," said a laughing Marcus in response to Simon's jibe.

"Oh man, sorry to hear that," Simon continued with the ruse, "she's just my type. You know I like the intellectual ones, you know the bookworms, right Marcus?"

"That surprises me, considering you can't read, Chief!" Marcus burst into laughter and was quickly joined by his friend. Marcus had gotten Simon's blessing to nickname him Chief, but somehow it still seemed derogatory, so by and large, it was mainly reserved for joking times such as this. Marcus always had a good time at the shop with Simon. He had loved working with Louie, but Simon was just a different breed of personality. He was not the typical Midwesterner; he had an edginess and humor that Marcus found refreshing. Aside from Cassie, he'd never met anyone whose personality seemed such a good and natural match to his own.

"Hey, speaking of reading, Marcus. Did you see this flyer?" Simon held up a soda-stained paper that was advertising the *Kaisenreicher Family Prayer and Salvation Ministry*.

"Yeah, a few weeks ago actually. I'm surprised that one is still surviving after this long," Marcus said in response to Simon's question.

"I went to the one last year," Simon reported. "over in Hickory Grove, just a few miles outside of Quincy. It was pretty cool, that man can definitely preach a sermon."

"Oh yeah?" Marcus asked. "Cassie and I were planning to go. It's next Monday night over at the field north of town where they used to do livestock sales about forty years ago. Hey, do you think you might want to go with us?"

"Well now, I doubt I'd go with you, your car only seats two, don't it Shemp?" The cutting reference had passed right over Marcus' head the first time Simon had called him 'Shemp'. Simon had been forced to repeat it twice more before it dawned on him that Shemp was the most profound dolt amongst *The Three Stooges,* and that Simon had used the name teasingly to point out whenever Marcus had said or done something dumb.

"Yeah, that's true, Simon, but what I really meant was attend with us, not go with us." Marcus attempted to clarify his language usage, but knowing it was too late. The damage was already done, the joke already made.

"I know, just messing with you," Simon said with his perpetual smile. "I might be able to talk Chester into covering my last hour next Monday. By the time I get home and wash up, I'd still be late, but if you'd save me a seat, I'd be glad to join you a few minutes after it got started."

"That idea will play," Marcus certainly wouldn't have an issue with holding a seat for Simon.

Cassie finally had managed to squirrel herself away from the attention starved members of the *Hopewell Oil* bowling team. The fellows had taken two of three games in their weekly league play and were having a quick grease-infused dinner before they retired to the lounge for a couple hours of serious Tuesday night adult beverage consumption. After Marcus and Simon had placed their orders, Cassie brought them a pair of fountain Cokes before beginning to pull the four wieners and buns from their respective warmers.

After two dogs apiece and a shared bowl of chips, they made their way to the pinball machines, where Marcus soon learned he had made a mistake in wagering a quarter a game. After dropping five of the six games, Marcus was about to be tapped out of cash.

"Okay Chief, so this is why you didn't want me to buy your dinner, you planned on winning it all back on *Hearts and Spades* didn't you?" Marcus said while laughing.

"I guess I never told you I was a pinball wizard, huh? And that us Injuns excelled at it because we've got strong wrists, did I Shemp?" Simon joined in the fun. "They got that way from firing arrows at the cavalry all those years. It's hereditary."

Since Marcus was about out of pocket cash, Simon forgave him the one dollar he had lost. "Just buy me another one of those free Coca-Colas that Cassie dispenses and we'll call it even," Simon figured his suggestion was a method for settling Marcus' gambling debt.

"Fair enough," Marcus responded with a smile.

"So tell me more about yourself and your family, Simon," Marcus said as they retook their seats at the snack counter.

"I don't know Marcus, pretty much told all there was to tell, I think."

"Well okay, but I remember you told me your tribe got run out of Michigan and Wisconsin, and that some of you ended up in Quincy while most went further west. I just don't know much about how any of that worked. What happened to your land? Did the government just move your people out and then just claim it and give it away to white Americans? I don't get it, that wouldn't have been fair." Marcus was far from being any type of social activist, but from what he knew of the Indian wars and the tribes' relocations to reservations, things just seemed wrong.

"Okay, here's one story that's been passed down, Marcus." Simon decided to relate one thing that he had heard since childhood. "Supposedly this tale goes back to when my ancestors first settled in Quincy somewhere around 1837 or 1838. It was about the time when my great-great grandfather was born, but this is the story that he was told by his father and it has been passed down ever since, going from generation to generation."

Marcus was really interested in hearing this, especially in light of the fact that he had absolutely no stories from his ancestors. Margaret had some information about his prior relatives, but basically it was just names that Elijah had told her and after he had died, she had written down for him from memory. Judy had kicked in some information, but much of what he knew from times past he had actually gotten from Jeremiah Paige or through Opa.

Simon embarked upon a lengthy telling of his ancestral saga. "The story goes that a U.S. Army wagon and soldiers rolled into Quincy on a summer afternoon in 1840 looking for the Pottawatomie tribal chief. At that point we actually no longer had one, but one our elders met with the leader of the troops. They asked how many of our families were located in our community and were told twenty-four. The elderly spokesman was grateful when the government officer told him that as a result of a treaty they had signed several years prior, our people were now going to be fairly compensated for the loss of our land. The government was offering one gold bar for each family that had been forcibly relocated, payable immediately. The gold was taken to the elder's hut and a meeting was called for the heads of all twenty-four families so they could decide what to do with the gold."

"Do you think one gold bar per family was a fair price for the land they had lost, Simon?" Marcus asked.

"As things turned out, I'd say no, Marcus." Simon told him his opinion. "A vote was taken and twenty-two families wanted to hold onto the gold, let it accumulate value. Two of the men wanted their bars immediately. The elder granted their wishes and presented a bar to each man. Of course, none of my ancestors even considered trusting the government banks with their investments, so the elders gathered again and decided to do as they always had when they'd accumulated valuables through trade or whatever. They sent three young warriors out with the twenty-two bars of gold, tasked with locating a safe and secure hiding place. One of two things then happened. Either they found a spot and successfully hid the gold bars or they didn't. They remained gone for four days. Fearing they either had taken off with the gold or had met with misfortune, a search party was sent on the fifth day. They were found a morning's ride north of the village, probably six to seven miles away. They had been slain."

"Oh my God, Simon, that's terrible," Marcus exclaimed. Cassie had come in halfway through the story and covered her mouth in shock at the fate of the warriors.

"Were the killers of those poor men ever caught?" Cassie wanted to know.

Simon answered the question negatively, "Never. Rumors spread that the two families that had received their share had immediately packed up and left within days. But before leaving, and on the very day of receiving their payment, one family member had revealed to local residents the plan that the remainder of tribal families had agreed upon. Speculation amongst the tribe was that robbers had either killed the warriors before they had hidden the gold and stolen it, or they had successfully hidden it and were on their way back when they had been attacked."

"What did your ancestors believe, Simon. Do they think the gold was stolen?" Marcus was curious what Simon's forefathers had concluded.

"My tribe had very brave warriors," Simon said with pride. "They most certainly would not have allowed the gold to be taken. From the stories passed down, they were tortured before death, which according to legend would indicate that someone had tried to find out where the gold had been hidden. Pottawatomie warriors would gladly die before revealing a tribal secret. Those warriors are revered to this day and celebrated as tribal heroes."

"An amazing story," Cassie remarked.

"Truly," Marcus agreed. "Such brave men. You should be proud of your forefathers, Simon. You have evolved from courageous stock."

"Thank you, Marcus." Simon said, grasping Marcus' forearm with his right hand. "That means a lot to me, my brother." Simon stood, the smile returning to his face. "It's almost ten, time for you and Cassie to go home. I'll see you back at the shop tomorrow afternoon, Marcus."

By the time the two of them had reached the Metro for the ride to Cassie's house, she couldn't contain herself any longer. She hadn't wanted to bring any of it up at the snack bar or on their walk through the building and parking lot, but after Marcus let her in and then got in himself, the floodgate opened.

"Marcus, Simon was absolutely describing the gold that you and Ellis found, and that I saw with my very own eyes. That stuff belongs to his tribe, Marcus! Can you believe it?" Cassie was almost beside herself with excitement. The puzzle that Marcus had struggled with had finally been solved. Now all their worries were almost over. Marcus would turn eighteen in a few months, and even though his inheritance had been stolen, everyone would know soon enough that it was all just a big hoax anyway. There was no inheritance. And now the mystery of the gold had been solved. Everything was going to work itself out. At long last they would be able to bury all the heartache and anguish, the unnecessary deaths. Cassie was relieved that they could put everything behind them and start concentrating solely on their future. She was so, so happy.

Until Marcus dropped the hammer.

"Don't be so rambunctious, Twigs. There's no evidence at all that the gold that we found is the same gold that Simon's ancestors lost. I would guess there have been hundreds of gold bars stolen over the past one hundred years or so." Marcus wanted to try to be a voice of reason here and keep Cassie from jumping to premature conclusions.

"You have to remember, Cassie. A hundred or so years ago, the Midwest was home to a bunch of bank robbers. You had the James Gang, the Dalton Gang, heck I know there were others," Marcus knew they couldn't just assume the gold belonged to Simon's tribe. There had to be a way to verify it. Maybe the bars were numbered or marked and could be positively identified.

"Marcus, how many bars are in that cave?" Cassie asked him.

"Twenty-two was what Ellis and I counted. Twenty-two," was his reply.

"And how many families did Simon say got gold bars from the government?"

"Aha, there you go, Cassie." Marcus had her on this one. "The government paid twenty-four families. So see?"

"Oh God, Marcus. It's no wonder Simon calls you Shemp." Cassie sometimes got so frustrated with him. Marcus was an intelligent young man, but sometimes the simplest of things seemed to escape him. "Yes there were twenty-four families, but two of them took their gold right away, which left twenty-two, Marcus. And that's how many bars you found. Gee whiz, smart guy!"

"Okay, you have a point there, Cass, but," Marcus had to further explain his hesitation to just take Simon's words at face value. "I haven't even known Simon for a month yet. How do I really know I can trust him?"

"Marcus, you two hit it off right away, it's almost like you've been friends all your lives." Despite hardly knowing him, Cassie appeared to have no qualms about putting her trust in Simon.

"I just don't know Cassie. We've seen too much deceit in the past. I need to be sure. What if Simon heard about our gold and he's actually nothing more than a slick shyster. Maybe it's a big elaborate plan for him to show up, get hired by Walt and then sidle up to me and earn my confidence. What if it's all just a ruse to use me and get his hands on the gold? What if his whole family history is a bunch of malarky and he's just in this to get his hands on the gold? I mean, what if, Cass?" Marcus felt torn and suddenly, over the course of the past thirty minutes, he no longer felt the security in his friendship with Simon.

"Give it a few days, Marcus." Cassie relented from her previous insistence that the gold belonged to Simon's tribe. "Let's take some time to logically think this through. I'm sure you'll come to the realization that Simon is a true and trustworthy friend. And then you'll be able to put this conspiracy theory talk to bed. And maybe Marcus, just maybe it's time for Opa to step in and provide us with some direction. Maybe he will give us a sign."

* * * *

It was a warm evening as the early May sun bore down, the tent was already slightly crowded with folks milling about chatting, and there was a palpably excited

188

buzz in the air. As Marcus and Cassie located and made their way toward a small batch of empty folding chairs, they shared in the aura of anticipation. This particular revival had never appeared locally, but the reputation of the visiting minister had preceded him. Word had spread of his fiery preaching and the number already present in the expectant crowd threatened the final total to exceed the planned capacity of two hundred. Reverend Heinrich Amadeus Kaisenreicher was a visiting German citizen, and although he was not widely known in North America, he had made it his mission to spend five summers in America spreading his unique vision of the word of God. He had a normally calm manner, but when delivering his message, he presented an image of a man completely overtaken by the Holy Spirit. Of course there were naysayers who would claim he was nothing more than a common charlatan, preying on the weak and desperate. But, in the end, that judgement would ultimately be made by a power much stronger than the Reverend's critics.

The grand production was set to commence at seven p.m. At five minutes past the anointed hour, Marcus sat in anticipation, with Cassie to his left and two of the very few remaining seats to his right. Several couples had inquired about the empty chairs, but when informed that the third member of their party had yet to arrive, all had moved on in search of alternate accommodations. It almost seemed to Marcus that the good Reverend was extending every consideration possible to allow Simon the opportunity to not miss a moment of the sermon. According to his watch, it was twelve past seven when his friend the took seat next to him.

"Ah, haven't missed a thing, have I?" Simon whispered as he leaned forward, patted Marcus' thigh and gave a small wave and smile to Cassie. At seven-fifteen sharp a lay member of the Reverend's group gave a short invocation and welcomed all in attendance. As the layman briefly spoke, Simon again whispered in Marcus' ear.

"Who are you saving this fourth chair for? Is your friend Denny coming? Should I move down one?" Simon asked.

"No, you're fine," Marcus whispered back. "When we sat, there were four empty seats here. Anybody who wants the fourth chair is welcome to it, I wasn't saving it for anyone in particular."

Cassie could overhear the whispered conversation centered on the unused fourth chair. In her mind she said a quick silent prayer that Opa would be the one who would take the seat. With so much religion, faith, and goodwill in the air tonight, she wondered if it wouldn't be the perfect time for him to give her and Marcus the sign they were hoping to receive.

When Reverend Kaisenreicher began the transformation from a mild and calmy reserved pastor, as to which he was accustomed, Marcus instantaneously felt the intensity of the entire crowd increase. Simon had definitely been correct in his assessment of the heavily accented preacher's ability to mesmerize. The man was able to thoroughly engage his audience, playing on their need to receive the salvation about which he so eloquently spoke, and almost seemed to guarantee would be delivered.

"If you truly fear that you may someday find yourself condemned to hell, then should you not first be made aware of the dreadfulness you that may expect to face?" The preacher practically screamed as he held a bible high overhead.

Simon had surely been right; the man did absolutely deliver fire and brimstone such as Marcus had never before witnessed. But it wasn't just the fear of hell and damnation that he warned of. Kaisenreicher was also unafraid to make everyone aware of the wrath of God as well.

"As we are forewarned in the book of Hebrews: 'For we know Him who said, Vengeance is Mine, I will repay, says the Lord' and we must hear His word my good friends." The preacher continued with, "The Lord will judge His people. It is a fearful thing to fall into the hands of a living God."

Marcus found himself moved by the preaching of this man who had traveled from halfway around the world, his purpose seemingly to deliver the words that spoke directly to him.

"As angry as God may ever be with us, we must continue to remind ourselves that His love is unfailing. As the words of John 3:16 tells us, 'For God so loved the world, that He gave His only begotten Son, that whoever believes in Him shall not perish, but have eternal life.' He gave his son my friends, can we not repay that gift by giving our hearts and souls to Him in return?"

For all the strong, inspiring, and truly powerful words spoken by the Reverend Kaisenreicher this evening, the part that touched Cassie the deepest was when the man appealed directly to the younger members of his flock. In a lowered, calm and somewhat soothing voice, the man wisely brought his sermon to today's generation.

"Many of you listen to the modern music of today and draw messages of false hope and despair. Believe me children, the world is not on the brink of destruction but rather the eve of resurrection. The best the world has to offer has not yet come to fruition, but it is your time now to spread the Word. As expressed in the lyrics of a man called Pete Seeger and sung by musicians you youngsters will know as the Byrds, there is and always will be

'A time to be born, a time to die
A time to plant, a time to reap
A time to kill, a time to heal
A time to laugh, a time to weep

To everything turn, turn, turn
There is a season turn, turn, turn
And a time to every purpose under Heaven'

These words are credited to Pete Seeger, but he will readily admit that they are taken directly from the Good Book. Almost word for word, this song is drawn from the book of Ecclesiastes, chapter 3, verses 1-8. When you hear this song, please listen to and pay attention to the lyrics. A time to every purpose under Heaven."

At the conclusion of the benediction the three of them were completely exhausted. Cassie hugged Marcus and thanked him for bringing her. As she had her arms wrapped around his neck, she could see over his left shoulder and past Simon who was stretching his arms overhead. During the course of the service it had gone unnoticed to either her or Marcus that an old man had occupied the fourth chair, the empty seat next to Simon. The man was now walking away and she could only see him from behind as he began to blend in with the crowd that was filing out of the tent. But there was no doubt in her mind as to the man's identity.

Cassie grabbed Marcus' chin and abruptly turned his head to the right so he would be able to see what was behind him.

"There's the sign we were waiting for, Marcus."

Baggage Dump

Marcus and Cassie sat on the porch swing in her front yard discussing the incredible sermon that they had been blessed to hear tonight. Neither of them had ever before experienced a good old-fashioned traveling tent revival, and while they had been somewhat excited and looked forward to hearing some fiery preaching, their expectations had not been exceedingly high. Even though Simon had highly recommended the work of Reverend Kaisenreicher, they had still entered the tent harboring some reservations. However, the energetic Reverend had proven to be all that Simon had promised and then some. All in all, it had been a marvelous event to witness. And they were in agreement that it had been well worth the ten dollar donation Marcus had forked over when a number of hats ranging from cowboy to fedora to bowler had been passed among the attendees. Marcus also seconded Cassie's opinion that they had not been blown away by obvious evidence that anyone had actually been healed or saved, but he did tell her that there surely must have been a healthy number of fence sitters who most certainly had been converted by the Reverend's promise of heavenly green pastures. The teens were emotionally worn down, and with school coming up in a few short hours, both were in desperate need of sleep. But while tired, they both were too wound up to call it a night. Their hope was that thirty minutes or so of calming conversation would serve to lower their adrenaline levels enough that they would be able to mellow a bit. The topic of the revival itself had gradually diminished, but Cassie had not yet expressed all of her intended talking points.

"Marcus, why didn't you say anything or even acknowledge the sign we were given, even when I pointed it out to you?" Cassie had waited patiently until they had returned to her house and had sufficient and ample opportunity to chill a bit before deciding to bring up a subject that had been sticking uncomfortably in her craw. She had been vastly disappointed in Marcus as she had received no reaction whatsoever from him when she had initially tried to draw his attention to the man whom, by his mere presence on the scene, she had perceived as the sign they had hoped for. Of course, she had understood that Marcus might have thought, in that exact moment, that the matter could not have been spoken of, nor discussed freely and openly, in the company of his friend Simon. But her dismay was further compounded when Marcus failed to mention it on the short drive home. She had fully expected to hear his thoughts when they were alone in the car. After asking her question, the thought crossed her mind that perhaps he had not even noticed the man. She had discreetly tried to alert him as soon as she realized who had been sitting in the fourth chair. But, by the time Marcus had turned his head and focused on the scene she'd referred him to in the outer aisle, it was quite possible that he couldn't even distinguish the man as he was merging into the human montage.

"Oh, you meant the man that was sitting on the other side of Simon?" It was just now coming to him precisely who she had been trying to identify to him. During the revival, Marcus had not actually gotten a look at the man; he had only taken brief notice of the properly crossed legs on the opposite side of Simon. But the sight had demanded a spark of Marcus' attention simply because of the unique off-white, rather pale shade of silky seersucker fabric. He remembered asking himself why in the world would anyone from around here be wearing a silk seersucker suit? "Cassie, I did see him walking away, but I never saw his face," he replied. "In that split second, how was I supposed to know who you were talking about?"

"Then you did see him," Cassie breathed a sigh of relief. "That's good. Marcus, you know that was him, that was Neville."

"No Cassie, I don't know that, at least not for sure." Marcus could not readily confess that he might be somewhat convinced but did have to concede that the suit definitely did fit the profile of the prim and stately Englishman he had recently met at the bowling alley.

"How could you not be sure, Marcus?" Cassie was flustered. "He had been less than three feet away from you, sitting right there next to Simon. Ask him tomorrow at work; I'd think they would have had to have spoken, at least said hello."

"Ask him what exactly, Cassie? Ask him if that had been an otherworldly being or ghost that sat next to him at the revival last night?" Marcus couldn't just idly and out of the blue ask, *"Hey, Simon, who was the character sitting next to you in that fourth chair last night?"* without some type of legitimate reason for the question.

"Just throw in a little white fib, Marcus. Ask him if he spoke to the old man next to him because you thought that you might have overheard an English accent." Cassie thought the question was simple enough and wondered why Marcus hadn't thought of it himself. Sometimes it just seemed that he lacked the initiative to get things done.

"So what if he had an English accent, Cassie," Marcus argued, although he knew Cassie was right. "That still doesn't prove his identity."

"Marcus, I saw him from behind and I knew it was him. Same haircut, same gray hair, same type of suit he wore at the snack bar. There's isn't one iota of doubt that it was Neville." Marcus wished he had gotten a better look or been able to hear his voice, just to be unconditionally positive. "We asked for a sign and him sitting in that fourth chair next to Simon was it."

"Cassie, you keep bringing up the words 'fourth chair'. Why are so hung on that term? What significance are you attaching to the chair anyway?" Marcus could not anticipate the correlation she was inferring.

"Marcus, I saw it as soon as we sat down. Four empty seats in the middle of the row. Four empty seats all in a row. I saw the connection almost instantly," she explained. "I felt it walking down the row. I would take the first empty seat and you would follow me. Then, when Simon arrived, he would sit to your right opposite me. That left one open chair, the fourth chair. No one would take that empty chair. Just about everyone there were couples or families. Single people don't go to revivals, so it would remain empty. I knew it would be Neville who came and sat there. I knew that would be the sign, Neville in the fourth chair. Or Opa, but Marcus, it couldn't have been a dog."

"I still don't get it Cassie. Why did the sign have to be the person in the fourth chair?" Marcus felt like he was missing something about that chair.

"I knew it right away, Marcus. Do you remember the first time Ellis came for dinner at your apartment? It was usually just you, me, and Margaret. The fourth chair was always empty. Do you see the significance now, Sherlock?"

"Ellis took the fourth chair," he said as the imaginary light bulb came on above his head.

"Exactly Marcus! Ellis was the missing piece of the equation, but with him gone, that chair is empty again." Cassie had solved the puzzle. "The fourth chair was open again, and Opa couldn't be the one to fill it and provide us with the sign because he is a dog. But now Neville is the new mystery being that has entered our realm. Don't you see Marcus? Neville showed up at the revival tonight and sat right next to Simon. He filled the void and that showed us the connection. That was the sign to let us know that Simon was telling you the truth. That gold, Marcus... it belongs to Simon and his people."

* * * *

Marcus held his timecard in his right hand waiting for the big hand to move one final tick and point straight up to the number twelve. As the clock clicked once again to signify the top of the hour, Marcus slid the card in and pulled down on the small lever. Removing the card he checked to verify his punch. *Tues May 13 16:00* it read in faded red ink. He made a mental note to check the stock room for a replacement red ink ribbon.

With it being Tuesday and Chester's day off, Marcus sauntered over to Simon to find out if there was a repair job or any tire work that needed his attention.

"No, nothing's pressing, Marcus," Simon said as he slipped a hose clamp into place. He had just replaced the upper radiator hose, and as he positioned the clamp he asked Marcus, "Hey, will you hand me that screwdriver? When this is tight, I'm taking a break. Why don't you grab us a couple of Nehi's for a change of pace?"

Retrieving the red shop towel from his back pocket, Simon wiped his hands and walked over to take a seat at the break table. Marcus set the cold drink on the table in front of Simon, who thirstily took a deep swig of the grape Nehi, wiped his mouth with his right shirt sleeve and flashed his customary smile.

"So, what did you think of the revival last night?" Simon asked the question with a touch of an *I told you so* intonation.

"Pretty much just what you had predicted," Marcus replied. "That preacher was really good. He sure knew his scripture; I don't even remember him hardly reading at all. He had everything memorized. Impressive."

"Oh yeah, he's good, Marcus. But you know what? I can see why he travels all the time. Could you imagine having to listen to that wild and exciting kind of sermon every Sunday?" Simon shook his head from side to side. "That would flat wear you out, don't you think? I couldn't take getting that worked up every week, could you?"

"No, I think you're right about that." Marcus agreed with a nervous laugh.

"Tell you what though, Marcus. I'm sure glad I went to see him last year. He really did me a huge favor. Talking to him probably saved my life." Simon wasn't smiling right now and Marcus sensed that what he was about to hear was going to be something either heartfelt or soul-baring.

"Gosh Simon, I mean..."

"Let me speak, Marcus. I've gotten to know you, and I like you. You and your girlfriend both. You are good people and you've got good souls and you're both pure of heart. Those are important traits. You might think I'm a little loco, but me and my people, we have a way about us. We can feel.... I guess we can sense things. And Marcus, there are things I sense about you.

201

You have secrets that you are holding back, keeping inside." Simon stopped and looked deeply into Marcus' eyes.

"I don't know what those secrets are, but there is pain and hurt. And that is why I have to tell you my story." He closed his eyes and Marcus wasn't sure if Simon was trying to think or remember something, or if he was falling into a trance.

"Marcus, I went to the revival last year because I was troubled. I was unhappy. I didn't like or enjoy my life." Simon opened his eyes. They had reddened and were moist. "I had grown to hate my stepfather and I didn't like my mother for allowing my father to die when I was a boy. Somehow I wanted to blame her because my father was mentally weak and couldn't face life like a man, like the Pottawatomie warrior from which he was descended. My father took his own life and I knew I was on a path to end up with the same fate. I knew I needed guidance but knew it wouldn't come from Frank or my mom. I didn't know where to turn. And then I saw a sign. It was a flyer advertising Reverend Kaisenreicher and his family revival. Very similar to the one at the snack bar that I showed to you. So, I went to the revival, and I swear to you Marcus, I swear I felt like he was speaking to me and me alone. Almost as if I was the only person in that tent. I got baptized that night, and afterward I requested to see and talk to the Reverend."

"And you were able to talk to him, Simon? Did he help you?" Marcus asked.

"Yes, Marcus. He's very wise. He explained to me that you do reap what you sow. And you know what else? He read to me from the Book of Ecclesiastes, just like he did last night. Those words mean so much to me." Simon actually had tears forming in his eyes.

"And that solved your problems, your talk with him?" Marcus was enthralled with Simon's tale.

"Oh no, not totally. He told me that God would be there for me in the hereafter, and that God would help me day to day, but that I still needed help from mere mortals as well. He told me to seek the help of a mental professional, and you know what, I did. Alan Copeland is his name. He's a psychotherapist over in Quincy." Marcus was amazed that Simon was sitting here, really baring his soul to a seventeen year old kid. "Marcus, I only had to see Dr. Copeland three or four times. I explained my issues, I was very open with him and he helped me almost immediately. He taught me to be myself, to take care of what I could control and to take with a grain of salt what I couldn't. I don't worry about things anymore, I don't feel any guilt or anger about my father, and I know that my mother did all she could to understand and support him. Now I know it wasn't her fault and I can accept everything without any remorse. I've learned to smile, to realize life is a gift. I've learned to recognize signs when they're presented and to appreciate all that I have. Does that make sense to you?"

"Yeah, Simon, it does. Maybe I'm just not always open to seeing the 'signs' as you say." Marcus was definitely pleased to know that Simon had found his path to happiness.

"Marcus, I've got a brake job to finish tonight and you've got four tires to rotate on that Rambler in Chester's bay. But first, take this." Simon pulled out his wallet and took out a worn business card. Handing it to Marcus, he smiled once again. "I don't need it anymore. Try him. Once or twice. You'll be glad, I promise."

Marcus took the card and looked at it. 'Dr. Alan Copland' it read in bold font. Smaller print gave the telephone number. He looked back up at Simon. Having no reason for why he did, Marcus held up the card and asked Simon, "Is he English by any chance?"

"Yeah, actually he is Marcus." Marcus had no idea why he had even asked the question, but the reason became clear when Simon answered, "He speaks just like the old man that sat next to me last night."

At seven-thirty, Marcus didn't even bother going home to clean up. Tonight he was in a hurry, and instead he opted to wash up carefully at the shop and change back into his school clothes. He sped over to the *Riverwalk Lanes*, anxious to talk to Cassie. His first words to her were to put her mind at ease by verifying that she had been absolutely right about Neville. He had to have been the person who Simon had identified as an Englishman and who had occupied the fourth chair in their grouping at the revival. They still could not grasp the exact significance of his appearance aside from just being a visible 'sign' to them. Nor could they establish a possible cause or reason for his existence. It had not taken them long to learn the how and why of Opa's role in their lives, but Neville was a complete mystery. However, they both were positive that he had been unquestionably real and not imaginary. Although his motivations were beyond their understanding it apparently seemed that he would continue to be an integral cog in their lives. Marcus' admission, and agreement with Cassie, that Neville's presence must have been the sign that they had requested meant the two could now retire that subject. Or at least put it to rest for the time being.

Whenever spare moments arose between Cassie serving her customers, Marcus would eagerly relate to her snippets of Simon's remarkable story of meeting Reverend Heinrich Kaisenreicher and then his subsequent visits with a psychotherapist. When Marcus showed her the worn business card that Simon had given to him, she looked at Marcus questioningly.

"So what exactly are you implying, Marcus?"

"I'm implying, Cassie, that I'm going to make an appointment. If it worked for Simon, maybe Dr. Copeland can help me to shed some of my guilt over Ellis." Marcus assumed that Cassie would be totally onboard with his decision. "I mean, that's what you suggested a few weeks ago wasn't it?"

"Yeah, Marcus, it is, but I never thought you'd agree to do it." Cassie almost sounded disappointed that he had decided to seek help from someone.

"Well, then why do you seem to be mopey about it, Cass?"

"I don't know. Maybe it makes me feel a little jealous," she more or less snorted her answer to Marcus' question. "When I suggested it, you got your drawers all up in a wad. But when Simon gives you this guy's name and number, all of a sudden now you're all set to go. I guess that bothers me. It's like you trust Simon's opinion more than mine, you know what I mean?"

"No, that's not it at all, Cassie." Marcus knew he had better smooth this out as quickly as possible.

"It's just the simple fact that Simon was in a worse way than I am, and he was man enough to face up to his problems. And then look, it worked for him," Marcus was making an attempt to rationalize his decision without diminishing Cassie's influence over him. "It's not that I didn't cherish your opinion Sweetie, I think I probably just took it the wrong way. But when Simon told me that the therapy worked for him, well, I think that was the validation that allowed me to accept that you were right all along."

"Okay Marcus, I suppose I can see how you came to the realization of the truth." Cassie was no fool, she could see right through to the reason for his buttery words. But, regardless of what had prompted this revelation, she was happy that he had finally come around and agreed with her assessment and suggestion.

Cassie had to break away to provide snacks for another hungry bowling team that had just finished for the evening. Seeing she would be busy for a bit; Marcus took the opportunity to play two games of pinball and then dropped three dimes in the jukebox. Upon retaking his seat at the snack bar, he sat in a contemplative mood, carefully listening to and absorbing the lyrics of his new favorite song, *Turn, Turn, Turn.*

When Cassie finally returned, serving a fresh refill of cola to Marcus, she was ready to resume the topic with which they had originally begun. "Now, let's change the subject once again," she said, "and get back to the fact that you agree with me that Neville did provide us with the sign we had requested. Now that you know you can trust Simon and believe the story about his ancestors and their lost gold, when are you going to tell him that you know where it is hidden and figure out a way to return it to him and his people?" Cassie was anxious to settle this part of the story and put it behind them.

"I think I'm going to tell him tomorrow. But, you know he's not going to believe me, Cass. He'll probably just figure I'm a lunatic." Marcus wondered how he could deliver such wonderful news without it sounding like he recently fallen straight off the funny farm wagon.

"Come on, Marcus. What's the surefire way to make him believe you?" Even though she knew he would eventually see the answer, Cassie somehow felt the need to lead the horse to water. "Seeing is believing, right?"

After clocking in on Wednesday afternoon, Chester had put Marcus to work on one of his least favorite tasks, performing inventory on the most common items that were routinely stocked in the shop. He stayed busy counting spark plugs, radiator hoses, oil filters and other items that were used more or less on a daily basis.

Parts that were more specialized, such as water pumps and alternators, or other items that were too expensive to merit the investment dollars to stock, were normally ordered and delivered to the shop, or in extreme emergencies, Walt would have to drive out to the supply houses down in Hannibal or Quincy to pick them up. As Marcus worked, he kept an eye over his shoulder, watching for Simon to take his afternoon break. Most days, he would try to take his break with Simon so they could chew the fat for fifteen minutes or so.

When Simon finally did pull out a rag and began wiping his hands, Marcus made a beeline for the soda machine. "Coke, Nehi, or Seven-Up?" Simon asked as Marcus approached.

"Coke," Marcus replied. "Thanks, Chief."

They pulled up chairs at the break table. Simon took a sip of his drink, but Marcus just sat holding his while watching his friend. He was trying to frame the question in his mind. He knew it had to be asked in just the right way.

"Simon, remember the story you told me about the three warriors that got killed all those years ago?" Marcus wasn't sure exactly what words should be used, even though he had rehearsed and framed his general thoughts several times while he was taking inventory.

"Yeah, I remember, why?" Simon asked.

"Was that true, you know about the gold and somebody torturing them and everything?"

"Well yeah, Marcus why would I lie about something like that? Those were my ancestors, it's my history. Of course it's true." Simon spoke with his usual grinning face.

"And there were twenty-two bars, you're sure about that, Simon? You're sure there were twenty-two?" Marcus asked.

"Yeah, Marcus, twenty-two gold bars. Why? What's up with you anyway, Shemp?" Simon thought there was something funny going on here. "What the hell are you grinning about, Marcus?"

"Simon, remember how honest you were with me yesterday? How you unloaded all that heavy baggage on me that you said you've been carrying? You know, about your mom and dad and the therapist and all that. You told me a lot, you know?" Marcus really felt for what Simon must have gone through.

"Yeah, of course, Marcus. You know, I just feel comfortable talking with you, my man. You're a good friend, Marcus."

"Simon, do you believe in signs?" Marcus asked.

"Yeah, I do," Simon said. "Hey, the day I interviewed with Walt, before I got out of my car, this cardinal landed in the parking lot, not ten feet away from my door. A cardinal is a sign of good luck, did you know that? I knew when I saw that cardinal that I would get hired. It was a sign, Marcus. I knew that was a sign."

"Well, Simon, I saw a sign too. And I've been carrying some baggage for a few years now that I've been wanting to unload, too." Marcus took a deep breath. "Don't like get loud or nothing, you might give Chester a heart attack." Simon, looking perplexed, lost his smile, tucked his chin in, furrowed his brow and drew his head back a couple of inches, wondering what in the world Marcus' baggage could possibly be. Marcus took another, even deeper breath. "Simon, I know where your gold bars are hidden."

To Marcus' amazement, Simon sat in stunned silence. He didn't look happy, excited, or elated, none of the emotions Marcus would have expected him to display.

Without an obvious or demonstrative reaction, Marcus decided to proceed with unloading the whole and *nearly* complete story. Some of the details were quite irrelevant to the discovery of the gold, especially since Marcus' supposed inheritance was now known to be non-existent. Marcus told Simon that he and Ellis had found the old treasure map his grandfather had drawn and explained how and why it had come to be. He explained how his grandfather and Jeremiah Paige had been the first to have discovered the bars but had left them undisturbed for all these years. And that now, after hearing Simon's story, he was sure that the gold had remained hidden there and untouched for over a century. Marcus told Simon that he and Cassie had visited just last summer, and that the treasure still remained intact. Marcus told Simon that he had vowed to Cassie that he would one day locate the rightful owner, and they had only recently tried and failed. They had only one suspected possibility, but it had turned out that Jeremiah's family had not claimed responsibility for it. Looking back, Marcus realized that he had left a door wide open and a dishonest Wanda could easily have lied and reported that Othello had indeed told her about its existence. But, thankfully, she had been honest in her denial. But when Simon had related the story to Marcus of the ancestral warriors, everything had become crystal clear. And on Monday, when the presence of the Englishman had been the sign delivered to Marcus and Cassie... well, that had sealed the deal. Both Marcus and Simon had far exceeded their allotted fifteen minute break, but Walt had already gone home for the day and Chester could not have cared less that they had overextended. Unless the place was extremely busy, or customers were waiting while their vehicles were being serviced, the shop was a pretty loosely run ship. Marcus promised Simon that they would take a river cruise this coming Sunday, assuming that he could arrange to borrow a canoe from his friend Denny's father. Simon would have the opportunity to see the gold bars with his own two eyes. After all these years, the fortune that had been so elusive to his ancestors would finally become a reality. They agreed that Simon would drive his Ford pick-up, gathering Marcus and the canoe before departing at one o'clock on Sunday afternoon.

* * * *

It was sunny and quite warm and calling it a beautiful afternoon would not be a stretch of anyone's imagination. Wading into the rippling muddy waters along the bank, the two adventurers carefully boarded their borrowed canoe and embarked on their current driven journey to the south. For the first time in nearly a year, Marcus would revisit the cave that Cassie had dubbed "Opa's Hideaway". But for Simon, the trip would culminate in his initial discovery of a sacred hiding place, the site of the Pottawatomie Tribe's long overdue reward. After more than a century, Simon's people would finally reclaim what had rightfully belonged to their ancestors. With the ultimate destination being only a few miles downstream and knowing that they had not discussed or even considered exactly how they were planning to retrieve the treasure, Marcus figured now would be a good time for him to inform Simon of some important facts that he had looked up, studied, and calculated. He doubted that Simon had taken into consideration any of what Marcus was about to impart. He hoped that it was not Simon's plan to just load the bounty into the canoe and just happily paddle their way back upstream. The enormity of the task was beyond anything they were equipped to handle today.

"Listen Simon, before we get there, I've got a few things I need to make clear to you. I checked in the school library and got a ballpark number for the weight of the gold. A standard gold bar weighs right in the neighborhood of about twenty-seven and one-half pounds. When Ellis and I first discovered the bars, he checked and said he was pretty sure he counted a total of twenty-two bars, and that matches precisely the number you told me that your ancestors had hidden," Marcus told him.

"Wow, that sounds like a lot of weight for this canoe doesn't it?" As Marcus had suspected, Simon hadn't thought of how heavy the gold might be.

"Yeah, that's exactly right, Simon," Marcus continued with what he had gotten from his factfinding. "So, with twenty-two bars that would be roughly six-hundred and five pounds, give or take a few. If you add the total weight of the gold along with our combined four hundred or so pounds of body weight, and that puts us and the cargo at a grand total just in excess of one thousand pounds."

"This canoe can't handle that much, can it?" Simon asked.

"Nope, I had Denny to ask his dad, and he said a fourteen footer like this is rated at about seven hundred pounds. But, and mind you Simon, this is a big but, this thing is at least twenty years old and Doug said it's had several cracks and holes patched already. I also had asked Denny about hauling cargo and he told me his dad said he wouldn't advise carrying more than a hundred pounds in excess of our own weights. That's why he said they usually just use it for fishing." Marcus hated be the bearer of bad news, and he was sure that Simon had hoped to bring the gold back with him today if it could have been possible.

"Definitely not worth the risk," Simon took the disappointing news in stride. "Especially going back upstream against the current. But it's okay, Marcus, don't let it get you down. I'll be satisfied today just to see something that my people haven't laid eyes on in almost one hundred and thirty years."

"Simon, do you know anybody with like a cabin cruiser or ski boat or anything like that? Maybe we can get somebody to bring us back to get it." Marcus didn't know of anyone who owned one, but he had certainly seen enough people out there water skiing and otherwise enjoying themselves as they boated up and down the river.

"You know, Marcus, now that you suggest it, I think I have a cousin that just might still have a ski boat." Simon remembered going on an outing a few years back and watching some of his relatives comparing their skill levels at skiing and tubing. Assuming he still owned it, Simon felt that he could surely talk his cousin Melvin into driving his boat out here, especially when he found out the purpose that was behind the request.

A couple of miles south of the sandbar that would eternally haunt his memory, Marcus recognized the overgrown shoreline on the Illinois side of the river. The two gently landed the canoe, pulled it a safe distance out of the water, and tied it to the trunk of an ash tree. Making their way through the brush, they eventually reached the mouth of the shale cave. After casting aside the dead and dried branches that served to camouflage the small entrance, Marcus lit his lantern and knelt down in preparation of entering the cave.

"Do we have to crawl all the way?" Simon asked.

"About half a mile," Marcus deadpanned before looking back at the worried look on Simon's face. Easing Simon's concern with a broad smile, Marcus said, "This is just nature's way of protecting the gold, Simon. It looks like a tiny opening, but once we're inside it gets a lot bigger. We'll even be able to stand up."

"Whew," Simon whistled softly. "You had me worried there for a minute."

Followed closely by Simon, who carried along a heavy duty flashlight, Marcus crawled on hands and knees for less than three feet before entering into the front main chamber where they both were able to stand. Having twice before been to the treasure room, Marcus didn't hesitate to start toward the artery to the right, brushing aside the cobwebs as he held the lantern at head's height.

"Are you sure which doorway is the right one, Marcus? I don't want to get lost in here." Simon spoke with sincerity.

"Haven't you heard it before Simon?" Marcus said before reciting what he could only assume to have been a nursery rhyme that Margaret used to chant to him back when his father was still alive. "The door on the right is the one you go in, go out on the left, you're as neat as a pin." Laughing to himself, somewhat surprised that he had remembered the words, Marcus then said in an assuring voice, "This is it. Third time I've been here. The other two arteries are dead ends."

Confidently, the pair started down the corridor. It was a long and winding hike, the damp, sweaty walls alternately narrowing and widening, but the ceiling consistently maintaining a height of just over six feet. After traversing a distance roughly equivalent to three football fields, or nearly one thousand feet, Marcus at last was able to usher Simon into the great room. He couldn't help but wonder, that many years ago and without the aid of artificial light, how Simon's ancestors had been able to locate such a safe haven. And then, without modern tools and equipment had been able to chisel and cut the wall to prepare the hiding place that had served to protect their assets for all these many years.

It only took Marcus a few moments to locate the two slightest of edges that identified the secret false rock in the wall.

"Your ancestors were ingenious, Simon. I don't know how they managed to cut this rock, but they did an unbelievable job in carving this hole in the shale or rock, or whatever you would call this material. The stone fits into that hole so perfectly; it is barely noticeable. If it weren't for these two little finger grips that they cut into it, it would be impossible to know it was even there." Marcus marveled at the outstanding workmanship the tribal warriors exhibited more than a century ago.

Simon brought his flashlight closer and examined the surprisingly accurate fit of the stone in the wall. Marcus was right in his assessment that the rectangular hole had been meticulously cut into the wall.

"Pay special notice to the two small edges they cut into the stone, Simon. They are a perfect size for someone to use a finger from each hand to wiggle the rock outward until it could be gripped solidly and then removed altogether." Marcus knew for a fact, even using power tools, that he could not have produced work matching such demanding detail.

"Should I remove the rock, Marcus?" Simon asked, giddy with excitement.

"It's your gold, Simon. Be my guest," Marcus could hardly contain the upsurge in excitement that he was feeling for Simon. He felt it even more so than the day when he and Ellis had initially seen the gold. It had definitely been exhilarating to rediscover the secret that the wall had managed to keep hidden for over a century, but in retrospect it had paled to what he was feeling today. For the gold to be returned to its rightful owners; the feeling was just incomparable.

Simon gently wiggled the rock just as Marcus had instructed. When he was able to maintain a firm grip, he grasped with both hands and slowly lifted out the stone, placing it gently on the floor of the cave. Sensing the historical significance of the moment, Marcus brought the lantern closer as Simon angled the flashlight carefully in anticipation. Tiptoeing for a better view and bringing his face closer and right alongside his flashlight, Simon wore an enormous and enthusiastic grin. He was nearly in a state of delirium as he peered behind the wall to gain his first ever view of real gold.

But his grin of expectation was quickly replaced by a look of utter confusion and disbelief. Simon could hardly control his eyes as they desperately searched, darting alternately up and down and then side to side. He frantically moved his flashlight around, inspecting every nook and cranny of the relatively small space. In a span of seconds, Marcus' excitement had turned almost instantaneously to dread. His stomach dropped and he was consumed by the urge to vomit. The sudden and obvious change in Simon's expression had told the entire devastating story.

Simon's arms dropped to his side as he closed his eyes and rested his forehead against the cold, damp wall.

"Marcus, it's not here. It's gone." Simon's voice carried such a depressive depth that Marcus hardly recognized who was speaking the words.

The Note

"How could it happen, Marcus? Weren't there any signs that someone had been there?" Cassie was in a state of shock and disbelief. Her degree of amazement and disappointment nearly rivaled that of Simon a few hours earlier. After the canoe had been returned, Simon had graciously rejected Marcus' offer to accompany him and Cassie to dinner at the *River's Edge*, instead opting to simply return to his room at the boarding house.

"No Cass, nothing seemed to have changed." Marcus picked idly at his house salad. Looking up from his plate he said, "Everything was just like it was when we were there last year. Exactly like it was. Nothing out of place. I mean it's like it was never there at all. Like it was just our imagination or something."

"You don't think Simon thought you had lied to him, do you?" Cassie asked in earnest. "My God, I hope he doesn't think that you stole the gold, Marcus. You don't think he would suspect that do you?"

"No, Cassie. Why would he think something like that?" Marcus was bothered that she would make such an outlandish suggestion.

"Think about it for a minute, Marcus," she reasoned. "Assume for a minute that you have figured out that Simon is entitled to the gold, but you have already taken it. And the best way to divert suspicion from yourself is to volunteer to take him to it. And voila! The gold is missing."

"Cassie, that's kind of ridiculous isn't it?"

"No, it makes perfect sense, really," she countered. "You think you've avoided suspicion by taking him to it, but if I'm Simon, I've figured out that you're just creating a diversion and I suspect you. What do you think now?"

"Honestly? I think you need to stop watching so much *Hawaii Five-O*. It's just a tv show, Cassie." Marcus wasn't at all impressed with her speculation. "Your theory makes for a good story line, but it's not reasonable at all. Simon is smart enough to know that if I had any designs on stealing that gold, I would never even have told him about it in the first place."

"Yeah you're right, Marcus. Simon knows you and trusts you. I just wish I knew who did steal it." Cassie had so much sympathy, not just for Simon, but for all of his relatives and other members of his tribe.

"Me too, Cassie, me too."

Marcus resigned himself to the fact that even though he had displayed the best of intentions, there was just nothing that he could do to correct the situation. What was done, was done, and the consequences would be as they are. Marcus swore he could almost see Louie sitting in Cassie seat in the booth and hearing his romantic voice *"C'est la vie, Marcoos, c'est la vie."*

Cassie snapped Marcus from hid trance by asking, "So I guess I forgot to ask you Friday, were you able to make an appointment with Dr. Copeland?"

"Oh yeah, yeah I did, Cass. I got one for Monday, June 9," he replied somewhat unconvincingly.

"Are you sure, Marcus? You don't sound so sure," Cassie said.

"Yeah, I'm sure Cassie. It's at ten in the morning. Actually, they're mailing me a form to fill out," he explained as he snapped out of his temporary malaise. "I was afraid Mama would have to go with me, but all she has to do is sign a waiver and mail it back. You know, like a permission slip since I'm not eighteen yet."

"Well, I'm really glad you decided to go, Marcus. You've been carrying a lot of baggage for a long time, and it got even harder after Ellis died. I mean it bothered me a lot, so I know it was harder on you." Even though her suggestion that he see someone had caused a temporary rift in their relationship, she was glad she had broached the subject. Marcus carried a lot inside and she feared if he didn't talk things out with a professional that eventually he would suffer to a larger degree, both emotionally and psychologically.

"Yeah, I guess now when I go telling him all about my hangups I'll have a nice fresh one to throw on the pile won't I?" Marcus laughed sarcastically, but he knew that today's revelation had metaphorically been just one more stone thrown onto wagon.

Marcus thought about going by the shop after school on Monday, but just couldn't bring himself to see Simon, to have to look him in the eye. He decided to give it another day and would apologize once more on Tuesday when he had no choice but to go to work and had no excuses left to avoid his friend. He and Cassie had instead decided to make a jaunt over to Quincy, ostensibly to locate Dr. Copeland's office so Marcus would know exactly where to go for his appointment in three weeks. On the drive, Cassie went on and on about her parents' Memorial Day barbeque next week.

The discussion led to a question that she had been wanting to pose ever since her mother had brought the rumor to her attention on Saturday morning.

"By the way, Marcus, when were you going to tell me about your Mama dating Buster Finkel?" Cassie asked the question with a bit of an edge, implying that Marcus had been purposely keeping the news from her.

"What are you talking about Cassie? Where did you hear that from?" Marcus was actually affronted by the question. If Cassie had heard this, it was certainly news to him.

"From my mother, that's where. We were talking about the barbeque Saturday morning and she told me that Margaret had asked if she could bring Buster along. Of course, mother said that was fine." Then Cassie reiterated her disappointment to Marcus. "But how come you never told me they were an item? I would certainly have told you if my mother was seeing someone."

Marcus had to laugh at the analogy. "Cassie, your mother is a married woman. If she were *seeing* someone, I doubt that you would know about it, and if you did, you absolutely would not be telling me."

"That's funny, Shemp," she responded. "You know exactly what I meant. Let me rephrase your honor. With all things being equal, in a similar situation, I would have told you. But instead, you kept it from me."

"No, actually, Cassie, I didn't know anything about it, even if it is true." Marcus spoke the truth.

Marcus was fully aware that Margaret had recommended Buster for an open chef's position a few months back at the *Gold Mine*, and that he had gotten the job. So the two of them were both working at the same place again after the years they had spent together at the *River's Edge*. Looking back, Marcus knew that they had always been friendly. Heck, Buster had often even given her rides home when she had worked late shifts. And whenever he had visited the diner, Buster seemed to always treat him a little special. He'd never really thought about it, but a few extra onion rings here, an extra scoop of ice cream there. When he ordered a milkshake, he not only got the milkshake in its customary glass, but usually he was presented with the stainless steel malt cup that contained a leftover two or three ounce bonus serving. Maybe there had been hints that Buster had a shine for Margaret that he'd never picked up on.

After taking a moment to contemplate, Marcus came to a somewhat suspicious conclusion. "Wow, I was remembering some things and I think your mom might be right, Cassie."

"Might be? Marcus, she asked my mother if she could bring Buster. There isn't any *might be* to it, is there, Shemp?" Cassie couldn't believe that Marcus had doubted her for even a second.

"Well, I'm asking her when she gets home tonight," Marcus said. "I'm going to demand the truth."

"Well, when she fesses up, and she has too, she can't just drop a bomb on you next week at the barbeque, I'll expect you to call and apologize for doubting my mother's word. Deal?" Cassie asked.

"Deal," Marcus replied, and they tapped elbows to seal the agreement.

When Marcus picked Cassie up for school on Tuesday morning, her first words were, "I didn't hear the phone ring last night."

"That's because Mama didn't get home until after midnight, it was too late to call. Your dad would have had a conniption fit if the phone rang that late," Marcus meekly replied.

"Okay then, Marcus. What was the verdict?" Cassie was anxious to hear her vindication.

"Well, it seems that Buster usually has his sister's family over for Memorial Day, but one of her sons has the chicken pox and so they had to cancel." Marcus was relishing this opportunity to zing Cassie. "So, Buster had already ordered steaks from his butcher and had no one to feed them to. And Mama had told him about us coming to your parents' house and so he offered to give your mother the steaks."

"So, what's that have to do with the price of tea in China, Marcus. The fact remains that Margaret still asked about bringing Buster." Cassie pointed out that her original evidence still stood.

"Well, Twigs, Mama didn't think it was right for Buster to spend all that money on the steaks, and then spend the holiday at home by himself. So, she asked your mother if he could join in at your house." Marcus was having so much fun. "So, I guess the bottom line is, you are wrong. They are not dating. Now don't you feel bad for spreading false rumors. I think you owe me an apology."

Cassie did feel bad for giving Marcus grief over something that now looked as though she had blown way out of proportion. "Okay, Marcus, I'm sorry. But I didn't spread any rumors. I didn't tell a soul besides you."

"Okay," Marcus said with a shy smile. "Apology accepted."

That afternoon Marcus had to be at work by four p.m. As was habit on days he worked, he pulled up in front of Cassie's house, shut the car off and raced around to the other side to open her door. A quick kiss and he was on his way back to the driver's side. As Cassie started up the sidewalk, and before he got back into the Metro, Marcus called out, "Hey Cass." When she turned, he smiled broadly and said, "Just kidding, Buster Finkel doesn't have a sister."

"So that means they are dating? I knew it." She called back, laughing.

"You win, Twigs." Marcus said as he got back into the car.

"I knew you were joshing me, Shemp," Cassie yelled, making sure she got in the last word.

When he first walked into the shop, Marcus didn't immediately spot Simon. He headed straight to the back, grabbed his shirt from the rack and made his way into the employee restroom. Marcus hurriedly changed and proceeded out onto the floor. He stood next to the timeclock waiting and precisely at four o'clock he punched in. Marcus turned from the clock and walked toward Simon's bay. He saw the open toolbox and a Ford Fairlane with its hood up, but still no Simon. Although Marcus had a pretty good idea where he was. He waited patiently, leaning against the Ford's left front fender until he saw Simon emerge from the employee restroom.

"Hey Marcus," Simon yelled across the shop. "Coke or Nehi?"

"Coke. Thanks Simon," Marcus responded. From twenty feet away and from all indications, Simon appeared to be his normal self. He had smiled when he had called out Marcus' name, so Marcus took that as a good sign. He was afraid Simon would be upset with him. And he was slightly apprehensive that Cassie's theory might have been correct.

Marcus walked over to the break table, took a seat, and picked up the bottle of Coke. Before he could open his mouth, Simon spoke.

226

"I know just what you're thinking, Marcus," he began.

Marcus felt relieved. As nice of a guy as Simon was, Marcus was almost certain that he was going to say that Marcus shouldn't feel bad, that he certainly wasn't his fault that the gold had been stolen. But Simon's words were not at all what Marcus had expected and was prepared to hear.

"I was on the toilet and heard you come in the bathroom to get dressed, and I thought to myself, should I or shouldn't I?" Simon paused and Marcus was truly afraid of what he was about to say. "And I decided against it." Simon picked up his Coke and casually took a long swallow.

"Okay, Simon, what did you decide against?" Marcus asked, expecting the worst.

"Courtesy flush, Marcus," Simon smiled. "I know it smelled pretty rough in there, but I decided against a courtesy flush. Call me sick, but I thought it would be funny, and a damned righteous decision, don't you agree?" Simon could not even sit up straight and he bent over in laughter. Marcus joined in, perhaps laughing more out of relief than because of the humor. And even though the joke was on him, it really was quite funny. After being pranked himself, he felt a little bit of remorse for pulling the earlier joke on Cassie. *What comes around, goes around* he thought to himself. Or maybe *you reap what you sow.* Marcus shook away the thoughts. This particular moment did not feel like a good time for moralizing.

But Marcus did want to get serious. "Simon, I feel really bad about the gold. I swear it was there last summer when Cassie and I went out to check on it. If I had known it belonged to you and your tribe, I would have brought it back and put it in the bank or something. You know I would have saved it for you. If I had only known."

"I know you would have, Marcus. And it's okay. It's not your fault. I prayed to my ancestors last night. I put my faith in their hands and I'm sure everything will turn out fine. If we are meant to have that gold, it will still happen. We just need faith that's all." Simon exhibited his perpetual smile and Marcus was overcome by a sense of calm. Somehow he knew Simon was telling the truth.

"Hey, Marcus, speaking of faith, at the revival last week, did you see the old man that was sitting next to me?"

Marcus wasn't sure how to respond. He couldn't very well acknowledge the old man because, even though he was certain that it had been Neville, there was no doubt that he would only be opening a proverbial can of worms. Marcus knew he was in no position to even attempt an explanation of the Englishman's existence nor could he admit to how he would have known him. Therefore, in the grand scheme of things, Marcus failed to see a single reason to admit, or benefit from, an acknowledgement of anything about the man.

"No, I didn't see him, Simon. Why?" Marcus asked innocently.

"Well, obviously the old man knew you," Simon explained. "He came in here this afternoon. Wasn't in a car or anything, he just kind of showed up at the open bay door. He asked me to give Marcus a message."

"I definitely don't know who this guy is," Marcus spoke unconvincingly, "but what was the message?"

"Whether you know him or not doesn't really matter, I don't suppose. But he sure as heck knew your name. Either he wrote it on here or maybe somebody else just gave him the note to deliver, but either way, here it is with your name on it plain as day."

"What does it say?" Marcus was hesitant to take the folded sheet of paper that Simon had removed from his breast pocket.

"I don't know, Marcus. It's got your name on it, not mine. Far as I can tell, it ain't none of my business." Simon pressed the note into Marcus' hand.

Marcus unfolded the paper and silently read the few words that were carefully hand printed in very neat and legible block letters. The style was not exactly what Marcus would identify as calligraphy, but with the detailed letter formation that was used, Marcus was reminded of historic items that had been written with perhaps a quill or old-fashioned fountain pen.

"Jacob Timmons. Have Deputy Daniels run background."

* * * *

Monday, June 9 had finally arrived and Cassie had accompanied Marcus to his appointment with Dr.

Alan Copeland. Aware that she would have to remain in the waiting room while Marcus was seen, she had hoped that her presence would provide a psychological boost and help him to remain calm and confident. She was also quite sure that had she not come along, there stood a very real likelihood that Marcus would have gotten cold feet and bailed at the last minute. Cassie was mildly surprised when Marcus was led into the doctor's private office at exactly ten a.m., just as scheduled. The receptionist carried a thin folder in her left hand as she escorted Marcus in and introduced him to Dr. Copeland.

The doctor stood and offered a firm handshake. Marcus made his own amateur assessment of a man who obviously possessed extreme self-confidence. He wondered if the doctor had formed a reciprocal opinion. Along with the heavy English dialect, one of Marcus' initial observations was that the doctor's hairstyle and round-rimmed glasses reminded him of John Lennon's image on the *Sgt. Pepper's Lonely Hearts Club Band* album cover, sans the elaborate uniform, of course. The first words the doctor spoke were an immediate cause to put Marcus at ease. The protocol for every prior visit to a medical doctor that Marcus had experienced had demanded that the provider be addressed as Doctor So-and-So. But Dr. Copeland was quite different.

"From today on, Marcus, you and I are on a first-name basis. You are required to call me Alan, or Al if you prefer. I want you to feel free and calm. We will become friends, you and me. You will speak your mind freely, whatever thoughts occur to you, express yourself with absolutely no qualms whatsoever. Nothing you ever say will be cause for judgement on my part, and please know that you are totally free of embarrassment. Nothing you would ever say could shock me or cause any ill will toward you. I am here to help you, that is my only goal. Your intake paperwork indicates to me that you are dealing with issues regarding guilt. Your initial appointment provides for a two hour window for you to get all of your preliminary history out into the open. I'll need you to start wherever you feel may have been the beginning of your perceived issues. I prefer not to waste your valuable time, so if everything I've expressed and explained to this point is satisfactory with you, why don't we get down to brass tacks?"

Wow, what an introductory speech, thought Marcus. Feeling relaxed and at ease, Marcus started with his parents. Marcus described the loss of his mother and father and the feelings of extreme loss. He explained the love, care, and nurturing he had received from his stepmother and stressed the importance of her insistence that they attend church regularly. He told the doctor how his prayers had provided solace, that he visited the graves of his parents regularly, and that he had reached inner peace with their loss. Dr. Copeland listened intently, and despite the fact that Marcus was detailing what he thought was an enormous amount of information, the doctor had failed to jot a single note on his notebook. The only thing Marcus could discern from his angle on the couch – just like in the movies, he was lying on a couch – was that the doctor, Alan, had carefully printed as a header at the top of the page his name, Marcus Clemens.

Dr. Copeland asked a few mundane and routine questions before Marcus began relating the events of 1963 when Oliver and Ellis Compton had attempted to filch an inheritance that Marcus had been designated to receive on his eighteenth birthday. The surreptitious plan that Ollie had carefully devised was to have Marcus eliminated or sentenced to jail. According to information Ollie had received, either result would lead to Ellis being the only surviving and legally eligible descendent of Mark Twain. Marcus described how he and Cassie had nearly met their demise in the mausoleum of the cemetery, and how Cassie had later been kidnapped and held hostage before the plan was ultimately thwarted.

"It was devastating, Alan," Marcus said with tears in his eyes. "Cassie had done absolutely nothing to have deserved being pulled into things. When we found her that night was when I realized that she was the most important thing in the world to me."

"Marcus, it's been six years since those events. With the passage of time, have those feelings changed or lessened?" Dr. Copeland asked as he tried to gauge the depth of Marcus' feelings toward Cassie.

"Oh no, Doc, not at all. If anything they have grown stronger," Marcus wanted to be crystal clear in explaining his dedication to Cassie. "We will be together forever, there's no doubt in my mind. We've been told that we share a lifelong commitment to one another."

"And who told you that, Marcus?" the doctor asked, delving ever so much deeper.

Marcus was stymied. He had revealed too much. Alan had convinced him to open up, to hold nothing back, and now he had gone too far.

"I guess you could say, we received word from above," Marcus tried to dance around the truth.

"So you're saying that God spoke to you?" Alan wasn't dancing, he wanted to reach the gist of the matter, to learn the truth, find out the real motivating factors behind Marcus' thinking.

"In a manner of speaking, yes, I guess so. I mean, I guess like in a roundabout manner." Marcus was wavering, but still found himself dancing.

"So how did you feel about Ellis? I mean you learned that he was related to you, and my guess is you never knew about that did you?" The doctor was interested in every aspect of Marcus' makeup.

"No, I didn't. And I hated him, I wished he was dead. He might have killed Cassie and I, both of us, although he told me later that he wouldn't have done it, that I guess, it was just a threat." Marcus found himself with tears beginning to well up again. "I know he wouldn't have because I found out later that he also had a lifelong commitment to me. I didn't really understand any of that at first, I guess it took a while. But now I do, I get the whole picture. And that's a lot of the reason I'm here to see you, Alan."

"I don't know that I understand all you're saying, Marcus." Dr. Copeland was playing coy but using the coyness to extract deeper feelings and emotions from his subject. "Can you fill me in a little more? Marcus, are you telling me that after all the terrible occurrences that

233

you have already described and attributed to Ellis, that he had the nerve and gumption to come back into your life once again?"

"Yes, he did, Alan." Marcus proceeded to give a full accounting of both his and Cassie's initial confrontation and then Ellis' second attempt to reconcile with Marcus. He told Alan of the forgiveness he and Cassie had extended and of the bond the three of them had developed. The saga had culminated with their discovery of the gold bars in the cave and their subsequent capture by the goons employed by Max Schoenfeld. The most difficult part of the story for him to relate were the events that had transpired at the pond, especially the final scene when he had crested the small incline and witnessed Ellis' lifeless body cradled in the arms of Marcus' friend, Deputy Mitchell Daniels. With the final words, Marcus burst into uncontrollable tears.

Giving Marcus a moment to regain control, Dr. Copeland offered up an unexpected question.

"Marcus, you've told me of Ellis' father, but what of his mother? What can you tell me about her?" Marcus had neglected to even mention Alicia.

"Not very much, Alan. Ellis barely mentioned her. She was very quiet when we all went to her house after the funeral, which I suppose was only natural." Marcus thought back, remembering that her red hair was touched by flecks of gray and he even recalled thinking that she had probably been attractive when she was twenty or so years younger. Looking back now, it dawned on him that she might even have represented a peek into his own future. He could see a slight resemblance in the profile and it occurred to him that her appearance might have been a prelude to Cassie's look in another twenty years. The thoughts and recollections seemed to help alleviate and release the past ten minutes of intensified grief and Marcus somehow felt a slight sense of relief.

"Here is a suggestion, Marcus. Go and visit her, Ellis' mother. I'm sure she would welcome seeing you. And it might be good for both your souls to sit for a few moments and reminisce."

"You might be right, Alan. I had never thought of talking to her about him. There's a lot that I'd like to know about him, you know about his childhood and growing up and all." Marcus felt a touch of inspiration in learning more about his cousin.

"Well, I think today has been a watershed moment for you, Marcus. I think what you have been seeking is the release that you have just experienced." Dr. Copeland was being truthful in his assessment. He felt that the pent-up emotions had been at the root of Marcus' emotional discomfort all along. "This has been a marvelous session for you Marcus. You have made unbelievable strides in just this one extended session. Your time is nearly gone, but I do want to know something else. I still can sense some reservation on your part. Is there another current issue or problem that is troubling you? Is there anything that might relate to Cassie perhaps?"

"No, Alan. Cassie and I are fine and we are very much in love." Despite getting the whole story involving Ellis out into the open, Marcus still felt the heavy weight of the guilt he was carrying in regard to the gold that had been stolen and he was still saddled by sorrow over the disappointment that Simon had suffered because of his carelessness. If he had only removed the gold. There had been so much time and opportunity over the past two years. He only wished he would have done something proactively.

Marcus spent the last ten minutes of his session explaining the discovery and subsequent loss of the gold bars. He briefly told Alan of his grandfather's treasure map, of him and Ellis finding the cave and its bounty, and of learning that it had belonged to his friend's ancestors. Attempting to present the depressing tale of lost fortune, Marcus was also striving to express the guilt, angst, and remorse that he bore as a direct result of what he viewed as his dereliction of responsibility.

"There is no need to feel guilt or responsibility, Marcus." Dr. Copeland made the effort to reassure his patient. "Those bars had remained safely hidden for over a century and should obviously not have gone anywhere. You had no control over the fact that, for no rhyme or reason, someone happened upon them just as both you and your grandfather had. The only difference was that this person did not have the moral conscience of you and your grandfather."

"Maybe you're right, Alan," Marcus replied glumly.

"Of course I am, Marcus. I get paid to be right," the doctor said with a smile.

The two of them rose and returned to the waiting room, where Dr. Copeland warmly greeted Cassie.

"You, my dear, must be the lovely girlfriend Cassie," Dr. Copeland said as he took her right hand in his, covering it with his left hand. "You two make a marvelous pair, I must say." The words brought a broad smile to Cassie's face.

Marcus interrupted to profess his need to use the restroom before beginning the drive back. "The lavatory is located back through that door and just at the end of the hallway on the left," the doctor directed as he pointed back to the open door they had just passed through. Marcus excused himself and headed toward the hallway.

After Marcus had disappeared from sight, Dr. Copeland put his hand gently on Cassie's shoulder and said in his most reassuring manner, "Marcus will be just fine. I think one more visit and his minor little hangups will be a thing of the past."

"Oh that's wonderful to hear, Dr. Copeland," Cassie gushed.

"But do me a favor. And do keep in mind not to tell him that I advised you of this, you know patient-doctor confidentiality and all, he can't be told that I spoke these words to you." Dr. Copeland leaned in close to Cassie's ear and spoke softly to minimize any possibility of being overheard. "Marcus informed me of a note that he was given and that he keeps folded in his wallet. I need you to somehow make sure that he does what the note has instructed him to do. The message was delivered in earnest and it is a very important request that he comply with the words therein."

The Big City

Marcus had been both pleased and relieved by his visit with Dr. Copeland, but by the end of the week he had reached the conclusion that further sessions were not really necessary. That was not to say that he was no longer wracked with guilt over the disappearance of the gold bars, but he had taken the doctor's words to heart. The bars had been safely stored in the cubby hole behind the wall for over one hundred years. The cave itself had been well hidden, the entrance was extremely small, and there was positively nothing that could possibly have drawn attention to it. There was no reason on earth that anyone would ever have suspected what might have secretly been hidden three hundred yards down in its dank and dark recesses within. The fact that the gold had been discovered and taken had been an absolute one in a million shot if ever one existed. The only other possibility being that someone, somehow, also had knowledge of it being there. Marcus and Cassie had discussed that scenario, but the likelihood or possibility seemed infinitesimally remote, at best.

When leaving Dr. Copeland's office, Marcus had scheduled a second session for two weeks in advance, on Monday, June 23. The doctor had recommended that he return the following week, on the sixteenth, but he and Cassie had already made plans for the Monday and Tuesday of that week. She and Marcus, along with her parents Jack and Debbie, were going to make a two day trip to St. Louis. Cassie had planned for a scheduled a visit to Washington University where she had hoped to begin her pre-med program. Marcus was more or less just tagging along. They were going on Tuesday for his unscheduled, impromptu visits at the University of Missouri's St. Louis campus and time permitting, possibly St. Louis Community College. Both of Marcus' potential schools were less than a fifteen minute drive from where Cassie was hoping she would be applying. On this particular visit, dormitory accommodations would be discussed, especially for Cassie. When the time came, Marcus had dreams of perhaps finding some form of part-time employment at a tire center or auto repair shop and renting himself a small apartment. Of course, they both harbored the very real ambition of sharing an apartment in St. Louis but had dared not initiate that conversation with her parents. Jack and Debbie were still very protective of Cassie, and while she was approaching her senior year of high school, she was still viewed as their *little girl*. The subject of their possible cohabitation would be one well worth remaining off the table until after graduation next summer.

Marcus sat at the snack bar on Sunday evening, the night before they planned to drive to St. Louis, chatting idly with Cassie. Marcus was well aware that Cassie's education was the main and overriding focus of tomorrow's trip. Encouraged by her parents, Cassie had long held aspirations of becoming a medical doctor. She hadn't yet made a decision on a specialty and was far from thinking that far ahead. The main concentration during her senior year was going to be to maintain her 4.0 grade point average and ensuring the likelihood of her acceptance at Washington University. During her undergraduate studies she could gain more insight and seek additional knowledge in regard to the various medical fields that may or may not serve her interests and desires. Marcus was fairly certain that his future would most likely be along the lines of what he was currently doing. While he enjoyed working on cars, and he did find it both challenging and satisfying, he wasn't totally sold on the prospect of still getting his hands greasy every day when he was Chester Bernstein's age. Marcus' expectation was to get a degree in business administration and, at the very least, eventually open a repair shop of his own. His pipedream would be to own his own car dealership, and specifically he yearned to be an auto broker for an upscale foreign manufacturer. It would be Marcus' absolute dream come true to one day own a BMW or Ferrari dealership.

"Excited about tomorrow?" Cassie asked, breaking Marcus away from the dreamy illusion he was envisioning of sitting behind the wheel of his very own green twelve cylinder 365 GTS convertible.

"Oh yeah, for sure. You too, right?" Marcus answered as he brought himself back to the reality of having dinner in a bowling alley and still being the proud owner of a well-worn turquoise and white 1959 Nash Metropolitan.

"I'm really looking forward to seeing to the big city itself more than anything. I can't believe I'm going to be eighteen and haven't been to St. Louis since I was like in the fourth grade. I hardly even remember it at all. I've got faint memories of the zoo, but not very much except for Phil the Gorilla." Cassie said with a sad and forlorn look in her eyes.

"Who is Phil the Gorilla?" The moniker was definitely one Marcus had never heard before.

"You never heard of Phil the Gorilla? He was this famous gorilla that they had at the zoo, but he died a few years before I got to see him," Cassie's explanation only served to confuse Marcus.

"I don't get it, Cass. You just said he died before you got to see him, but before that you said he was one of your few memories from the zoo. I guess I don't follow what you're saying," Marcus wasn't exactly asking a direct question, but he obviously was requesting some elaboration on Phil the Gorilla.

Cassie laughed, "Yeah, I suppose that was like an Abbott and Costello routine kind of explanation wasn't it?" Cassie drew a deep breath and said, "Let me try again in plain English. Phil the Gorilla was a big attraction at the zoo, up until he died. But because he had been so popular, they had him stuffed and then they put him out on display. That's when I saw him, when he was already dead and stuffed. But anyway, he was huge and I was fascinated by him. Which I guess is why seeing him stuck in my memory."

"Good gosh, Cassie, that sounds gross to me. Why would people want to look at a stuffed dead gorilla? Yuck!" The whole idea seemed revolting to Marcus.

"Well, they claim he was like a local icon. I guess people didn't want him to be gone. But personally, I thought it was pretty cool." Cassie attempted to defend her long held fascination with Phil the Gorilla.

"I don't know, Sweetie. To me, that would be like if Walt McMurphy died. He's an icon around here, right? Do you think they should stuff him and then stand his stuffed corpse in the waiting room at the shop, for Pete's sake?" Marcus asked as he drew what he felt was an accurate analogy.

"No, Marcus. That would be gross," Cassie exclaimed.

"Why? What's the difference, dead is dead isn't it? You're the one who's going to be a doctor. Would you want one of your patients to die and then his family just get him stuffed?" Marcus knew his question was more rhetorical than actual.

"You're talking about moral issues now Marcus. Different people are going to have different opinions." Cassie was taking umbrage with Marcus' stance. "It's one thing to stuff an animal but it's quite a different matter with a human being."

"Cassie, I'd bet a dollar to a doughnut that there are people out there right now that have dead relatives stuffed and then they keep them right there in their homes." As much as Cassie disagreed with what Marcus had been saying, she had to admit that he did have a point.

"Okay Marcus, I'll concede that there are whackos in the world who just might possibly do something like that, but let's face it, they would have to be crazy. No sane person would ever revert to that type of behavior. That's just not normal, it wouldn't be acceptable. No society would never condone stuffing human beings," Cassie said emphatically.

"What about the mummies?" Marcus asked. "Isn't that the same thing?"

"I meant modern society, Marcus. And mummies aren't the same thing as you're talking about anyway. Enough about stuffing either people or animals. The whole subject is making me sick to my stomach." Cassie was ready for one of them to turn the conversation in a different direction.

"Cassie, will you fix me a burger? And make it rare please, with lots of blood." Marcus almost choked from laughing so hard at his joke.

After throwing a wet dish towel at Marcus, Cassie turned the talk back toward him, "So Marcus, speaking of whackos, what did you decide about appointment your next week?" Marcus had been wavering all week long about returning for his session with Dr. Copeland that was scheduled for next Monday. He had been weighing the pros and cons. Cassie felt it wise for him to continue and that he should go at least once more, but Marcus had been resistant to returning. In the end it had been his decision to make and Cassie had vowed to support whatever conclusion he reached.

Marcus had made up his mind as he lay in bed Thursday night, although he had not shared his plans with Cassie.

"I cancelled the appointment on Friday," he said.

"Why Marcus?" She asked. "The doctor said you had made great progress. I really thought you would go back at least once more."

"Cassie, you said you'd support me whatever I decided to do, remember?"

"And I do, Marcus. I really do. I'm fine with you not going back." Cassie said one thing, but her facial expression certainly told a different story. Marcus thought the word *disappointment* may as well have been written in bold black letters across her forehead.

"Really?" Marcus asked.

"Yes," was the one word solemn response.

"Hey, now I'll have an extra forty dollars to spend on you in St. Louis!"

"Now you're talking," Cassie said laughing. "I love you, Marcus."

"Love you, too, Sweetie," he said with a wink.

* * * *

They got off to a bright and early start on Monday morning. Marcus parked at the curb and checked his lucky Timex watch. It was the same watch that Margaret had given him on his twelfth birthday and it still was perfectly accurate, even though it was now almost a full six years old. The time shown was precisely five-fifty-six a.m., and after taking a couple of moments to gather his duffel bag and umbrella (sadly, the forecast called for intermittent showers throughout the Midwest for the entirety of the week), Marcus cruised up the sidewalk and was ringing the doorbell at six o'clock sharp.

Cassie opened the door and stood with the doorknob in one, her red toothbrush in the other, and a smiling mouth that was overflowing with Colgate's finest. When it came to dental care, Cassie was quite fortunate to have not grown up with Margaret as a mother. Marcus had spent his first thirteen years brushing with *Arm and Hammer Baking Soda*, before finally convincing Margaret to spring for actual toothpaste. After setting his bag and umbrella on the floor just inside the door and being cautious not to get the white froth on his face or in his hair, Marcus gave Cassie a warm hug.

"Breakfast is about ready," Cassie sputtered the words with a protruding chin as she struggled not to spew toothpaste all over the floor. "Go ahead to the kitchen while I rinse my mouth," she instructed.

Marcus entered the kitchen and greeted Cassie's mother as he pulled out a chair and sat down.

"Good morning, Marcus," Debbie Worthington said as she turned and brought a plate full of pancakes to the table. "Are you excited for today?"

"Yes ma'am, you bet. I've never been to St. Louis; I'm looking forward to having my first look see at a big city." Marcus had survived now for nearly eighteen years and had never been to St. Louis. In fact, he never remembered having ever been further south than

Hannibal. For that matter, he had hardly seen anything east of the Mississippi River either, beyond infrequent visits to Quincy. Admittedly, he was a country boy through and through.

"Wow, Marcus, that's interesting. I never realized you were such a homebody. In all these years of speaking with you, you always seemed very worldly. I suppose I had just naturally assumed you had done some traveling at least." In Debbie's mind, Marcus had always appeared knowledgeable in regard to geography and landmarks and such.

"Nope, just good teachers and a lot of reading I reckon," he said with a wide and toothy grin.

"Well, it's too bad we won't have time for a lot of sightseeing while we're there. Cassandra has already mentioned the zoo, but I had to decline her request. I mean, that would take an entire day in itself. The St. Louis zoo is a sprawling complex." Debbie regretted having to nix Cassie's desire. "That girl still swears that was her most favorite place she's ever been."

"Cassie was just telling me about that last night," Marcus replied. "She seems to have quite an infatuation with Phil the Gorilla."

"She actually loved that display," Debbie said. "I, myself, found it horrific. That creature looked like an absolute monster to me. It was so huge. I don't know, maybe because it brought back memories of that movie *King Kong*." Debbie had to wrap her arms around herself as she shuddered. "I watched that movie when I was twelve or thirteen and I swear to you that I had nightmares for at least two weeks."

"Oh, it wasn't as bad as you're making it out, darling." Marcus hadn't noticed Cassie's dad, Jack, leaning against the door jamb with arms folded across his chest listening in on the conversation. "Phil just looked like a big old monkey standing there. Heck, I doubt he was even as tall as you, Debbie. And they say when he was alive, he was gentle as a lamb."

"Well, I thought he looked mean, like a smaller version of King Kong for sure." Debbie maintained the frightening demeanor that Phil had represented to her.

Catching the tail end of her mother's words as she was approaching the kitchen, Cassie had to chime in with her two cents worth, "I loved Phil. I wonder if he'll still be there the next time we visit the zoo?"

"We'll find out when we start school there next year, Cass. I promise that one of the first things we'll do is spend a Saturday at the zoo." Marcus' words put a smile on Cassie's face. The only drawback to his promise was that would have to wait for more than another year.

After breakfast, and right on schedule, the Worthington's car was loaded and they were southbound on U.S. Highway 61 by seven-thirty. There was a slight drizzle for the majority of the drive, and Jack was forced to adjust his speed accordingly, but they still made pretty good time and arrived more than twenty minutes early for the ten-thirty a.m. appointment with Cassie's potential student counselor.

Compared to what they were accustomed to at Lewis and Clark High School, the Washington University campus was nearly a sprawling city unto itself. To her parents, with the complex commanding an area in the neighborhood of two thousand acres, the thought of Cassie trying to locate buildings and classrooms on her own seemed that it would be a daunting proposition. But confident as always, Cassie shrugged away any of those concerns with a simple sentence or two.

"I know how to read maps, and I'm not afraid to ask for directions," was her calming response when Debbie voiced her concern. "And I'll always have Marcus to rely on if I do encounter problems. You both know that Marcus would never let anything happen to me, he would defend me with his life. That's true right, Marcus?" Cassie asked as she looked over at her boyfriend.

"Absolutely. I would fall on me sword for you, m'lady," he answered with a bow and in his best Shakespearean dialect.

"Laying it on a little aren't you, Marcus?" Jack joked as he glanced into the backseat at his future son-in-law.

After a delicious steak dinner at a restaurant called *The Flaming Pit*, a popular local establishment that had been highly recommended by the clerk at the hotel where Jack had arranged for them to stay, the five of them took a ride around the city. They took a few photographs of some of the landmarks like the historic Old Courthouse (the site of the famous Dred Scott trial which ultimately served as a steppingstone of sorts to the Civil War), the still relatively new Gateway Arch (a 630 foot tall monument that celebrated St. Louis' rightful place in the nation's expansion to the west coast), and Jack's personal favorite, Busch Memorial Stadium (home to the local major league baseball and football teams, with both franchises ironically sharing the name of St. Louis Cardinals).

Other than photographs in books and magazines, Cassie and Marcus had no recollection of anything like it. They were in awe of the size of the city itself as well as the massive enormity of the buildings, all the impressive architecture, and the sheer mass of human beings occupying the streets and sidewalks. The experience was only serving to whet their young appetites. They had come to St. Louis not yet entirely sold on the idea of continuing their respective educations there. But after tasting just one day of big city life, their minds were nearly made up.

Tuesday morning was again essentially spent riding around the city. The first obligatory destinations were the St. Louis campus of the University of Missouri and St. Louis Community College. No official visits had been scheduled, Marcus had merely wanted to get an eyes on, firsthand look at the schools. He had plenty of time to make a decision and apply for admission. It wasn't a particular matter of importance to him which if either of those two he attended. There were other options in and around the city and time was on his side. The important purpose of the trip had been satisfied yesterday. Cassie's education had been the primary focus of making this excursion and Marcus knew he would be satisfied with whatever crumbs he was afforded. His only interest was in being there with Cassie, wherever the journey might lead.

They had a quick lunch at a *White Castle* chain restaurant. The hamburgers sold there would have brought tears of laughter to someone like Buster Finkel. Buster prided himself on the size, texture, and flavor of his hamburgers and cheeseburgers. He took great pride in serving a burger that was worth every penny that his customer invested. Even at a price of only a dime apiece, he would have viewed these tiny things as nothing more than appetizers. He certainly would not have labeled them in the category of *hamburgers*.

While having their lunch, Debbie entered into a conversation with a lady at the next table. Trying to decide how to spend a few hours before heading home, she asked the woman if there were any unique shops or boutiques in the immediate area.

"I always like to bring relatives from out of town over to Cherokee Street," she suggested. "I don't think anything there would qualify as being a boutique, but you will find some pretty unique shops featuring out of the ordinary items."

When they returned to the car, Jack opened the floor for suggestions, "What would everybody like to do for about two hours?"

"Let's go up in the Arch," Cassie's now eleven year old brother begged.

"No, son," Jack said, "I'm afraid that might take too long and I'm sure it will be busy, probably tons of people down at the riverfront. Between the crowd for the Arch and the tourists checking out the riverboat and sightseeing everything, that place will probably be a boondoggle. We'll need to do that another day when we have more time to spend down there. Sorry champ."

"Well Jack, the lady I just spoke with said we're only a few blocks from an area she said was good for shopping for out of the ordinary stuff called Cherokee Street. Why don't we spend a little time window shopping before we get on the road?" Debbie knew that Jack would not be overly enthusiastic about wandering through a gaggle of shops for a couple of hours, but she thought the kids might enjoy looking at things that might be different and unique compared to the mundane fair they were used to seeing at their local dime store.

Jack merely shrugged and asked, "Which way did she say to go?"

They parked and Jack dropped a quarter in the parking meter to reserve his space for the next three hours, plus the eight minutes that the car before him had left unused. The first storefront they entered was slightly reminiscent of *Franklin's Five and Dime*. Once passing through the door, the cash register was located to the right and there was a soda fountain on their left with a magazine rack behind the swivel chairs. Jack happened to notice the menu board above and behind the soda counter.

"Yep, kids, we're in the big city, alright." Looking up at the sign, Jack went on to read aloud the item that had captured his attention. *"Frozen Coke,"* the sign had been hand-lettered in bold red letters. "Any of you ever had a frozen Coke before?"

None of them had ever heard the term before, but the description itself did sound appealing on a hot June afternoon. Jack proceeded to order five of them as everyone planted on a cushioned swivel seat, identical to the ones at *Franklin's*.

Being the youngest, Charlie was the first to be stricken. "Ow," he yelped as he set his drink on the counter and squeezed both palms against his temples.

The soda jerk immediately turned his head to Charlie. "First frozen Coke?" The young man laughed as he looked toward Jack and Debbie. Jack nodded in the affirmative. "Brain freeze," the soda jerk said nonchalantly. "Happens if you drink too much too quick. Feels like your head is gonna explode, but don't worry, it goes away in a minute."

Charlie began to show signs of relief, but Jack couldn't resist laughing at his misfortune.

Marcus looked at Cassie and said, "I gotta try it for myself." He sucked down as much as he could in one long draw on his straw. It only took a couple of seconds to register. "Oh my God." Marcus squeezed his temples in complete agony and Cassie began laughing uncontrollably. After a few seconds, Marcus looked to Cassie and said, "Your turn."

"No way, I'm not stupid like you two. I've seen enough that I don't want to know what it feels like." Cassie had made a quick decision and told Marcus, "In the words of William Shakespeare's Falstaff, *caution is preferable to rash bravery.*"

"Who is Falstaff?" Marcus asked. "I only thought that was a beer."

"Geez, Marcus. Didn't you pay any attention during English literature?" Cassie asked. "He was a character in *King Henry the Fourth, Part One*. That's who the beer was named after, I would think. And that's the line that evolved into the saying *discretion is the better part of valor.*"

"Oh, okay," was the only response Marcus could muster.

Finishing up their frozen Cokes without further incident, the group left the store and began exploring other shops. Becoming bored with the knickknacks and antique boutiques that all seemed the same to him, Marcus' attention was drawn to a storefront on the opposite side of the street.

"Hey, look over there, Cass," Marcus said as he pointed to the unique business with the clumsily shaped words *Dunberry's Taxidermy* painted in its shop window.

"Let's go check that out while your folks are looking at more antiques," Marcus suggested. "You won't see Phil the Gorilla this trip, but you might find something else even more memorable in there."

The thought of a taxidermist's shop did pique Cassie's interest. She informed her mother as to where they were going, promising to be back in ten minutes. The two of them blatantly jaywalked across the street and a small bell chimed as they opened the door and entered the dark and dimly lit shop. There was a strangely pungent odor in the air that Marcus could not identify. He had initially suspected it to be the smell of death, but soon decided it wasn't that nasty or grotesque. He had smelled dead animals in the woods, and what he detected wasn't close. This was more acidic, perhaps more along the lines of acetone or some other chemical. Surprisingly, Cassie didn't seem to be bothered by the odor, in fact she appeared quite interested in the scattered variety of animals that were on display. They had only been in the shop for two or three minutes when a middle-aged gentleman made his appearance, slowly limping through gray curtains that apparently served to separate the display floor and the back room where the actual work was performed.

Wiping his hands on a heavily soiled apron, the shopkeeper studied the two teenagers for a brief moment before asking, "Can I help you kids? You looking for a trophy for one of your fathers, or just looking? I'm kind of busy, but lots of folks like to just check this place out, find out how I do what I do."

"Um, well actually, I guess we were just kind of looking," Marcus stammered.

"Actually, sir," Cassie chimed in, "I'm the one that was interested. I think what you do is fascinating. I'm planning to go into medicine when I graduate high school and I think there's kind of a correlation between people and animals, you know?" Cassie was afraid she might have come off as a dopey teenager who had no clue as to what she was trying to say and probably appeared to be an idiot.

"You gonna be a nurse?" The man asked.

"Oh, no sir. I'm going to be a doctor," she replied.

"That's pretty uppity for a girl, being a doctor. Don't think I've ever seen one. You know, I mean a girl was a doctor." Cassie couldn't read the salt and pepper whiskered face; the man could have been expressing disdain or it could also have been that he was impressed with Cassie's ambition.

"My name's Dirk, Dirk Dunberry. Been owning this place since I got throwed out of the army. Probably woulda stayed in, but they wouldn't let me after a bastard Gerry blasted my leg up with machine gun scatter. Such is life though, right?"

"It's good you found a trade that keeps you going Mr. Dunberry," Marcus said.

"I didn't find the trade, young fella. It was bred into me. My pappy did the same thing, taught it to me when I was a little kid. He had a place up north, right up until he passed. I kept it for a spell, but then got drafted in '41 and the bank ended up taking it. Hard to keep up a mortgage on the seventy-one dollars Uncle Sam was kind enough to pay me whilst I was over there in Europe fighting his war for him."

Considering some of the first words out of Dirk Dunberry's mouth was that he was busy, the man sure seemed to be more than happy to chew the fat and give his unsolicited life story.

"So anyhow, yeah, between what I pull in here and my disability and veteran's benefits, I get by okay. Thanks for asking."

Marcus and Cassie were both beginning to suspect that the old timer just might be a five of diamonds short of a full deck. But at the same time, Cassie was interested in both the man's story and what he did for a living. It dawned on Cassie that it might be the chemicals that he worked with that had affected his mental capabilities.

"If you don't mind me asking, what is that chemical smell in the air, Dirk?" Cassie asked innocently.

"Arsenic," he calmly replied. "Main ingredient, goes under the skin, helps keep insects and other critters away."

"Arsenic is poisonous isn't it?" Marcus asked.

"Well, yeah, if you was to swallow it, but who'd be foolish enough to do that? You just make sure to keep your hands wiped clean and there ain't nothing to it."

Dirk Dunberry had been using arsenic all his life and was still around to talk about it. But Cassie did wonder about its possible effects. She wondered if it could be a long term cause of mental diminishment. She also had noticed the terrible condition of the man's teeth. It appeared they were literally rotting in his mouth. If he had been drafted, probably as a teenager in 1941, he couldn't have been much more than fifty years old now. And yet he looked more like seventy.

Marcus diverted her attention when he asked a question relating to something they had just been discussing.

"Dirk, I know they had Phil the Gorilla stuffed and put on display over at the zoo and it made me wonder." Cassie could not believe Marcus was going to go there, that he was going to drag this conversation irretrievably down into the gutter. "Since a gorilla and other members of the ape family are so close to humans, would it even be possible to stuff a human being? I mean, I was just wondering."

Cassie looked anxiously to Dirk, assuming he would make some type of remark to let Marcus know what a stupid and insensitive question he had just asked. But Dirk's response took her totally by surprise and was not at all what she had expected to hear.

Dirk paused for a few unnerving seconds before saying the words Cassie never would have imagined that she would ever have heard spoken.

"Sure, it can be done. I've seen it done, I've seen the results of it being done, and I've..." Dirk suddenly stopped himself. Cassie got very scared and was overcome by a nervous feeling that caused her stomach to begin to knot up.

"I seen my pop do it. And it's a sad thing, especially if they ain't freshly dead. It takes a sick sum bitch to wanna do something like that." Dirk chewed his bottom lip and wiped his eyes as tears began to well. "And it takes a worse human being to agree to do it." Looking down, Dirk raised the tail of his apron and wiped his eyes.

Looking back up he said, "If you kids ain't buying you need to get on out of here. I'm busy, got a lot of work to do."

Without a word, Marcus took Cassie's hand and opened the door. As the tiny bell clanged once again, Cassie tool a parting glance back at Dirk before following her boyfriend back outside. They crossed the street in silence, but upon reaching the other side, Cassie spoke.

"Marcus, that man is crazy, you know that don't you?" Cassie had been deeply touched by Dirk

Dunberry, his apparent mental and physical problems, and the dark secrets he was carrying deep inside.

"Should we call someone?" Marcus asked.

"Who, Marcus?" she asked, "Who would we call?"

"Unless he opened up to someone and told them everything he just told us, there's no reason for anyone to suspect he's mentally ill. I'm getting tired, Marcus, I'm getting tired of it all. When is it going to end? When? I'm telling you; I can't take it much more."

"Take what, Cassie? Tell me, what is going on?" Marcus' heart was hurting for Cassie. It had been a long time since he'd seen her acting so vulnerable and he knew there had to be something she wasn't telling him.

"Marcus, it's just everything. It all started with Ollie and Ellis and Opa. Then it was Jeremiah and Ellis getting killed. And then the inheritance that wasn't an inheritance. Finding the gold, then Simon coming along, and then somebody steals the gold. And now there's Neville. And on top of that this happens. It's supposed to be a happy day for me. I'm making plans to go to college and become a doctor. And then we run into this whacko and you ask him stupid questions about stuffing dead people. I can't take it, Marcus." Cassie burst into tears and Marcus grasped her firmly in his arms.

"It's okay, Cass. Everything is okay, I promise," he pulled Cassie closer; he wanted her to feel protected and secure. "I'll always be here for you, Cassie. Each and every day for the rest of my life, I swear."

Cassie rubbed her face against his shirt, inadvertently wiping some of her now runny nose drippings on his chest. Looking up, she softly spoke, "Sometimes Marcus, I think maybe you are part of the problem."

Marcus was stung. Cassie had never, ever before said words to him that had hurt so badly, dug him so deeply. Did she really feel that he was part of the problem? Yes, everything had started because of his inheritance. And Cassie had always been there, she had stood by his side every step of the way. He owed everything to her, he could not have handled any of it without her support. And now, after everything, she has come to the realization that it was all his fault. Marcus could feel it, he could sense the end coming. He was going to lose her and he couldn't allow that to happen.

"I love you, Cassie. Please don't say that I'm losing you. I can't live without you." Marcus was at a loss for words. This was probably the worst he had ever felt in his entire lifetime.

"Marcus, you have to be more honest with me if you want me to be here for you. You can't go on keeping things to yourself." Cassie had no intention of breaking up with Marcus, but she wanted him to act in a manner that she knew was in his best interests.

"What do you mean, Cassie? I don't keep anything from you." Marcus didn't know what she was talking about.

"Marcus, give me your wallet." Cassie demanded.

"What for?" Marcus was totally at a loss. He pulled out his wallet and handed it to her, no more questions asked.

Cassie quickly rifled through the wallet and was not at all surprised to find a folded up piece of paper. She hurriedly opened it and read the words. *Jacob Timmons. Who in the world is Jacob Timmons?*

"Where did you get this paper, Marcus? Who is this person?" Cassie was demanding an answer.

"I don't know who it is, Cass," Marcus said.

"Did you contact Mitchell, like it says to?" She wanted to know.

"No, not yet," he offered meekly.

"Why not?" Yet another question demanding an immediate answer.

"Because I wanted to figure out who it was first," Marcus explained.

"Where did the note come from, Marcus?" Marcus asked himself if the questions were ever going to end.

Taking a deep breath, he opted for the truth, as disconcerting as he realized it was going to be.

"I got it from Simon..."

"What?" Cassie was caught off guard by this revelation.

"Wait, Cassie. Simon gave it to me, but he doesn't know what it says. Someone else gave it to him to give to me."

"And..." If this were a cartoon, Cassie would have been tapping her foot right now.

"Neville gave it to him to give to me," Marcus gave her the truth.

"Why didn't Neville just give it to you himself and explain to you who this Jacob Timmons is?" Another in the long line of unanswered questions.

"I don't know, Cass. He came to the shop when I wasn't there. He gave it to Simon to give to me, and that's all I know. I swear on the Holy Bible."

They both stood in silence.

"Marcus, you have to give this to Mitchell." Cassie was right and Marcus knew it. He didn't really know why he was delaying; he had not made any attempt to determine who Jacob Timmons was.

"I will. After school and before work tomorrow, I'll give it to him." Marcus raised his right hand and looked skyward. "I swear."

They stood in silence for a few more moments watching the traffic flow past.

"I've got a question, Cassie. How did you even know the note was in my wallet? Do you snoop through my wallet when I'm not looking?" Marcus was pretty sure that Cassie had not found it by snooping. If she had, she would already have read it and the topic wouldn't have waited this long before being brought up.

"Honestly, Dr. Copeland told me about it and he told me to make sure you acted on whatever was written in the note, but that I couldn't tell you that he was the one who had told me. You know patient-doctor confidentiality and all that jazz. He wasn't supposed to tell me because of that, but he did anyway." Cassie felt somewhat relieved to have let the cat out of the bag.

"Nope, this doesn't make sense, Cassie. How could he have known about the note?" Marcus asked aloud.

"Because you told him, I guess," she said.

"No, I didn't. The only person that knows about it is Simon and he couldn't...."

"Simon told him, Marcus. Simon had to of been the one. Simon used to be his patient, heck he's the one who sent you to him. Simon read the note and he called Dr. Copeland." At least Cassie had resolved that mystery.

"No, I disagree, Cassie. I don't think Simon would have done that. Plus, I'm just about positive that Simon didn't read the note."

"Why do you say that?" she asked.

"Because he said so and I believe him," was Marcus' feeble response.

"Whatever," Cassie said.

"There's something about that Dr. Copeland. I can't put my finger on it though," Marcus said as he put his hand to his chin as if in deep thought.

"What makes you think that, Marcus?" Cassie was curious what prompted Marcus' sudden doubt in Dr. Copeland.

"I don't know. For one thing he suggested I go talk to Alicia to learn more about Ellis' past," Marcus relayed Alan's suggestion.

"For what reason? I would think you should trying to put Ellis out of your mind and getting over him, not dredging up more memories to have to contemplate and sift through." Cassie was right. Why give himself even more to think about?

But Marcus couldn't shake the thought that there was something about Alan. There had to be some subconscious reason that he should talk to Alicia.

"You know what, Cass. As soon as we get back, I'm going to Alexandria to see Alicia. Do you want to go with me?" Marcus asked, hoping she would say yes.

"Absolutely. Maybe whatever she has to say will give me better nightmares than Dirk Dunberry and his creepy shop."

Alicia

"I hope she still lives in the same place," Cassie said as they motored north on U.S. 61. The only time they had visited Alicia's home was following the conclusion of Ellis' funeral back in July of 1967, nearly two full years ago. At that time, she and her son had resided in a two bedroom rental located on a dusty gravel road south of County Road 323, just a couple of miles west of Alexandria proper. Marcus was fairly confident of having an accurate recollection of the exact location. He knew it would take roughly thirty minutes and was approximately a twenty mile drive from Cassie's house. With them hitting the road just past seven-thirty, he hoped they would arrive in the neighborhood of eight p.m. The plan was to arrive safely ahead of dusk and yet well past anyone's normal dinner time. As such, neither of them believed that their unannounced appearance would serve as a major inconvenience to Alicia. Originally, Cassie had suggested that they call her in advance rather than just dropping by and unexpectedly ringing her doorbell, but Marcus had respectfully digressed. He was concerned that, despite whatever the mysterious reasoning had led to Dr. Copeland's insistence that he go and talk to her, giving Alicia advance notification might possibly be ample cause to arouse alarm or suspicion on her part. He feared that Alicia might suddenly realize that she had been harboring some secretive information that perhaps she should not divulge or share and would then refuse to meet with him. A surprise and totally unforeseen appearance at her door seemed the more intelligent and effective plan of attack.

"Me, too," Marcus answered. "I'm sure she's probably still there, but then, I guess it's possible that after Ellis died, she might have found it difficult to remain in the same house. There's only one way to find out for sure."

"Well, like I told you, Marcus," Cassie reminded him, "We could have called ahead and made plans to come see her."

"And like I've already explained that to you Cassie." Marcus retorted. "If we called first and it turns out she is hiding something from us, we might never get the opportunity to talk to her. I don't know how or why he told me to, but Dr. Copeland must have had a solid and valid reason to tell me to go and see her."

"I sure do hope so, Marcus," Cassie replied. "I hope this isn't a wild goose chase."

There was no doorbell, so Marcus had to knock. Again, with this not being an everyday type of moment, he skipped his signature knock and instead rapped firmly three times and waited. There was a twin pair of slender windows in the front door, each backed by a sheer curtain. While Marcus stood looking down at his feet, Cassie noticed one of the curtains pulled aside and then released. The woman's voice came from behind the unopened door.

"Who is it? If you're collecting for the high school, I already donated," Alicia spoke, obviously not wanting to be bothered by the teenaged couple standing outside of her front door.

"No ma'am," Marcus replied. "I'm Marcus Clemens, I'm Ellis Compton's cousin and this is my girlfriend Cassie Worthington. I hope you remember us. We had become very close with Ellis before his passing."

There was a slight pause prior to the sound of the deadbolt being disengaged and the door opening slightly. Holding it open only a few inches, Alicia peeked out for a brief instant before opening it wider.

"I remember you now. You are Elijah's boy aren't you?" It had taken her a few seconds, but Alicia remembered Marcus from the gathering after Ellis' funeral. Cassie did not seem familiar to her but Alicia trusted that she was the boy's girlfriend.

"Yes ma'am," Marcus answered politely.

"Well, come on in before the flies and mosquitoes figure out the door is open." Alicia led them to the living room and pointed toward the leather couch. Taking the gesture as an invitation, Marcus and Cassie took a seat.

Alicia adjusted a pillow on the seat of an antique wooden rocker before picking up a pack of cigarettes and book of matches and sitting down to face her teenaged guests.

Lighting her cigarette and exhaling the initial inhalation heavily to her left, Alicia asked, "So what brings you young'uns up here? Unless you're headed for Keokuk to party, you're quite a ways from your stomping grounds, aren't you?"

"I'm going to be straight up honest with you Mrs. Compton." Marcus said.

Alicia immediately held her hand up to stop Marcus before he could go on.

"First off, young fellow, please never refer to me as Mrs. Compton. I don't know if you're aware, but Ollie and I were divorced way before he went and pulled that stunt of his with you. And I hope I'm not out of bounds here Marcus, but is this young lady the same girl that was involved in all that as well?"

"Yes, ma'am, that was me," Cassie chimed in.

"Then I apologize to the both of you," Alicia said, seeming to speak sincerely. "Ollie was a sick man, and I'm truly sorry for what he put you kids through."

"It's okay, Mrs...." Marcus quickly realized he hadn't been told yet what he should call her.

"Just call me Alicia. I took my maiden name back, it's Davenport. But because you had become friends of Ellis, just call me Alicia," she spoke in a tone that was obviously meant to convey reassurance.

"Yes, ma'am," Marcus and Cassie said almost in unison.

"Honestly, I don't know how you two ever forgave Ellis, but I thank you that you did. I think the last few months of his life were undoubtedly his best," she said. Not leaving time for either to respond, Alicia continued,

"So what were you about to say, Marcus? You said something about being honest."

"Yes ma'am, um, Alicia. I'm going to be honest with you. I, well, we have been through a lot the past few years, and we've lost a lot of people that were close to us both, and especially Ellis. But anyway, because of all that, I started seeing a therapist over in Quincy."

"Well, I'm sure that's a good thing. Might be something I should think about. I got a pretty good sized load of crap I've been totin' around myself." Of course, Alicia had never considered seeing a therapist, but she felt like at this particular moment, these were the right words to use. She figured that the poor kid might be struggling with a complex, feeling kind of non-masculine since he was seeing a psychiatrist and all that stuff.

"It might be good for you Alicia," Marcus said earnestly. "Two hours and it did wonders to help me." Marcus regrouped his thoughts, trying to find the best way to express himself. "You know, when I saw Dr. Copeland, we talked about a lot of things, and one them was Ellis. Alan, uh, Dr. Copeland, he told me it would be a good idea to come and have a talk with you. He never told me why, but my guess is to learn more about Ellis. You know, how he grew up and everything, and maybe to understand him and our relationship better."

Alicia seemed perturbed as she snuffed out her cigarette. "Look, I don't feel like talking about Ellis or his childhood if it's all the same to you. And besides, it's nearly eight-thirty and I gotta get ready for my date."

"Oh, I'm sorry, Alicia. We didn't have any idea you had a date tonight. We should have called you first before driving up here," Cassie offered an apology for their rudeness in showing up announced. She gave Marcus a sideways glance to accentuate her displeasure with his insistence not to call first.

"It's alright," Alicia just as suddenly reassumed a more calm demeanor. "Jacob and I go line dancing over in Keokuk on Tuesday nights. He'll be here in half an hour or so."

The concerned look that Cassie had displayed while apologizing to Alicia now suddenly deepened as she stole a quick look to see if Marcus had caught what she had just heard. He had also turned toward Cassie in the same instant, a lightbulb seemingly and meta-phorically flashing over his head.

Thinking quickly, Marcus dove in headfirst hoping to elicit a response that may or may not be to his liking. "Is Jacob from down our way?" Marcus asked before continuing with an outright fib. "There used to be a Jacob that worked at my tire shop and I remember him saying he used to drive to Keokuk to line dance. I wonder could it be the same guy? If it is, that would be neat, I haven't seen him in nearly a year."

"No, not the same guy, I'm afraid," Alicia almost felt sorry to disappoint Marcus. "He ain't never worked in a tire store", she laughed. "But close though. The last few years he's been running a body shop in Monti-cello, probably a good forty-five minutes or so from here. It's called Timmons' Auto Body."

270

"Wow, that's interesting, I've never heard of it. I remember a body shop over there, but not by that name." Of course, Marcus knew that Max Schofield had owned the only body shop over in Monticello, but Max had been Ellis' murderer, and there was no way he would allow himself to be so uncouth as to mention that man's name in front of Alicia.

Marcus suddenly stood and took Cassie's hand to pull her up from the couch. "Well gosh, Alicia, we sure don't want to keep you from your date." Echoing Cassie's apology, Marcus said, "And I am sorry that we showed up at your door without any warning or nothing. That was really rude on our part and I really am sorry."

"That's alright, Marcus," Alicia said. She was actually glad that they appeared ready to leave. She had been ill-prepared and in no mood to discuss Ellis, and she had been telling the truth when she told them that Jacob was on his way to pick her up to go line dancing.

Marcus didn't want to seem obvious or appear suspicious, but he was in more than an extreme hurry to get out of Alicia's house and back on the road. They started toward the door, but before Marcus could reach to open it, Cassie turned back toward the slowly approaching Alicia and said, "Thank you for inviting us in, unannounced as it were, Alicia. Perhaps we can get together to reminisce another time when you're not so busy."

"Let's do that, my dear," Alicia said as Marcus and Cassie walked out the door.

Alicia stood in the doorway watching them as the two teenagers got into the tiny blue and white vehicle.

As they pulled out of the driveway and started down the gravel road, Alicia wondered what the actual motivation had been for their visit. The idea that Marcus' psychiatrist had recommended him talking to her as part of his therapy had somehow rung hollow with her.

Cassie tried to stay calm until she was positive they were out of Alicia's sight.

"Marcus, I know you heard that, that's why you were in a hurry to leave wasn't it?" Cassie was practically squealing with excitement.

"Yes I did. And thank you for keeping yourself under control when she said it. I was scared to death you would say something and the last thing we would want her to know was that that was probably the reason we were sent here." Marcus certainly would never have suspected that the name given to him by Neville, through his friend Simon, would be the ultimate reason that Dr. Copeland had recommended he talk to Alicia. None of it made sense, but it obviously all fit together.

"Don't worry, Marcus, I wouldn't have said anything, but isn't it remarkable that Dr. Copeland told you to come here and that Alicia has a boyfriend named Jacob Timmons?" Cassie was incredibly amazed. "Marcus do you believe it? That had to have been the absolutely most absurd and improbable coincidence in the history of mankind."

"Or..." Marcus said hesitantly.

"Or what?" Cassie asked.

"Face it Cassie, that's not the most inconceivable or fantastically preposterous thing we've ever seen is it? Not by far."

"Opa." Cassie uttered the name, almost reverentially.

"Yeah," Marcus agreed. "Opa. Where has he been? I haven't seen him anywhere lately, have you?"

"No, but Marcus, what do you make of Neville?" she asked.

"I don't know, Cass. We see him at the snack bar, he recommends going to the revival. We're both revitalized by attending and then he shows up there. And then he hands the note with Jacob Timmons name on it to Simon." Marcus was stumped and hoped that with her superior intelligence, Cassie could connect the dots and come up with a solution.

"And you're missing something else, Marcus. What do you really know about Simon?" She asked the question, hoping Marcus could expound on his knowledge of his newest best friend. "Do you know anything beyond what he has told you?"

"Well, no Cassie, but he has to be legitimate. I mean, Walt did a background check on him. He checked his references, and Simon drives a car, so he must have a driver's license. Simon is a real person, Cassie." Marcus was convinced that he needn't doubt Simon Macawi. "He's not a ghost, or anybody's guardian angel or anything supernatural."

"Probably not, but you have to consider this, Marcus." Cassie was reverting back to debate club as she began compiling evidence and talking points. "Neville

273

comes in the snack bar. He points out to you the *Kaisenreicher Revival* flyer. Then who recommends the preacher from the revival, saying he went to it last year?"

"Simon," said Marcus.

"So you invite Simon to the revival with us. There is a fourth chair that sits open next to Simon. No one sits in it until after the revival gets started. Who ends up sitting in the fourth chair, next to Simon?" Cassie asked again, anticipating Marcus' participation.

"Neville sat there," he replied.

"Neville comes to your shop to present you with a note, but you're not there. So he conveniently gives it to Simon to pass along to you." Cassie was definitely on a roll. "You and Simon discuss personal matters, he suggests you see *his* therapist, Alan Copeland, and you do. Now you have a three way connection. You, Simon, and the man who is the therapist to both of you. Dr. Copeland suggests you talk to Alicia."

"And Alicia has a boyfriend named Jacob Timmons, the name that was on the note Neville had prepared for me. But Cassie, Dr. Copeland knew about the note, he told you to make sure I acted on it. How did he know it even existed?"

"I explained that to you already, Marcus." Cassie reminded him once again, "Simon had to have seen it and called Dr. Copeland and told him."

"But Simon wouldn't know the significance of that name and neither would Dr. Copeland. Why would it mean enough that he would tell you to push me on it? Why wouldn't he just tell me himself?"

"Because he didn't want you to know he was aware of it, I guess. I don't know Marcus, it's all just too complicated." Cassie thought, quietly thinking it over. "All I know for sure is that there is some kind of connection between you, Simon, Neville and your therapist. I can't explain it, but it's there."

"Where is Opa when we need him, Cass? We could sure use his guidance right now, couldn't we? Are you sure he hasn't like come to you at all, I mean in your dreams or anything?" Marcus asked.

"Nope, he hasn't," she said regretfully.

The drive seemed longer on the way back. It was beginning to get dark when they were finally approaching *A & W*. They had planned to stop for root beer floats and as he was parking, Marcus suddenly asked, "It's after nine o'clock, do you think it's too late to call Mitchell?"

"I don't think so. The note says you're supposed to ask him to do a background check on the guy, and now that you've found out who he is, I wouldn't put it off. I think you should call him, Marcus." Cassie had emphatically cast her ballot.

After parking and ordering, Marcus left Cassie a five dollar bill to pay for the refreshments and strode purposefully to the payphone that was located just outside the restrooms. He dropped in a dime and dialed Deputy Mitchell Daniels' number. The phone was answered promptly on the second ring and though he was nervous as all get out, Marcus proceeded to make his unusual and quite unorthodox request.

"Mitch, I have a name that I was told to give you, that it was important to have you run a background check on this person."

"Okay, Marcus give me the name, I'll write it down, but then I have to ask you some questions," Mitchell had several already forming.

"Jacob Timmons," Marcus said.

"Is that the Jacob Timmons over Monticello, Marcus? The guy that runs the body shop?" Mitchell asked.

"That's him," Marcus replied. "Do you know him?"

"Not well, but I know of him," was the response. "He took over the shop after Max Schofield, you know." Mitch waited an appropriate few seconds before continuing, "Okay, Marcus. So why am I doing a background check on Jacob Timmons?"

"Honestly, I don't know, Mitch," was Marcus' unsatisfactory answer.

"Okay, Marcus. Let me ask you who gave you the name and why?" The second question was expected, but Marcus' answer was still going to be vague.

"A mechanic I work with gave me a note. That's where I got the name."

"So how does this mechanic know the name and what's he got against this guy?" Mitchell asked another innocuous question, and again expecting yet another evasive answer.

"He doesn't know the name. Someone else, an old man named Neville, gave him the note to give to me.

I know it sounds crazy, Mitch, but there's something up and we need to figure out what it is."

"Marcus, you're not making this easy, you know? What's the mechanic's name? and who is this old man you're calling Neville?" Mitchell was fishing, but once again doubted he would get a bite.

"Simon Macawi is the mechanic. He's my friend, but you don't need to bother him. He doesn't know anything, he's just a messenger, you know, like a middleman. And Neville, Naughton is his last name." Marcus told Mitchell the little about Neville that he actually knew. "He's an Englishman."

"Figures, judging by the name," Mitch commented. "Where do you know this Englishman from, Marcus?"

"He came in the bowling alley once, to the snack bar. He sat and talked to me and Cassie for, I don't know, half an hour or so, ordered french fries and then he left. Didn't even eat them after he'd ordered them. That was strange." There really wasn't much more to say about the man.

"Have you seen him since then?" Mitchell wondered.

"Yeah once, when the revival was in town. Cassie, me and Simon took our seats and there was a fourth chair open. But after the service started, Neville came and sat there. Aside from telling Simon hello, he never said a word to anybody though. And then as soon as everything was over, he just left again. Not a word, left as quietly as he had arrived." Marcus had explained as best he could.

"And I guess that's it, right Marcus?" Mitchell was a bit flustered. "You haven't given me much to go on. I really don't have a legitimate reason to pull up anything on this guy, you realize that don't you, son?"

"Yes sir, I do," Marcus acknowledged. "But, you know Mitch that there have been a lot of things over the years that, yeah, maybe they defied logic, but they always seemed to prove out in the end didn't they?"

"Yeah, like the guy that broke into your footlocker. Your friend Denny spotting him leaving your house was a big, unexpected arrow pointing at the guy." Mitchell had to admit that when it came to Marcus Clemens, he had learned to always expect the unexpected.

"Whatever happened to him anyway, Mitch? Did he ever go to trial?" Marcus asked innocently.

"I never told you, Marcus?" Mitchell couldn't believe he had never relayed the news. "He got beaten to death with a tire iron. Same day he was bailed out of county jail. He went to the *Bar None Saloon* out there west of La Grange. We suspect he crossed some bikers and he got his wings handed to him. Another one unsolved. Whenever anything happens at that biker bar, nobody ever fingers anybody. The mantra out there is always *nobody seen nothin'.*"

"Gosh that's terrible," Marcus said, truly feeling bad for the man. Yes, Jimbo Burgess had broken into his house and tried to steal his inheritance that wasn't, but that certainly wasn't a crime worth dying over.

"Well, you know the old saying, Marcus, *sleep with dogs and you're gonna get fleas.* Keep in mind

Marcus, when you turn twenty-one and have a hankering for a beer, steer clear of that place. It's no place for a good clean-cut kid like you, never." Mitch hoped that when the time came, Marcus would heed the advice.

"No sir, I don't expect I'd ever have call to go near that place," Marcus said.

"I'll look into this Jacob Timmons tomorrow, Marcus. I'll let you know what I find out." Marcus knew Mitchell Daniels was a man of his word and would delve deeply into the man's past. With all the clues and hints leading to Timmons' name, it seemed inevitable that Mitchell would uncover something.

Hanging up the payphone receiver, Marcus returned to his car. Removing his mug that now contained a melted root beer float, he carefully opened the door, got back in, and then gently reclosed the door without either spilling a drop of the root beer or knocking the tray off the partially open window.

"Well?" Cassie asked.

"It was tough because I couldn't give him anything to go on," Marcus explained. "But he agreed to look into the guy's name and background." Marcus felt satisfaction that he could at least tell Cassie that Mitchell had taken his word and promised that Jacob Timmons would at least be checked out.

"I can't wait to find out what he did, Marcus." While Marcus had been on the phone with Mitchell, Cassie had been busily imagining scenarios that would implicate Jacob Timmons as some master thief or bank robber, or at least a surviving member or descendant of Al Capone's old Chicago mob gang.

279

"Me too," said Marcus as he laughed at Cassie's perceived enthusiasm.

Jacob's Web

Mitchell Daniels reported for roll call fifteen minutes early, making it a mission to seek out and corner his fellow patrol officer, Helen Wilcox. He quickly located her in the officer's lounge gulping down a croissant and cup of coffee.

"I don't think we could survive without the caffeine, Helen," Mitchell said as he poured himself a steaming cup of what was most likely the strongest blend available west of the Mississippi River. The early morning duty officer that prepped the three pots of coffee every weekday almost certainly must have originally hailed from the state of Louisiana because the brew that he concocted, at least in Mitchell's humble opinion, seemed to be the closest thing to chicory coffee he had ever consumed. The only discernible difference was that officer's coffee was still potently caffeinated as opposed to chicory, which happens to be caffeine free.

"This gruel is the only thing that gets me going in the morning. I need to have Stu come and make my coffee at home on the weekends. Compared to this stuff, the coffee I make requires three cups just to get my eyelids propped open." Whether Helen's evaluation was a testimonial to Stu's brew or actually a back-handed compliment of her home preparation was open to interpretation.

Mitchell took a seat opposite Helen, took a sip from his cup and said, "I've got a feeling that the little incidence of the break-in and theft at Marcus Clemens' house a while back might only be a prelude of something happening all over again."

"How so, Mitch? What's up now?" Helen asked. Her interest was instantly drawn by the mention of Marcus Clemens' name. "It does seem like something comes up with that boy every couple of years, doesn't it?"

"Yeah, seems to, doesn't it? I'd rather hoped the break-in was just a little one time situation. I mean, he'll be eighteen in a few months, this whole thing about Mark Twain and the inheritance should all just dry up soon, wouldn't you think?" Mitchell asked with a slight shake of his head. "Marcus called me late last night with a strange request. He asked me to do a background and a wants and warrants check on Jacob Timmons."

"Timmons Auto Body over in Monticello?" Helen asked.

"One and the same," Mitchell answered.

"Why did he ask, Mitch? What's his connection to him? Does he know we're already keeping a suspicious eye on Timmons?" Now Helen's interest truly was piqued.

"I'm sure he doesn't know anything about us watching the guy, and I don't sense there being any connection. Marcus doesn't hang out in Monticello, he's too busy with his work, school and football, and the Worthington girl. He's too busy to be wasting his time running around." Mitchell had been bothered for years about Marcus and Cassie and their seemingly endless saga; what with everything that had suddenly come to light when the whole episode with Oliver Compton had exploded. Beginning with the discovery by the two of the Wozniak girl's corpse on the riverbank, it seemed there had always existed an aura of mystery and intrigue, a perpetual underlying sense that there was more to the story, that secrets were being kept. Mitchell had made a point of befriending Marcus, Cassie and their families, had become close with everyone involved, but for the life of him, he could never put his finger on the hidden aspects of their situation.

"So he didn't give you any explanation for why you should check on Timmons?"

"No, he just asked me to trust him. He pretty much told me that he'd never steered me wrong before and to just take him at his word." Mitchell thought back to the phone call. "A lot of things have defied logic, but they worked out."

"What do you mean?" Helen asked.

"That's what Marcus said when he told me to trust him. A lot of things defied logic, but they always seemed to work out," Mitch repeated the words.

"I'll be honest with you, Mitch. Sometimes I think those kids are a little creepy, you know?" Helen looked at her watch and began gathering her gear. "We're going to be late for roll call, let's get moving," she said as she arose.

The National Crime Information Center had been created by the FBI two years ago, in 1967, and while the Lewis County Sheriff's Department was linked into the system, it was a tool rarely needed or even used in their rural, loosely scattered and thinly populated jurisdiction. But today, immediately after roll call and the morning briefing, Mitchell decided he would pull out all the stops and take a deep dive into Mr. Jacob Timmons.

There was some valuable information that came from Mitchell's database search. There were no glaring facts to be gleaned from the NCIC records, no major arrests or convictions noted. However a search of Timmons' military records produced far more revealing information. Mitchell found that his subject had been the recipient of a dishonorable discharge from the U.S. Army, back in February of 1953. and shortly after returning from an abbreviated tour of duty in Korea. The listed grounds for the discharge were repeated drug related offenses. While in Korea, the report indicated that Timmons had served three separate stints in the brig at the installation known as the Pusan-West Air Base. With another sixty day sentencing for his third infraction, the army had apparently seen enough. After the completion of his third and final visit to the brig in Korea, Timmons was shipped home and prepared for discharge. Mitchell noted the apparent drug abuse but didn't actually connect any obvious dots with that knowledge at this particular point. But upon further research, he realized that with Timmons' third and final arrest by the military police, there had also been both the apprehension and sentencing of an accomplice. In the same military proceeding, Private Maxwell H. Schofield had also been ordered serve thirty days for what was his first offense.

Realizing that the two had both been in Korea at the same time, and strangely enough, arrested together, Mitchell developed additional curiosity. He decided to check on some items in the local county records. Mitchell spent almost three hours at the computer and uncovered even more interesting details. He found that Schofield's Auto Body in Monticello had not been owned solely by Max Schofield. Mitchell learned that the business had, in fact, been owned equally by a triumvirate. Max and Jacob had been in partnership along with a third, and unidentified, silent investor. Upon Max's death, and with Jacob named as the legal heir in that event, ownership had been transferred to Timmons and the mystery partner, although the property and business itself was deeded solely in Jacob's name. Apparently, the silent investor was free of any legal or tax related responsibility, but in return for what must surely have been a sizable initial investment, was now reaping the benefits from revenue and dividend sharing. *Nice work if you can get it*, Mitchell thought to himself. He sat silently contemplating who the silent partner could possibly be. There were some farmers in the area with very large and healthy spreads who obviously possessed the necessary resources. One of them might have been so inclined to partake in an investment in a business that enjoyed a virtual monopoly in the county. The more Mitchell considered that possibility, the less likely it seemed as an appealing option. He even considered the possibility that Alicia Compton could be the mystery investor. She had worked in the employ of Max Schofield for years and had been married to Ollie. There had even rumors of a potential dalliance between the two. Many folks pointed that out as the probable cause for her and Ollie's divorce. Mitchell knew that no one could have known more about the ins and outs of the workings of the business than Alicia, but he also knew that she lacked the resources to allow that feasibility.

After Oliver Compton and Max Schofield both had passed, the respective investigations that were performed revealed that they were connected via a partnership in the local drug trade, with Ollie in the employ of Max. Mitchell's search of the county's property records also led him to discover that Jacob Timmons had not only been in position to assume ownership and control of Schofield's Auto Body, but he had also been Max's beneficiary regarding the Schofield homestead. This immediately raised a red flag and garnered Mitchell's attention. He knew that Jacob was living in a single wide mobile home located on the southern edge of the Schofield property and it was common knowledge that he had rented the mobile home from Max. So far as Mitchell had been aware, that arrangement had continued after Max's death and he assumed that Jacob was continuing to pay rent to whomever now owned the property. But if it was true that Timmons was now the rightful owner of the entire property, why did he still reside in the mobile home and not move into the luxurious house?

Mitchell dug up reports detailing the surveillance that the department had performed on Timmons. Not being an active participant in that investigation, Mitchell had no firsthand knowledge of the information contained in the reports. However, he soon learned that there was indeed a strong suspicion that Jacob Timmons had not only taken control of the body shop, but also was suspected of stepping into Max Schofield's unfilled shoes as the mastermind and new ringmaster behind the apparently burgeoning marijuana and methamphetamine distribution network. Mitchell was easily able to make the obvious connections between the reasons behind Jacob Timmons' military discharge, his previous and continued relationship with Max, and the fact that he now owned, but did not reside in Schofield's old house. Paired with the surveillance reports, Mitchell came to the logical conclusion that Jacob perhaps might be using the old Schofield home as a warehouse for his illegal contraband. Mitchell gathered all the information and documentation he had accumulated and ventured directly to Detective Bryan Reynolds' office upstairs.

Fortunately for Mitchell, Detective Reynold's had been anxiously awaiting a breakthrough in the investigation of Jacob Timmons.

"I knew it was only a matter of time," Detective Reynolds said as he poured over the pages that Mitchell had spread before him. "What was the clue that prompted you to check his military records? That's the real nail in his coffin, I mean aside from his stupidity. If we find contraband in that old Schofield house, he's headed up the river, no doubt about it. I knew he would do something dumb and screw up eventually, but it just wasn't happening. How did you put it together Daniels?"

The last thing Mitchell wanted to do was implicate Marcus' true involvement. If not for the phone call last night, it is almost a definite certainty that not a shred of this evidence would ever have seen the light of day. But the reality of the situation would have to remain cloaked in secrecy.

"Just a hunch detective. I remembered that Schofield had claimed to be an army veteran, and I got thinking about those two bikers that had worked for him and it dawned on me that all three of them had served in Korea, and it made me curious about Timmons. You know, I hear his name every so often in the morning briefings and just got to wondering, that's all." Mitchell hated not giving credit where it was honestly due, but perhaps sometime in the future he would be able to see that Marcus was properly recognized. Even though Detective Reynolds was ecstatic with his work and the discoveries he had made, Mitchell was still unsettled and felt disconcerted over Marcus' unexpected suggestion; no not suggestion, make that insistence that he take the time and effort look into Jacob Timmons. Marcus was either unwilling or just unable to provide a plausible reason for the how or why. Why did the old Englishman, Neville, send the note to Marcus? Mitchell knew he would eventually need to confront Marcus and get to the bottom of the matter. Mitchell had a plethora of unanswered questions and this had been escalating now for years. Mitchell shook himself from his thoughts as the Detective concluded the animated phone conversation in which he had been engaged.

"A search warrant is in the works and should be available this afternoon. Would you care to partake in a raid tonight on the Timmons residence and Max Schofield's former house and property, Deputy?" Detective Reynolds asked, offering the opportunity as a reward for Mitchell's initiative and hard work.

"It would be my pleasure, Detective," Mitchell replied with a gracious smile.

Before beginning his patrol duties, Mitchell returned to the officer's lounge and went to the phone bank on the west wall. He dialed a number and after four rings, Walt McMurphy answered. Quickly identifying himself, Mitchell asked to speak with Marcus Clemens. He had promised Marcus he would let him know whatever he had discovered about Jacob Timmons, and being a man of his word, Mitchell would fulfill that commitment. When Marcus picked up the receiver and expectantly greeted him, Mitchell began by demanding that Marcus swear to secrecy the information he was about to impart. He then immediately went into an abbreviated report on the basic highlights of his findings. He concluded by telling Marcus that he would know more tomorrow morning and that he would stop by the shop then and give him any updates that were available.

"You may have broken an investigation wide open, Marcus, and I thank you for your assistance. But, I must tell you that I have been asked multiple times already how and why I was able to link Jacob Timmons and Max Schofield and their possible mutual involvement in this drug conspiracy. The definite connection was not there until you pointed me in that direction." Mitchell was grateful, but he still longed for answers to his lingering questions.

When he was pressed, Marcus could only respond similarly to last night.

"I can't really tell you anything, Mitch. It's a mystery to me, too. The man sent me the note and it said to contact you and so I did. That's all I know, Mitch," Marcus swore he was telling the truth.

He was dissatisfied and annoyed by Marcus' reluctance to provide the answers that Mitchell believed he knew, but clearly Marcus, either voluntarily or involuntarily, was not yet in a position to divulge further information.

* * * *

There were twelve participants scheduled to take part in the raid and search of Jacob Timmons' property. They had all gathered at six o'clock p.m. in the briefing room of the sheriff's office, and now at six-twenty they had completed the appraisal, examination, and scrutinization of all the final details and assignments of the mission. Detective Muchnik and four deputies would approach the mobile home, present the warrant to the property owner and detain him while searching the structure. In the meantime, Detective Reynolds, along with Deputy Mitchell Daniels, and the five remaining deputies would proceed to the main dwelling, which they expected would be unoccupied. Two of the deputies had been assigned to sweep the premises before the other four could enter and initiate the search.

Jacob Timmons had only recently arrived home from his shop, was drinking a Budweiser, and planning to throw together a bologna sandwich when his dinner preparations were put on immediate and indefinite hold. He was imminently surprised by the barrage of police cruisers and unmarked sedans, all with lights flashing, invading the property just moments ahead of seven p.m. Startled by the sudden sound of the approaching vehicles, followed by car doors opening and slamming shut, Jacob found himself instinctively grabbing the shotgun that he kept conveniently propped next to his couch. Quickly peeking out the window and realizing the severity of the situation he was undoubtedly facing; Jacob calmly laid the shotgun down on the couch. He made his way to the front door and pushed it open with his foot. With both arms raised and his fingers laced atop his head, he gingerly walked down the short set of stairs and waited patiently for instructions.

Detective Muchnik told Jacob he could drop his arms. Reaching out with the paperwork in hand, Muchnik presented the search warrant and explained the purpose of the visit. Jacob momentarily smiled, because he was confident that nothing would be found in the mobile home, save for one smoke he had rolled to help him sleep later tonight. *Surely that insignificant amount of possession would be dismissed or at most satisfied by a small fine and some court costs,* he thought to himself. At least until he looked closer at the search warrant and realized that three other cruisers and an additional unmarked car had proceeded to the main house on the property. Sweat beads soon began to form as long ago memories of the army brig flashed across his brain.

When the all clear was announced by the two deputies who had been assigned to sweep the structure, Mitchell and the others sprang into action. Because of his previous experiences at this house, first with Ollie Compton and then in '67 when it belonged to Max Schofield, Mitchell had volunteered along with Deputy Clyde Latham to take care of the garage and long abandoned workshop. He had plenty of memories to contend with, fortunately most were good. Mitchell had feared the worst on both occasions. In 1963, he had opened the back of the old van, discovering the motionless, and luckily only unconscious, Cassie Worthington and pulling her to safety. Four years later, it was discovering the two mutilated bodies and then finding and releasing the kidnapped and bound Marcus Clemens. Of course, that discovery had been followed by the events at the pond. Still to this day, his having to fire the shot that killed Max Schofield remained the only time, while on duty, that Mitchell had ever pulled the trigger on his service revolver. And he prayed to God every night that he would never again be required to use it.

Clyde had turned on all the overhead lights and they carefully searched all the shelves and cabinets. With the overriding odor in the garage, they both knew it was only a matter of time. Indeed, less than ten minutes later Clyde was beaming with pride. When he had pulled back a green canvas tarpaulin that seemed to be serving as a curtain, he discovered what they both assumed to have been a drying rack. The wire shelving was covered in single layers of plant branches. Neither Mitchell nor Clyde had any experience in the area of marijuana cultivation, so they were both completely unsure whether what they were looking at was freshly cut or dried and ready for market.

After briefly examining Clyde's find, Mitchell moved on to the workshop where, rather surprisingly, much of Ollie's old locksmithing equipment still remained. Dust covered; it was obvious that no one had used the equipment in the past several years. Mitchell noticed another green tarp over in the corner that appeared to have been thrown over something. After Clyde's discovery, Mitchell could only assume that this tarp was also concealing some item or items of value When he pulled the tarpaulin aside, Mitchell was expecting more than marijuana or perhaps some related paraphernalia, but instead he was shocked to an extent that qualified as beyond amazement. When he became fully aware that what had only been haphazardly hidden, Mitchell regained his composure. What he was staring at, in his mind at least, was without a shred of doubt infinitely more valuable than any of the drugs they had expected to seize. Not even bothering to notify Clyde, Mitchell instead went immediately outside to locate and alert Detective Reynolds. Mitchell felt that, unquestionably, this revelation was far more significant and easily outstripped the importance of the simple search they had planned to conduct, or the drug bust they had hoped to pull off. This discovery was indicative of a major crime and perhaps even the involvement of some big-time organized crime mob. This was going to be major and might eventually even lead to the involvement of the FBI and maybe even the Treasury Department.

When Mitchell notified him, Detective Reynolds hurriedly left the comfort and security of his air-conditioned unmarked car and, with his arms swinging to and fro, almost seemed to speed walk into the workshop. Mitchell pulled back the tarpaulin to reveal the bonanza.

"That had to be stolen from a bank. That's probably a fortune we're looking at," Bryan Reynolds marveled. He had personally never seen an actual gold bar, not to mention fifteen or twenty of them.

Jacob Timmons was cuffed and taken to the county jail. The crimes he would be charged with were, without a doubt, going to be both multiple and severe. Among the counts should also be several felonies. In addition to the drying marijuana found in the garage, two storage rooms had been located at the back of the house, each containing blocks of cocaine, bags of heroin, and assorted papers, pipes, bongs and associated paraphernalia. Concealed in the basement was a virtual hothouse, designed and equipped with lighting, stocked with soil, fertilizers, and equipment. The basement ran the gamut, from A to Z, everything necessary for growing marijuana. Over the course of the night and following day, all the drugs and paraphernalia were photographed and seized. Later on Thursday morning Wells Fargo dispatched a truck to transport the eighteen gold bars that had been carefully counted, organized, and had all the serial numbers annotated and reported to the authorities in Washington, D.C. Detective Reynolds was promised that the Treasury Department would notify him of the outcome of their research as soon as it was completed and they had been able to determine exactly when and from whom they had been stolen.

Jacob Timmons had no argument or excuses for the drugs and paraphernalia other than to claim they simply were not his. He admitted to owning the property of course but asserted that since he did not live in the house, he had no idea about what was going on inside the structure. He professed that he only held onto the property as an investment, that he was perfectly happy remaining in his mobile home. He was steadfast in his assertion that squatters must have taken over the house and it was them who were responsible for everything that was found during the search.

Interestingly, Jacob Timmons did allow for one exception to his claims of ignorance. He did want to claim as his own the gold bars. He insisted that spelunking, the exploration of caves, was a hobby he had taken up as a teen. Timmons attempted to explain to the deputies that he had merely found the gold one day while spelunking along the banks of the Mississippi River. He even had offered to show authorities the exact location and cave in which he had found them. When he was informed that each bar was stamped with a serial number and could be traced back to their origin and rightful owner, he did not appear either swayed or dismayed. Even if they had been stolen, at least he honestly knew it wasn't by him and it would be impossible to prove otherwise. Worst case scenario, Jacob felt like he would surely be due a reward for finding them. He could also rest easy knowing he had already managed to unload four of the bars and had pocketed nearly sixty thousand dollars, even though he had unloaded them at a price well below market value.

As promised, Mitchell stopped by Walt's on Thursday morning to give Marcus an update.

"Your tip proved valuable, Marcus," Mitchell said as he shook Marcus' hand. "We have now taken one more known drug dealer off the street. I don't foresee any way he avoids some really serious jail time."

"I'm really glad to hear that, Mitch. I guess Neville knew what he was talking about when he sent me that note," Marcus replied.

"Now I wish you would allow yourself to come clean with me, Marcus. I'd like some honest answers and I'd also like to meet this Neville character. I'd like to have somebody let me in on where he got his information, who his source was." Mitchell looked Marcus directly in the eye, searching for a clue that would tell him if Marcus was being honest with him.

"Honestly, Mitch, I've told you the truth and really, I wish the same thing. Whether you believe it or not, I'd like to know for my own sake, exactly who he is as well, because right now, I don't have a clue."

Mitchell nodded, hoping Marcus was being truthful with him and feeling a touch of sadness because he did sense emotion in the young man's voice. As he walked back to his cruiser, he remembered something, some news that he had planned to share with Marcus.

"Say, Marcus," Mitch called. When Marcus turned in response, Mitchell motioned for Marcus to come back, that there was more to discuss.

Marcus returned to hear what Mitchell had to say. "I forgot to tell you, Marcus. You might be in for a reward, but I don't know yet, for sure."

"For what? I didn't do anything to earn a reward, Mitch," Marcus said.

"Well, you suggested I look Timmons up. But here's the thing, Marcus. We found more than drugs. Timmons also had a stash of gold bars in his workshop." Marcus froze. *It can't be*, he thought to himself. "Treasury Department picked them up this morning," Mitchell continued as Marcus' heart raced. "They're all stamped with a serial number, so they'll get them researched, find out where Timmons stole them from and then get them back to where they belong. But personally, if I had them stolen from me and somebody was responsible for their return, yeah, you could bet your bottom dollar there would be a reward."

"You said they were gold bars, Mitch?" Marcus asked. He had to make sure he had heard correctly.

"Yep, that's what I said. Marcus. Gold bars, and heavy ones at that, too," Mitch verified what he had said.

"How many?" Marcus almost felt like he was in a trance as he asked.

"Eighteen I think. Why? You want to calculate the value?" Mitchell asked.

"Oh no, just curious," Marcus waved off Mitchell's question a little unhappily. He had desperately wanted for the gold to be the bars that were stolen from the cave, but there were only eighteen, not the twenty-two he had hoped to hear.

"Well, I called the bank this morning out of curiosity, if you're interested," Mitchell continued. "They're worth at least three hundred thousand, maybe four they said, depending on the exact weight of each of the bars. Pretty penny, that's why I say they ought to be worth a hefty reward, I'd guess, Marcus. Keep your fingers crossed."

"Are you sure there were only eighteen, Mitch?" Marcus asked again.

"Well, Marcus, I guess there were more originally, but Timmons admitted he had already sold four of them."

Alicia's Revenge

Though he didn't really feel up to it, Marcus was back at work Friday morning, doing his utmost to exhibit and project a cheery outward appearance. But the fact of the matter was that he had suffered through a restless night and the infrequent sleep he had managed to steal had been fitful. He had picked Cassie up from the snack bar at the conclusion of her shift and they had gone to the *River's Edge Diner* to share a late snack. Afterward, they tried going to the dam. Visiting the lock and dam after dark, quietly sitting there just watching the boats and barges with their soothing lights, usually served as a calming influence and helped to ease the stresses brought on by psychologically uneven days. Not that Thursday had been a bad day by any means. By most measures, it had actually been an excellent day. Mitch Daniels had stopped by and gifted Marcus with refreshing news. News that should have been cause for joy and jubilation. The revelation made by Deputy Daniels had provided Marcus with the much needed answer to his burning question of why Neville had chosen him to deliver the note containing Jacob Timmons' name. The psychological effect produced by Neville's simple tactic had been immeasurable. By selecting Marcus as the conduit to pass that name along, Neville had correctly surmised that, in the eyes of Deputy Daniels, there would be an automatic attachment of importance and a sense of credibility. The resulting enhanced regard for the note had been the key instigating factor that had prompted Mitchell to investigate more deeply and eventually connect the existing dots. In the end, Neville's choice of who performed the act of relaying the most basic of messages had culminated in the arrest of a drug dealer and true menace to the populace. Marcus should have felt extreme satisfaction because of the role he had played in corralling a man whose actions were so detrimental to society. Without the impetus Marcus had provided, Mitchell would not have been compelled to fit together the pieces of the puzzle. Without Marcus providing the name, the gold that Jacob Timmons had stolen from the Pottawatomie Tribe would never have been recovered and would have been lost forever. As good as Marcus should have felt, he was still saddled with a disposition that bordered on demoralization.

While Simon had outwardly made a supreme effort to shrug off and not make an issue of the disappointing reality of the gold being stolen, Marcus knew the truth. There was no question of how much the loss of potential riches had saddened and affected Simon. He had been so excited, not for himself, but for his family and for his people. Marcus had been quite taken with Simon's reaction when he had informed him of the existence of the gold and the fact that it was still available after all these years. Simon had not given a single thought to his own personal benefit or gain. The knowledge of what was out there just waiting to be reclaimed had produced nothing but visions and dreams of what it would mean for his tribe. It had been right there, within Simon's grasp, but before he could even lay eyes on the prize, it had been snatched away. Marcus was positive that he would never shake the image of trauma nor the despondency reflected in Simon's eyes when he looked behind the wall and saw not his people's saving grace, but mere emptiness.

Marcus had shared in the disappointment of the lost fortune, and then for a brief and fleeting moment yesterday, he had felt that the hope and promise had been resurrected. Mitchell's initial words, his report that a number of gold bars had been discovered on Timmons' property, had served to briefly raise Marcus' spirits and had sprung hope that the recovery and return of the gold had been the real reason Neville had produced the note. But as quickly as the hopes had risen, they had also been dashed. It was similar to the roller coaster at the county fair. *Yes, we found gold bars* (the high), *but no, they're not yours* (the low). *You were missing twenty-two* (high) *but we only found eighteen* (low). *The eighteen might be yours* (high). *But the government will have to investigate. Sorry, guess they might not be yours after all* (low). Marcus had endured the extreme highs followed by depressing lows. Mitchell had closed the conversation with more words that served to arouse his expectations and provide a sparkling sliver of optimism. "Timmons admits he had already sold four of the bars." Mitchell had said. For a moment, the coaster seemed to have started tracking back up the incline. The inclusion of those four meant that Timmons actually had possessed an original total of twenty-two, matching the number that had been stored in the cave. Marcus' hopes soared when he realized there was a likelihood that they indeed were the stolen bars. But those aspirations were immediately tempered when the realization hit him that the bars had already been dispatched to the Treasury Department. Mitchell had informed Marcus of the government's promise that serial numbers would be tracked and the gold eventually returned to whoever had been its rightful owner. Thinking in realistic terms, Marcus discounted the chances that the gold bars would actually be traced to an inconsequential tribe of Native Americans back in the mid-nineteenth century. It would be much simpler and cost effective to simply sweep the matter under the rug and return the gold to a storage facility in Fort Knox. As much as he hoped to be wrong, Marcus figured that the odds of Simon and his tribe ever receiving their just desserts would fall right in the neighborhood of zero and nil.

Based upon a likelihood that he perceived as nonexistent, Marcus elected not to even present Simon with an inkling of what would again, most assuredly, be nothing more than false hope. He decided against even mentioning Mitchell's revelation that the gold had been recovered during the search. There was surely no point in raising expectations only to see the specter of disappointment once again raise its ugly head. Better to hold off until Mitchell relayed the findings of the Treasury Department. Then, when the expected bad news came, the matter could be put to bed once and for all and with no regrets and no second guessing.

It was fast approaching the noon hour and Marcus was busy rotating tires on a Chevy Bel-Air when Simon called over to him, "Hey Shemp, I feel like a Papa Burger. I'll buy if you'll fly."

"Sure thing, Chief," Marcus hollered back. Marcus wished so badly he could make things right for Simon. He was such a good and honest person. Marcus put the finishing touches to his project by double checking the lug nuts before strolling into the restroom to wash up before going to *A & W*. When he came out, still drying his hands with paper towels, Marcus noted that Simon was still busily under the hood of a car. But in Marcus' absence, he had scattered one dollar silver certificates on the break table. Marcus folded and slipped them into his pocket. He had no idea why, but Simon always left five dollars whenever Marcus did the flying. The Papa Burger was only ninety-five cents and the fries thirty-five. Lunch for the both of them, even with tax and a small tip included, generally amounted to only three dollars. They would always purchase their drinks from the shop's vending machine. Unless someone opted for a milkshake, Marcus would typically return with two of the one dollar bills. When he made mention of the excess two dollars, Simon's standard comeback was, "One of these days inflation will hit and the prices will skyrocket. I don't want you caught off guard."

Marcus pulled into a parking space at *A & W*, placed his order and was waiting patiently for the car-hop to skate out with his food. He was mildly pleased when he noticed the front end of the familiar Sheriff's Department cruiser nose into the open space to his right. Glancing to the left and realizing who he had parked next to, Mitch Daniels got out and walked around to the driver's side of Marcus' Metro. Leaning back against the support pole of the menu board, Mitchell said, "Fancy running into you, Marcus. I was planning to stop by after lunch, but it looks like you saved me the trip."

"Hi, Mitch," Marcus said. "How is your day going today?"

"Real good, Marcus, really good actually," Mitch replied. "You know, Marcus, I wasn't what you would call an exceptionally good student back in the day, you know when me and Elijah and your mama were all in school. But you know what, I got a history lesson today that I never knew anything about."

Marcus didn't have a clue what Mitchell could be referring to but was pretty certain that he would soon find out. "What kind of history lesson, Mitch?"

"You ever heard of a Native American tribe called the Pottawatomie?" Before Marcus could answer in the affirmative, that yes, he not only knew of them but that his friend Simon was himself a Pottawatomie, Mitchell had continued, "Well, I hadn't either. But I found out today that they used to live up in Michigan and

Wisconsin and that the government forced them off their land, I guess like they did to all those Native American tribes. Anyway, they got run out when they signed the Treaty of Chicago in 1833. I'd never heard anything about it but they forced all these poor folks off their land and made them move west. I'm told they all got paid some cash for their land and their trouble, and they got put up on some nice reservations out in Kansas and Nebraska. Except for a small band called the Pokagon faction. They settled across the river, over there in Quincy, and somehow they sort of fell through the cracks. So then it turns out that the government finally found out about them and sent a delivery of gold bars to them in 1839, you know to settle up with them like they had the others. Nobody knows what ever happened to their gold, or if they ever even got it at all, but guess what, Marcus? The Treasury Department called this morning and those eighteen gold bars that we confiscated, in no small part due to your help, well guess who they belong to?"

"The Pottawatomie!" Marcus whooped with excitement.

"Thanks to you, Marcus, they're getting all that gold they should have received more than one hundred years ago. And all because you gave me that one name." Mitchell was happy that he could be the messenger delivering the good news. It had occurred to him that Marcus had behaved strangely when they had discussed the gold yesterday. But now that he'd had the opportunity to put things together it had registered to him that Marcus had somehow already found out, probably through

305

his friend Simon, that the gold had disappeared a long time ago. Looking back and remembering, it had dawned on Mitchell that when he had initially told Marcus about finding it, he had seemed happy, as if he had somehow already known that it was the gold the Pottawatomie tribe had never received.

"I can't wait to get back to the shop to tell Simon," Marcus said, still grinning with exhilaration at the great news.

"So he is part of that tribe? I suspected that. Well, let him know that the Treasury Department is planning to contact tribal representatives today, so hopefully it won't be too long until it either gets returned or arrangements are made for a cash payout. I'm sure they'll work it all out, though." Mitchell reached out and patted Marcus' shoulder through the open car window, "Congratulations, Marcus. Those folks owe you big time."

"Thanks, Mitch, thank you," Marcus said with a smile. Out of the corner of his eye, right on time and with a bag of burgers and fries in hand, the carhop was skating his way. He was unbelievably anxious to get back and have a word with Simon.

* * * *

Margaret had picked up her purse and was ready to head out the door for work on Saturday morning when the turquoise Princess phone began chirping. She laid her keys and purse down atop the small bookcase that housed the oft used and well-worn set of

306

Encyclopedia Britannica volumes and crossed the room to the small telephone table. An unfamiliar voice spoke softly.

"Is this Mrs. Clemens?"

Not recognizing the caller, Margaret politely replied, "Yes, how may I help you?"

"You don't know me, Mrs. Clemens, or at least we've never properly met, but you've no doubt heard of me. My name is Alicia Davenport, I think you'll remember me because I am the ex-wife of Oliver Compton. I'm sure you remember my son Ellis." The tone and clear annunciation employed by Alicia projected her desired aura of calm.

"Yes, Mrs. Davenport, I do remember your name. Ellis used to mention you quite often. As a matter of fact, he spoke very highly of you, he was very complimentary. And please accept my belated condolences and my apologies for not being free to visit with you after the funeral." In reality, Ellis had rarely mentioned his adoptive mother and had actually projected more of an indifference toward her and her hand in his upbringing. As far as the post-funeral gathering was concerned, at the conclusion of the service, Margaret had been forced to rush off to work and been unable to attend.

"Well, I appreciate the kind words, Mrs. Clemens," Alicia replied cordially. "The reason for my call is because of the visit I received from your son, Marcus and his young lady friend on Tuesday evening. I wanted to express my regret for not being available to spend ample time with them, as I had prior obligations that particular evening. However, I was calling to let Marcus know that I am free this evening if they would be interested in returning. I'd be more than happy to bake some cookies and we can reminisce about Ellis as they had hoped to do on Tuesday. I've gotten down a family album with pictures of Ellis that I'm sure they would be delighted to look through."

"That's kind of you to offer Mrs. Davenport..."

Alicia briefly interrupted Margaret to offer a correction, "Please, Mrs. Clemens, do call me Alicia."

"Alright, Alicia," she said. "I was just about to leave for my job and Marcus is gone right now at work as well, but he'll be in just past seven-thirty. I can leave him a note, though. If you'd just be kind enough to give me your telephone number, I'd be more than happy to jot it down for him. And, by the way, I'm Margaret."

"That would be wonderful, Margaret. Just please ask Marcus to call so I will know whether or not to expect him." Alicia slowly and clearly recited her number and then asked Margaret to please repeat it, just to ensure she'd taken it down correctly.

Marcus clocked out at seven-thirty and hurried to his car. He was in an excellent mood and in a hurry to get home, bathe and meet Cassie back at her snack bar. As usual on a Saturday night, he would while away a few hours talking to and ogling his girl. He spirits were high, still up on a cloud after learning yesterday that Simon and his people were finally going to receive their just rewards. Marcus was sure that Opa and Jeremiah were smiling down from above, pleased that justice had been served and he hoped they were proud of the small part he had played.

After he had returned to the shop from the *A & W* run yesterday, Marcus had enthusiastically passed along the exciting information he'd been given by Mitchell. When Marcus told him the news, Simon had nearly choked on his burger. Within a few moments Simon was able to regain his composure and catch his breath. The gravity of the situation had finally managed to sink in and he was positively ecstatic.

"We owe our good fortune to you, Marcus," a smiling Simon said as he first grabbed Marcus by the shoulders and then pulled him into a bear hug.

"No more than you owe yourself, Simon," Marcus said as he wrestled free of Simon's grasp, struggling to regain the breath that had been squeezed out of him. "You gave me the note, I just passed it along."

"Not for that, Marcus," Simon clarified. "For discovering the gold in the first place. If you and your cousin hadn't of found it, we would have never known that it even existed. And you were honest Marcus, you could have just claimed it for yourself, but you didn't, you waited to see if the real owner would have returned for it."

"So could my grandfather and his friend Jeremiah," Marcus replied solemnly. "Listen, it was all meant to be Simon. Powers that are stronger than anything we know have been in charge all along."

After work last night, Marcus and Simon had met up with Cassie at the bowling alley snack bar and marked the occasion with hot dogs, fries and Coca-

Colas, enjoying a lighthearted and jubilant bit of merriment in celebration.

Arriving home from work and hurrying to get to the bowling alley to again meet up with Cassie, Marcus had literally run up the sidewalk and into the house. Stripping off clothing, he had raced into the bathroom, quickly turning on the shower, and in an immature act of impatience, jumped in without even waiting for the water to warm. Within a mere fifteen minutes, he was dressed and ready to head for the front door. But before leaving, Marcus decided he was thirsty and detoured into the kitchen to grab a bottle of soda from the fridge, figuring he could easily drink it on the way to the *Riverwalk Lanes*. Opening the refrigerator door, his attention was drawn to the sheet of pink stationery that he knew had come from the pad that Margaret kept religiously stationed on, and which never strayed from, the telephone table. Stationery taped to a refrigerator door, in an empty house; a universally understood notification of a waiting and possibly urgent message. After pulling down and reading the note, his face flushed and he felt a slight tightening in his chest. Marcus pulled out a chair and sat at the table, rubbing his forehead. *How had he not given any consideration to the possibility that Alicia was going to be upset?* Marcus wondered. Alicia had just inadvertently told him on Tuesday that Jacob Timmons was her boyfriend. Now he was being held in jail, a situation for which Marcus was at least partially responsible.

But the more he thought about it, the less consequential it seemed. There was no way in the world that Alicia knew that Marcus had been responsible for delivering Jacob's name to a Sheriff's Deputy, nor of the prodding it had instigated. She could not have known that his involvement had ultimately led to the arrest of her beau. *Or could she?* No, that would have to be considered an impossibility. Marcus had to logically think this through. With Jacob having been arrested, she was probably feeling down and out and in turn, that had caused her to again start thinking about Ellis. Then with Ellis on her mind, she had probably remembered Marcus and Cassie having shown up completely unannounced, and she might have decided it would be comforting to talk to them about Ellis. That had to be it. The fact that he and Ellis had been close was why she wanted to talk to him and Cassie. Perhaps she saw that as a way to ease her mind and achieve some degree of comfort. He decided he would call her.

"Alicia, this is Marcus Clemens," he said in response to Alicia's hello. "My Mama left me a note that you had called."

"Yes, Marcus," she replied as she took a drag from a menthol Kool cigarette. "I was sitting around this morning and got to thinking. I felt bad for rushing you kids out the other night and I think I did promise to sit with you and reminisce about Ellis. So, I'm not busy tonight and I thought, what the heck, good a time as any, right?"

"Well, Cassie is working tonight, but I guess I could drive out and stop by for a bit," Marcus offered hesitantly. On one hand, his preference would not have been to go without having Cassie along, but on the other hand, he did want to talk to Alicia. He still hoped it might help to clear his own mind in regard to Ellis. "I can probably get there by eight-thirty, would that be too late?"

"No, actually I'm a bit of a night owl, Marcus. That would be fine," Alicia seemed almost suspiciously cordial.

Alicia had made no mention of Jacob Timmons at all. Marcus reasoned that she either had no any inkling or held any suspicion of a correlation between him and Jacob's arrest, or the highly unlikely possibility existed that she was still unaware of him being jailed.

After hanging up from the call with Alicia, Marcus immediately dialed the number for the bowling alley to talk with Cassie. Marcus was in a hurry, but quickly gave her a brief synopsis of his conversation with Alicia, promising to get back from seeing her in plenty of time to pick her up at ten-thirty.

Cassie had expressed her only two true concerns. "Are you sure you don't want to wait until Monday when we can go together?" she asked. Before he could answer, she had followed up with the second, "What if she decides to blame you and give you a hard time about Jacob getting arrested?"

"I'll be fine going alone," Marcus said trying to reassure her. In response to the second question, Marcus said, "First of all, I don't think she has any idea that I even know who her boyfriend is. And besides, even if I did know him, there couldn't be any way for her to know that some mystery man had given me Jacob's name in order to have his background checked."

Before ending the call, Marcus assured Cassie that he would be back to see her in two or two and a half hours. Feeling that he had everything and everybody under control, Marcus locked up the house and went out to his car.

When he arrived in Alexandria, Marcus was relatively surprised to see Alicia waiting on her front porch appearing quite relaxed. His first thought was that they weren't far removed from the river, and with it being just beyond dusk, that she was probably being eaten alive by mosquitoes. As he had turned into the driveway, he had noticed the yellow bug light in the porch lantern and assumed that may have been a mitigating factor. Getting out of his car and approaching the porch, he picked up on the lemony scent of citronella wafting through the air. The use of citronella was a very efficient method of controlling insects, especially effective in deterring mosquitoes. Marcus quickly realized that Alicia had also employed another tactic to protect herself from the effects of insect invasion. On a small utility table next to her lawn chair sat a tall bottle and large glass tumbler half-filled with a brownish liquid. From the slight odor he was able to detect as he stepped up onto the porch, Alicia was not enjoying a glass of iced tea.

"Well hello, Marcus," Alicia said as she snuffed out one cigarette before deftly reaching with one hand for the open pack and extracting another. "Welcome to the Davenport spread," she said.

"Thank you," Marcus replied warily. He immediately began to question the wisdom in making the drive. He sensed an enveloping cloud of foreboding.

"Well, come on inside, before you get ate up," Alicia said as she picked up her glass and bottle of bourbon, or perhaps whiskey, Marcus had no clue which it might have been. She opened the door and started to lead the way inside.

"Do you need your cigarettes, lighter and ashtray?" Marcus asked politely.

"No honey, those are my outside smokes," she said. "I have more in here."

Marcus reassumed the position he had taken on Tuesday, sitting on the couch while Alicia plopped down on the adjacent love seat. They both sat for a moment in silence. Marcus was heedful of exactly what had prompted Alicia to call and invite him to visit. He was also uneasy with the fact that she was drinking, wary of the many avenues down which this could lead. Finally, Alicia broke the silence.

"Marcus, I've been doing a lot of thinking since you were here the other night, and there are a few things I need to get off my chest. I hope you have a little time to spare," Alicia said, as she reached for her open pack of 'indoor' smokes.

"I've got until about ten o'clock to listen, Alicia. I have to pick Cassie up from work when her shift is over, but I'm free until then." Marcus had no idea what baggage was about to be unloaded, but he hoped it would be something concerning Ellis that would allow for a deeper and better understanding of his cousin.

"Okay then," she said as she took a swallow from her tumbler. "I'd offer you a glass Marcus, but I'm afraid you're too young and besides, you're driving. I don't want to have to carry the guilt of destroying the life of another young man."

Marcus was slightly shaken by the last sentence and feared he was about to hear confessions that he would eventually wish had remained unspoken.

"To start with Marcus, I should have been a better mother. I should have put my foot down about a lot of things. I think my lack of responsibility is what allowed Ellis to begin the journey down the path that my lunatic ex-husband Ollie led him on."

"But Alicia..." Marcus started to tell her that he didn't need to know all the morbid details of Ellis' relationship with Ollie, and he certainly didn't want her to suffer through reliving any of her nightmares. But he was immediately cut off.

"Listen, Marcus, I have a lot to say, and if you consistently interrupt me, you're going to be late picking up your girl. So please let me just get it all out. Sit quietly and listen to what I have to tell you." Alicia seemed deadly serious, and with Marcus being unsure how long she had been drinking or how much liquor she had already consumed, he decided to shut his mouth and take in as much as he could for as long as he could handle listening.

"Marcus, you were there the day Ellis died and I'm sure you know the whole story about Max Schofield, don't you?" She asked, while not even realizing she was already violating her own edict by asking him a question and inviting him so speak.

"Well yeah, I know he was trying to get to my inheritance, I guess just like Ollie had wanted to do. That's why he had me and Ellis brought to his house that day," Marcus gave the rather simple explanation he had understood of the case's resolution.

"You haven't heard anything about the drugs?" Alicia was surprised. From all the scuttlebutt she had managed to hear, she had assumed that Marcus had inside connections with the Sheriff's Department. She and Jacob had always worried about the extent of law enforcement's knowledge of Max and Ollie's involvement in the drug market and the possible ramifications that could bring down upon them.

"No ma'am," Marcus answered honestly.

"Well then, I'm going to fill you in, son," Alicia said as she once again topped off her tumbler. "Max Schofield was the big dog, all the way from Hannibal and up into Iowa and then on to the west central parts of Illinois. All of the weed, cocaine, amphetamines, methamphetamine, that got sent and sold, that was his exclusive market and Ollie worked as a mule for him."

"How do you know all this, Alicia?" Marcus asked, curious as to how she knew so much, who her source of information had been, aside from Ollie.

"Because I worked for Max Schofield, that's how," she said without hesitation. "I was his bookkeeper at the auto body shop, but my work wasn't limited to the shop's business. I tracked his shipments, the cash flow, took care of payroll, even the ones who were under the table employees, I took care of everything. After Ollie's arrest, I was glad he never turned on Max, and they were never able to trace any of it back to him. Because of that, in the end, it made the transition easier for Jacob. We always worried that somebody out there knew something that they would one day use against us, but I guess those worries don't really matter anymore now, do they?"

Marcus felt his face flushing, he was nervous about where Alicia was going next.

"Did you hear the rumor that my boyfriend got arrested?" Alicia asked.

"No," Marcus said, hoping the word *liar* wasn't plastered across his forehead.

"Yeah, busted. Dead to rights," she reported nonchalantly. "Guess I won't be seeing him for a few years."

Marcus was surprised that Alicia displayed such a calm demeanor and kind of wondered if her lack of emotion was due to embarrassment or if perhaps she was nonplussed by the certainty that Jacob was certainly going to prison.

"To get back to what I was saying about Max and Ollie," she continued as if she had only stopped to take a sip of her refreshment. "After all the crap involving you and your girl and my idiot ex-husband's conviction for murder, which is another whole story unto itself I might add, Ellis had to do his two years in that reform school down in Boonville. I even moved to Fulton so I could be close and visit with him while he was in lockup. Anyway, when he got out and was on that one year of probation, I thought it would be good for him to earn some money, you know, some real money. I wanted him to be able to live at home for free and to sock away some cash, you know? I wanted him to be able to build a solid foundation because I knew it was going to be hard for him. So I asked Max if he could help out by giving him a job, and he did. He put Ellis to work with a legitimate job delivering car parts. He did that for just a few months and Max saw that he was a good and reliable kid."

Marcus was glad that Alicia was actually imparting some good and useful information about Ellis that he found interesting. Until she continued with more.

"Max had an eye for talent and he saw something in Ellis. So one day, he calls me up and asks if Thor, Thor was what Max always liked to call Ellis, he asks if Thor is ready to take the next step. Well, the next thing I know, Ellis is galivanting all over the state of Missouri delivering marijuana shipments. Max had him handling Ollie's old route, can you believe it?" Alicia was obviously torn while describing Ellis' shady, but lucrative, employment situation.

"Why did he call Ellis. Thor?" Marcus asked, innocently enough.

"Another story for another day, it came from his time at the *Missouri Training School for Boys*," Alicia said with a wave of her hand. "So anyway, one day when Judy was visiting. You're related to Judy, right? And you know that Ellis found out that Judy was his real father and that his mother had died, Ellis told you all of that, right?"

"Yeah, he did." Marcus was all too familiar with all the grizzly details of Paula Sue Schaeffer's death.

"So when Judy was out in Fulton to visit with Ellis one day, I told him that he needed to talk to Max and tell him he needed to come up with something else for Ellis to do, something that wasn't illegal and wouldn't risk him going back to jail. But Judy never did anything about it. So, in a way I blame him, I think in a way it's Judy's fault that Ellis is dead."

Marcus was noticing that Alicia's words were beginning to slur a bit. She was obviously reaching the point where she would be well advised to put down the liquor and perhaps put on a pot of coffee. Beyond his concern with her sobriety though, he was curious why she had expected Judy to talk with Max about Ellis' situation, especially in light of the fact that she was the one responsible for arranging his employment in the first place.

Suddenly, Alicia did an about face and returned her attention to her boyfriend, Jacob Timmons. "You know, Marcus, if Jacob hadn't of been ratted out, he was on the verge of getting out of the drug business. He was on to something else that would have provided us steady income for many years to come."

"What was that, Alicia?" Marcus inquired, although he felt as though he might already know the answer.

"Gold, my friend. The good old reliable monetary standby. Cash might come and go, but gold will always hold its value, there will always be a market for it," she said with a knowing smile. "Jacob went and dug up and harvested the gold that Ellis had found and kept hidden. We would have been rich, just selling it a little at a time. Except that now it all got taken away from us. It should have been Ellis' but with him gone, then it should have be mine. It ain't fair," Alicia said as she drained the final contents of the bottle into her glass.

"That's not true, Alicia," Marcus protested, letting emotions override common sense and good judgement. "Jacob didn't have any right, that gold wasn't his to take. And besides, Ellis didn't find it. I was the one who showed it to him. It belonged to my grandfather and his friend Jeremiah. They found it when they were young, a long time ago. But none of that matters because I found out who it really belonged to."

"What the hell are you talking about, Marcus? How do you know anything about it?" Alicia demanded.

"I just told you, Alicia," Marcus said with growing frustration, both with Alicia and with himself for flapping his own gums. He should have just kept his mouth shut, but now the damage was done. "What I'd like to know, is how did Jacob find the gold, and how did he even know where to look for it?"

"We have Ellis to thank for that. I didn't know it, but Jacob figured it out. I guess I found out on the day Ellis died." Alicia unwittingly admitted.

Marcus was incredulous. Of course, it didn't matter now because the bars had been recovered and the Pottawatomie Tribe was going to reap the proceeds, but he was devastated that Ellis had told Alicia about it. "I can't believe Ellis told you about those gold bars," Marcus mumbled.

"Well, he didn't exactly tell me. He had an old treasure map folded up and stuffed in his pants pocket. I found it when I picked up his belongings from the coroner's office," she said.

Marcus had never considered that when they had been accosted on the sandbar and the map had been left lying in plain sight atop one of their bedrolls, that Ellis might have picked it up to keep it from being stolen, lost, or destroyed. Marcus had gone the last two years thinking the treasure map had inadvertently met its demise. Hearing the revelations Alicia had made tonight, Marcus was experiencing revengeful delight that Jacob Timmons had been exposed and arrested.

"With what you have told me, Alicia, I am doubly pleased that your boyfriend is behind bars. Neither you nor he deserved a penny's worth of that gold's value, not a penny. And right now, I'm tickled to death that I did my part in getting him arrested." As soon as Marcus uttered his final words, he wished again that his mouth contained some type of filter.

"You?" Alicia flew into a momentary rage. "You are the one that turned him in? You little bastard. After all you've done, all the pain and heartache you have caused and you had the gall, the nerve to rat Jacob out and cost me what I deserve, what is mine?"

Marcus was confused, unsure of what he should do, what recourse he had. He knew he should do something to stabilize the situation. He contemplated just getting up and bolting for the door before Alicia could attempt to attack him, but in assessing that potential, he realized that Alicia was not a very big woman and she was severely intoxicated. He was aware that because of the alcohol she could be unpredictable, but he also seriously doubted that she posed any real threat of danger or of causing him any physical harm. Calming himself and deciding there was no imminent risk or peril, Marcus opted to remain seated and prepared to merely ride out the storm.

"Listen to me Marcus Clemens, Mr. High, Mighty, and Moral. Don't you see the devastation that you have caused? If it had not been for you and that inheritance that is going to make you a wealthy man, sooner rather than later, didn't you ever think of the number of people that would still be alive? If not for you, Ellis and Ollie would never have done what they did and would never have gone to prison. Ollie would still be alive; Ellis would still be alive. Hondo and Mooch, the guys that worked for Max, their wives would still have husbands and their kids would still have fathers to take care of them. Hell, Max would still be alive and running his body shop. I hate him for shooting my son, but if not for you, none of that would have happened, none of it. It's all your fault, Marcus. You are responsible for all those deaths."

The words stung, they burned deeply into Marcus' conscience. The words were especially haunting because they were almost identical to the last words Opa had imparted to Cassie and that he had been instructed to deliver to his Cousin Judy. Her words and syllables were nearly verbatim.

Alicia wanted to lash out even more, searching her mind for anything she could use to further punish Marcus. The answer came in a dazzling flash.

"Do you know why I was so made at Ellis' real father and your cousin, Mr. High and Mighty?" Alicia asked as she prepared to unleash further fury. "Because he is a fraud. Your Cousin or Uncle or whatever Judy is to you, that man is a total fraud. Oh, he would never show that side of himself to you, Marcus, but that man has multiple personalities. Ellis knew him as his hero. He saw Judy as a loving, caring, doting, and generous father who had miraculously come back into his life. Judy acted like he was Ellis' personal savior. He was a role model; a shining example of what Ellis could do with his life. All it took was a work ethic, a desire to be all he could be. But that wasn't the real Judy. I wonder what he was to you, Marcus? Did he present himself as a successful businessman? A world traveler who'd had a multitude of exciting and exotic experiences? A kindly old mentor with a wise demeanor? And to your girlfriend and your mother, a debonair man with expensive taste and a flair for the dramatic? I've seen all those facades that Jude Allensworth used to put on display. All of them. But do you want to know about the real Jude Allensworth, Marcus?"

Marcus said nothing, he just stared coldly at Alicia, taking in her every word.

"I'll tell you about the real Judy, Marcus. He is a ruthless and uncaring ass. He is vile and evil. He would slit his own mother's throat if he thought for a minute he could extract and sell her dentures for a dollar. Let me ask you a question, Marcus. When Judy began showing up at your house, how long had it been since you had seen him? Tell me, Marcus, how long?"

"I think six or seven years," Marcus replied as he thought back to his first memory of Cousin Judy sitting at the kitchen table of their old apartment. He had never seen Judy before, or at least had not remembered ever seeing him.

"Another question, Marcus. When Judy came into your life, was there anything in particular going on around that time?"

"Yes, that's about when everything got started with Ellis and Ollie," he replied.

"Thought so. Would you like to know why? It's because he got wind that you were going to receive an inheritance. You see Marcus, I worked for Max Schofield and Ollie was my husband. And Ollie worked for Max, too. Marcus, I knew everything and everybody. Do you know who Max worked for back then and who Jacob had been working for until you caused his arrest?"

Marcus didn't know the answer, but at this point, he could have ventured a fairly educated guess to whom Alicia was referring.

"Yeah, Marcus. Did you know he doesn't go by Jude or Judy in his business dealings? He has this tremendous ego and insists that everyone calls him *Boss-man*. He runs one of the biggest rings in the country, almost all of the illegal drug trade from Memphis, through St. Louis and just about all the way to Chicago. I'm telling you, Marcus, the man is ruthless. He's schizophrenic or whatever that word is. I'm telling you; he has multiple personalities. He would just as soon shoot you between the eyes as to talk to you. Do you remember when Ollie died in prison, not long before Ellis was killed?"

"Yes, I remember that," Marcus replied.

"Well, Judy had visited Ollie in prison the week before he was killed." Alicia was about to unload a long story that she was sure Marcus was not prepared for. "Then he came to my house and told me that Ollie had threatened to turn him in, claiming he'd seen Judy kill Ellis' birth mother. I don't know if Ellis told you, but her name was Paula Sue Schaeffer."

Of course Marcus had known who she was, but not from Ellis. He had learned from newspaper clippings and research done on the micro fiche machine at school.

"Well, I knew Ollie had seen him do it, he'd told me about it when it had happened, but I kept my mouth shut because I knew what that man was capable of. Judy didn't know it at the time, but Ollie had been a witness, he had seen it all. Of course, Judy was a suspect right away and he knew he had to find a way to take the heat off of him, so with Ollie being the good friend that he was, Judy came to him. He pleaded and begged, eventually holding some stuff over Ollie's head, until Judy was able to convince him to lie in court. Judy had arranged to frame some hobo that had been camping over on the riverfront. And then, when Ollie testified against him, the poor schmuck never had a chance. He ended up getting executed. The poor guy got killed while Judy and Ollie, they were both young and carefree, they just wrote it off like it was nothing. This all happened right around the time Ollie and I had gotten married. But fast forward to two years ago, to that day when Ollie threatened to turn him in from prison. Although I didn't love Ollie anymore, I still felt like I had to try to protect him from Judy. I told Judy that Ollie was bluffing, that when Paula was killed we had been in California on our honeymoon, so there was no way he could have seen any such thing. But I was lying and I guess Judy knew it. I'm telling you Marcus, Judy has tons of connections all over this state, and somehow he had Ollie murdered inside those prison walls. Judy had Ollie killed because he was worried that Ollie was going to expose him as Paula's real killer, which he was. The man has absolutely no heart and wouldn't know what a single normal human emotion was." Alicia felt she had shed a huge burden telling all of this to Marcus.

Marcus, of course, was stunned by all of Alicia's accusations. Marcus' dad, Elijah, had saved all those newspaper clippings relating to Paula Sue's murder for a reason. He had foreseen and had planned ahead for the possibility that this day would arrive. The reasons behind the contents of the footlocker were beginning to come into focus.

Marcus had hundreds of questions now floating through the recesses of his mind, but he had glanced at his watch a few minutes ago, as Alicia was talking and noted that it was nearly ten minutes past ten o'clock. When she had paused to light her umpteenth cigarette,

Marcus stood to announce that he was going to have to leave. He was mildly surprised that Alicia seemed understanding. All of the anger and raw emotion she had displayed earlier had subsided and she had mellowed quite a bit since initially beginning her rant against Judy. Marcus stood, telling Alicia that he would see himself out.

As he drove down the gravel road toward the intersection with County Road 323, Marcus launched into an internal debate centering on both the truthfulness and the reliability of Alicia's recollections and accusations. Had she been telling him the truth? Had she been honest and direct with him, or had Alicia been dealing in fluff, merely a pathetic effort to create a chasm between Marcus and Judy? He was sure that Alicia felt she had numerous reasons to cause problems for Marcus. Especially after she had learned that he had played a part in the investigation and arrest of her boyfriend and benefactor. Assuming Alicia was still working under the guise of being the body shop's bookkeeper, Jacob and his business ventures were her only apparent source of financial support. With the probable loss of her employment and associated benefits of dating Jacob, Marcus was certain that Alicia had only chosen to tell him about Judy as way to enact her revenge upon him. The subject of Judy may never have even come up, and the entire night likely would have continued to revolve around the memory of Ellis, if Marcus just kept his trap shut about Jacob. Yes, he was fairly positive that Alicia had only railed against Judy in an effort to extract her pound of flesh. He couldn't wait to sit down with Cassie and afford her the opportunity to dissect all that he had to tell her.

Alicia hadn't even waited for Marcus to start his car before she had picked up the phone receiver and begun dialing.

"That little fink cousin of yours was just here again," Alicia said. "He's the one that ratted Jacob out. I hope you're going to take care of him for good this time."

"I don't have a clue what you're talking about Alish." Judy remarked.

"He's the one that's responsible for Jacob getting arrested, Judy. If you get dragged into this too, it's all going to be because of your stupid little nephew ," Alicia explained.

"I wonder how Marcus is involved in Jake's arrest? And he's a second cousin, not my nephew," Judy clarified for her.

"Because he admitted that he gave up Jacob's name," said Alicia.

"But how did he know anything about Jake's involvement? How would he even know who Jake was?" Judy wondered.

"I don't know, but he did," she said, before adding, "You need to do something about him."

"I hate it, but you're right Alish. Sarge told me about all the inheritance stuff the kid had been holding, the stuff we all thought was supposed to have been worth a king's ransom. It turns out it's about as valuable as a used wad of toilet paper. Since Ollie's promise of Twain's treasure is out of the picture, Marcus is no longer of any use to me. My major concern now is the risk I'm facing with Jake in the clink. If that little worm decides he wants to drop a dime on me to save himself a year or two on his sentence, he's got another thing coming." Judy Allensworth, aka the *Bossman*, was well aware and concerned with the precariousness of his present situation. Ollie had been a good and trustworthy foot soldier, had kept his lips zippered and not given up anything on Judy. At least, up until the moment that he realized Judy was not going to provide him with a last minute rescue. The fear of his impending execution was what had changed him. Jacob wasn't facing possible punishment nearly as severe as Ollie, but Judy did not have the same faith in his commitment. A single wrong chess move could mean the collapse of the sizable empire he had spent more than fifteen years cultivating. He needed to figure out just what would be required to appease Jake Timmons, to convince him to take one for the team. Judy had been fortunate to have avoided a major calamity when Max Schofield had decided to go rogue. Max had created a firestorm with his carelessness and the resultant carnage he had induced two years ago.

Earlier, with Marcus, Alicia had been unable to hold back her disdain for Judy and her attempt to calm herself with liquor had backfired, proving to be an even more effective catalyst for her diatribe against Judy. In retrospect, she knew she had made a huge mistake unloading twenty years of pent-up anger and unreleased rage, but it definitely had been a relief to finally have had a sounding board. Being solidly locked into the inebriated state in which she currently found herself immersed, Alicia was free of inhibition and had no problem continuing on with her invective onslaught. She proceeded by admitting to Judy that she had disclosed to Marcus all of the disturbing and surreptitious facts she had for years kept under wraps. Truths that Judy would have preferred to remain hidden behind the mask that he always managed to so effectively wear publicly. She informed him that Marcus had been made fully aware of a host of secrets and skeletons that Judy had accumulated and so carefully and effectively kept stashed away in the closet. Choosing which concealment could prove to be most damaging would have to be considered a toss-up, the possibilities falling between his murder of Paula Sue Schaeffer and the fact that he was the *Bossman*. What could be worse? To be revealed as a cold-blooded murderer? Or the revelation that he had been presiding over the most successful illegal drug and contraband cartel operating along the length and on both sides of the Mississippi River?

To Alicia's dismay, Judy seemed to take her words in relative stride. She had hoped to provoke him, or at the very least, rankle him enough for an angry response. But, there was no sudden outburst or even mild expression of consternation on his part. He quietly listened to what Alicia had to say and, when he was quite certain she had divulged all of her grievances, he thanked her for being so honest with him. Judy did manage to subtly register one small admonishment. He informed Alicia that, while he appreciated the fact that she had taken the time to privately express to him her thoughts and feelings, he did truly wish that she had not chosen to air his secrets and dirty laundry with anyone else. He also made abundantly clear his disappointment that she had also chosen to share with this particular young man.

In her compromised state, Alicia left the call somewhat unsure of how her words had been received. Judy, on the other hand, hung up harboring definite thoughts, some of which required his immediate attention. Judy dialed a number in Jefferson City and dictated specific orders for a small job that needed to be handled in the morning. His second call was to a local small business owner in St. Louis to make arrangements for a project that would need to be performed posthaste, sometime later tomorrow evening. The handling of the final item on his list would be a fairly simple matter. Judy decided it best for him to handle that final detail himself.

The Fourth Chair

Neither Marcus nor Cassie had gotten to bed before the extreme wee hours this morning. Of course, with them being teenagers, it was normal to stay up late on a weekend night. With Cassie's Saturday night shifts lasting until ten-thirty, it was common for them to knock around for an hour or two before getting back to her house. A typical Saturday night called for them to watch a late movie on a nearly muted television until the broadcast stations signed off at one a.m. But last night had been an anomaly, and for very good reason. After leaving the *Riverwalk Lanes*, they had dropped by *A & W* to pick up take-out root beers and then driven over to the dam. Arriving at the riverfront, and with Marcus' promise that they had a lot to talk about, they opted to remain in the car. Their discussion carried on until nearly midnight, at which point they returned to Cassie's house, flipped on the television, which was showing *Creature Feature with Chuck Acri*, and lowered the volume. Pretending to watch, the two continued talking in hushed voices until the Star Spangled Banner played and the screen went blank, filled only by static.

Relocating to the wooden swing on the front lawn that had borne witness to a great many serious discussions in the past, Marcus and Cassie continued rehashing the disturbing revelations and accusations that Alicia had leveled. Initially, Cassie's off-hand casual advice to Marcus had been to dismiss everything that Alicia had told him about Judy. In many regards she saw the situation as merely the ramblings of a sad and lonely woman who was desperate for attention. But the longer they talked and shared recollections of the many questionably strange events of the past, the more inclined she came to consider that perhaps Alicia had been forthright. Both of them had been troubled years ago by the dubious behavior Judy had displayed. Almost from the get-go, his character had seemed suspicious. His arrival had been a total and complete surprise, coming without any prior warning or notification, and after a multi-year absence. And just as Alicia had correctly pointed out, his appearance and sudden apparent interest in the lives of Margaret and Marcus actually had coincided with the terror inflicted by Oliver and Ellis Compton. Cassie agreed that the peculiar timing was enough to warrant suspicions pertaining to Judy's motives.

But, as Marcus pointed out, "Cassie, we have to remember that Judy was the person who was responsible for saving Mitchell's life that night. And more than that, his actions probably saved yours and mine as well." Marcus certainly had a valid point. That night at the Compton's, as Mitchell was being held at gunpoint, it had been Judy who had slammed the trunk lid down on the back Ellis' head, rendering him unconscious. He had then distracted Ollie, causing him to turn slightly and squeeze off a shot in Judy's direction. It had been enough of a diversion that Mitchell had the opportunity to disarm and subdue Ollie. "He was even wounded, Cassie. I cannot begin to imagine why someone could or would have done what he did that night if it were true that he was in partnership with Ollie."

"Didn't you tell me that Alicia explained that to you, Marcus? That Judy had learned of Ollie's plan and that he wanted to get in on the action as well, and perhaps even collect your inheritance for himself?" Cassie had brought up valid points.

They sat talking on the swing until two-thirty, arguing the ins and outs, the stack of evidence for and against Judy, without ever reaching a satisfactorily agreed upon conclusion. After checking his watch and realizing the hour, Marcus walked Cassie back to her front door, kissed her goodnight, and drove back home deep in his thoughts.

On Sunday morning, Marcus and Cassie were both quite listless after a short and restless night's sleep. Debbie's breakfast of scrambled eggs, accompanied by crispy bacon slices, had helped to provide some much needed energy.

Jack noticed their lethargic behavior this morning. "Looks like you two might have burned a little too much midnight oil last night." Jack had been up in the

335

middle of the night and glancing out the window had seen them sitting out on the swing.

"Yeah, Daddy, we did kind of lose track of time," Cassie said with a sheepish grin.

"Well, I'm sure you'll be paying for it today young lady. I'm guessing it will catch up with you later on in your shift today," Jack warned as he spread oleo on a slice of toast.

The sermon at church this morning, revolving around the promise of eternal life had seemed to drag on eternally. With his eyelids heavy and drooping, Marcus was glad he had today off and would be able to enjoy a much needed nap this afternoon. Poor Cassie had to face the prospect of enduring a five hour shift at the bowling alley. Marcus doubted she would still be game for going to the *Meridian* tonight. They had planned to see Sam Peckinpah's *The Wild Bunch* this weekend, but he thought that if Cassie felt anything like he did, he might suggest they wait until tomorrow night to go.

After church, Jack, Debbie, and Charlie went to the *Red Roof* in LaGrange for their customary Sunday lunch, while Marcus and Cassie returned to the Worthington house. Cassie had about an hour to grab lunch, change into her work clothes, and have Marcus drive her to the *Riverwalk* for the start of her shift at one p.m.

Alicia Davenport had awakened early on Sunday morning, suffering from a massive headache as a result of her uncontrolled drinking the night before. After four aspirin and a tall glass of water, she had crawled back under the covers and was sleeping soundly. She was oblivious to any sounds as the lock was silently being picked at her back door.

On the way to the bowling alley, Marcus made an unexpected announcement that Cassie could sympathize with, but was disappointing to her, nonetheless. "Cass, I'm beat. I think I'm just going to drop you off and go home to catch a nap. I'll come back around four though, and I'll sit with you until you get off at six. If it's okay with you, I mean."

"Well gosh, Marcus, I'm beat too, you know," she made her best attempt to whine and make him feel guilty.

"Aw, Sweetie," Marcus said sympathetically.

Cassie laughed and said, "No, it's alright, I'd be saying the same thing if I was in your shoes and our situations were reversed. Go get yourself some rest and come back later."

"Thanks, Cassie. I do appreciate you; you know. You're such a perfect girlfriend," Marcus said, both gratefully and in earnest.

Marcus drove Cassie right up to the front door, giving her a quick smooch and hug before she let herself out of the car. He watched her briefly as she strolled toward the entrance. Reaching up to the steering column, Marcus pulled the gearshift into low and motored away.

Cassie stepped through the door and was immediately met by a strange man in a business suit who seemed to carry an authoritative air.

"Cassandra Worthington?" the man asked as he displayed his badge.

"Yes," she answered meekly, glancing quickly at the badge and then back to his face, while wondering what in the world was going on.

"I'm Detective Burgess," the man said as he fought the urge to smile at his personal inside joke. "I hope you don't mind; I need to ask you a few questions about Marcus Clemens." Cassie was taken back by his words. She certainly was clueless as to why a police officer would be inquiring about Marcus. "I'd rather not talk here, in public, like this. Would you mind stepping just outside the door?"

Cassie's face told the story of her hesitation without the utterance of a word.

"I won't bite, Cassie, I swear," he promised with a reassuring smile. He turned, and with an open hand, motioned toward the door.

As Cassie started that way, the detective moved quickly to politely push the door open for her. She stepped through and walked three feet to the right before she suddenly stopped, hands on hips. "You have to hurry," she said, displaying a touch of attitude. "I'm going to be late for work." She hadn't an inkling of what this man was about to ask her about, but she sure wished Marcus hadn't chosen today to just drop her off like he had. Marcus almost always walked in with her and then generally stayed a little while before going to spend a couple of hours with Denny or Simon.

Aware of the attitude in her voice, Detective Burgess assumed one of his own. "Young lady, I didn't ask

338

you out here for you to stand right next to the door with your hands on your hips like this. My intent was to avoid any attention in regard to your boyfriend, the last thing I wanted was to make a scene and cause him embarrassment. Whether you noticed or not, we are standing right here next to the doorway. From this position, anyone walking in or out of that door is invited to listen in on our words."

"I'm sorry," Cassie said. "Do you want to move further away from the door?"

"I have a better idea," he said. "My car is right over there and it has air conditioning. Let's sit for a moment and talk like two adults. I promise it will only take five minutes. If you'd like, I'll even go in afterward and explain to your boss why you are running late and smooth everything over for you."

The prospect of getting into a stranger's car did not initially sound appealing to her, but Cassie recalled that when she was a young girl her mother had told her that if she ever felt in trouble, she could always feel safe with a police officer. *A policeman is always your friend* were her words a dozen years ago. Buoyed by her mother's advice, Cassie relented and joined Detective Burgess in his car.

Marcus had set his alarm for three o'clock, figuring that would give him plenty of time to get back to Cassie's snack bar by four. That had been his plan but plans sometimes change. Marcus was awakened just a few minutes past one-thirty by the ringing telephone. His first instinct had been to ignore the noise, expecting it would eventually cease. But the telephone had continued ringing incessantly. Unable to take it any longer, Marcus got up and staggered into the living room.

When he answered, the voice on the other end was that of a person he would least have expected.

"Marcus, it's Alicia Davenport. I have good news for you," she seemed to speak solemnly, but Marcus attributed that the aftereffects of last night's drinking binge.

"Alicia?" Marcus asked, totally surprised.

"Marcus, do you remember when we talked about those gold bars last night? Did you know that four of them were missing?" Alicia hadn't mentioned that last night.

"Yes, I knew that," Marcus said. "I was told that Jacob had already sold four of them."

"Well, truth is, he kept four, he didn't sell four," Alicia said. "I thought about things later on last night and I felt a little guilty. Marcus, I know where they're at and I want you to have them. You can do with them whatever you want. But it's not right for me to keep them."

"I don't know what to say, Alicia," Marcus was flabbergasted by Alicia's change of heart and attitude.

"Don't say anything, just come and get them before I change my mind."

"I can't come right now," Marcus told her. He had promised Cassie he would be at the snack bar at four. He didn't want to drive all the way to Alexandria and back this afternoon.

"Now or never, Marcus. If you can't do it now, I'll have to rescind the offer," she said in a tone more reminiscent of last night's Alicia.

"Okay, okay. Where are they? At your house?" Marcus asked.

"No, they're at Jacob's house, you know where Max used to live in Monticello? You remember where it is, I'm sure." It made sense that Jacob would have had them at his own place, but it surprised Marcus that they hadn't been discovered during the search.

"Alright," Marcus said, "I guess I can be there in about half an hour or so."

Marcus put his shoes on, grabbed a Pepsi from the fridge and headed out the door. Marcus started the car and headed in the direction of Monticello. It would be his first time returning to the scene where he had been held hostage and Ellis had been killed almost exactly two years ago. It was also the same house where Cassie had been kidnapped and held. An absolute house of horrors and dreadful memories.

Little did Marcus know that after getting in and starting the car, the telephone had begun ringing inside his house. Jack Worthington was calling, and he continued to call repeatedly, desperate to talk to Marcus. The manager of the *Riverwalk* had just phoned to check on Cassie, to see why she had not yet reported for work.

Marcus pulled into the familiar driveway. His attention was immediately drawn to the red Corvette Stingray in the driveway. He hadn't noticed any cars at Alicia's house last night but had no choice other than to assume this prized vehicle was hers. Marcus figured she must have had a garage or shed that he had failed to notice, his assumption being that she kept it stored inside and out of the weather. The thought did briefly cross his mind that Judy had a silver Vette, almost just like this one, but he chalked that up as just a weird coincidence.

Marcus parked and got out of his Metro. Looking around, he saw no one, the place looked completely deserted. Alicia hadn't told him where he was supposed to go to meet her when he arrived. He supposed he should just go to the front door and knock. As he started in that direction, a familiar voice spoke from behind.

"Marc," the call came. Marcus stopped and turned around.

Judy stood in the doorway of the workshop, an unfiltered cigarette dangling from his lips. Judy removed the cigarette with his thumb and forefinger, smiled, and said, "Long time, no see."

"Judy?" Marcus asked, quite surprised. He had arrived expecting to meet with Alicia, and after the manner in which she had spoken of him last night, Judy had to have been the last person Marcus would have thought he would encounter today.

"One and only. How have you been, Marc?" Judy questioned. "You look like you just saw a ghost. What, are you surprised to see me? Sorry it's been a while, but I've pretty busy."

"Yeah, I... I'm good," Marcus replied. He didn't understand Judy's comment about it being a while, he had just seen him on Easter, when Judy had helped with the move. "And yeah, I am surprised to see you, I guess. I mean, someone had called and asked me to meet them here."

"Oh, you must be talking about Alicia." Obviously, Judy must have been aware of Alicia's earlier call. "Yeah, she's here Marc. And anxious to see you, too. Come on, why don't we take a walk in the back yard? I got something to show you that I think you'll really find interesting." Judy started around the corner of the workshop, toward the back. Marcus felt nervous and hadn't yet budged. Judy stopped and looked back, "C'mon Marc, don't be a scaredy cat. Your dad and I, we used to play back here by the creek when we were kids. Come on, let me show you," he said, motioning again with his hand for Marcus to follow. Marcus was completely in the dark as to what was happening, but he decided to follow.

Judy strode across the backyard with Marcus close at his heels. After walking a couple of hundred feet, the yard gave way to a thinly treed, woodsy type of area. It didn't seem dense enough to be considered forest. There were a few scattered trees and plenty of weeds and briars. Judy weaved his way knowingly. There seemed to be a bit of an ages old path, but it appeared to have not been much traveled for years. Although Marcus did notice some slight indication that someone had very recently been through here. Some twigs had been snapped and some of the weeds appeared to perhaps have been freshly trampled. About ten minutes into the journey, they had reached a clearing that contained what Marcus assumed was a cellar.

"This is what Elijah and I used for our fort," Judy said with pride as he pointed to the ancient twin cellar doors. There were matching rusty metal handles, one on each door with what could be described as either a small branch or large twig jammed through the handles. Marcus' first impression was that it reminded him of what someone would do to keep a prisoner being held down in the cellar from escaping by opening the doors from the inside. "About another half mile or so through the woods is where we used to go creek swimming." Judy motioned further to the west. "Matter of fact, that's where my sister Elsie died. Yep, it was in that creek, all those years ago."

Judy removed the branch and pulled the doors open, one at a time. They were pulled back the full 180° on either side and both now lay flat on the ground. Judy started down the wooden steps, ten or twelve of them. Marcus stood up at the entry watching as Judy looked around in the dim light, finally locating a kerosene lantern. Using his Zippo, he lit the wick and the small area flickered with light.

"Come on down, Marcus," Judy said as a form of invitation. "You have to see where we used to play and store our fool's gold and the like."

Marcus was hesitant, but he nervously went down the steps. It was a small room, dank and musty. The walls were formed by hardened dirt and the floor was also earthen, but a rough ceiling had been formed in, supported by 4" x 4" horizontal and vertical beams. There were a few shelves on the wall to the left of the foot of the stairs. Judy pointed to the shelves saying,

"My mom used to can fruits and vegetables, she'd make jelly and such and we stored them in Mason jars on those shelves. Kept them cool in the summer." That made sense to Marcus. He was sure there were no refrigerators back in those days.

Judy drew Marcus' attention to the wall to the right of the stairs. There was a crude, wood-framed doorway that led into a side room. "That was our fort, in there, Marc. We'd steal away out here and eat our lunch in there," Judy said as he seemed to remember happy times.

"This must have been a lot of fun, Judy," Marcus solemnly commented.

Judy didn't reply as he walked into the darkness of the adjacent room. He was gone thirty seconds or so before Marcus notice the flickering, dancing light that was obviously not produced by another lantern. Apparently, several candles had been lit in the room. Judy appeared back in the doorway, smiling. "It became my trophy room a few years later," he said. "Elijah wasn't allowed down here anymore and I told him he better never tell anybody about it, or else. And, I guess he never did. But I wanted you to see it, Marcus. As Elijah's son and the only other living member of our family, you have every right to be in here, maybe even to be a part of this."

Judy came out of the doorway, put one hand firmly on Marcus' shoulder and motioned for him to go on into the room. As soon as he crossed the threshold, Marcus screamed uncontrollably as he stepped back and tried to turn and run. But Judy had grabbed his shoulders firmly from behind, held him forcibly and actually was shoving him forward a few more steps, basically holding him hostage. Marcus stood with his eyes closed, not wanting to continue looking at what was before him. He was literally frozen in place, held not as much by Judy, but by his fear, nausea, and repugnance.

It was all too much for Marcus to bear. He turned to his right and began to vomit violently.

"Come on, don't be so soft, Marc. You're a grown-up now. Man up, son." Judy said commandingly.

Marcus again returned his gaze to the horror before his eyes.

"How? How could you do this Judy? And why? Why would anyone do such a thing?" Marcus was completely repulsed by the scene. The shock had somewhat worn off, but the disgust and revulsion would remain for as long as he lived. "You have to tell me, Judy, why?"

"It's a matter of love, Marc, don't you see? It's all because of love," Judy tried vainly to explain and justify his motivation. "I loved my big sister, and I was just playing with her. I didn't mean to hurt her; it was an accident."

"How did you get her here? Like this?" Marcus asked as he looked at the remains of a little girl with faded and scraggily red pig-tailed hair that sat in a chair at the table, her head awkwardly tilted downward. Her face was so badly decomposed it could hardly have been recognized as human.

"I was about fourteen when the thought occurred to me," Judy related in a nonchalant manner. "We had a drunk out here in Monticello, a taxidermist by the name of Dunberry, I think the first name was Wilbur, although I'm not so sure anymore. But I made him do Elsie. Wasn't a lot to work with, she had been in the ground for six years or so at that time, but he did a pretty good job, seemed to make up for what was missing. I paid him well, and then a few years later, I brought him Paula Sue and made him fix her up. She looks lots better than Elsie, doesn't she? Almost lifelike, I think. I got to her just a few weeks after she was buried." Marcus could not believe that a man that he had once admired and looked up to would actually be harboring this heinous collection. "But, you know what? The old man, he got a little too big and ambitious for his own good. After he had prepared Paula Sue, he came back, trying to get even more money from me. He even threatened to turn me in. That's one thing I don't take is a threat. You make the effort to threaten Judy Allensworth, you just signed your own death warrant."

Marcus had seen and heard enough to realize that Alicia had been telling the truth about Judy. The man was completely insane. Marcus couldn't comprehend how a person with such a demented mind could have presented a public veneer that seemed normal and well adjusted.

"So Judy, are you telling me that you accidentally killed your sister Elsie?" Marcus asked as calmly as possible.

"Yeah Marc, but it *was* an accident. I'da never have hurt Elsie on purpose, never." He swore again.

"What about Paula Sue and the taxidermist?" Marcus continued.

"I didn't have any choice, Marc. When I found out Paula Sue was carrying the baby, I asked her to marry me. I loved that woman, Marc. More than the moon and the stars together. But she turned me down. Then Paula Sue threatened that she was going to put my baby up for adoption. I couldn't talk her out of it, told her even that I would raise it, but there just was no getting through to her," Judy spoke as if he were offering a perfectly reasonable explanation for killing her. "And the squirrel stuffer, he tried to blackmail me. Like I told you, Marc. Nobody threatens me and gets away with it."

Marcus was troubled, he had a myriad of thoughts racing through his mind when the memory of Cassie's nightmare had unexpectedly dawned on him. She had predicted this very scene. She had foreseen the little girl and the woman. She had feared that she might have been the little girl. Marcus remembered that she had seen Ellis as well. Her dream had actually been a premonition.

"What about Ellis?" Marcus had to know. Ellis occupied the third chair; he was situated between Elsie and Paula Sue.

"I had Ellis done because I loved him, he was my son," Judy said.

"But you didn't kill Ellis, did you?" Marcus asked Judy, wondering if perhaps it had been done on his orders.

"No, you know I didn't. You were there, Marc, you know," Judy reminded him of a fact that Marcus knew only too well.

"You didn't have it done, did you? Ellis hadn't threatened you or anything had he?" Marcus asked.

"No, of course not. I loved my son, Marc. I loved him," Judy said, seemingly displaying real emotion.

"Who did the work on Ellis?" Marcus had an inkling but wanted verification.

"I kept it in the family, Marc," he explained. "Old man Dunberry's kid, Dirk. Taxidermy, that's what he does now. Like father, like son. Lucky for me, he's a meth head. As long as I keep him high, I know he'll never talk. And he learned from his old man, he knows better than to ever threaten me. Matter of fact, I got him lined up to do another one tonight."

Marcus was gripped by fear all over again. "What do you mean, Judy? Are you gonna kill me and have me stuffed, too?"

"Don't know yet," Judy said as he looked toward the ceiling, thumb and forefinger to his chin, as if in really deep thought. "You see, Marc. There are three chairs filled. You'll notice that right now, the one on the left there, that fourth chair is still open. And therein lies my dilemma. My original plan, after I found out that your inheritance wasn't worth diddly squat, was to seat you in the fourth chair. It seemed like it was only logical that I give it to you. After all, you're family. The whole table would have been filled with family and people that I love."

Marcus was sweating bullets, trying desperately to think of a way to talk Judy out of his plans.

"But then things changed," Judy was about to add a twist. "I told you; I don't take kindly to being threatened. Alicia made the mistake of telling you a lot, gave you a bunch of information about me. Information and facts that I don't necessarily want to be made public. Wait here, Marc."

Judy, who had been sitting cross-legged in the doorway, suddenly stood and stepped out of the room momentarily. Marcus began to tremble; he was truly worried that this might be the end. Judy was quick to return, almost immediately in fact, dragging behind him a loosely bundled piece of green shag carpeting. Standing with his back against the dirt wall inside the door frame, Judy pushed with one foot. The carpet rolled and unraveled a bit, just enough to partially expose a lifeless body that Marcus instantly recognized as Alicia's. Marcus could only surmise that Judy had just gone and retrieved her corpse from beneath the wooden stairs. There was nowhere else where it could have been stashed in that barren room where it could possibly have escaped Marcus' notice.

"So, I thought to myself, I could put Alicia in the fourth chair," Judy said as if he still might be considering the possibility. "But then I thought no, definitely not. The fourth chair is reserved for someone who I love, or who at least is family. Which brought me back to you, Marc. But then, after talking to Alicia last night, another possibility surfaced, so I had an old friend of mine procure something for me earlier this afternoon."

Judy went to the darkest, far corner of the room, grasping something covered by an old army blanket, and drug it forward.

Oh God, Marcus thought, *I sure hope that's not another corpse.* "You killed someone else?" Marcus asked, not wanting to see yet another of Judy's victims.

"Oh no, quite the contrary. Very much alive," Judy reported. "Though, perhaps drugged a bit too heavily."

Judy pulled off the soiled blanket to reveal an unconscious Cassie Worthington. Marcus dashed immediately to her, and Judy made no effort to impede or stop him. He knew only too well, and completely understood, the power and raw emotion that came with true love. Marcus lifted Cassie's head, drawing her face close to his own. Satisfied she was indeed breathing, Marcus gently laid her head back down, propping a portion of the blanket underneath to keep her hair off the cold and filthy dirt floor. Standing, he then approached Judy who was now looking quite comfortable, sitting with his legs crossed in what had previously been the empty fourth chair.

"Oh, are you gonna bow up to me now, Marc?" Judy asked defiantly as he looked upward at Marcus. "Don't think I would advise that. What you need to do is go stand over there by the doorway and convince me who should occupy the mystical fourth chair. We know it's not going to be Alicia; she doesn't fit the bill. She meets neither the qualifications nor the requirements."

"And neither does Cassie," Marcus blurted. "She's not family."

"Well here's the little catch there, Marc," Judy explained. "Neither was Paula Sue, although she should have been my wife if she hadn't turned down my marriage proposal. However, I still loved her just the same. She didn't meet the requirement, but she was okay on the qualifications, do you follow me here, Marc?"

"The parameters seem pretty subjective to me." Marcus said.

"Ooh, big words, schoolboy," Judy mimicked Marcus' vocabulary. "How about this then? Cassie was destined to be your wife. That would make her family, which would then meet the requirement." Judy argued what he saw as a valid point.

"You just said Paula didn't meet the requirement because she didn't marry you," Marcus threw Judy's own words back in his face. "You said she was able to meet the qualifications because you loved her. You don't love Cassie."

"Oh contrare, mon frere, as you kids like to say," Judy replied. "Think back a few years, Marc. Do you remember when I said something, called her a redhead or something, and you asked me how I knew she had red hair? Remember that, Marc? And I told you she was standing on her front porch when I had dropped you off and I'd seen her? Now, I know Alicia probably told you that I'm partial to redheads, Marc. I fell in love with your girl that very day, her and those sexy little pigtails. So yeah, she qualifies. Now I just have to make up my mind who I want to see sitting here, in this fourth chair, for the rest of my life."

"You don't have to decide, Judy. It'll be me," Marcus volunteered. "But you have to promise me you'll let Cassie go."

"You never were very bright were you, Marc? The decision is who gets to sit in the fourth chair and stay young forever. The other person doesn't get *let go* like you're dreaming or something with that fairytale teenaged mind of yours. You're both going to die, the only question is ... who earns the chair?"

"It's neither of us, Judy. You're not God, you don't get a vote." Marcus said, suddenly flashing a tone of bravado.

Judy gave Marcus a strange look, obviously unhappy that Marcus' choice of words had been so disrespectful.

Marcus reached behind his back, raised his tee shirt and pulled his father's .22 caliber Ruger out of his waistband, and aimed it toward his cousin Judy, who still sat in the chair, a mere six feet in front of him.

"What do you think you're gonna do with that, Marc?" Judy asked as he laughed. "You ever even fired a gun before, son?"

"I will shoot you dead Judy, I swear. I don't want to, but I will." Marcus had never fired a gun and didn't want to now. But if that was what needed to be done to ensure that Cassie would walk up those steps and back out into the sunshine, well then so be it.

"You will not shoot me," Judy said sternly, as if giving an order, as he coldly stared into Marcus' eyes.

"You don't need to shoot anyone, Marcus," said a strange voice, that somehow, even though the speech

353

seemed impaired, Marcus understood clearly. He had never heard the voice before but it somehow seemed familiar. An undulating, pale, cloudy figure seemed to materialize to Marcus' right. *"You have proven yourself,"* the voice said firmly. A portion of the foggy form seemed to envelope Marcus' right hand and he felt his grip on the gun involuntarily relax. Marcus watched in disbelief as the Ruger seemed to flutter softly as it floated up and then slowly over toward Judy. Almost as if by magic, the gun had traveled six or more feet in a cloudy haze and now, to both Marcus' surprise and dismay, the Ruger .22 was being held in Judy's right hand and was aimed toward Marcus. *What is going on?* Marcus was shocked, his mind now consumed with fear. His pounding heart felt as if it was about to come bursting right out of his chest.

Judy seemed paralyzed, and Marcus watched in disbelief as Judy's eyes grew wide; the degree of widening was beyond belief. Tears had formed in his eyes as Judy's hand helplessly and hopelessly raised, slowly rotating the position of the gun until the muzzle was gently touching his right temple. In the small room, Marcus thought the sound was deafening.

"You have done well, Marc. You have done what you knew to be right. Go now, help Cassie." The voice spoke for the final time as the quivering, cloudy figure seemed to slowly dissipate before vanishing completely.

Marcus walked over and picked up the still unconscious Cassie in his arms. As he cradled her softly and carefully, he passed through the doorway, preparing to carry her a few feet toward the stairs. Marcus stopped to take one final glance back into Judy's trophy room. He sadly looked at the grotesque little girl in the first chair, Judy's sister Elsie. She may have had her way too short life ended accidentally, but it still had been at Judy's hands. Poor Paula Sue Schaeffer was seated across the table, in a second chair. She had no doubt come to realize who the real Judy was, and even though she carried his child, had refused his marriage proposal. As a result, she had been forced to pay the ultimate price. The third chair was occupied by Ellis Compton, the young man whose early life had been distorted and destroyed by all of the evil that had influenced his childhood. Once freed from those shackles, his true personality had been restored. He had saved Marcus' life and in that short time they were able to share, Marcus had grown to love him as a brother. Alicia Davenport Compton lay on the floor. Another soul that Marcus felt had been the victim of her evil environment. Perhaps deep down Alicia had not actually been a bad person. And finally, Cousin Judy. Now there were no more relatives, no more descendants of the Clemens bloodline. Judy had kept so much, so many dastardly secrets from everyone. And it was probably only fitting that he sat at his own trophy room table. That Judy himself had been chosen to occupy the hallowed fourth chair.

Just Rewards

Marcus punched the clock at seven-thirty and, as was customary, he hurried home to clean up and high-tail it to the bowling alley to join Cassie, who was working a seven hour shift today. She would get off at nine p.m. and they would have a couple of hours together to chill. Fortunately, tomorrow was the Fourth of July and both Walt's and the bowling alley would be closed in observance of the holiday.

This holiday weekend would mark two weeks since the events surrounding the death of Marcus' cousin, Jude Allensworth. Almost two weeks had now passed, but the memories were as fresh today as they had been in the nightmares of that very first night. As quickly as Marcus possibly could on that fateful day, he had carried Cassie into the backyard of the house and opened a water spigot. He had generously soaked his father's bandana, one of which he still religiously kept in his back pocket. Marcus had repeatedly soaked the bandana and had continually and gently wiped Cassie's face until her eyes had opened and regained focus.

Assured that she was fully awake and feeling no worse for wear, he had taken her to the car and hurriedly driven to the nearest pay phone, putting in a call to the Sheriff's Office. Marcus regretted having to report the latest carnage and he didn't revel in being asked to describe the grotesque details that were entailed. Mitch Daniels had not been the original officer to respond to the scene, but when he received radio notification indicating that Marcus Clemens had been involved, it became his business to make double-time in getting to Marcus and Cassie to offer his support.

After revealing all the grizzly details, including the plethora of information that he had gathered from Alicia, police investigations were rather quickly able to track down every aspect of Judy's intricate network of dealers and henchmen. Without her knowing, Alicia's last good deed had been to provide Marcus with so many of the important details that had proven to be essential to the police. Especially, and to the glee of Cassie, was the fact that *Detective Burgess* had been identified, and within days, apprehended. Cassie learned that the man had been a trusted associate of Judy's and that his true identity was that of Sergeant Oscar Roberts of Jefferson City. Surprisingly, the imposter had actually been a supervisor in the Missouri Department of Corrections at the Missouri State Penitentiary.

In order to explain Judy's use of Marcus' father's Ruger to take his own life, Marcus was forced to stretch the truth, reporting that as soon as he had pulled the weapon, Judy had charged him and managed to wrest the gun away. Marcus had been through enough scenarios in the past that he had become quite adept at covering up for the infrequent supernatural occurrences.

In their subsequent discussions across the last few days, Marcus and Cassie had come to the conclusion that it must have been Opa who had once again been the guiding force behind all that had taken place. Marcus had attempted to book another appointment with Dr. Copeland, but when he had called, the operator had informed him that the number he had dialed was not in service. Hoping to locate the doctor, Cassie had made calls to other therapists in Quincy, only to be told in each instance that no one had ever heard of a Dr. Alan Copeland. Marcus wished he could have gone back to Simon, since he had been a patient as well, to find out if he knew anything about the doctor's disappearance or perhaps a new number or location, but when he had returned to work on the Tuesday morning after the incident, Simon was nowhere to be found. Chester had informed Marcus that Simon had come in early on Monday morning and promptly loaded all of his tools and belongings and left. He hadn't even bothered to tell Walt he was leaving. He had left a note thanking Marcus for being such a good and welcoming friend. And for his role in delivering hope, and with the return of the gold, actual means to provide a better future for Simon's Pottawatomie Tribe. Marcus had asked Walt for the number that he had called to get a work reference for Simon, but again was hit by an impasse when he was told by the operator that this number also was no longer in service. Cassie had tried calling the information operator in Quincy, inquiring about a number for either Simon Macawi or his stepfather Frank Bearcat, but there were no listings for either name.

The old Englishman, Neville Naughton, also remained a mystery. Marcus had mentioned him to Mitchell and asked for his help in tracking the man down, but once again, no records could be found. It appeared as if the man had never existed at all. It was very difficult for both Marcus and Cassie, but they had come to the conclusion, and were forced to face the reality, that no answers to any of their questions would be forthcoming.

In just over a month's time, Marcus' birthday was due to arrive. He was a bit disappointed that all the hoopla over his inheritance had turned out to be no more than empty promise, but at the same time he was sort of glad. He had a job, he had friends and family, and most importantly, he had Cassie. Finally, Marcus was able to rest assured that everything had actually come to a close. He and Cassie were at last in a position to live their lives in peace, with no more reason to worry or forced to be constantly looking over their shoulders. They suffered with only two lingering regrets. One being that Marcus had lost a good friend in Simon. The other, and by far the more painful, was that they were forced to face the reality that they had probably seen the last of Opa, forever.

Marcus was strolling from the front door to his car at the curb, looking forward to seeing his girl, when he spotted the approaching cruiser. It only took a second to recognize his friend, Mitch Daniels, behind the wheel. This evening, Mitch was being accompanied by his sometime partner, Deputy Helen Wilcox. They both got out of the car and approached Marcus, who raised both hands overhead, mocking his surrender.

Marcus jokingly said, "You got me officers, what are the charges?"

"No charges." Helen said laughingly before adding, "This time."

"Actually, Marcus we've got this little package for you. It came in the mail this morning. I guess whoever sent it didn't have your address and figured by sending it to the station we'd somehow get it to you. With it being a holiday weekend I didn't want to wait until Monday to get it to you, just in case it was important or was something time sensitive, or whatever," Mitchell said, in explanation for why they'd hand delivered it this late in the day.

Marcus accepted the package, and with no idea of its contents, checked the sender's return address looking for a clue. He immediately recognized the person's name and the city of origin. Wanda Paige, Fairfield Iowa.

Curious as to its contents, Marcus tore the package open. There was a rolled up piece of paper, bound by a pair of rubber bands, and a folded note, along with a bulky and worn old leather pouch. Marcus opened the note first. It didn't contain a salutation, just a brief hand-written paragraph.

I wish I could have been of more assistance with your questions about the gold. After you had left, I found these items that grandpa had been given after Jeremiah's passing. As you see, one is map. I've no idea what it's for or about. Probably a remnant of them playing as pirates when they were kids. The other is a pouch that grandpa said that Jeremiah once told him had been stolen from the James Gang. Grandpa told me that Jeremiah and your grandpa had been the owners. There were two identical pouches. As you and I are the only descendants of Jeremiah and your grandpa, I think that makes us the rightful heirs. Therefore, I think it's only appropriate that we split the bounty. I kept one pouch and I believe that you are entitled to the other. God Bless, Wanda.

Marcus loosened the drawstring, opened the pouch, and sifted through its heavy contents. There were dozens of solid gold and silver coins, apparently dating back at least to the Civil War era. Marcus estimated the weight of the pouch at two or three pounds.

"Well, Marcus, looks like you did earn an inheritance after all," Mitch remarked. Marcus looked up from examining the coins and smiled at Mitch's comment. As he turned his attention back toward the contents of the pouch, Marcus was forced to do a double take. He would have sworn that out of the corner of his eye he had seen a familiar mangy dog staring at him from across the street. But before he'd had sufficient opportunity to refocus, the animal had suddenly darted between houses and disappeared.

Thanksgiving, 1972

Marcus had opted to spend some idle time on Thanksgiving morning over at Randolph Park rather than sitting in front of the television watching the *Macy's Thanksgiving Day Parade*. With the exception of a few sporadic visits with Denny to knock a few balls around the field in the summer after high school graduation, it had been a long time. From today's perspective, the field now appeared tiny, with the glory days nothing but a distant memory. He and Cassie had sat here a countless number of times on days just like this, occupying the very same bench and letting another cool late autumn afternoon drift by as they watched the migrating ducks swim and frolic in the chilly waters of the lake. Over his shoulder sat the rustic pavilion that had served as their rendezvous point when they had met up at the park to spend their first real time together. On the neighboring playground, Cassie had surprised Marcus with her speed and agility; she had proven to be a very competitive lass. She ran well for a girl and had handled herself admirably in nearly all the games and challenges they had undertaken. Looking back, Marcus realized that Cassie's athletic abilities had been but the first of many qualities that had endeared her to him. And of course, Marcus now knew that Cassie's performance that day was merely a foreshadowing of all that she would become. She had also proven to possess well above average intelligence, courage, daring, and was also blessed with an extraordinary gift for compassion and human understanding. Plus, and in spite of the ill-advised Pixie haircut she had once experimented with, Cassie had grown into a beautiful and desirable woman.

Marcus had been sitting quietly, silently wrapped in his thoughts, memories, and personal musings for nearly an hour when the tall elderly gentleman sporting a trench coat and matching black bowler hat had taken a seat at the far end of the bench. Marcus stole a glance to his right as the man had taken a seat and removed his hat. Perhaps sensing Marcus' gaze, the man turned to his left, and using both hands to carefully place his bowler down onto the bench, smiled and nodded toward Marcus.

"I know you," Marcus said softly. Quietly though he had spoken, Marcus had been unable to mask his astonishment. "You're Neville, no, let me correct that. You are Opa. You are my grandfather, aren't you?"

"Call me what you will, Marcus," the man sagely replied. "I suppose I can be anyone, or anything for that matter, that you would fancy me to be. Whatever it may require that would merit your trust and belief."

"I don't understand what you mean, Neville.... Or, um, grandpa." Marcus paused as he dealt with the lump in his throat. "Grandpa is how I would really like to know you."

"Whatever suits you, Marcus." The man smiled in response to Marcus' words. "I would be honored to be referred to as grandfather by such a fine and up-standing young man."

"I haven't seen you as Opa since the encounter with Judy more than three years ago," Marcus said before asking the burning question that was on his mind. "And please don't misinterpret my intentions, but I can't help but wonder. Is something else bad about to happen? I mean, to be perfectly honest sir, just about every time you or Opa has come into my life, it has been a harbinger of unpleasant circumstances to come."

"No Marcus. Not today, not today. Actually, I was sent because this will most likely be the final time you will see me." The gentleman elaborated, "You deserve to be made aware of the truth. You have seen me in several forms, although I have purposely allowed only allowed two of them. This, the one you know as Neville. and the other that Cassie has affectionately referred to as Opa. But there have been others of which you were unaware."

"I'm afraid I don't understand Neville ... Grandpa." Marcus was flustered. At this point, he was unsure how he should even address the man.

"Let me try to further explain," the gentleman said softly. "I am but an aberration to you. As I was in the cellar. Some might describe me as a ghost, or a spirit. Whatever the preferred connotation, it is true that I am from the hereafter. That much you have already deduced. What you have failed to comprehend, and through no fault of your own, are the multitude of reasons for which I was sent to, I suppose it could be said, to meddle in your life."

"I don't think meddle would be the word," Marcus said earnestly. "You have saved both mine and Cassie's lives on numerous occasions. You *have* been a Godsend to us."

"Exactly, Marcus. That's exactly what I was, and you need to understand that. I literally am a Godsend." More explanation was now in order. "I must admit to you, I initially misrepresented my purpose and duty, although I never intended to do so. When souls, like myself, are dispatched amongst mortals, it is always so done with a decidedly specific purpose. Often times, those purposes change or become altered. Yes, when I first arrived, you were my sole charge. But as time and circumstances evolved, so also did my purpose. Such that Cassie ultimately became my responsibility as well. Even I was initially unaware of the redirection of purpose."

"So, you became Cassie's guardian angel as well as mine?" Marcus was taken back by this new revelation.

"Yes. Although I was not even aware of that fact. Actually, at some of those moments during which you believed that I was acting on your behalf and saving your life; well, in reality, the purpose of my actions had ultimately also been for Cassie's benefit." Marcus found himself hanging on Neville's – or Opa's – every word. It seemed that with each sentence that had been uttered,

Marcus had found himself with a more clear understanding of Opa's mission. The truth had become obvious to him prior to the words being spoken. "You had to be cared for, Marcus, because ultimately, it would be you who were to ensure Cassie's survival and eventual purpose."

"I understand now, Grandpa. I don't think it had ever been me that you were sent to watch over and protect," Marcus now had a grasp on what everything had been about. He'd always been aware of how special Cassie always had been, and now the realization that there was something so infinitely unique about her that God himself had sent an angel to protect her was a sobering thought indeed.

"To an extent, you are correct, Marcus. Everything on earth is according to God's master plan. Unfortunately, the best laid of plans can still be interrupted by evil forces. There are times when those disruptions to plans cannot be corrected; it is an eternal struggle between good and evil. But through my assistance, He has provided that at least some may be." Marcus was relieved to know that he had been the person chosen to be placed in the position of Cassie's mortal protector.

"It is your responsibility now, Marcus, to care for and help guide Cassie on her journey. It was her destiny for you to sire and for her to birth a leader who will ensure the continuance of a peaceful world. For years to come, they will desperately be in need of your support and care. Be there for them, Marcus."

"I will, I ..." Marcus was forced to stop mid-sentence, succumbing to sheer and utter amazement. Just as he had begun to speak, and within the blink of an eye, Opa, Neville Naughton, Dr. Copeland, Simon, Grandpa, John Clemens, or perhaps even God himself, whomever had been seated on the far end of the bench had faded and vanished. Suddenly, and once again, sitting alone, Marcus was sickened by the thought that this had been the last time. All that remained was the black bowler hat. It was left, Marcus was certain, so that there would never be any doubt, and that he would forever and always know, that the conversation had truly taken place.

Marcus felt tears welling in his eyes. The cause of the tears? He could not be sure. Tears of sadness because he knew Opa was probably gone forever? Perhaps they were tears of joy and gratitude for all that Opa had done for both he and Cassie? Or maybe, just maybe, they were tears of Marcus' sincere thanks that a higher power had brought Cassie to *Franklin's Five and Dime* on a Saturday in May nine and one-half years ago. Maybe they were tears of happiness that Cassie had found the spunk and gumption that he had lacked, and had approached and spoken to him? Cassie's boldness had served to kick-start a budding relationship that had only strengthened with each passing day.

Realizing that he had spent enough time away from his family this morning, Marcus stood and picked up his grandfather's abandoned hat, caressing it gently to his bosom. He was instantly aware that the treasured item would become, from this day forward, a family heirloom. Marcus thought of the family back at the Worthington house. Cassie's mother, Debbie, was probably still busily cooking and baking. She was surely being aided by his still new stepfather, Buster, while his stepmother – no, *mother,* Margaret, would either be setting the table or tending to Marcus' new four month-old baby sister, Eleanor. Margaret had never gotten over her infatuation with the Beatles and insisted the baby be named after her favorite song, *Eleanor Rigby.* Jack Worthington was probably in his easy chair, shoes kicked off and enjoying a cocktail, anxiously awaiting the kickoff of the Detroit Lions and New York Jets tilt and wondering when Buster would leave the kitchen and join him. And Cassie, Marcus' lovely wife Cassie, is probably at this very moment nursing their two month old son, John Elijah Clemens. Walking toward the car and wearing a broad and heartwarming smile, Marcus thought to himself, *Oh, what a glorious time to be alive.*